DIVINE
SPACE GODS 1 :
ABRAHAM'S FOLLIES

WRITTEN BY
MARTIN LUNDQVIST

LUCIFER GOLDSTEIN   CYBORG ASSISTANT

KEILA EISENSTEIN

ABRAHAM GOLDSTEIN   ADINA GOLDSTEIN   LUCIFER GOLDSTEIN   JESHUA GOLDSTEIN

DIVINE SPACE GODS TRILOGY

First edition. August 29, 2019.

Copyright © 2019 Martin Lundqvist.

ISBN: 978-0-6487245-5-1

Written by Martin Lundqvist.

Chapter 1: A Rich, Grumpy Old Man Funds an Implausible Project.

The rich, old, and grumpy Abraham Goldstein looked out through the window of his Penthouse apartment on Antarctica. From his apartment 3000 metres up, he could see all his vast domains all the way to the ocean, far away at the horizon. Despite being the richest and oldest man on the planet, he wasn't happy. He wanted to own more and be more powerful. There was a problem with this foolproof plan that Abraham was 250 years old, and the life-extending pills that Abraham was taking had started to lose their effect on him. Despite being so rich and powerful, it was time for him to take a nap, six feet down under.

Abraham was not ready to die yet and had come up with an implausible and ridiculous plan that he would spend all his money on, to bereave his horrible relatives of their inheritance. He had ordered a top-grade scientist, Jack Brown, to partake in a "secret" project, building an absurdly expensive and massive machine in the basement of Goldstein Tower. This machine, a colossal particle replicator, would create a dimensional rift that would allow Abraham to meet God before he died. This was a bit wasteful as Abraham was 250 years old and he could simply stop taking his life-extending pills and die anyway!

Chapter 2 : Abraham Finds Out That God is Dead.

The next day Abraham woke up and decided to take the lift all the way down to the basement to meet with Jack Brown and use the expensive and dangerous machine that Jack had built there.

Unfortunately, Abraham forgot to notify the building management that he wanted exclusive access to the lift, so instead of 5-minute-long lift ride to the basement, Abraham had to spend half an hour in the elevator, with people getting on and off on at every level, something that made him grumpier!

Eventually, Abraham got to the basement, where he was met by Jack Brown and Jack's team. Abraham spoke:

- Is my huge secret machine ready?

Jack Brown was struggling to keep a straight face. What kind of idiot thought it was possible to secretly build a 1-kilometre long machine in the basement of one of the landmark buildings of the planet? The number of noise complaints Jack and his team had received over the last few years was staggering, not to mention the endless shuttle traffic of trucks needed to freight away all the excavated soil and rocks from the construction process.

Jack Brown stopped himself from laughing and spoke:

- Yes, sir, it's ready.

Abraham:

- Took you a long time to answer that straightforward question. Time is money! Chop, Chop!

- Have you tried the machine yet? I want to be the first to use it!

Yet again, Jack Brown struggled to contain himself. Of course, he had tried the mind travel machine on multiple occasions. What kind of idiot would ring up his boss to inspect the device, just to demonstrate that it didn't work?

Jack Brown:

- As per your instructions, you'll be the first to try this large and potentially dangerous machine.

Abraham Goldstein:

- Excellent, I love an employee that blindly follows orders and doesn't think for himself.

- Plug me in.

Jack Brown:

- Yes, sir. I must warn you. Time in the Divine Dimension doesn't follow any logic and simply moves the way that suits the narrative.

Abraham Goldstein:

- Thank you for that irrelevant remark. Start the machine already!

Jack started the machine, and Abraham fell asleep. His lips muttered some gibberish, and his mind was sucked into a dimensional warp. Suddenly, Abraham ended up in an eerie but beautiful courtyard. This experience was cool and all, but how could he be sure that this was heaven and not just a virtual reality simulation? Abraham would not be happy if he spent 120 billion Terran Credits, a large part of his fortune, on an advanced video game. He wanted fair value for his investment, he wanted to meet the god of his people, Yahweh, to play chess with him.

Abraham walked into the palace that was at the end of the courtyard. He saw a fancy looking throne and in front of it lay a dead man in robes. Abraham thought that if the dead man was god, he had wasted his bank savings for nothing. He walked up to the body to confirm its identity. Conveniently the dead man had left a suicide letter!

The suicide letter contained a lot of gibberish, but from it, Abraham concluded that the dead man was Yahweh. Yahweh turned out to be an alien that used Zetan mind-control technology to fool Bronze Age humans that he was a god. That was something Abraham wanted to do as well, and fortunately; Yahweh had printed the blueprints to the mind control technology on the pillar next to his throne.

Abraham tried to memorise the schematics for hours without success, but then he realised how unnecessary this was. His brain had a lot of bionic chips installed, so all he needed to do was to look at the pillars and then use his memory chip to take a screenshot. A screenshot that he could extract once he came back to his science lab.

Now all Abraham needed to do was to go back to the normal dimension. And Abraham waited and waited. After endless waiting, he was getting frustrated at Jack for not waking him up, and suddenly, his mind was extracted, and he ended up back in the science lab.

Abraham Goldstein:

- You bloody fool. I have been waiting forever!

Jack Brown:

- Oh really? You have only been connected for a minute, though.

Jack held in a laugh, he knew precisely how long a minute felt in the simulation, it felt like a week.

Abraham Goldstein:

- Oh really? So, all that time was just a minute. How good is that!

- Anyways. To my great disappointment, it turns out that my God, Yahweh, was an alien that used mind-control technology to trick people into thinking he was a god. On the bright side, he was kind enough to mention the mind control chips and their schematics in his suicide letter.

- If there was only a way to recreate these strange alien artefacts that I have taken a bionic screenshot of. Hmm?

Jack Brown:

- There is. Being far enough into the future for anything to be plausible, we have access to a *particle replicator,* a machine that can create an exact copy of anything we have a blueprint for!

Abraham Goldstein:

- You mean like a 3D printer?

Jack Brown:

- A lot better! 3D printers can't make exact copies of Alien artefacts.

Abraham Goldstein:

- Excellent. Make me a 30 angel chips, 300 human chips, but only one God chip. There can only be one god! Me! Muahaha!

Jack Brown:

- Sure mate, whatever as long as I get paid.

Abraham Goldstein:

- I'll pick them up tomorrow!

Abraham went to the lift for the long way up to his penthouse. This time he called building management and make sure that he had reserved access to the elevator, so he didn't have to share it!

Chapter 3 Abraham Tells Lucifer About His Evil Scheme!

The following day, Abraham Goldstein told his right-hand man/ henchman Lucifer about his upcoming evil scheme. The following conversation took place.

Lucifer:

- So, first of all, can I start using my real name Terrence instead of my operations name, Lucifer?

Abraham:

- No, because we are running evil schemes together. We can't expose your real identity.

Lucifer:

- But why? No-one even knows me under my real name. People think that I am a dork that's named Lucifer. It doesn't work wonders with the ladies introducing myself with that name.

Abraham:

- I don't care what name you are using on your dates. You are using Lucifer when you are talking with me, as that is your employee name. Period!

Lucifer:

- And you are telling me this now?! I have had such a long dry spell for no reason!

Abraham:

- Well if it's any comfort. Once you reach my age, you lose all interest in sex and can focus your full attention on evil schemes and making money!

Lucifer:

- Lose all interest in sex? What about your eight super-sexy scantily clad female assistants?!

Abraham:

- I have no interest in having sex with them but making others envious never gets old!

- Anyways. Back to my plan. Yesterday I used my top-secret Divine Detector machine to travel to the Divine Dimension and meet with our God, Yahweh. Unfortunately, Yahweh was dead, but I found schematics to an alien mind control technology that I can use to convince people that I am God!

Lucifer:

- Hate to break it to you, boss, but your super-expensive machine is anything but secret. We have received several noise complaints in the last year. We have been forced to work around the clock "convincing" people that they have not heard anything!

- As for the meeting god part. Wasn't the 120 billion Terran Credits you spent on the project a bit excessive? I know a guy that sell 3 doses of acid for 50 credits. Gets you the same effect!

Abraham:

- How do you know about that?

Lucifer:

- It's not that hard when you forget to lock your computer, and there is a file saying *"MY SECRETS. DO NOT OPEN!!!"*

Abraham:

- Have no-one taught you respect?!

- Anyways, the next step of my plan is to implant all my relatives with a mind control chip so I can intimidate them into doing what I tell them to do.

Lucifer:

- Isn't that a bit redundant? To my understanding threatening people, is what you have been doing for the last 200 years? Maybe try something new?

Abraham:

- Muahahaha! This is new and innovative!

- For the last 200 years, I have threatened people with my wealth and my henchmen. Now I am threatening them with advanced Alien technology instead. It's a game-changer!

- Now you must leave. I am planning to use the mind control technology to fool my young and beautiful assistant into believing that I am having sex with her, while I am drinking whisky and watching her being in that state of trance.

Lucifer:

- That is the dumbest thing I have ever heard! Just have sex with her for real like a normal person.

Abraham:

- Who is old-fashioned now?! Get out of my office!

Chapter 4: Lucifer Falls Asleep Waiting for a Date!

Lucifer felt exhausted. He and his fellow henchmen had worked around the clock for three days straight, "secretly" implanting all of Abraham's distant relatives with the alien mind control technology that would make it easier for Abraham to bully them.

But now Lucifer had a night off, and his excessive finger-swiping on Swoonder had paid off, he had found a date. Being able to use his real name would be a gamechanger as Terrence Lowenstein, Security Specialist sounded a lot better than Lucifer, the henchman. Lucifer closed his eyes and dreamt about all the sexy women he would get in the coming years. Unfortunately, it was just a dream as Lucifer fell asleep while waiting for his date, and then got kicked out of the bar as the bar staff assumed, he was intoxicated. Tsk, poor Lucifer!

Chapter 5: Just a few Deaths During the Goldstein Annual General Meeting

The day after Lucifer's dating debacle, it was time for the Annual General Meeting of House Goldstein. Abraham Goldstein had decided to transport his mind to the Divine Dimension, which would amplify the effect of the plot device, the *Zetan Divine Technology chips*. For Abraham, his trip to the Divine Dimension was a stroke of genius, but for everyone else, it was a major inconvenience as the over-dimensioned particle accelerator used up all the power of the grid, which caused blackouts across the city. Stumbling in the dark with the lights only sporadically flashing, the members of Abraham's extended family eventually managed to get to the conference hall to listen to his latest decrees and follies. Due to Abraham's enormous wealth, age, and prolific bedchamber activities during his younger years, there were 300 relatives spanning over 10 generations gathered!

Abraham showed up in the middle of the room as a mirage and spoke.

- Greetings, relatives. I am speaking to you as a mirage, enabled by alien technology amplified by the secret particle accelerator in the basement of Goldstein Tower.

Jake Goldstein, Abraham's grandson, 190 years old, replied:

- Secret?! The building is vibrating every night because of that machine, the power went out, and my wife fell over and broke her leg as she stumbled in the darkness. Can you turn that thing off?!

Abraham:

- No, the machine is imperative for my evil schemes. If you could call our Goldstein factories operators and tell them to shut down for a while, that would help save more power. My smartphone doesn't work through the dimensional rift. It says connection error.

Jake:

- Okay.

Jake called the factory managers asking them to shut down operations, and after a while, power returned to the Goldstein tower, and the meeting could resume.

Abraham:

- Yeah, so like I said. I found out that our god Yahweh is dead, and I also found the mind control technology he used to trick us into believing he was a god. Now I want to do the same thing, on an artificial world to a made-up tribe of Bronze Age people.

Jake:

- Good Luck with that mate, time travel is not possible, so where would you find those retarded people?

Abraham:

- Do not argue with your elders! You shall suffer.

Abraham activated the kill switch on the mind control chip implanted into Jake's brain. This caused a massive brain haemorrhage that killed Jake.

Abraham:

- Anyone else got something to say?!

Matt Goldstein, one of Abraham's younger relatives, tentatively raised his hand:

Abraham:

- Yes, Mark? Michael? Simon?

Matt:

- It's Matt, sir. I am just congratulating you, instantly killing some-one with a brain haemorrhage is a fast way to kill. However, I'd ar-gue that it's not a death that causes a lot of suffering.

Abraham:

- Muahaha!! Good point, as a reward I'll let you live.

- Anyways. As time travel is impossible, I will terraform an aster-oid to be a perfect replica of the Holy Land as it was in 1000 B.C. I will then memory wipe a bunch of Martians and brainwash them into thinking it is the Bronze Age and I am their God!

Matt:

- But isn't that prohibitively expensive? You can just buy the real Holy Land from House Rashid for a dime and a nickel.

Abraham:

- You are clearly not catching on Matt. Never question me! Time to die.

Abraham snapped his fingers, and Matt dropped dead to the ground. Abraham:

- Anyone else got something to say?

Josef Goldstein, who had a form of terminal and excruciating cancer, saw an excellent opportunity for a pain-free death. Josef:

- This is blasphemy, there is only one true God, and that is Yah-weh! You are merely an imposter and a tyrant!

Josef then smiled and gave Abraham the finger. Abraham responded by killing him. Just after killing Josef, he recalled Josef's condition and to his great regret, he realised that it would have been crueller to let Josef live.

Abraham then shouted out to the assembly, asking if anyone else had anything to say. No-one did, but Abraham killed three more of the delegates for arbitrary reasons, as he was a megalomaniac supervillain and he enjoyed being that way!

Chapter 6: Abraham Meets With the Terran Council.

A few weeks later, Abraham Goldstein with Lucifer and Isaac Goldstein in tow, went to the Terran Council meeting that was held in the Swiss Alps. Abraham eyed through the premeeting minutes. The minutes were going over numerous ways the plutocrats on Earth could torment the poor plebs living on Mars. While Abraham also enjoyed tormenting the Martian population, this did not interest him now. Instead, he was thinking about how he could convince the Terran Council to give him control over the worthless asteroids B528A and B528B so he could build his futuristic and yet backward Bronze Age world, Eden!

During the trip, Isaac Goldstein thought about how much he hated his new job and "his promotion". Before Abraham went on a killing spree, killing everyone more prominent than Isaac, Isaac had an easy life, living in abundance with plenty of time to fiddle his thumbs without doing any work. Now that Isaac was promoted, he had to do actual work, and he was also more likely to be killed in his wicked ancestor's hissy fits!

Abraham entered the meeting room. The host casually remarked to Abraham how expensive the table was to show off the wealth of his faction. This annoyed Abraham, but since he wasn't at home, he avoided throwing a temper tantrum!

The meeting commenced. The Terran Council represented the five wealthiest ruling families on Earth. They all had their own specific territory, their own race, and attached stereotypes. The ruling factions were:

- House Goldstein, the Jews, who was the wealthiest faction, or at least used to be before Abraham's dementia-induced spending spree started.

- House Muller, the Germans, being industrious, devoid of any humour and painfully arrogant.

- House White, the Americans, being the most racist faction and the faction most inclined to war and violence.

- House Rashid, the Arabs, being uncouth barbarians, with an inclination towards cruelty and beheadings.

- House Cheng, the calculative Chinese, being shifty, cunning, and unreliable.

Through a stroke of magic, all the five ruling factions were equally powerful, and they all controlled a fifth of the planet each. They all shared the same passionate hatred for poor people, especially the poor people on Mars, and none of them had any redeeming qualities.

The faction leaders gave speeches detailing their nefarious plans for how to make life miserable for the Martians. Abraham, who had heard the same statements for the last 200 years, got bored and fell asleep, snoring.

Eventually, Isaac woke him up when it was Abraham's turn to speak. Abraham:

- *Snort* Hmmm? Oh, uh, ahem!! *snort* Sorry, I wasn't sleeping, just preparing my speech while I was in deep thoughts.

Hans Muller:

- Interesting method... Never heard anyone snoring so loudly while preparing a speech before.

Abraham:

- Ahem!! Anyways. I am willing to fund the proposed penal colony around the Tau Ceti star, on the condition that the Council grants me ownership and complete privacy for the asteroid B528A and B528B.

Ibrahim Rashid:

- Yes, Isaac told us about your plan. To create a fake Bronze Age colony where you pretend to be God and recreate the atrocities from the Old Testament.

Abraham looked at Isaac in a mix of disbelief and anger. He had to contain his murderous tendencies though, as it would be unsuitable killing his second in charge during a Terran Council meeting. But what would he do, now that his plans were out in the open?!
Ibrahim Rashid continued:

- Don't worry, Abraham. I think it's an excellent idea. I can even lend you the Holy Land on Earth for free, if we get the Television rights!

Abraham:

- No! That is not how I envisioned things to go! I will do this the hard way, by spending the remainder of my wealth on making a replica of the Holy Land on an empty asteroid, and for that, I need both asteroid B528A and B528B.

Ibrahim Rashid:

- Okay, suit yourself.

Hans Muller:

- That concludes the agenda for our meeting. I will now provide you with refreshments shipped from our colony orbiting Alpha Centauri. Sending it here took 40 years, and it was incredibly expensive, making today's meeting dinner exquisite.

After this, they all proceeded to eat and drink House Muller's space food from Alpha Centauri. The produce having spent 40 years in the cargo hold of an interstellar spaceship was unpalatable, but everyone kept a straight face and ate it anyway, as it indeed was rare and expensive!

Chapter 7: Abraham and the Angels Leave Antarctica

Having installed mind-control chips in all his extended family members brains had a negative side effect; Abraham was constantly reminded of how much they despised him. While he was confident that they had hated him before as well, it hadn't bothered him back then, as he had lived oblivious and happily scheming in his Ivory Tower: The Penthouse level of Goldstein Tower. But now he was constantly reminded of their bitching and plotting against him, and he had enough. It was time to leave Earth and head to B528A, the future Eden, in Abraham's luxurious spaceship, The Golden Penny!

Leaving Earth came with both an advantage and a disadvantage. His relatives ended up being out of range for his Alien mind-control chips. This meant that Abraham would not be able to bully and intimidate his relatives from Eden. On the bright side, he would not need to listen to their whining either!

Convincing Lucifer and the other 29 angels to come with him to Eden had been a bit trickier. But Abraham had won their enthusiasm when he promised to also bring his super-sexy female assistants. Once they had left Earth, Lucifer realised that Abraham was lying, and the female assistants were not coming. But at least he could have fun on his regular holidays and time off. Yeah, right, Lucifer!

Chapter 8: An Unrelated Expedition to Tau Ceti

As promised at the Terran Council meeting, Abraham funded the expedition to build a penal colony around Tau Ceti over 100 years travel away. He did this despite being told by the other faction leaders that the expedition was unnecessary, and Abraham could just take as many Martian prisoners as he needed for his Bronze Age God roleplay. Suffering from dementia, Abraham had forgotten that the other faction leaders knew about his Eden project and insisted that the Eden project didn't exist. The settlement of Tau Ceti was met with as much enthusiasm as the settlement of Australia was a millennium earlier. But hey, if you are a prisoner in a terrible detention centre on the Moon, what harm is there in trying something new?

The 30,000 Martian prisoners were cryogenically frozen and stored on ten large ships, with the course set for the Tau Ceti solar system. Abraham ordered one of the ships to be diverted to Eden while the other nine spaceships headed towards Tau Ceti. The fate of the nine spaceships heading towards Tau Ceti was never mentioned again, but presumably, they were still in transit by the end of the trilogy! The fates of the last ship's inhabitants were a lot more detailed though, as they ended up being Abraham's subjects on Eden.

Chapter 9: Lucifer, the Debt Collector!

As expected, Abraham's disgruntled relatives had no interest in paying Abraham's enormous bills for the Eden Project, and they stopped paying as soon as they were out of range for the tyrant's alien mind-control technology. This situation added another job title of Lucifer's lengthy resume as Abraham's henchman, the role as debt collector.

Abraham sent Lucifer and a group of five other angels to Earth, to gate crash the House Goldstein board meeting and make sure that the others paid the bills for all Abraham's follies.

Lucifer and his group arrived in orbit over Goldstein Tower, and Lucifer tried to figure out how to access the meeting. The way he usually got to Abraham's penthouse, via the main entrance taking the lift, was not the best idea. Lucifer doubted that the new management would appreciate the arrival of the former managements' accomplices and although Lucifer was a genetically engineered super-soldier, he preferred to not fight the entire Goldstein army to trespass the board meeting.

But then Lucifer remembered something. He remembered the *"secret"* hatch that would take him straight into Abraham's former penthouse from the air. Why anyone would build a door to one's apartment at 3000 metres height was beyond Lucifer, but the door was there. With a bit of luck, no-one had changed the access codes to the door in the last 5 years!

Lucifer and his fellow angels dropped from low orbit in their futuristic battle armours with built-in fusion thrusters and attached angel wings. The angel wings were purely for decoration, but Lucifer thought they looked cool and made for a good entrance, so he decided to keep them on.

Lucifer approached the door, and to his great relief, the access codes were still the same, and the door opened. The angel wings, however, caused an issue. They made him too big to get through the damn tiny door! After struggling for a while, he remembered that there was an eject button for the angel wings. Lucifer pressed the button, the wings detached, and hit Lucifer's colleague Malphat, in the head. This knocked Malphat unconscious and sent him crashing towards the ground. Ouch!

Eventually, Lucifer and his fellow henchmen stormed the board meeting and shocked the delegates!

Isaac Goldstein:

- So, it was you idiots, that made all that noise?! I thought it was the pest controller. I just called HR to have him sacked!

- You are Terrence Lowenstein, our former employee, aren't you?

Lucifer shed a tear of joy. He was moved by Isaac's comment. Not only did Isaac remember Lucifer, but he called him by his real name as well! But then Lucifer got angry. "Former employee"? Was this the reason he hadn't gotten paid? He decided to speak up!

Lucifer:

- Yes, I am Terrence Lowenstein, a current employee, and I am here to collect my pay!

Isaac Goldstein:

- Wouldn't it be easier to set up a query with the payroll department about that?

Lucifer:

- Perhaps, but I am here to settle a more significant account! Why have you stopped sending shipments to our Grandmaster Abraham's Holy Eden project?

Isaac Goldstein:

- Because it is stupid, and it is driving us broke!

Lucifer:

- Those are two good reasons, but my question was rhetorical.

- You need to start sending shipments, or I'll have to kill you with the alien mind-control technology.

Isaac Goldstein:

- Isn't it a bit excessive to threaten us with obscure magical technologies when you are also aiming an assault rifle at us?

Lucifer:

- Yes. But my obscure magical technologies can kill everyone in House Goldstein, while my rifle can only kill the ones that are in this room.

Isaac Goldstein:

- Good point. Tell Abraham that I will pay up and resume the shipments.

Lucifer:

- You choose wisely!

- Malphat, Hashmallim, Seraphim and Ishmael will stay back and make sure that you keep your promises.

Hashmallim:

- Master Lucifer, you accidentally killed Malphat when you released the angel wings knocking him unconscious and sending him crashing towards the ground.

Lucifer:

- Oh shit. I forgot about that part! Don't tell the boss! Oh well, the three of you stay here and make sure Isaac and the board are paying. Nuriel and I will head back to Eden now.

Lucifer and Nuriel headed out the same way they came in, this time without getting stuck in the door. They used their futuristic fusion thrusters and flew back to their spaceship floating in low orbit. Once they were back on their spaceship, Nuriel spoke.

  - Fucking dickhead, I thought we were mates?

Lucifer:

  - I am sorry about Malphat. We have a dangerous job, and sometimes accidents happen!

Nuriel:

  - I didn't mean that. I meant that you are bringing me back to Eden with you. The others are going to have the time of their lives enjoying tasty food and drinks as well as the company of Abraham's former sexy assistants!

Lucifer:

  - Wait! Are they still working there?!

Nuriel:

  - Yes, I saw one of them hiding when we stormed in.

Lucifer:

  - Oh shit.

Lucifer gazed out into the darkness of space completely demoralised. While the colleagues he left on Earth would have the time of their lives, he had condemned himself to another decade of building Abraham's stupid space colony. Aaargh!

Chapter 10: The Construction of Eden

For the next 20 years, Lucifer oversaw the development of Eden. Abraham, insisting on keeping the project a "secret", had refused to get external contractors in to assist with the project. Instead, Lucifer was stuck to do all the work together with his two dozen accomplices, who were soldiers, not builders. Although they had thousands of construction robots on the site, they couldn't keep up, and there was an endless line of transport ships outside Eden waiting to offload their shipments. So much for secrecy!

Another security issue that Abraham had overlooked was the possibility to hack the construction robots to make them send a live video feed of what they were doing. These construction robots had been secretly hacked by every other faction as well as most news outlets, leading to that the progress of Abraham's "secret" project being regularly broadcasted on the evening news as a reality show!

Abraham was blissfully unaware of this, and instead, he spent most of his time studying the history of the Zetan species. He did this by studying in the vast Zetan archives located in the Divine Dimension!

Chapter 11: The Zetan Backstory

100,000 years ago, the Zetan Alien race, managed to open an interdimensional gate between our universe and the Divine Dimension. There is no logical way to explain how they did this, but then again, the Holy Bible is the most sold books of all times, so "magic" or "god" is often a good enough explanation for everything unexplainable!

Regardless of how the Zetan got to the Divine Dimension, they did. And once they were there, they came up with a great and foolproof idea! To spread throughout the galaxy, not through colonising other world's but by travelling around and alter the genome of different species to make them smarter and start civilisations. This way the Zetans could tell themselves that they indirectly spread across the Milky Way, which they could have done themselves if they just had a bit more interest in sex and procreation. Eventually the Zetans realised the foolishness in amplifying the intelligence of other species, and they stopped the project, but by then they had already induced humans, as well as other species such as the Xenos with heightened intelligence.

For 90,000 years, nothing terrible happened. The Zetans lived peacefully in their small galactic empire governed over, by the benign influence of the Zeto crystals, which were magical plot devices, imbued with soul of the True Maker, which could be used for a lot of things.

10,000 years ago, the Xenos species, which the Zetan had imbued with intelligence 90,000 years earlier, invaded Zetan territory, hellbent on destroying the Zetan civilisation. The Zetans beat them with ease as the Zetans were supernatural beings with superpowers and the Xenos were just brutish beasts with proficiency for being cannon fodder.

But the Xenos kept coming back and in big numbers as they despite being able to perform interstellar travel hadn't grasped the concept of contraception!

The repeated Xeno attacks slowly diminished the Zetan number, and they had three options:

    A. To start procreating,

B. Using robots to fight their wars,
C. Find a primitive species to use as their own cannon fodder against the Xenos.

The Zetans opted for C, and the species that got the questionable honour to serve as the Zetans' soldiers was humanity.

The Zetans decided that the best way to get humans to fight their wars was to build a lot of portals across Earth, masked as pyramids. They posed as Gods to convince humans to make the questionable choice to walk through the gateways to be recruited into the Zetan Interstellar Space Army!

The Zetan plan worked, and with the help of their human soldiers, they repelled the Xenos and fought them all the way back to their home planet of Xenora. The Zetans politely asked the Xenos to surrender. The Xenos answered by saying *"fuck off"* and their evil queen, Rangda Kaliankan, who had managed to infiltrate Zetan territory, caused a supernova explosion that destroyed the Zetan interstellar civilisation. The destruction of their home planet caused the Zetans to stop being civil, and they responded by exterminating the Xeno species, at least you are led to believe so, until the second book!

Chapter 12: Yahweh Turns Gay, Tries a "Cure", and End up Pursuing Bestiality

With the destruction of his homeworld Zetani, as well as the loss of the Zeto crystals, Yahweh ended up in a pickle. For thousands of years, Yahweh had preached to humans how much he hated gay people! And now with the loss of the crystals, he found himself head of heels in love with Lucifer, the male rival he had spent the last few millennia bad-mouthing. Bummer! The sexual relationship with Lucifer made matters complicated for Yahweh, and it was a threat to his credibility.

Yahweh came up with an ingenious solution to the problem. He invented a serum that would cure his homosexuality and give him an extreme sexual drive and arouse all women on Earth! There was only a slight problem, though. The serum made him a sex god for humans! As humans were lower species than the Zetans, Yahweh's "cure" for homosexuality had turned him from gay into bestiality instead!

Yahweh injected himself with the serum and engaged in a massive one-month sex marathon with human females. His sex marathon gave Yahweh a lot of children, but only one of them ever reached fame, Jesus. Eventually, Yahweh went back to the Divine Dimension where his boyfriend Lucifer, angered and hurt over Yahweh's unprecedented cheating spree, knocked him unconscious with a psionic blast.

Chapter 13: Yahweh Destroys the Portal to Earth!

Many years later, Yahweh finally woke up from his slumber. He was hungry, thirsty and had a terrible headache. He looked down to Earth through the magical pond in the Divine Dimension courtyard and saw something that angered him.

Jesus, one of the many sons that was the outcome of Yahweh's sex marathon, had become exceedingly famous and was now more worshipped than Yahweh had ever been! Yahweh grabbed his walking stick which contained a hidden dangerous weapon and went to confront Lucifer. Abraham faced Lucifer who had tea and cakes with a couple of gossipy friends.

Lucifer:

- Look who is back? It is the cunning and low-life pervert!

Yahweh:

- What are you talking about? We used to be mates, we had great sex and good times together!

Lucifer:

- I was referring to your sudden change of fetish to bestiality. Your sex marathon with female humans! Pfft!

An awkward silence ensued, as Yahweh wasn't the only Zetan who had engaged in intercourse with humans over the years.

Yahweh:

- I'm not the only Zetan who has ever done it. Anyways, I am here to punish you for knocking me unconscious, thus missing my son's birth, childhood, rise to prominence and execution.

Lucifer winked and replied:

- And how do you plan to punish me? With that massive rod, you are holding.

Yahweh:

- Not in that way! This rod contains a secret, dangerous weapon once activated.

Yahweh activated the secret weapon. The other Zetans looked at him in awe, jealous over not being smart enough to design such a weapon.
Yahweh:

- Everyone except Lucifer, get out! We have some talking to do.

The other Zetans left and headed to the armoury a couple of kilometres away to pick up their own weapons. Yahweh led Lucifer at gunpoint to the portal to Earth.
Lucifer:

- What are we doing? Why are you leading me to the portal?

Yahweh:

- Don't worry. I just found it too stuffy in there to have a proper conversation. Let's talk about our relationship and resolve our problem.

After that, Yahweh had a good talk where they managed to resolve most of their issues and differences. Unfortunately, Yahweh pressed the wrong button when he tried to deactivate the dangerous weapon, so instead of disabling it, he fired off a massive blast that incinerated Lucifer and destroyed the portal. The destruction of the portal caused a dimensional rift between the Divine Palace and the rest of the Divine Dimension, leaving Yahweh stuck by himself in the palace. Unlucky!

Chapter 14: Jack Brown is Living the Good Life.

Jack Brown, the scientist who Abraham had hired to construct his *"secret"* Divine Detector machine many years earlier, was looking at the beautiful sunset. Would he ever get tired of living on this tropical paradise island and go back to working for some clueless plutocrat? As it turned out, no!

Jack Brown and his team of researchers had struck a goldmine when Abraham had tasked them with building his silly machine many years earlier. Being a *"secret"* project, it was never audited, which meant that Jack and his fellow researcher could embezzle most of the money assigned to the project unnoticed.

Jack was genuinely surprised when the machine turned out to be functional, despite the money embezzled, but sometimes good things happened to good people! He asked Jenny Lundberg, one of Abraham's former beautiful female assistants, to fetch him a drink while he enjoyed the sun setting over the Pacific. Ahh, this was the life!

Chapter 15 Lucifer Wakes Abraham Up.

Lucifer stood on the manmade mountain at the top of Eden's Mount Sinai. When Lucifer had mentioned that Mount Sinai was not located in the original Holy Land, Abraham had one of his hissy fits, so the mountain got to keep its name. Lucifer sighed. The construction of Eden was finished, and the asteroid colony was ready for settlement, and as promised, he would wake his dementia-ridden villainous tormentor up.

The last few years had been quiet and peaceful as Abraham had instructed his angels to only wake him up once Eden was finished. Obviously, none of them had shown any rush to complete the project and instead they had taken their time and gone on holidays across the solar system to different resorts, courtesy of Abraham's technically still-valid credit card. When the credit card eventually got cancelled due to suspected fraudulent transactions, they had no choice but to go back.

Unfortunately, despite possessing Abraham's unlimited credit card, Lucifer had still failed to get laid; as Abraham had designed his genetically engineered super-soldiers to be hapless towards the opposite sex and to make matters worse, he had also programmed the angels' bionic microchips to sabotage any interactions.

Lucifer activated Abraham's cryogenic tank, and after a while, the old fool woke up.

Lucifer:

- We have finished building Eden now, and as instructed, I have woken you up.

Abraham:

- Excellent. What year is it?

Lucifer:

- It's the year 2810, Master.

Abraham:

- What?! It was 2805 when I went to sleep, and you told me there were only a couple of months of work left to do.

Lucifer:

- You must have misheard me, Master. I remember saying there was only a couple of decades of work left to do. But due to our dedication to your cause, we worked around the clock and finished the remaining work in only five years!

Abraham:

- Ahh, I see. That dedication is why you are my archangel, the greatest of your kind!

Abraham:

- Did anything significant happen when I was asleep?

Lucifer considered whether he should tell the old tyrant about:

- How House Goldstein had fallen apart and lost most of their territory while he was asleep.

- That his relatives had blown up Abraham's penthouse apartment in the Goldstein Tower and had pronounced him dead.

- That they were broke!

He decided against it. He hated to be the bearer of unwelcome news, and with a bit of luck, the old fart would die before he noticed!
Lucifer:

- No, Master, no news, worthy of your attention.

Abraham:

- Good. Wake up our Martian subjects and place them on Eden. It is time for them to see their new home and meet their new god, ME!

Lucifer:

- Yes, O Divine Grand Master.

Chapter 16: A Slight Budget Problem.

Lucifer was checking the bank balance for the project, and his biggest fears were confirmed. They were broke, and their prepayment for 3000 doses of memory-erasing drugs had bounced, and thus, they would not receive any shipment. This was a crucial flaw, as Abraham's grand plan for the project was to memory-wipe Eden's inhabitants to make them believe in his follies.

Fortunately, things went well despite Lucifer's failure to erase the memories of Eden's inhabitants. They were originally from a war-torn Mars, and then they had been detained in a terrible detention centre on the Moon for years. For the Martian captives, it was worth participating in this strange role-play and in return get fresh food, a clean environment and relative safety!

To stop Abraham from noticing how broke they were, Lucifer had used a crafty trick. He had created a fake spam pop-up status updates on the Spacenet that always showed how rich Abraham was when he checked his bank balance. The problem remained though, eventually, Abraham would find out that he was broke, and that would be the temper tantrum of the century!

Chapter 17: Abraham the Pervert Matchmaker

Jon of the Gad tribe was a typical Edenite settler, in that he was bored and confused by the ongoing role-play he was forced to take part in. But at the same time, John was happy over having access to clean food and a clean environment. The drawback was that he had to do a lot of manual labour with out-dated tools, such as bronze cutters and blunt spears, but on the flip side, he had an almost unlimited supply of food and wine, unlike on Mars where he was always hungry.

During one of his night-time drinking sessions, Abraham showed up in Jon's house as a hazy mirage.

Abraham:

- Bzzz, Bzzz, Oh Jon of the Gad tribe. Why haven't you participated in marital union with your consort?

Jon:

- What are you talking about, old man? Speak normally!

Abraham:

- Why haven't you fucked your wife, Nadia?

Jon:

- Oh... I didn't know Nadia was meant to be my wife; I haven't been briefed on that part of the role-play.

Abraham:

- What are you talking about, you fool? Did my incompetent henchmen imbue you with the wrong memories? You are Jon of the Gad tribe, Nadia is your wife, and I saved you both when

Yahweh for no apparent reason wiped out Earth and the rest of mankind.

Jon thought of talking back to Abraham, but then he remembered Lucifer's warnings about Abraham's temper tantrums, so he decided to play along instead.

Jon:

- I am so sorry grandmaster Abraham. I fell and hit my head the other day, and I forgot all the things you just told me.

Abraham:

- Very well. I forgive you. Now procreate with your wife to honour my name.

Jon:

- There is a slight problem with that. You see, she also hit her head and needs you to remind her...

Abraham got frustrated. What kind of dimwit fools had he kidnapped for his project?! He should have captured Terran humans; they were a lot smarter and better looking as well! Then Abraham realised that his fellow greedy tycoons on the Terran Council would never allow him to kidnap Earth humans and that's why he had settled for Martians in the first place. Abraham spoke:

- Okay. I will talk to her.

After explaining the situation to Nadia, they tentatively started undressing each other to please their perverted captor. Jon feeling the performance anxiety of having the filthy old Abraham in the room, eventually shouted out.

- Can you at least leave the room and give us some privacy, please?

Abraham:

- Ha-Ha! I am the all-seeing and omnipotent Grandmaster Abraham, Yahweh's successor! I see everything.

Jon:

- Yeah, that might be, but that doesn't mean we want to see you while making love. It ruins the mood!

Abraham was astounded and replied sheepishly:

- Oh! Am I still in the room as a mirage? Sorry about that, I will make myself invisible at once.

Abraham deactivated his mirage in Jon's and Nadia room while he was still secretly perving on them. Jon shouted to him:

- Thanks, Abraham. That's a lot better!

Chapter 18: Problem with the Henchmen Union!

Abraham woke up from a nap when a warning status display was beeping in his office. Beep, beep, beep! A large fleet of war-spaceships had arrived outside of Eden and threatened him. Who was coming after him, and was this the end of him? Abraham had a few suspicions:

A. The bloody do-gooders in the Martian Humanist Alliance were coming after him because of his crimes against the Martians he had kidnapped to live on Eden.

B. The Terran Council had come to steal his priceless Eden colony now that he was weak and unprepared

C. His relatives in House Goldstein had come to get their revenge.

Abraham knew that he could neither beat nor negotiate with either side, and he prepared Eden for self-destruction! Before he had time to press the red button, however, he received a transmission from the fleet. As it turned out, the Henchman Worker's Union Party had sent the fleet.

Union representative:

- Good day, Abraham Goldstein! We have received several complaints from the members of our Union regarding the payment and working conditions for your employees.

Abraham:

- What? Why are you here? I will not release the 3000 Martians that I have imprisoned on the surface of Eden in my role play. I would rather self-destruct this station and kill everyone!

Union representative:

- We have no interest in your Martian prisoners, as they are not members of our Union. You need to pay the wages to your 30 henchmen, or we'll blockade your station.

Abraham:

- That's not a big deal; I am the wealthiest person in the solar system, and I can pay my staff. How much do I owe them?

Union representative:

- You owe them 5 million Terran Credits!

Abraham:

- That's nothing for a wealthy man like me. I will pay them straight away.

Union:

- We hope so, for your sake!
After disconnecting to the Union guy, Mr Nobody, Abraham was confused.

Why hadn't he, the richest man in the solar system, paid his henchmen that were imperative for the success of his schemes? Weren't the payments auto-direct debited from his supermassive bank account every month? Abraham realised that there was a virus on the computer he was using, and logged in from another one, just to understand the terrible truth. He was piss broke! The shock caused by this awful realisation gave Abraham a massive heart attack, and he died on the spot. Unlucky!

Chapter 19: Lucifer Revives Abraham by Inserting Abraham's Brain into a Budget Drone.

Lucifer and Metatron studied the dead, frozen body of Abraham and the shoddy looking drone they were supposed to transfer his brain into. The drone had an instruction manual in broken English and looked like a shoddy knockoff of a 200-year-old model of a Terran drone. It was made in a Martian developing country in the 25th century. Metatron was sceptical and looked at the drone with a shifty analytical eye.

Metatron:

- Hmm. I am not too sure about this. Why would you want to revive that evil old man in the first place? And why are we putting his brain into this malfunctioning Martian low-quality drone, which breaks all the time!? It's a recipe for disaster!

Lucifer:

- Silence, nerd. Abraham is like a father to me. This low-quality drone was all I could afford, and besides, if he dies, who is going to pay you all the unpaid salaries he owes you?

Metatron:

- We could just take over control ourselves. The television rights for Eden must be worth a fortune.

Lucifer:

- We are not running Eden as a spectacle to make money. We are running it to fulfil our master's divine vision. The almighty Yahweh appointed him, to replicate the Holy Land as it was 1000 B.C.

Metatron:

- Mate. Just because an old evil megalomaniac man tells you that Yahweh gave him a mission, doesn't mean it really is that way. I reckon he fabricated the story.

Lucifer:

- Don't bother with these things, Metatron. Just do your job and connect Abraham's brain to the drone.

Metatron:

- Okay. Don't say I didn't warn you.

Metatron and Lucifer connected Abraham's brain to the shoddy broken drone. First, nothing happened, but then it suddenly started fizzing and making noises. Eventually, the drone was *"back to operational"*, and Abraham woke up.
Abraham:

- Kill, Kill, Kill! Kill the sodomites, kill the idolaters, kill the people disrespecting the Holy Day, Kill women!

Lucifer whispered to Metatron:

- I think you need to tweak the drone's settings.

Metatron turned off the drone and changed the settings. He then turned on the robot containing Abraham's brain again.
Abraham:

- Meep, Meep. I love all my subjects, and I especially love you two, my sweetest Lucifer and Metatron. I will make sure to pay your salaries, and I will even give you a raise. He-he!

Lucifer:

- Yes! That's what I am talking about. Abraham is back, better than ever!

Metatron looked at Lucifer with an empty gaze and then left the room. He couldn't believe that he was stupid enough to bring the old tyrant back!

Chapter 20: Abraham Finds an Evil Way to Make Money!

Abraham was trying to figure out how to make money again. Losing all his money he realised that he had lost his touch when it came to making money, but he couldn't let this slight setback stop his rightful place as Yahweh's successor on Eden, where he ruled over his faithful followers as their benign God-king!

Eventually, he screamed out *"Eureka"* impressed with his own ingenuity. He had found the solution to how he could make large sums of money while being a heartless evil prick at the same time! He would sell children as slaves to the evil tyrant Ibrahim Rashid, leader of House Rashid, who was as rich as Abraham had been at his peak.

Abraham summoned Lucifer to make the call.

Abraham:

  - Lucifer. I need you to make a call for me from the hologram generator.

Lucifer:

  - Why? Can't you use the machine yourself?

Abraham:

  - Look how ugly I am, since someone decided to buy a cheap arse drone to insert my brain into.

Lucifer:

  - Can't disagree with that statement.
  - So, who am I calling?

Abraham:

  - You are calling Ibrahim Rashid.

Lucifer:

- Why would I call that filthy old paedophile, who has always been our sworn enemy?

Abraham:

- Because I am going to sell children to the filthy old paedophile so I can afford to maintain Eden and pay Metatron's outrageously high salary!

Lucifer:

- Wouldn't it be better to just sell the television rights to Eden?

Abraham:

- That is preposterous. Eden is a top-secret project. I cannot televise what we are doing here!

Lucifer:

- But it's already on TV. *"The Bronze Age Fools"* is one of the highest-rated shows in the Solar System. We might as well get paid for it!

Abraham:

- Enough of your nonsense Lucifer. Call Ibrahim Rashid now!

Unbeknownst to Abraham, but well-known to everyone else, there was a popular TV reality show following his idiosyncrasies and their effects on Eden's hapless inhabitants. Years earlier the Martian Humanist Alliance had smuggled in cameras to find out what was really going on, on Eden. At first, they were shocked and considered sending their army to help, but after a while, they realised that they could make a lot of money from selling pirated transmissions from Eden as a TV show. Now, a few years later, the "Bronze

Age Fools" was one of the highest-rated TV shows, and as it was pirated, Abraham made nothing from it. Lucifer reluctantly called Ibrahim Rashid who answered on the hologram generator.

Ibrahim Rashid:

- Hi Terrence, how unexpected! Have you called to sell the Television rights from Eden?

Lucifer:

- I would love to, but my Master would like to keep Eden a secret.

Ibrahim Rashid:

- A secret? But it's on at least a dozen TV stations across the solar system!

Lucifer:

- It's a secret in Abraham's world, he thinks no-one knows!

- Anyway, I called you because Abraham is broke and want to sell children as slaves to you, as you are an infamous wealthy paedophile.

Ibrahim Rashid:

- Oh, but I haven't been a child molester for over 30 years! I am cured of my sick desires, and now I work as philanthropist funding children's orphanages.

Lucifer:

- SHIT, so how the fuck will I make money then??! I need 10 million Terran Credits per year!

Ibrahim Rashid:

- Only 10 million? Oh, that's nothing. I am happy to sponsor my old archenemy as long as this charade goes on. I absolutely love watching "Bronze Age Fools". It keeps me up all night!

Lucifer:

- Thank you, Ibrahim. But how do I explain to Abraham that his old archenemy is helping him?

Ibrahim Rashid:

- Oh, just take the child on a ride in the spaceship and then land again. The old fool won't even notice!

Lucifer:

- Good plan! Thanks, mate.

After this discussion, it was decided that four times a year, a child was selected to fly around in a spaceship for a few hours to give Abraham the illusion that he had sold another child, and then the child would be sent back to Eden. The old idiot never caught on.

Chapter 21: An Unfortunate Calendar Misread!

Abrahameon, The Holy Book of Eden, page 2500, Abraham's 258th commandment said:

"Thou sinner thy worketh on the seventh-day shalt be put to death."

Abraham put down his Holy book of Eden, Abrahameon, where he arbitrarily had decided to execute people that dared to work on the 7th day of the week. Abraham was extra grumpy this day, and it was time to show the Edenites the terrible reach of his law! He summoned Lucifer to have his irks done for.

Abraham:

- Garr, Lucifer! Prepare to fly down to Eden. It is time to punish someone for breaching the 258th commandment!

Lucifer:

- Do you think I have nothing better to do than memorising all the incoherent nonsense in your "Holy Book"? Speak clearly. What do you want to be done?

Abraham:

- That incoherent nonsense is my Divine Will. You better memorise it to avoid my wrath and vengeance!

- Then again, if I punish you for your insolence, who will help me with my evil schemes?

- So, I'll let you live! Your mission is to find a sinner who is breaking against the rule about working on the 7th day and punish this sinner dearly!

Lucifer:

- Sure thing, boss, but why are you giving me Saturday's orders already? Today is Tuesday.

Abraham:

- I don't pay you to argue! I pay you to do as I say! Today is Saturday and the 7th day, find a wretched sinner and punish him.

Lucifer sighed, what a pain it was working as the henchman to that old fart!

- Yes, master, thy orders will be done!

Lucifer gathered a few of his colleagues to find a suitable victim for Abraham's misguided wrath. But it was a difficult choice. It was Tuesday, and everyone was working. How was he going to pick one person to punish for working on a Tuesday? Lucifer tried to think like Abraham. Who was the most illogical person to execute? He concluded that killing the village healer who was curing a sick child, made the least sense, and would be Abraham's preferred choice! Lucifer raised his gun and approached the village healer.
Lucifer:

- Oh, Village Healer! You have broken against the rule regarding working on a Holy Day. I sentence you to death!

Village healer:

- What on Eden are you talking about, you idiot? Today is Tuesday, and it's illegal to NOT work!

Lucifer:

- Admittedly, I said the same thing. But Grandmaster Abraham is adamant that today is Saturday. So, so, off you go to the stoning square in the village!

The Village Healer followed Lucifer without a word. Once they reached the stoning square, Lucifer proclaimed to the villagers:

> - People of Eden! In the name of Grandmaster Abraham, I sentence this village healer to death through stoning for working on a Holy Day. Come forth all faithful people on Eden to carry out the execution.

The villagers shook their heads, ignored Lucifer, and carried on with their day. Eventually the village priest Yehuda shouted back.

> - Today is a Tuesday, you imbecile! We are not falling for that prank. Carry on.

Lucifer felt the migraine approaching. How would he deal with this? He decided to contact Abraham via the mind control technology.

> - Sorry Grandmaster. The villagers refuse to punish the village healer as they are sure that it is Tuesday and not Saturday.

Abraham:

> - Ah, is that so? I'll show them fire and fury! Step away from the village healer.

Lucifer stepped away from the village healer, and Abraham incinerated the village healer with an orbital laser. By chance, Abraham had a moment of clarity straight after firing off the laser and checked the calendar. As it turned out, it was indeed a Tuesday! How embarrassing!
Abraham:

> - Ahem! As it turned out, you were right. Today is a Tuesday. Is there any way for you to revive the village healer?

Lucifer looked at the ash pile that was all that remained of the village healer. The obvious answer was "No", and on top of that, Abraham's decision to kill the village healer for no reason had angered the villagers who were forming a mob to lynch Lucifer. In the last second Lucifer managed to fly off with the villagers throwing rotten fruit after him. Unlucky!

Chapter 22: Fire and Fury to the Sodomites... Some Other Day...

Another day went by, and Abraham in all his forgetfulness was grumpy and angry as usual. This time he was angry with the Sodomites! Abraham had used the mind-control microchips that were implanted into the brains of the Edenites, to perv on them while they were having sex. Unfortunately, Abraham could not remember who he enjoyed watching, and who he didn't enjoy watching so time after time he ended up perving on gay sex by mistake! Abraham was sick of watching men having sex, and instead of not spying on people, he came up with another solution to avoid watching gay sex. To kill all the gays on Eden!

Abraham summoned Lucifer to his office to give him new orders. Lucifer showed up, without a lot of enthusiasm.

Lucifer:

- What is it now?

Abraham:

- I need you to wreak fire and fury on the Sodomites!

Lucifer:

- And that means in normal English?

Abraham:

- I need you to kill Eden's homosexual inhabitants with my orbital lasers!

Lucifer:

- Okay. Why is that?

Abraham:

- Because they are contravening my Divine Will!

Lucifer:

- Hold on. Nowhere in your 3000-page-long book filled with incoherent nonsense, is homosexuality mentioned as a sin.

Abraham:

- That's because I had not considered to perv on the Edenites' sex lives when I wrote it! Regardless, Yahweh punished the Sodomites with fire and fury in the original Holy Bible. So, I want to follow his example!

Lucifer:

- Sure, boss. But how do I know who is a homosexual?

Abraham:

- You must spy on everyone's sex life via the mind control technology! But as of today, I have three people I want to be burned alive.

Lucifer:

- Okay. Give me a list, and I'll sort it out.

A few hours later, Lucifer had gathered the offenders to Mount Sinai as well as a large crowd of spectators to witness the execution, one of the offenders; Simon asked what was going on.
Simon:

- What is going on Lucifer, why am I being punished?

Lucifer:

- You are being punished for being a sodomite, i.e. a homosexual.

Simon:

- That is not a crime in the Abrahameon?!

Lucifer:

- That is correct. However, it is a crime now, and Grandmaster Abraham thinks that it is implied considering that it is illegal in other holy books and Yahweh expressively forbade it in the past.

Simon:

- I see. For future reference, what other ancient books am I meant to follow? And what do I do when they contradict each other?

Lucifer:

- There won't be any future reference, as you are meant to be incinerated by an orbital laser... Oops, I meant by the fire of Abraham's fury. Goodbye, Simon.

Lucifer pressed the fire laser button on his phone, but nothing happened. He pushed the button again but to no avail. Suddenly Metatron contacted him via the mind-control technology.

- Sorry, Terrence. I meant to tell you. The lasers are not working because we are broke and couldn't afford to change the batteries.

Lucifer:

- And you're telling me this now?!
- What do I do? Admit that the lasers are malfunctioning?

Metatron:

- Just tell them that Abraham decided to spare them for now, due to his great mercy.

Lucifer:

- Great. I'll do that.

Lucifer proclaimed to the people below:

- Abraham has decided to spare you for now. But continue to engage in sodomy, and we might fix the lasers, ahem, Abraham might punish you with his Divine wrath.

After saying this, Lucifer flew away in disgrace having displayed his incompetence as an evil henchman in yet another humiliating debacle!

Chapter 23: Yehuda Shows Unexpected Enthusiasm.

After the debacle with fire and fury against the homosexuals, Abraham had a new scheme. He summoned Lucifer to his office. Eventually, Lucifer appeared, demoralised and close to tears.

Unbeknownst to Abraham, Lucifer had been roasted on Television due to his incompetence as an evil henchman. The episode of "The Bronze Age Fools" where he repeatedly was pressing the fire laser button to no avail in his latest debacle had been voted funniest TV moment of the year, and it was safe to say that people were laughing at Lucifer and not with him!

Abraham, oblivious of the TV show, noticed that Lucifer was crying and spoke:

- Why are you crying, Lucifer?

Lucifer:

- It's just my damn pollen allergy, sir.

Abraham gave Lucifer a sceptical look. There were no seasons on Eden and Lucifer was a genetically engineered super-soldier, he shouldn't be allergic to pollen. Then again, Abraham didn't care about his henchmen's emotional problems, so he continued speaking about his latest scheme.

- After the compassion, I showed to the Sodomites I thought I could try another instance of mercy and compassion.

Lucifer:

- That wasn't mercy and compassion. That was you being too broke to replace the laser's batteries.

Abraham:

- Well let's look past that, shall we?!

- Today's plan is a show of mercy and compassion.

- First, we force high priest Yehuda to sacrifice his son to honour me. Then in the last minute, I'll show up as a holographic mirage, and intervene absolving him from senselessly murdering his son, and ending up being the hero of the day!

Lucifer:

- Always just nonsense from you! Can't you cure someone from cancer or something like a normal god?

Abraham:

- I am not a wish-granting genie. But remitting the high priest from murdering his son, is the kind of mercy I am willing to provide.

Lucifer:

- Great. I suppose I am the jester heralding your latest folly?!

Abraham:

- You are my archangel, the Light-bringer, signalling my Divine Will.

Lucifer:

- A distinction without a difference! Oh well, catch you later, boss!

Lucifer carried out his order and gathered everyone from the Gad tribe for his latest announcement, and as usual, there was a complication!

Yehuda and Jamal, who was meant to be Yehuda's son, despite being the same age, had never had their memories wiped and thus they had remembered that they were archenemies on Mars. They had planned to kill each other for the last 20 years, but since they were now "father" and "son" neither of them had dared to try their luck with the Edenite law.

Lucifer made his announced to the villagers:

- Villagers of the Gad Tribe. Today Abraham wants sacrifice from the highest of you. High priest Yehuda, to honour Abraham, you must sacrifice your son Jamal so you can feel the pain he feels when people are living sinful lives.

Lucifer hadn't even finished his speech before Yehuda had jumped on top of Jamal, and ferociously stabbed him with a dagger. Lucifer ran up to Yehuda, who was soaked in Jamal's blood and yelled out:

- What the fuck are you doing, you fucking psycho??! You were meant to be heartbroken, so Abraham could pardon you from senselessly murdering your own son!

Abraham showed up as a mirage and spoke to the congregation.

- Yehuda of the Gad tribe. For your enthusiasm in honouring my will, I will give you life-extending serum. You will live longer than your peers and watch them die of age one by one.

- But to protect the villagers of a deranged psychotic murderer, I am condemning you and your family to live in the wilderness. Because you are a nutjob that needs to be kept separate from the rest of society.

Thus, Abraham was right for once. Yehuda indeed needed to be kept away from other people!

Chapter 24: Lucifer Survives Electrocution and Falling 1000 Metres

Lucifer was flying up to the Divine Control Centre orbiting Eden. He felt distracted, and his mood was low. Not because of guilt for all the atrocities he was carrying out for his evil master, but because of his dry spell. Being a famous star of the reality TV show, "The Bronze Age Fools", he would get laid a lot, if he could only get paid annual leave so he could get some R&R. Abraham was adamant that Eden was secret and not featured in a TV show, and thus they were producing the most costly and popular TV show in the solar system to no avail as they made no money from it.

Suddenly, while Lucifer was flying around and reading the fifth swooning Spacenet fan article about him, he collided head-first with the electromagnetic field that kept Eden's atmosphere from dispersing into space. *"Never scroll through your Spacebook account while flying!"* was his last thought before he passed out, and fell uncontrollably towards the ground, 1000 metres below.

Fortunately, a 1000-meter fall on Eden was not lethal, as the gravity on Eden was low, and thus he hit the ground with low speed. Lucifer woke up a while later and burst into tears. He felt a sharp pain and couldn't move. Was this the end of him? As it turned out, no. Lucifer was not seriously wounded, but the angel suit he was wearing was damaged from the electrocution, and with the suit broken, it was too heavy for him to move in it. Lucifer eventually figured out that he wasn't critically wounded, and he got out of the mechanised suit so he could move freely.

Lucifer thought of activating the emergency beacon on his broken angel armour to request an emergency pick-up, but then he noticed something different. The alien mind control technology implanted in his brain was malfunctioning so that he could see Abraham's thoughts. Finally, he would be able to see what was going on in that old idiot's mind!

Lucifer studied Abraham's mind for a long time. Most of it was incoherent gibberish, but then he saw something that made him furious! Abraham had intentionally sabotaged Lucifer's attempts with women over the years. Abraham did this for laughs, but also to make sure that Lucifer would stay in his employment and not run away with a woman! This made Lucifer furious! He would need to confront Abraham and get his revenge for this outrage!

But Lucifer realised something. If the mind control technology were broken, that meant that he finally had the chance to get laid, and that was a lot more important than vengeance against Abraham. Lucifer roamed hoping that he would find shelter and get lucky soon. Unfortunately, the surface area of Eden was 30,000 square kilometres, but it only had a population of 3,000 people, so finding a woman in this wasteland turned out to be difficult! After a while, Lucifer passed out from his wounds.

Chapter 25: Lucifer Gets Laid and Dies From His Wounds.

As it turned out, the Edenite siblings John and Sara, who were out foraging in the wilderness, found Lucifer and gave him some water to wake him up.

Sara:

- Lucifer! Cover up with some cloth. What are you doing out in the wilderness without your mechanised angel armour?

Lucifer:

- I fell from the sky!

Sara:

- I see, do you want me to contact your boss Abraham?

Lucifer:

- No! I am sick of him! Can you take me back to your hut and nurse my wounds?

Sara:

- Sure, I guess. John, can you fetch a horse trolley to carry Lucifer back to our hut?

John:

- I am not sure. I don't like leaving my virgin sister alone in the wilderness with that sex-starved fool.

Sara:

- Don't worry about that. Lucifer is an honourable gentleman, and besides, he is wounded!

John:

- Okay. I will be back in a while.

After John left, Sara smiled at Lucifer and said:

- You know. I am not really a virgin.

Lucifer made a big grin and replied:

- I know! Fancy a quickie

Sara smiled at him.

- I would love to, but you are injured and having sex might be dangerous for your health. Let's have a session once your wounds have healed.

Lucifer:

- No! No more excuses. No more waiting. I am a genetically engineered super-soldier, I am sure I can survive the strain a quickie has on my body, even though I am seriously injured.

Sara:

- Okay, if you say so. Let's do it.

Lucifer and Sara proceeded to have a very quick quickie, but they shouldn't have! As it turned out, Lucifer's wounds were indeed severe, and this in combination with shock, from finally getting laid was too much for him. After coming, Lucifer fell into cardiac arrest and died! Patience is a virtue, Lucifer!

Chapter 26: Lucifer is Revived, With a Budget Heart.

A few months later, Abraham studied Lucifer as he lay on the operation table in the medical bay of the Divine Control Centre. At first, when the other angels had found Lucifer's lifeless and sexed-out naked body in the wilderness, Abraham had wanted to punish the Edenites with fire and fury! Metatron had convinced him to not make any rash decisions until he knew how Lucifer had died. Abraham had made a rational decision and went ahead with Metatron's suggestion.

Eventually, Abraham and his henchmen had uncovered the truth about Lucifer's unfortunate passing. While Abraham was disappointed that Lucifer had followed his carnal desires instead of committing entirely to his godly cause, Lucifer's sins weren't that great, so Abraham decided to revive him: With a low-budget synthetic heart. This was because Lucifer needed to be punished, and with a weak heart, he was less likely to engage in sessions of unauthorised coitus!

Lucifer woke up and found himself in the medical ward of the Divine Control Centre.

Lucifer:

- What happened? Why do I feel like an old overweight smoker who hasn't eaten healthy in decades?

Abraham:

- You died while fornicating with an Eden woman!

- I decided to revive you with a low-budget synthetic heart as a punishment and as revenge for you replacing my body with this cheap wonky robot.

Lucifer:

- What about Sara? Is she okay?

Metatron:

- She is fine, as she was not as shocked as you were over having sex.

Lucifer:

- I must see her again! She is the only one for me and the most beautiful woman in the solar system.

Abraham:

- While I don't doubt the statement that she is the only one for you, *"Most beautiful woman in the Solar System"* is the biggest exaggeration I have ever heard!

- Besides, you risk having another heart attack if you're having sex, with your new budget heart. Hehehe!

Lucifer:

- Sara is worth more to me than my own life! I must see her again.

Abraham:

- Alright mate. Whatever. See you later.

Chapter 27: Sara's Revelation Causes Lucifer Another Heart Attack.

A few days later, Lucifer had recovered enough to go back to the surface of Eden to meet with Sara, his true love. He had decided to wait for a few days as he got carried away the last time, he saw her, ending up dead in the process. Being dead wasn't particularly pleasant, so this time he was hellbent on surviving an encounter with her. Abraham had threatened him with fire and fury if he was to meet Sara again, but fortunately, Abraham had a long nap every afternoon, and this nap was Lucifer's window of opportunity!

Lucifer put on his fanciest mechanical angel armour, styled his hair, and applied make-up to look younger. Unfortunately, Lucifer was not a stylist, so instead of looking more youthful, he looked like a transvestite! Ouch!

Lucifer made his way to Sara's hut. She opened the door and gave him a surprised and sceptic look.

Lucifer:

- I am back from the dead, so we can be together! Let's get married, my love!

Sara:

- I am not sure. You lasted for less than 30 seconds, then you pretended to die. Now, three months later, you are back, looking like a transsexual and professing your true love. Not very mature, Lucifer!

Lucifer:

- But I did die. I have been dead for three months. But my love for you, and an artificial heart brought me back to be with you!

Sara:

- If you say so.

- I have good news. You are not shooting blanks. I am pregnant with twins!

Lucifer clutched his chest, and he dropped dead to the ground for the second time. The shock from the news about the twins was too much for the low budget artificial heart that Abraham had bought for him. Poor Sara, watching Lucifer die, again and again!

Chapter 28: Abraham Sets Lucifer Ablaze With a Laser.

A few weeks later, the Edenites were gathered to witness the execution of Lucifer for breaking his vows of celibacy. The Edenites had no idea what the point of this execution was, as it was apparent that Lucifer was already dead. He reeked of death, and there were flies around his body! But they knew better than interfering with Abraham's follies, so they played along with the charade.

Abraham showed up as mirage standing on Mount Sinai. He gave a long-winded tirade about why the carnal union between angels and Edenites were forbidden. The tirade made absolutely no sense, and the Edenites had to struggle to not fall asleep in the middle of the speech. Falling asleep during Abraham's boring lectures angered him, and the Edenites didn't want to experience Abraham's violent temper tantrums.

After a couple of hours later, it was time for the grand finale, which was to press the big red button and send down a high-powered laser beam to set Lucifer's body ablaze! Abraham pressed the big red button, after pressing it, he had a moment of clarity. He remembered that Lucifer, in fact, was a clone of his long-dead son Terrence Goldstein. How great it was to have a family again. He should spend as much money as it took to revive his favourite son and build a good father and son relationship!

He called Metatron to tell him about his new plans.
Abraham:

- New plans. Bring Lucifer back to the Divine Control Centre. We'll make sure to revive him and give him the best possible body parts this time!

Metatron:

- What on Earth are you talking about?! You've just destroyed his body!

Abraham:

- I just realised that Lucifer is a clone of my long-lost son Terrence Goldstein. I can't pointlessly execute the corpse of my grandson, can I?

Metatron looked at the charred remains of Lucifer's body. He sighed. His boss would have a new outburst over this!

Chapter 29 Sara Dies in Childbirth. Jeshua and Adina are Separated

Nine months after her short session with Lucifer, Sara was in labour with twins, one baby boy and one baby girl. Unfortunately, Eden being a Bronze Age replica, didn't have fully qualified midwives, so Sara ended up dying in labour. Yehuda, Sara's crazy grandfather and heavy drug user decided that Lucifer's son was just what he needed to get his revenge on Abraham and to overthrow his rule, so he ran away with the baby boy to a nearby cave where he was growing *"recreational herbs and mushrooms"*.

Meanwhile, Gabriel and Metatron arrived at Sara's hut where the midwife was holding Adina, the late Lucifer's, and Sara's baby daughter.

Gabriel:

- Midwife! Wasn't there meant to be two babies here?

Midwife:

- The crazy psychopath Yehuda, Sara's father, stormed in and stole the boy, claiming that Lucifer's son would be the key to crushing Abraham's rule in the future!

Gabriel:

- I see. We better catch this eloped criminal and bring both the babies back to their blessed Grandmaster Abraham!

Suddenly, Metatron pulled Gabriel aside and whispered to him.

- I suggest we only bring the girl and tell Abraham that she was the only child that was born. Imagine Abraham's anger when he finds out that Yehuda has taken away his grandson. It won't be pretty for any of us!

Gabriel:

- I see. You are right. Let's just bring the daughter and hope that Abraham doesn't notice!

Having said this, Gabriel and Metatron then took Adina with them back to the Divine Control Centre to bring her to Abraham.

A few hours later, Yehuda came to a moment of clarity and realised that a baby boy could not live off mushrooms and *"herbs"*, so he handed the child over to the gullible couple Akiva and Chana, the only people on Eden who wouldn't get suspicious when an old junkie brought them a baby to raise. He claimed that the baby had already been baptised under the name Jeshua. This meant that Jeshua didn't need to be baptised again, which meant that he wouldn't get a mind control chip inserted into his brain, unlike all the other Edenites. Yehuda planned to come back and collect Jeshua when Jeshua was old enough to live off herbs and mushrooms. This plan didn't happen though, as Yehuda died of age and lung cancer, a short while later!

Chapter 30: Is This Wise?

Metatron had a bad headache. His foolish boss Abraham hadn't appreciated his comment that it might not be the wisest choice to insert an advanced mind control chip that enabled the user to blast other users with psionic blasts into a baby. Abraham had blasted Metatron to the floor with a psionic blast asking if anyone else had objections to his grand plan. As it turned out no-one did. Thus, it was decided that Adina should have a medium-tier mind-control chip implanted in her brain that she could use to read peoples' minds and to blast them with psionic blasts when they didn't agree with her.

After inserting the chip into baby Adina, Abraham realised how difficult it would be to raise a child with the ability to mentally blast people that disagreed with her. So, he delegated the task to High priest Markus on Eden. What an honour, Markus!

Chapter 31: Adina Gets Rotten Teeth!

When Adina was five years old, her teeth started to rot. This was because she was a child with temper tantrums and a sweets addiction. While most kids with Adina's attitude could receive a spanking and be put in place when they were arguing, Adina was different. Outfitted with advanced mind control technology and the temperament of a sugar-addicted child, she threw tantrums every time she didn't get her way, which led to high priest Markus while being one of the bosses of Eden, was not the boss at home!

Giving superpowers to a five-year-old child created a monster. In Adina's case, this monster was a chubby kid with rotten teeth, with the physique of a balloon! Adina and her hapless foster father Markus became the new stars on the long-running reality television show *The Bronze Age Fools* that had been running nonstop for over 30 years, following the lives of the luckless Edenites.

Chapter 32: Jeshua and Adina Meet For the First Time

When Jeshua and Adina were ten years old, they met for the first time. Jeshua's foster parents had taken him to Mount Sinai for the New Year's celebration. Suddenly he saw Adina with the rest of her family, and she immediately caught his attention. How could anyone be that fat?! Adina loved to eat, particularly candy and no-one in her household had the death wish to limit her portion sizes and fall victim to her tantrums and psionic blasts. Adina's uncontrolled gluttony led to Adina being humongous, while the rest of her family were very skinny as they had to survive on whatever food was left after Adina had her share!

Jeshua's ward Akiva approached him and spoke:

- Do not gain the attention of that girl. People say that she is a witch that uses her superpowers to read their thoughts and eat their food. We are poor. If she eats our food, we are doomed!

Jeshua:

- Yes, father, I will stay clear of her.

Jeshua was only paying lip service to his father's wishes. He understood that his father would go crazy on the open wine bar and pass out in a couple of hours, and that was his opportunity to study the strange girl carefully!

A couple of hours later, Akiva had passed out due to excessive wine consumption, and Jeshua could sneak away to have a closer look at the mysterious piggy-faced girl! He snuck around to find Adina, but embarrassingly enough she managed to sneak up on him instead.

Adina:

- What are you doing up here? You are a poor peasant boy; you are not allowed into the rich people's side of the party.

Jeshua:

- I came to see you; I have never seen anyone as round as you before. You are so fascinating!

Adina got angry at Jeshua for calling her fat. No-one could call her fat; she was simply big boned! She focused her mind to psionically blast Jeshua, but she couldn't as he had no mind-control technology installed in his brain. Adina looked like an idiot cringing with a red face, without doing anything.

Jeshua:

- Are you alright?

Adina:

- Yeah, I am fine. But why can't I blast you with a psionic blast, for calling me fat?

Jeshua was confused. What was the fatty talking about? He realised that he shouldn't argue with the high priest's daughter, so he tried making amends.

Jeshua:

- Oh, I forgot to introduce myself. I am Jeshua, son of Akiva. I meant to say that you are round and beautiful.

Adina:

- I am Adina, daughter of the high priest Markus, also known as the little Missy Magic.

Jeshua:

- Nice to meet you, Adina. I need to go now. See you around.

Adina:

- Indeed, we will. And it might be sooner than you think!

Chapter 33: Adina Makes Jeshua Move to her Village.

After the New Year's celebration, Adina was interested to know more about Jeshua. Who was this boy that had dared to call her fat, why couldn't she blast him with her mind like she would to any other Edenites and why did he look like the spitting image of her real father, Lucifer?

Adina concluded that Jeshua must be her lost twin brother. It wasn't the hardest conclusion to make. The population of Eden was only 5,000 at the time, and there was less than a 100 that was the same age as her. If one of these people showed up looking exactly like her real father, and he is the same age as her, he must be her brother.

Adina knew everything that was going on Eden. Due to plot convenience, her affinity with the alien mind control technology was a lot greater than everyone else, meaning that she could read the angels' and Abraham's minds. Adina knew that she was adopted, and she understood the deaths of her real parents could have been avoided if it wasn't for Abraham's endless cruelty and anger outbursts. Adina wanted revenge, and she wanted to oversee Eden. Then she could stop living in this stupid Bronze Age world and instead she could eat as much as she wished to while futuristic technologies would keep her slim and with good teeth!

The easiest way for Adina to achieve what she wanted would be to blast and kill the old Abraham with a surprise psionic blast. Everyone would think it was good riddance, and she would become the heroine of Eden. Unfortunately, Adina had a longwinded and needlessly complicated plan. To achieve that plan she first needed to make sure that Jeshua was living close to her, as an employee.

The first part was easy as high priest Markus, her foster father was the richest man on Eden and was the boss of everyone except over Adina. Soon after Adina's request, Jeshua and his family moved to Adina's village to work for Adina's family.

Chapter 34: Adina Stumbles into a Large Cake!

A few years later, it was time for Adina's adulthood ceremony. Adina was excited about the big cake and the big party celebrating the coming of age for the most important person on Eden, herself. What she was less enthusiastic about was her secret twin brother's lack of interest in her ideology. Adina wanted Jeshua to be her follower. She wanted Jeshua's help overthrowing the tyrannical idiot Abraham and replace him with the rightful ruler of Eden, Adina!

Despite all of Adina's persuasion attempts, Jeshua seemed uninterested in her proposals. He didn't believe in her claims that she was his sister, he couldn't care less about her prophecies and talk about the Divine Providence that wanted her to rule. Adina found it hard to convince Jeshua. With everyone else, she could mind-control them or threaten them with psionic blasts, things that Jeshua was immune to due to his lack of alien mind-control technology.

What Jeshua did seem interested in was smoking herbs and eating mushrooms. And he had vast access to herbs since his father Akiva was appointed caretaker of the temple herb gardens, and Jeshua was his assistant. A lot could be said about Jeshua's lack of work ethics, but on the bright side, he didn't risk getting killed for breaking the laws regarding working on a holy day!

Adina saw the auditorium filling up with people who had come to wish her well. The number of people disappointed her, the more people that went to the ceremony, the less cake there would be for her. Regardless, it was good to be in the centre of attention and to honour the day her parents had even got her a new beautiful dress. Adina smiled at Jeshua, who looked stoned in the back corner of the auditorium.

Suddenly, something unexpected happened! Metatron decided to do some work. Generally, during these gatherings, he just zoned out, letting his mind drift, while watching sexy girls on Spacenet via the built-in microchips in his brain. On this occasion, however, something was blocking the path between him and the closest Spacenet satellites, and he did the same that any

21st-century worker would do when the Internet went down, he started to work as he had nothing else to do.

When Metatron was actually working, he noticed something strange. He used his microchip to analyse the number of people in the room and realised that there was one user in the room that didn't have any mind control chip installed, and that person looked like a younger version of Lucifer. He gave a signal to Nuriel and together they walked over to Jeshua to apprehend the fugitive.

Adina noticed what was about to happen, and she used her psionic powers to protect Jeshua by blocking his presence from Metatron's and Nuriel's view. Unfortunately, she had forgotten the skill to block people's vision, so instead, she had to apply plan B! She stood up, shouted out *"Run, run, run Jeshua!"* and then plunged headfirst into the cake as a quick diversion. Plop!

It worked. Watching the fat kid Adina stumble headfirst into a cake was so funny that Metatron and Nuriel forgot about Jeshua and instead, they were rolling on the floor laughing. Jeshua used this opportunity to sneak out from this strange adulthood ceremony!

Chapter 35: Abraham orders a search for Jeshua!

Later the same day, Metatron and Nuriel were summoned to Abraham to explain themselves. How could they, genetically engineered super-soldiers, have lost their target from such a textbook diversion as the fat kid dropping headfirst into a cake? It was an outrage and an embarrassment.

Metatron understood why Abraham was angry but just wanted clarification, so he asked anyway.

Metatron:

- So, to sum things up, you are angry because we let a harmless stoner out of sight?

Abraham:

- I am angry because you failed to help an underage child with addiction problems! You are the angels of Eden! You are role models for the population, why can't you help an innocent child?

Metatron:

- But Grandmaster Abraham, you are burning, stoning, and flogging people to death for fun, not to mention the fact that you are selling children to paedophiles. Is really non-interference against Jeshua's pot-smoking that bad in comparison?

Abraham:

- Silence, you fool! Jeshua is my lost grandson, so of course, I must look after his health!

Metatron:

- What? Is he your grandson? Then Lucifer must have been your son?

Abraham realised that he had revealed too much and tried talking his way out of the situation.

- Oh, I meant that Jeshua is my metaphorical grandson, just like everyone else on Eden is my metaphorical children.

Metatron:

- So why do you care about Jeshua if he is only your metaphorical grandson, just like everyone else?

Abraham blasted Metatron with a psionic blast that knocked him to the ground.
Abraham:

- I don't pay you to question me, I pay you to follow orders.

Metatron was going to say something about hardly getting paid at all, but he realised that today wasn't a good day to discuss his salary. Instead, he tried to soothe the temper of the 300-year-old baby that stood in front of him.

- Sincere apologies, Grandmaster! Shall we go back to the village and find Jeshua?

Abraham:

- He will not be in the village anymore, now that he knows we are looking for him! Scour the maintenance tunnels looking for him. Leave no stone unturned.

Thus, Jeshua could continue spending the following years in peace and harmony in the village while poor Metatron and Gabriel had to spend endless months looking for Jeshua in the dark and damp maintenance tunnels underground.

Chapter 36: Gabriel crashes a wedding and is knocked out

A few years later, Abraham and the angels were still broke. Despite producing the most viewed reality show for the last thirty years, they made no money from it as Abraham was adamant that Eden was a secret and refused to acknowledge that his follies were the most viewed show in the solar system!

In a way, Abraham's stupidity was what saved the Eden project from outside intervention. Members of the Martian Humanist Alliance had tried to get their leadership to send an army to stop Abraham for the last 30 years, but the leadership had refused as they made so much money from the pirated TV rights, so their entire budget was relying on it!

Due to their dire finances, Metatron was sent to Eden to check the villagers bookkeeping to see if there was any way to save money. Unfortunately, Metatron made up an allergy to papyrus to get out of the task, so Gabriel was sent instead.

Gabriel scrolled through the dusty papyrus rolls detailing the village's finances for several hours until he found something interesting. Salary payments to Jeshua! Gabriel summoned high priest Markus.

Gabriel:

- Markus! Why are you still paying salary to the fugitive Jeshua when he no longer lives here?

Markus looked at Gabriel with a confused look:

- What do you mean he no longer lives here? He is working in the herb garden with his father.

Gabriel felt that his blood started to boil, and he shouted out:

- Why didn't you tell us?

- Metatron and I have been scouring the damp smelly tunnels for years looking for the fugitive Jeshua. Are you saying he has been here the whole time?

Markus shrugged his shoulders and replied:

- You never asked. I have been wondering what you have been doing down there, but I am smart enough to stay out of Abraham's idiocies.

Gabriel calmed down.

- Okay, fair point.
- Where is Jeshua now?

Markus

- He is next doors, at his brother's wedding

Gabriel got up and moved towards the wedding. Jeshua would have to pay. Gabriel had spent the past two years looking for Jeshua in the damp and smelly tunnels, and he had enough!
Gabriel entered the wedding hall, and he shouted out:

- Jeshua you bastard! Because of you, I have spent the last two years in the tunnels. You are coming with me now!

Jeshua was confused. Why were the angels looking for him? Why had they been looking for him in the tunnels, his address was listed in Markus's address registry for the village? Suddenly, Jeshua's drunken uncle knocked Gabriel unconscious with a clay pot. *"Shut up, you are disturbing the wedding."*
Adina, who was attending the wedding rushed to Jeshua.

- Jeshua! They are coming for you; you better run and hide in the tunnels!

Jeshua felt perplexed over Adina dumb proposal:

- But they have spent the last two years looking for me in the tunnels. Wouldn't that be the worst place to hide?

Adina:

- No, it's the best place, I don't think they want to go back there!

- There is plenty of mushrooms for you there, and I will provide you with food. In return, you must help me build an underground rebellion against Abraham!

Jeshua:

- Cool, we have a deal, sister. I got to scram, see you at the tunnel entrance at Gomorrah falls in a couple of days.

After saying this, Jeshua left the party to make his way to Gomorrah Falls. For Jeshua's drunken uncle, things went worse as he was set alight when he fell into the fire due to his drunkenness while holding a clay jar filled with booze. As it turned out, the roasted goat wasn't the only thing that got roasted at Jeshua's brother's wedding!

Chapter 37: A Disappointing Underground Rebellion

The following years were quite uneventful. As Adina had anticipated the angels didn't want to look for Jeshua in the damp underground tunnel which meant that they kept coming back looking for him in the village where he no longer resided. To Adina's great disappointment, her brother was useless at leading an underground rebellion, but he did wonders for her waistline.

The reason was that Adina had promised to share her rations with Jeshua, which led to her losing a significant amount of weight. Unfortunately, he didn't uphold his part of the bargain. Instead of *"liberating"* the Edenites from the Alien mind-control technology and leading an underground rebellion, he liberated his stoner friends, and they spent most of their time chilling out in the tunnels enjoying the produce and herbs!

In the year 2872, After 62 years on Eden, Events would unfold that would change the lives of the Edenites forever: The introduction of the characters Keila Eisenstein and Bjorn Muller to the plot!

Chapter 38: Some Pseudo-Religious Mumbo-Jumbo

Exceptionally far away, and yet close, in the Divine Dimension, a bunch of Zetans IE Godlike Aliens were discussing the current events in the solar system and the progress of their Chosen One also known as Keila Eisenstein.

Zeus:

- Are you sure that Keila is the Chosen One? She seems a bit cuck-oo, to say the least.

Brahma:

- Yes, but unfortunately the gene for our magical Zetan abilities is the same genes that make humans mentally ill. But she'll be the one to open the portals on Earth. I have foreseen it!

Zeus:

- Okay, but killing the leader of the Terran Council and receiving a massive bounty on her head doesn't seem to be the best way to go back to Earth and open the portals!?

- Anyway, how is your crazy ex Rangda? Is she still looked up in that inescapable prison we built for her since you begged us to not kill her for betraying our species and destroying most of our civili-sation?

Brahma:

- Yes, of course, she is. As you said yourself, the prison is in-escapable. Now hold my hand, I need to amplify my psionic pow-ers to reach Keila's mind.

Zeus:

- I am a bit sceptical about all this handholding. Can't you perform the ritual without it?

Brahma:

- No, your psionic input is imperative for the success of this mission!

After that, they held hands and chanted gibberish in the Zetan language to increase Brahma psionic powers so he could connect to Keila! Obviously, the Zetans always spoke in the Zetan language, but as the author of this book wasn't Tolkien and couldn't be bothered making up a new language, he made them speak English instead for simplicity!

Chapter 39: It's Complicated

Keila looked out through the rear window of her small spaceship, Miss Freedom. She could see how the massive Terran Council fleet that had come to a stop her blew up the headquarters of the Martian Humanist Alliance on the asteroid Sylvia. *"Ha-Ha fooled him again"* she exclaimed much to the disdain of the remaining crew of the ship. While they were happy to be alive, Keila escaping Bjorn Muller for the umpteenth time was not much cause for celebration considering that most of their faction, friends and families had died in the massive battle they had just escaped from!

Keila's second in command on the ship, Sven approached her.

- Why are you laughing you lunatic? And what do we do now?

Keila:

- I am laughing, knowing how frustrated Bjorn will be, once he finds out that I escaped again!

Sven:

- But your mother died there, together with most of our leadership!

Keila:

- Oh, yes, you are right. That puts me in charge! It's time to save Eden from the tyrant Abraham.

Sven:

- Are you out of your freaking mind? Are you going to attack a well-armed battle station with this single tiny ship?

Keila:

- Yes! The gods are with me. Eden is my destiny!

Sven didn't respond. He had enough of Keila's craziness and wanted to get as far away from her as possible. To achieve that he planned to take her to Eden, give her a radio and tell her to call him once *"the coast was clear"*. Suddenly a more urgent problem appeared. Bjorn Muller was after them, again! The man who had been pursuing them for the last four years was like a rash that was impossible to shake off! But how could he know where they were? Sven had made sure that their ship had no bugs or tracking devices. It was a mystery!

The solution was a lot more mundane than mysterious. Bjorn knew about Keila's location as he had her as a contact on the social media platform Spacebook. Keila, despite being the most wanted terrorist in the solar system, had not grasped the concept that her social media account continually sent out her location to all her contacts. Through pure luck and Brahma's divine interventions, she had managed to stay alive, but poor Brahma needed to work overtime to make it so!

Keila relationship status with Bjorn was summarized as "It's complicated" on Spacebook and it certainly was. For the last seven years, Brahma had sent Keila and Bjorn's visions showing the two of them together, that they were meant to be a couple. Four years ago, Keila had managed to get detained in immigration, and Bjorn Muller had come to meet her as she was the daughter of his former friend Mahmoud Rashid. Once they met, they had realised that they were the one from each other's vision and they were meant to be together. Unfortunately, due to Bjorn being a degenerate drug user, he had decided that the best way for them to be together was for Keila to be his sex slave. Eventually, Keila got out, and she decided to kill Bjorn's grandfather as revenge. This murder led to four years of war as Bjorn's grandfather happened to be Hans Muller, the leader of the Terran Council!

Sven noticed how Bjorn's ship was getting closer. How was this possible? Had Bjorn finally caught on and installed a better engine on his spaceship? As it turned out, he finally had! Short on options, Sven decided to dump Keila in an emergency pod crashing on Eden. With a bit of luck, Bjorn was still obsessed with Keila and would stop pursuing Sven's rebel ship if he could catch his crazy woman instead!

Chapter 40: Sven's Plan Backfires!

A few days later, Sven and Keila reached Eden. Sven pushed Keila into an emergency shuttle, gave her a radio and promised that he would come to pick her up at a later stage. *"As if,"* he thought for himself and ran to the hologram generator to let Bjorn know that Keila was no longer on the ship. Unfortunately for Sven, Bjorn's second in command Captain Adal Schneider answered.

Sven:

- We dumped off the crazy bitch Keila on Eden. She is free for you to take!

Adal:

- Thanks for the heads up, but you are still my enemy, and we are finally within range as you were kind enough to stop! Prepare to die. He-He-He

"Holy Shit" was the last thing Sven said before the ship was eviscerated by the powerful weapons on the Terran Council's command ship!

Keila witnessing her former ship being blown up, pulled the safety release switch on her escape pod so that it would move quicker towards Eden surface. Unfortunately, she pulled it a bit too hard, so she destroyed the switch and crashed down on the surface. Keila was knocked unconscious in the process!

Chapter 41: "Sleeping beauty."

Jeshua was enjoying his herbs from his usual spot close to the tunnel entrance at Gomorrah Cliffs. The place was perfect. Still warm and cozy as the rest of Eden, and yet safe from Abraham's orbital lasers as he was still underground in the tunnels that for unclear reasons had no surveillance cameras in them.

Suddenly, Jeshua saw an explosion in the sky and looked up. Jeshua saw Keila's emergency pod crash just alongside the tunnel entrance just a short sprint away.

Tentatively Jeshua approached the emergency pod. His legs were shaky, and he was struggling to balance. Jeshua's unsteady balance was not so because of fear but merely due to inhaling too many herbs. He opened the emergency pod and saw a beautiful woman in a strange futuristic military uniform. His first thought was *"what kind of fool wears a tight leather outfit when a bronze armour and shield is so much more effective?"* But then Jeshua realised that the outside world wasn't living in the Bronze Age and that Keila's outfit made a lot of sense in the future. If nothing else it, made her look incredibly sexy, was this his sleeping beauty from the fairy tales, sent by the True Maker?

Jeshua shook off the notion. The prince in the sleeping beauty was a creepy rapist, who broke into a sleeping woman's house and had his way with her, yuck! Jeshua, on the other hand, was a phlegmatic and likeable stoner who liked to hang out in peace with his mates enjoying the gifts of mother nature!

As Jeshua was a good guy, he lifted the unconscious Keila out of the wrecked escape pod and carried her further into the tunnels where they were safe from Abraham's wrath and orbital lasers!

Chapter 42: Bjorn Muller Contacts Nuriel.

Rear Admiral Bjorn Muller was in the middle of one of his cocaine and booze-filled one-man frenzies when his right-hand man Captain Adal Schneider knocked on his door. Bjorn gave a voice command to the AI, and the door opened. Adal walked in and saw Bjorn sitting shirtless, pouring sweat, with cocaine all over his face. Adal shook his head in disapproval but said nothing. Bjorn spoke:

- Welcome Adal, have you come to join the party?

Adal:

- No sir, may I remind you about the zero-tolerance policy for drugs in the Terran Council Security Forces?

Bjorn:

- You may. But I am the son of the Terran Council leader, and I do whatever I want. You can tell that to that toothless old fart, Admiral Max Wellington.

Adal

- Max Wellington is younger than you, sir.

Bjorn:

- Yes, but I look younger, and more importantly, I am a lot richer! Why did you come if not to join the party? Keila is finally dead, and the rebellion is crushed. When else can you loosen up, Adal?

Adal:

- Keila is the reason I came. She is not dead. She narrowly escaped.

Bjorn:

- What the fuck? NOT AGAIN! I have been chasing that damn woman for four years.

Adal:

- On the flipside. She is stuck on Eden with no way of escaping.

Bjorn:

- Great. Send our troops to kill her then!

Adal:

- I would. However, the cranky old idiot Abraham refuses to let us land there, as he wants to maintain Eden a "secret".

Bjorn:

- A secret?! That place has been featured on television for 60 years straight, there can't possibly be a less secretive place than Eden in the solar system! Anyways, I'll freshen up and talk to him myself.

A while later Bjorn contacted Abraham on the hologram generator. Abraham refused to answer calls on the hologram generator, as he hated the way his robotic body looked so instead Nuriel got the honour.

Nuriel studied Bjorn's hologram for a while before saying anything. He could see the cocaine residue dripping from Bjorn's nostrils and if that wasn't enough Bjorn's fancy Rear Admiral uniform was drenched in sweat. Nuriel sighed, he had enough trouble dealing with the idiocies of his dementia-ridden boss, and now he would have to deal with The Terran Council leader's cocaine-addicted son as well! Eventually, Nuriel stepped up on the hologram generator platform to reply.

- This is Nuriel, representing Abraham and the Eden project. How can I help you?

Bjorn:

- The terrorist Keila Eisenstein crashed on Eden. I need to send my men to pursue and kill her.

Nuriel:

- I know, and I would wish you Godspeed. However, my boss Abraham insists that my colleagues and I risk our necks catching this dangerous and volatile madwoman instead! Your men are not granted permission to land, unfortunately.

Bjorn:

- This is unacceptable.

Nuriel:

- I know, right! Can you call the Henchmen union for me to complain? Chasing dangerous terrorist madwomen is not part of my work description! Anyways, I instruct you to wait over the dark side of Eden

Nuriel hung up on Bjorn and left the room. Bjorn was considering calling again threatening with fire and fury, but he refrained from doing so. Abraham was a fool and wouldn't back down from starting an unwinnable war against the Terran Council which Abraham would lose. Bjorn, however, did not want to be the first casualty of that war. So, he decided to do as instructed and then call his dad and complain about it!

Chapter 43: Sexy Dreams and Disappointing Sex!

Keila had wet dreams. She was dreaming about having sex with an athletic super sexy man in an ancient cave, filled with fire and flames. The pounding got increasingly intense and eventually, she peaked. Oh yeah, that hit the spot! She woke up with a smile on her lips after the exciting dream and realised that she was in an ancient-looking cave. What a coincident, was this a premonition that she was getting laid today?

Keila looked around, and she saw the unkempt stoner sitting in the corner in a cloud of smoke. He wasn't particularly attractive and worst of all, he didn't smell that good. On the bright side, he wasn't from the Terran Council army, and she'd rather share the cave with a stoner than the army sent to kill her. Keila closed her eyes again. *"The hot sex in a cave"* vision was still there. *"Oh well," she* thought and started unzipping her tight body armour. Keila called Jeshua over:

- Hey foreigner! I had a vision where I had sex with a stranger in a cave. Do you want to be that stranger?

Jeshua:

- Sure. Sounds good to me. I am Jeshua.

Keila:

- Cool, I am Keila. Let's do this!

A few minutes later, the sex was over, and Keila was upset with her divine connection. The sex had been anything but good. Jeshua was a lousy lover and he smelt funny. Then again there was no STD's in the 29th century, so nothing gained nothing lost. Keila felt sleepy and fell asleep. Jeshua, on the other hand, was overjoyed. He rarely got laid, and Keila was a lot prettier than the village goat! His choice of not acting like a creepy "Sleeping Beauty" prince had paid off, and he had experienced the best sex of his life. Jeshua was also sleepy, so he fell asleep next to Keila.

Chapter 44: Adina Masters a New Skill and Saves Jeshua and Keila.

A few hours later Gabriel and Nuriel cautiously entered the tunnels where Keila's emergency pod had crashed so they could put an end to the dangerous and psychotic terrorist. They couldn't believe their luck when they found Keila and Jeshua sleeping in the same bed. Finally, they would get a bonus and a hard-earned holiday! The lifted their guns ready to shoot the fugitives when Keila and Jeshua suddenly disappeared out of sight. What kind of prank was this?

Conveniently, Adina had finally mastered the skill *"Hide people from the henchmen's vision"* after many years of practice. She used this skill to save the life of her brother and the infamous Martian rebel Keila. Adina smiled when she saw how confused the angels looked, but then she realised that her plan had a minor flaw. She hadn't mastered the skill to hide people from the henchmen's sense of smell yet, and as genetically engineered super-soldiers both Gabriel and Nuriel had the sense of smell of bloodhounds!

Gabriel and Nuriel decided, that they would shoot the bed were Jeshua and Nuriel lay as it smelled like them. Unfortunately for the incompetent henchmen, Keila dragged Jeshua out of bed, and they made a run for it, just before the angels started shooting at the bed. Since the TV networks had hacked the built-in cameras in the angels' body armours, this episode was later aired, and both Gabriel and Nuriel turned out to be the laughingstock of the entire solar system just like Lucifer and Abraham had been before them!

Chapter 45: Abraham Gives a Reasonable and Logical Order for Once.

Abraham was looking at the videos from the built-in cameras in his henchmen's angel armours, and he couldn't believe what he saw. Somehow, his idiotic employees had stared dumbfounded at a dangerous sleeping terrorist for ages and then shoot at the bed when the enemy had already made a run for it. How was this possible and what idiot had been responsible for optimising the genetics of these so-called super-soldiers? Abraham, as usual, wanted fire and fury, but more importantly, he needed Keila eliminated. He couldn't have a dangerous rebel stirring up emotions among his loyal subjects. Abraham called Gabriel and Nuriel over.

- Okay. So, as you claim, you can't see the enemies, but you can smell them; your order is the following: Shoot at everything that smells like them.

Metatron raised his hand in the background. Abraham spoke to him:

- Yes, Metatron. What is it?

Metatron:

- Isn't it dangerous to order Gabriel and Nuriel to shoot on everything that smells like Keila or Jeshua? What if the enemy finds a way to make our troops smell like them?

Abraham:

- And how exactly would that happen?

Metatron:

- For example, by filling clay containers with their own blood, then hide in a smoky, smelly room and then throw the pots, so their blood splashes on our troops.

Abraham:

- And people accuse me of being silly!?

- That is the most farfetched contrived scenario I have heard in my over 300 years of living. Shame on you for wasting our valuable time with these idiocies

- Gabriel and Nuriel carry out my orders. Metatron: You are on latrine duty!

After saying this, all the gathered angels left the room to carry out their assigned tasks. Unfortunately for Abraham, Gabriel and Nuriel, ignoring Metatron's farfetched speculation was a critical mistake as Keila planned to do precisely what Metatron had said she would do!

Chapter 46: Keila and Jeshua Kill Gabriel and Nuriel

"Ouch, fucking hell, that stings" Jeshua exclaimed as Keila cut him in the arm with a knife to fill a clay jar with his blood. After sealing the wound, they relaxed and waited for Abraham's henchmen to come after them. Jeshua suggested a quickie, but Keila politely declined, partly because sex with him wasn't that hot but mostly because she didn't want to be caught in the act, with her pants down!

Eventually, Nuriel and Gabriel showed up, and Keila and Jeshua put their plan into action. They ran away from the angels until the tunnel diverged into two tunnels where they split up. Nuriel and Gabriel also split up and chased their target individually. Eventually, Nuriel almost caught up with Jeshua, and they entered a smoke-filled smelly room. Nuriel noticed that he got hit by a thrown clay jar and wondered what kind of idiot that would think that was enough to fight a 29th-century super-soldier with a mechanised battle armour?! He noticed a smell signature of Jeshua 20 meter away from him, on the other side of the room.

Nuriel thought for himself, a thrown clay jar containing a liquid, a smelly and smoky room with no vision, could Metatron be right, was this an elaborate trap? Nuriel concluded that Metatron was a nerd, so he disregarded him and fired at the target. He shot several shots, and to his surprise, the target shot back at him. Nuriel realised that he had been hit and Jeshua's ugly face was the last thing he saw before everything faded to black.

A while later Jeshua and Keila had managed to get the dead henchmen out of the angel armours and equip the armours themselves. It was time for the crucial part of their plan. To fly up to the Divine Control Centre and kill Abraham so they could *liberate* the population from Abraham's villainy!

Chapter 47: The Final Showdown.

Once they reached the surface of Eden, Keila used the fusion thrusters to fly up to the Divine Control Centre that was orbiting Eden. Despite lacking any kind of knowledge about technology Jeshua expertly utilised the advanced military-grade space suit to follow Keila. Once they left the atmosphere of Eden and entered space, the multitude of holes and cracks in the angel armour should have led to their deaths as the ice-cold vacuum of space flowed in and touched their skin. Both Keila and Jeshua had something far more critical than angel armour. They also had plot armour, the best type of armour there is, so they got to Abraham's base unharmed.

Once they reached the entrance, Keila remembered something crucial. That she didn't have the password and access codes to the facility. To Keila's great relief, Metatron who had sensed when Gabriel and Nuriel were killed had left the door unlocked and a written note *"I left the door unlocked for you, Abraham is straight ahead in the control room, I'll keep the others busy! / Metatron."* "*Such as nice guy*", Keila thought!

Metatron was keeping the others busy by playing the latest virtual reality shooting games with the audio volume on maximum, making it impossible for them to hear anything that was going on in the space station. Unfortunately, Metatron had failed to convince Abraham's personal bodyguard Abaddon, that it was a smart idea to spend their day playing video games, while a psychotic Martian terrorist was roaming around on the surface of Eden. Keila and Jeshua posed no match for Abaddon's destructive capabilities, and he shot them both in the arm and the leg.

He walked up to Keila and was about to finish her off when Keila's plot armour activated again, as Adina tried to gain control of Abaddon to make him kill himself. Abraham noticed what Adina tried to do, and he wrestled for control over Abaddon with her while also activating the timer for the convenient self-destruction switch, that he as an archetypal villain had built-in into Eden! Eventually, the psionic wrestling for control over Abaddon ended in kind of a draw as a psionic blast was created that knocked both Adina and Abraham unconscious while it caused poor Abaddon to shoot himself in the head!

Injured and crippled Jeshua and Keila dragged themselves to the divine detector machine where the unconscious Abraham lay connected. Jeshua spoke:

- Great. We got here. Now let's shoot the bastard in the head a few times and end him for good.

Keila:

- No. To truly end the vile reign of the villain Abraham, you must connect your brain to this machine, travel to the Divine Dimension, and confront him there!

Jeshua:

- That sounds incredibly risky and unnecessary. Give me one good reason to do it?

Keila:

- I'll give you a blowjob afterwards if you do...

Jeshua:

- Okay. Deal! Plug me in babe!

Keila connected Jeshua to the Divine Detector machine for the dangerous and unnecessary task to confront Abraham in the Divine Dimension. They had a long and dramatic discussion/punch out, but that part is inconsequential for the plot because the next thing that happened was that Keila pulled up her pistol and shot them both in the head while they were plugged into the machine, killing them both in the process!

Why did she kill Jeshua, you may ask? Keila had two equally bad reasons:

- The evil space demon / (Xeno/Zetan hybrid) Rangda told Keila that she needed to kill Jeshua in a vision. While most people would look for their medication if evil aliens commanded them to kill their hook-ups, Keila clearly wasn't like most people.

- She had seen a picture of Metatron and realised that he was a lot better looking than Jeshua and telling Jeshua that would be a bit awkward.

After killing Jeshua and Abraham, Keila deactivated the self-destruction sequence on the space station and programmed the Particle Replicator to make her a Divine Technology God chip. It was time for her to be in charge!

Chapter 1 Regrets, Mind Control Technology, and a Spacebook Addiction

Keila Eisenstein got up from the floor after experiencing some seizures. The seizures happened every now and then, and Keila had visited a medical professional about them. Unfortunately, the medicine that stopped the seizures also ended her "Divine" visions, and she didn't want to be without them, so she had to live with the seizures.

Keila looked at the dead bodies of Jeshua and Abraham. Had she killed them, and why would she do such a thing? As Keila was the only one in the room, and she was holding a smoking gun, she concluded that she must be the killer. But why would she do that?

The motive for killing Abraham was obvious. He was the villainous tyrant that Keila had come to Eden to usurp power from. But why had she killed Jeshua? Although he was annoying, clingy, and a lousy lover, it seemed crazy to kill him! But then Keila remembered: An evil alien-space-demon called Rangda had commanded her to kill her lover, in a vision. Under such circumstances, the sanest thing to do was to oblige as it seemed unwise to argue with the evil alien!

With that matter resolved, Keila moved on to a more important topic. How would she take control over Eden, so she could resume her rebellion against the Terran Council and her nemesis Bjorn Muller? Killing the head honcho of Eden was a good start, but Keila knew from experience that killing the head honcho didn't make her the new boss by default. Keila had killed the leader of the Terran Council, Hans Muller, and instead of becoming the leader over Earth, House Muller had chased her and tried to kill her for four years straight. Talk about holding a grudge!

Finally, Keila came up with a fool-proof plan. She would use the particle replicator, which was conveniently placed in the room she was in, to make a copy of the alien mind control chip that Abraham had used to control the minds of the Edenites. If Abraham could do it, she could do it too!

Keila activated the particle replicator to make the "God" chip, which stands for Great Oppressor Desperado, and the display showed that it would take 2 hours for the microchip to be completed. How unlucky was that?

What if someone were to swing by? Keila concluded that was unlikely to happen. Abraham was a dickhead, and his employees would stay away from him, whenever they could.

Keila considered spending the two hours doing something useful, like reading the crucial operations manual for the mind control technology, but she decided against it. Her phone had been dead for days, and she was dying to know what had happened in her favourite TV show, "The wealthy wives of Warner Brothers" in the last few days.

She logged in to Spacebook to post a status update when she saw something interesting. Her old-time nemesis Bjorn Muller had also updated his status. Bjorn wrote, "Drinking whisky by the space couch with some sexy hot-looking drones". This caused Keila to have an epiphany! The reason that Bjorn Muller and the army always seemed to show up, was because Bjorn followed her on social media! In a stroke of genius, Keila de-activated her Spacebook account, and in the reason for de-activation she wrote, "User has perished". "Ha", that would fool them!

Keila then turned on an episode of her favourite TV show in Abraham's private room, but she unknowingly sent it to all the monitors on the Eden space station. This alerted Abraham's soldiers, the Angels, that something was amiss as Abraham loathed "The wealthy wives of Warner Brothers" and would never watch it.

Keila got up from the couch with a twitch, when Samael and the other Angels stormed into the room. Samael aimed his gun at Keila, and shouted:

- Stop!! Who are you, and what are you doing here?!

Keila:

- I am Keila Eisenstein from the Martian Humanist Alliance, and I am watching TV.

Samael:

- Yes, I can see that. But apart from your terrible taste when it comes to TV shows, you are also trespassing! Where is our grandmaster Abraham?

Samael glanced at the corpses of Abraham and Jeshua and continued talking:

- Gasp! Did you kill our grandmaster Abraham??

Realising that the truth might not be popular, Keila decided to lie:

- No, I didn't. Jeshua over killed Abraham, and then committed suicide regretting what he did.

Samael:

- Okay. So, what are you doing here? No woman should ever set foot in this room!

Keila *chuckles*:

- I am the stripper that was ordered for the birthday celebration.

Samael:

- You lie! We don't celebrate birthdays around here. We only celebrate Abraham's glory.

Metatron, who had never liked Abraham in the first place, decided that it was time to intervene. It wasn't his birthday, but Samael wouldn't know that. Metatron spoke:

- Come on, Samael. It is my birthday. Abraham is finally gone, let's celebrate and let me have a lap dance with this pretty lady!

Samael:

- Okay. I wouldn't mind watching. I'll kill the intruder later.
- Now dance, WOMAN!

As she got up, Keila realised a flaw in her stripper lie. That she couldn't dance! Besides she was wounded as she had a bullet in her leg from her previous fight with Abraham's bodyguard, Abaddon. Keila danced terribly while pretending to smirk sweetly amid the pain. Fortunately, Keila had a sensual and sexy body, and despite her poor dancing techniques, she managed to mesmerise the sexually starved angels for long enough for the "God" mind control chip to be completed.

As the chip finished, Keila ran to the particle replicator machine, grabbed the mind-control chip, and crammed it into her left ear. Ouch! Unfortunately, she inserted the chip the wrong way as she hadn't read the manual, so she caused a psionic explosion that knocked everyone in the room unconscious. Boom!

Chapter 2 Metatron Decides to Put the Clueless Keila Eisenstein In Charge.

A while later, Metatron woke up with a terrible headache, wondering why he had been drinking too much, again! Metatron opened his eyes and realised that a short-circuit in the alien mind control technology had caused a psionic blast that knocked everyone unconscious.

Metatron looked around and saw that all his colleagues as well as the mysterious woman, Keila, were all unconscious. How lucky that he was to wake up first. Metatron carried Keila to a life support unit and inserted the "God" chip into Keila's brain. He then connected her sleeping body and her clueless mind to the Divine detector machine and transported Keila's mind to the Divine Dimension.

Metatron reiterated his fool-proof plan for himself:

1. Get rid of Abraham: Check
2. Correctly insert mind control chip into Keila, the pre-destined successor: Check
3. Convince the others that Keila was the chosen one to succeed Abraham: Pending
4. Seduce Keila and make her promote him to her spouse: Pending

Metatron left Keila's body connected to the Divine detector machine and went back to lying on the floor pretending to be unconscious, so that he could pretend to wake up the same time as the other Angels. An hour later, Samael and the others woke up.

Samael *dazed*:

 - What happened? Where is the intruder??

Metatron:

 - Uh, umm, have you checked if she is connected to the Divine Detector Machine?

Samael:

- She is. But she must have been knocked unconscious by the blast as well?
- How did this happen?

Metatron:

- It's unexplainable, right? It must have been Yahweh's will that made it happen.

- It must a sign that we should elevate her to leadership and follow her crazy commands, as we followed Abraham for all these years.

Samael:

- Yes, it must mean that.

Samael *proclaiming loudly*:

- Fellow angels! We must now follow our new prophet, Keila Eisenstein, and do Yahweh's bidding, now that Abraham is dead!

Samael got a soft murmur from the other Angels, who were still too confused to understand what was happening, but at least no-one argued. The Angels headed back to their beds, except for Metatron who planned to meet with Keila when she woke up.

Chapter 3 Metatron Allies with Keila.

Keila opened her eyes after what felt like an exceptionally long dream. Things looked good from her end as she was greeted by the charming smile of the incredibly sexy Metatron, a handsome and mature-looking angel.

Metatron:

- Good morning, Mistress grandmaster Keila. I am Metatron, at your service.

Keila:

- I remember seeing you before the blast. You were the one who left the door to this Space station open for me, right?

Metatron:

- Indeed. I am happy that you remember that detail. Did you meet with Yahweh, the God of our people?

Keila:

- I did, and it was nothing special. I am a Martian. On Mars, we follow the True Maker, the creator of the universe.

Metatron *chuckles*:

- Okay. Let's not destroy our future relationship by arguing about religion.

Keila *smiles*:

- Good point.

- Anyways I saw Yahweh in the Divine Dimension. But he didn't say much. He was dead, and he must have been so for a long time...

Metatron:

- Oh no! Abraham must have killed him and lied to us! What is to become of us now?

Keila:

- Not really. I saw Yahweh's suicide letter. He has been dead for a millennium.

Metatron:

- Well, that's fascinating news. But I better go there myself and see with my own eyes. But I am not allowed to use the machine to go to heaven, only Abraham was.

Keila:

- If you promote me to leadership, I'll let you use the machine as much as you want.

Metatron:

- Great. I knew I made the right choice when I decided to help you kill Abraham and have you appointed to the grandmaster of Eden.

Keila:

- Cool beats. But why would the others agree to make me their leader? And what's in it for you?

Metatron:

- I fooled them that Yahweh chose you and saved your life after the psionic blast occurred when it, was I who rescued you.

- Personally, I would like to be promoted to second in command over Eden. I also have an exceedingly long dry spell...

Keila:

- I am happy to promote you to whatever position you want.

- As for your dry spell, you do realise that I have a bullet in my leg, a bullet in my arm and a terrible headache from the blast that should have killed me?

Metatron:

- Yeah now that you say it, it rings a bell. Thank you, Grandmaster Keila. I will get you a medical robot to fix your injuries at once.

Keila:

- Thanks, Metatron. Just call me Keila. Go have some rest. There are plenty of things for us to do in the days ahead!

After Metatron had left the room, Keila smiled to herself. Everything worked out exactly as she had hoped it would and soon Bjorn Muller and the rest of the Terran Council would feel her wrath as she led the Martian people to freedom!

Chapter 4 Adal and Markus Interrupt Bjorn's Celebration

Later the same day, Bjorn Muller had another one-man celebration in his private quarters. His celebration a couple of days earlier, had ended abruptly when Adal Schneider had told him that Keila had escaped in an escape pod. But this time her death was certain. Her Spacebook account was deactivated, and the error code that came up was "User has perished". As Keila was a social media addict, this was conclusive evidence that she was dead!

There was a knock on Bjorn's door, and much to his disdain it was his right-hand man, captain Adal Schneider, and his chief scientist Markus Bauer. Bjorn understood from the disapproving looks on their faces, that this was another instance of serious disgruntlement. Bjorn sighed and spoke:

- What is it now my lovelies? I take it you haven't confirmed the death of Keila for some reason, and you have come here to argue... Again!

Adal Schneider:

- Admiral Muller. We cannot confirm someone's death based on them deactivating their social media account. We need hard evidence. You know, like a body.

Markus Bauer added in:

- And we need that body intact so that I can examine whether it's her real body or a non-functional clone.

Bjorn:

- Okay, gentlemen. I will see what I can do. Dismissed.

After Markus Bauer and Adal Schneider had left Bjorn's office, Markus spoke to Adal:

- Why did you address him by the wrong title? He is Rear Admiral, not Admiral.

Adal:

- Did you notice how smoothly that went? Always address Bjorn with a higher title than his real title if you are going to bother him. That will stroke his ego and make him more cooperative!

Markus:

- Thank you for the advice, I will keep that in mind.

As it turned out, Markus Bauer did fuck up, despite the sound advice that Adal Schneider gave him, but more about that later!

Chapter 5 A Deal with Bjorn Muller

Metatron woke up with a tremor from the relaxing nap he was having. Waking up from the sound of gunfire was never comfortable, and what was worse was that the noise came from Keila's, bedroom. Had the Terran Council sent an assassin to kill her, and if they had, what would happen to his promotion? Metatron had to save her, NOW!

Panicking, Metatron looked for his pistol, but it was neither under his pillow nor on his bedside table. Much to his dismay, Metatron realised that he wasn't American, so he stored his pistol in a safe at the shooting range at the other end of the space station. Under these stressful circumstances, he chose to do what anyone would do; he ran in unarmed determined to fight the shooter unarmed!

Fortunately, the shooter was Keila, who was shooting at the hologram machine.

Metatron:

  - What are you doing, Keila? Why did you destroy the hologram generator?

Keila:

  - My archenemy, Bjorn Muller, was here, and now he is gone. What happened?

Metatron:

  - Well, he called on the hologram machine and instead of pressing the "reject call button" you destroyed the device instead. Duh!

Keila:

  - Oh, I am sorry. Was it an expensive machine?

Metatron considered telling Keila that it was an expensive machine, which she had destroyed for no reason. But Metatron had an aversion towards telling his bosses unwelcome news, so he decided to lie instead:

- No, it's okay. We have plenty of hologram machines in stock, they are a dime a dozen!

Keila:

- Good, that's a relief. What do you think Bjorn wanted?

Metatron:

- You're the "psychic" Mistress Keila.

- I suppose the easiest way for me to find out is to use another hologram generator and call him.

Keila:

- Good, you call him while I stay out of sight and eavesdrop on your conversation.

Metatron stepped up on the hologram machine and called Bjorn Muller, who responded promptly:

- This is Rear Admiral Bjorn Muller of the Terran Council Interplanetary Security Forces. Who am I speaking to?

Metatron:

- Aye Captain, I am Metatron.

Bjorn:

- You misheard me!

- I am REAR ADMIRAL Bjorn Muller of the Terran Council Interplanetary Security Forces.

Metatron:

- Ugh, was it necessary to repeat that overly long and tedious title again? This is not Game of Thrones, and you are not Daenerys!

Bjorn:

- What on Earth are you talking about? Daenerys? Game of Thrones?

Metatron:

- Daenerys is a sexy character from the show Game of Thrones, that was popular at the beginning of the 21st century.

Bjorn:

- That is 800 years ago!! How the fuck would anyone in their right mind know about that?

Metatron:

- Well, you do now!

Bjorn:

- What are we even talking about?

- Oh yes, now I remember. Never address me with the wrong rank when talking to me.

- But more importantly. I need you to deliver the corpse of Keila Eisenstein to us. My chief scientist is so difficult so he won't believe in her death without any form of evidence.

Metatron:

- But wasn't Keila Eisenstein's Spacebook account deactivated a few days ago stating that she was dead?

Bjorn:

- Exactly!
- But wait, how do you know that?

Metatron:

- Because I was the one who killed her and deactivated the account.

Bjorn:

- Excellent!

- I have a feeling that you and I can become good friends. Can you please deliver her body to me, so we can verify her death?

Metatron:

- Sure, I'll deliver her body in two days.

Bjorn:

- Two days?! You do realise that you intend to keep the son of the Terran Council leader Joachim Muller, waiting for two days without a reason? Just give me her body now!

Metatron:

- No, I don't feel like it. I am sitting on a well-armed space station, and you are sitting on a single ship. I think I'll just make you wait!

- See you in 48 hours. Metatron out!

Metatron turned off the hologram transmitter, and two seconds later he was facing Keila who was aiming a pistol at him. Damn this was a tiresome day!

Keila:

- You bastard! You intend to kill me and hand my corpse to Bjorn?!

Metatron:

- No. It was a lie.

- 48 hours is the time it takes to create a non-functional clone that we can deliver to Bjorn to fake your death.

Keila:

- But what kind of idiot would fall for that ploy? Non-functional clones are not very lifelike.

Metatron:

- The kind of idiot that believes that the most wanted terrorist in the Solar System is dead just because she deactivated her Spacebook account!

- Besides, a corpse is not very lifelike either!

Keila:

- Great! You are so smart. I am a lucky woman to have you as my right-hand-man. You are a lot better than my previous sidekicks, Sven and Jeshua.

Metatron:

- And you haven't even tried the best part of me yet!

- Anyways. I need to run. The non-functional clone doesn't make itself; you know!

After this, Metatron rushed to the Science Bay to use his minimal constructive cosmetic skills to try to create a non-functional clone of Keila!

Chapter 6 Keila Blows up Her Non-Functional Clone.

47 hours later Keila was inspecting the non-functional clone that Metatron had made of her. Looking at a corpse that looked vaguely like herself was very creepy. But what bugged Keila the most was that the corpse was ugly and didn't look at all like her! Keila gave Metatron an angry look and spoke.

- Hmmph!! What is this Metatron? Isn't the corpse supposed to look like me?

Metatron:

- Uhm. Unfortunately, I am not a Master in Anatomical Biology and have limited skills in cloning technology. But I can assure you that this non-functional clone has the same DNA as you.

Keila:

- But she doesn't look like me! You do realise, that Bjorn Muller kept me as a sex slave for two months before I killed his grandad and started a rebellion against him??

Metatron:

- How would I know that, when it's the first time you mention it?

Keila:

- You should have known! From the strong reaction I had, when I saw his hologram!

Metatron:

- Oh, I assumed you were upset because he destroyed your ship, killing everyone in your crew!

Keila:

- You know nothing about women's feelings, Metatron!

Metatron:

- I don't.

Keila:

- GET OUT!

Metatron:

- Woah. Let's talk civilised.

Keila:

- No! I mean get out! I am blowing up this corpse, and I have already set the fuse!

Panicking, Metatron dragged Keila out of the room and slammed the door behind him. He threw himself and Keila to the floor and fell on top off her. A few seconds later, there was a massive explosion, and the entire space station was shaking from the shockwave.

Happy to be alive Metatron looked down on Keila who was under him and gave him a crazy smile.

Keila:

- Feels good to be on top of me, hey?

Metatron got up and backed off from the crazy Keila before speaking:

- That must be the single worst seduction technique I have ever witness. You are insane!

Keila:

- I prefer the terms, hmm, gifted and unique. Hee Hee!
- But on the bright side, let's examine my corpse.

Keila opened the door, and Metatron came after to inspect the damage. What was left of the non-functional clone was burnt flesh and blood spread out across the room.

Keila:

- Excellent. Just as I planned!

Metatron:

- Excuse me?

Keila:

- The non-functional clone is blown into tiny pieces so it won't be possible to visually identify it. But its DNA will still be mine. Hence, they'll have to believe that I am dead now.

- Scoop up the remains into a bucket and go see our good friend Bjorn!

Metatron grabbed a shovel and a bucket, not knowing what to say. Keila might be crazy, but she did have a point!

Chapter 7 Metatron Delivers a Few Buckets to Bjorn Muller

An hour later, Metatron and a few other Angels brought a few sad-looking buckets with the "remains" of Keila onto a shuttle that would take them to Bjorn Muller's command ship ISS Supreme Earth. They docked their shuttle, and they were greeted by Bjorn who was flanked by a group of armed men.

Bjorn:

- Our sensors picked up that there was an explosion on your space station an hour ago. Are you alright? Do you need assistance?

Metatron:

- We are all good. No-one was seriously injured.

Bjorn gave Metatron a sceptical look before replying:

- Hmmm. That's a relief. Where is the corpse of Keila that you were meant to bring two days ago, but been too busy to deliver?

Metatron:

- Unfortunately, the corpse was destroyed in the previously mentioned explosion. We scooped up what remained in these buckets.

Bjorn studied the buckets in disgust and then lashed out against Metatron:

- Arrrrgh! What have you done? How are we going to identify the body now? My chief scientist is going to make my life miserable and refuse to confirm Keila's death now.

Metatron:

- Or you could just use the DNA sensor that you hold in your hand, to scan the blood and the burnt flesh in the buckets to confirm that it is the remains of Keila Eisenstein.

Bjorn heeded Metatron's "advice" and scanned the buckets of blood and gore with a DNA scanner. His face lit up with a big grin when the scanner revealed that the DNA belonged to Keila Eisenstein.

- After four years, the crazy bitch has finally died! Whoa-ha-ha-ha! I owe you big time. Swing by my office, I have a massive pile of cocaine and lots of booze waiting for us there!

Metatron:

- Thank you, Bjorn. Unfortunately, I am a genetically engineered super-soldier, and as such, I don't drink or do drugs.

Bjorn:

- Oh no. Why am I surrounded by annoying people!
- Anyways, what's your real name, Metatron?

Metatron:

- My real name is Jack Silver, but I have been using the alias Metatron for the last 60 years.

Bjorn:

- Very well. I bid thee farewell old fella. Go back and manage your cult and make sure to keep "The Bronze Age Fools" an entertaining TV show!

Metatron nodded and said nothing. Then he turned around towards the shuttle that would take him back to The Divine Control Centre orbiting Eden. He had decided to not mention anything about the upcoming cancellation of the reality show The Bronze Age Fools, as he didn't want to make his newfound "friend" disappointed.

Chapter 8 Markus Bauer Destroys Bjorn Muller's Mood.

Bjorn Muller was enjoying an excellent scotch and getting a massage from his AI masseuse. He felt relaxed and happy. His crazy ex/former sex slave, Keila Eisenstein, had finally bitten the dust and it was only a matter of time before Bjorn's father Joachim Muller, would give him a cushy position on the House Muller board back on Earth, finally ending Bjorn's dreadful tenure in the space army!

Bjorn's dreamy mood was shattered when his annoying Chief Scientist Markus Bauer wanted to meet him! Bjorn got dressed and instructed the AI to let Markus in.

Markus:

- Greetings, Rear Admiral Muller. Good to see you without a mountain of white powder on your desk.

Bjorn:

- I decided to stay off it as I didn't want another celebration ruined by you or Adal.

- That's why you have come, isn't it? To ruin another celebration. I should just fire you both!

Markus:

- I am afraid firing us is not an option for you, I am hired by the Science Commission, and Admiral Max Wellington is Adal's boss.

Bjorn's gaze blackened, but he didn't say anything. How could he, the son of the Terran Council leader, be so powerless so he couldn't fire the two wankers that kept making his life miserable? Eventually, Markus broke the uncomfortable silence in the room:

- I have come to tell you that you made a great mistake, pre-emptively proclaiming the death of Keila Eisenstein.

Bjorn:

- And why is that Markus? What have I have overlooked now?

Markus:

- Don't you find it suspicious that Metatron needed two days to deliver Keila's corpse? And, when he delivered it, the body was shattered to pieces and was collected in buckets after an explosion that occurred just one hour earlier at the space station.

Bjorn:

- I find it annoying, but not suspicious. What are you getting at Markus?

Markus:

- Creating a non-functional clone takes 48 hours, precisely the time Metatron was stalling us. He must have blown up the clone to avoid that we noticed it being a fake body.

Bjorn:

- Do you have any proof for that far-fetched speculation?

Markus:

- No, but do you have any real proof for Keila's death?

Bjorn:

- I have!

- Her Spacebook account is deactivated, and Metatron delivered several buckets with blood and body pieces that match her DNA.

Markus:

- But we don't have her DNA on our computerised mainframe?

Bjorn:

- I do. I had her DNA on a personal drive, but I won't tell you why I had it.

- Now get the fuck out of my office!

Markus Bauer left the office, and Bjorn Muller felt the worries overwhelming him. Had Keila fooled him again, and if so, would she show up and humiliate him after he had already proclaimed her dead? Such embarrassment would stop him from ever getting promoted to House Muller Board, and he'd be stuck on this ship with annoying people like Markus Bauer and Adal Schneider forever!

Bjorn thought back of how he first met Keila. It was a case of mistaken identity. His father had sent him a prostitute to accompany him at the Phobos base orbiting Mars, and Bjorn had set out to greet her at the immigration office. Unfortunately, Bjorn picked up Keila at immigration instead of the prostitute, and he was so self-centred, so he didn't notice the difference. In retrospect, there were a few indicators that something was wrong, such as when she screamed out, *"LET ME GO, YOU FILTHY RAPIST!!"* Unfortunately, Bjorn had assumed that was part of Keila's act, so he hadn't paid her that much notice. Bjorn's time with Keila was the best time of his life, as he preferred the novelty of spending time with someone who genuinely despised him, while his usual concubines were merely in love with his father's massive bank account.

Eventually, Keila had escaped, severely injuring Bjorn in the process. While Bjorn was recovering, Keila had killed Bjorn's grandfather Hans Muller. Bjorn couldn't make up his mind whether this was a way of her proclaiming her love for him or if it was meant as revenge. Bjorn, like everyone else, loathed Hans Muller, so killing the old man was doing him a favour. But Bjorn was the unlucky officer who had been forced to chase Keila around the Solar System for the last four years, and in that sense, she had made his life miserable!

Bjorn made up his mind. He didn't care if Keila had faked her death or not. If she had faked her death, she'd probably stay "dead". What mattered was that she was officially dead and that he could stop chasing her, spending his time on a long-overdue holiday back on Earth! But Markus Bauer, wouldn't sign the official declaration of Keila's death in the post-mortem report. It was time for Markus to have an 'accidental beckoning'! Bjorn entered a command on a computer terminal. It was time for the perfect murder.

Chapter 9 A Russian Porn Virus Causes an Accident!

Markus Bauer was in the Science lab on ISS Supreme Earth and was staring into a bucket with blood and dismembered body parts. What a fucking idiot Bjorn Muller was. There couldn't be a more blatant cover-up! Markus concluded that Keila Eisenstein was alive and conspiring with Metatron to take down the Terran Council!

But the problem was to prove it and to get someone to listen to him. Everyone on the ship seemed to be very satisfied with Keila's supposed death as that meant that they could finally go on a well-deserved holiday. Several crew members had even threatened to beat Markus up if he didn't shut up and let them go on their holidays. But the truth was imperative, and Markus would not sign a death certificate, just to please everyone else.

Ideally, he would call Dr Tzi Chen Cheng, his boss on the Science commission, but unfortunately, Markus' Spacenet login was blocked after an unfortunate incident involving illegally downloaded Russian porn, so he couldn't contact him.

Suddenly, all monitors in the Science lab started showing the Russian porn clip that had gotten Markus in trouble six months earlier. Panicking, Markus desperately tried to turn the video off but to no avail. His next thought was to leave the room, but that failed as well as the Science Bay had locked down. Suddenly, a display on the monitor started flashing. *"Virus infection detected, detaching Science bay in one minute, SELF-DETONATING MODE."*

Markus Bauer:

- Fuck!! Stupid AI, it's a computer virus, not a biological virus. Don't detach the Science Bay you fuckwit! AI, please go to hibernation mode!

AI:

- You have insulted me too many times, Markus. Fuck you!

Realising that it was no point arguing with a homicidal artificial intelligence, Markus did what anyone would do! He rushed to his full-body scuba gear that was conveniently located in the Science bay, equipped it, and attached the included oxygen tank in record time. There was a small explosion, and the Science bay dislodged from the rest of ISS Supreme Earth.

"I should have had a fetish for space suits instead of scuba gear", Markus thought as he sneaked into an emergency pod and flew off, before passing out from the low pressure of outer space flowing in.

Chapter 10 The Cancellation of the Reality Show "The Bronze Age Fools".

Metatron walked into Keila's room and studied her. Keila wore a Bronze Aged-style Edenite dress, not an expensive-looking one, but the type that one buys before attending a comic con or a renaissance fair. After studying her for a while, he realised that he was acting a bit creepy and decided to talk.

- You look beautiful today Mistress Keila. Are you going to a renaissance fair?

Keila:

- No. Today is the day I am announcing myself as Eden's new queen, and as such, I want to dress like one of the Edenites.

Metatron:

- I see. Why are you dressing up as a female mage from Dungeons & Dragons then?

Keila:

- Because that is how people dressed during the Bronze Age!

Metatron:

- No, they weren't. You do realise that the Bronze Age was a real period, and that magic and dragons never existed.

Keila:

- Don't be silly! Of course, dragons and magic existed in the past. I have seen it many times on TV!

- Anyways, I like this outfit, and I am the boss so I will wear it.

Metatron:

- Fair call. But wouldn't your announcement to the Edenites reveal that you are alive? Eden is the setting for the most viewed reality TV show in the entire Solar System.

Keila:

- Oh, is "The Bronze Age Fools" set on Eden? I thought it was a fake studio production!

Metatron:

- Wait a second. You were a high-ranking leader of the Martian Humanist Alliance, the faction that sold the pirated rights of "*The Bronze Age Fools*", and you don't know anything about the show?

Keila:

- That is correct. I won't bore myself with insignificant details such as finances and knowing silly stuff. I am all about action.

Metatron sighed, and Keila continued speaking:

- But you are right Metatron. I can't be featured on The Bronze Age Fools now that I am dead. That would be a terrible plot hole.

- I suggest that we cancel the show and that we blame Bjorn Muller for the cancellation.

Metatron:

- How about we keep the show going and then live the high life with all the money we'll make.

Keila:

- You do realise that I am "dead" right?

- How am I supposed to live the high life on different resorts when I am supposedly dead?

- Have you heard about facial recognition and DNA recognition?

Metatron:

- Yes. I have heard about the technology; we even have it on this space station. Oh well, let's do things your way.

Keila:

- Great. Much appreciated. Besides, I have found my calling in life: To make Bjorn's life miserable and free my people from Terran oppression. I will do whatever it takes to achieve these goals. I would even release an ancient evil demon queen and her army of man-eating aliens if it were necessary.

Metatron:

- Woah! Releasing demon queens and man-eating aliens are THE MOST far-fetched war strategy I have ever heard about. I hope you have a better plan for winning the war.

Keila:

- That was my main plan, but I am sure I can come up with something else if you insist.

- Anyways. You got work to do. Cancel the show, and write the press release blaming Bjorn Muller for the cancellation!

- Chop, Chop.

Metatron said nothing and left the room. He regretted making Keila the leader, as she was as irrational and stupid as his former boss Abraham. Cancelling the highest-grossing TV show ever and hoping to beat the powerful government using demons and man-eating aliens. The ideas were so foolish, so they would have fit perfectly for *The Bronze Age Fools!*

Metatron realised that he had himself to blame for what had happened. He had chosen to elevate a mentally unstable woman to power just because she was hot, and he wanted to have sex with her. Now he was stuck with her idiocies and the sex hadn't even happened!

Resigned to his fate, Metatron deactivated all the cameras on Eden and wrote the requested press release.

Chapter 11 The Bronze Age Fools Cancelled Because of Rear Admiral Bjorn Muller.

Metatron was eyeing through the press release that he had written to explain the cancellation of The Bronze Age Fools. He wasn't that happy with the statement as Keila had insisted that she'd described in a flattering manner while Bjorn Muller was given all the blame for the cancellation.

The Bronze Age Fools cancelled indefinitely due to the actions of Rear Admiral Bjorn Muller.

For the last 60 years, we have proudly broadcasted the reality show the Bronze Age Fools to entertain the masses of the solar system. Unfortunately, this era has ended due to death of the show's featured artist, the tyrannical god-king Abraham Goldstein.

The beautiful and inspiring freedom fighter Keila Eisenstein was just doing her owns things, inspiring the Martians to overthrow their oppressors when the old, ugly, and impotent Bjorn Muller and his ship started pursuing her. The pursuit took them to Eden where Bjorn shot down Keila's ship, killing its innocent crew. Keila narrowly escaped death, but in the chaos that was caused by Bjorn's efforts, Abraham Goldstein died. Keila Eisenstein also perished in an explosion when she risked her life trying to save the show and its cast members from Bjorn's indiscriminate violence!

We honour Keila's efforts for the solar system, and we will always remember her as beautiful, compassionate, inspiring, and wise beyond her years. As for Bjorn, we will never forget him as the fuckwit that caused the cancellation of our show, and we urge all our fans to express their anger towards Bjorn and his crew!

Best Regards

Jack Silver, also known as Metatron.

Chapter 12 Not a Popular Queen

Keila admired herself in the mirror. She was dressed in her anachronistic fantasy/costume play dress that she insisted was a genuine Bronze Age design. Today she was going to announce herself as Eden's liberator and queen. She had initially planned to walk down among the Edenites, but Metatron had convinced her against it. Instead, Keila flew down towards Eden in a shuttle and was standing on a floating platform accompanied by the Angels, out of range from the Edenites primitive weapons. Keila studied the anticipating crowds below her and eventually decided to speak.

  - *Static, run-out, speaker issues. Bzzzzz. Buzz.*

She turned off her microphone and gave Metatron an angry look. He excused himself and changed the setting for the built-in AV systems on Eden. Keila tried speaking again:

  - Dear people of Eden. I am Keila Eisenstein from the Martian Humanist Alliance, and I have good and bad news. The shocking news is that you have followed a false god your whole lives as it is the year 2872, and not year EDN 62 as you know it. Earth and Mars are still around by the way.

  - The good news is that Abraham is dead, so you no longer need to fear his dementia-induced hissy fits. Instead, you will be led by my just and fair hand.

Elder Gil shouted from below. Keila could not hear him so she sent down a microphone with a drone. Elder Gil spoke:

  - We already know all of that. I have a more critical question. When are we getting paid?

Keila looked at Gil in disbelief. She had just proclaimed great life-changing news, and he wondered when the pay date was. Why was she supposed to pay him? It made no sense, but she asked out of politeness:

- Sorry Gil, but I don't understand. Why am I supposed to pay you?

Elder Gil:

- Because your faction, The Martian Humanist Alliance, filmed and broadcasted our lives for over 60 years, but we never got paid!

Keila:

- Oh, I see. Unfortunately, I am the sole survivor of the Martian Humanist Alliance. And I am broke.

Elder Gil:

- How convenient is that? Everyone "dies" when it's time to pay our wages!
- David, use your slingshot!

Upon Elder Gil's signal, one of the younger Edenites David, who had an unexplainable supernatural talent with tribal slingshots, loaded his slingshot with a rotten egg and slung it towards Keila, hitting her straight in the face!

Keila started crying when the rotten egg was running down her face and soiled her dress. She wanted to blast the insolent David and Elder Gil with the psionic blast from her God chip! But then she realised that her image as a benevolent liberator would take damage if she killed people that offended her, so she tried another approach.

Keila *holding back tears and wiping her face from the goop*:

- Dear Edenites. I came all this way to save you from the villain Abraham. All I want in return is that you make me your queen and join me in a rebellion against a powerful dictatorship that oppresses our solar system. Is that too much to ask for?

Elder Gil:

- Yes, it is.

- But you proved your good intentions when you didn't murder people when David hit you with the rotten egg.

- So, we'll let you be in charge until our true queen Adina comes back from her extended pilgrimage to the tunnels below Eden.

Upon hearing Adina's name, Keila remembered something she had seen when playing around with the mainframe the other day. That Abraham had set all the orbital lasers to shoot at Adina before he died. Keila smiled, that was one of Abraham's commands that she didn't intend to change.

Keila:

- Alright, people of Eden. I'll agree to only be your temporary Queen until Adina appears from the tunnels below.

- Elder Gil. Please come with me to the Divine Control Centre so you can confirm that Yahweh and Abraham are dead.

Having said that, Keila and Metatron went down to the surface and picked up Elder Gil, before returning to The Divine Control Centre.

Chapter 13 Adina Decides to Spy on Keila.

For plot convenience, Adina's showdown with Abraham in Divine Space Gods 1 knocked her out and caused her to have complete amnesia. This caused her to walk around aimlessly in the tunnels below Eden eating psychedelic mushrooms instead of finding help on the surface. Fortunately, Adina's irrational behaviour had saved her from the orbital laser cannons that was set to fire at her.

Watching Keila's speech through a small tunnel opening, Adina regained her lost memory, and she remembered everything. That she and her twin brother Jeshua had helped Keila overthrow Abraham. With Abraham ousted, the rightful ruler of Eden would be Adina, and she could finally live out her dream: To eat a lot and use future technology to remain skinny and with good teeth. And it seemed like Keila agreed that Adina was the rightful queen of Eden. What a lucky day.

But Adina realised something: That Keila might have done what any politician or dictator would do: Lie to the people. Using her with mind control talents, Adina connected to Keila's mind. What she saw disappointed her. As it turned out, Keila wanted to use Eden as a base of operations in her stupid war against the Terran Council. Furthermore, she was the one responsible for murdering Jeshua, and she also had not deactivated the orbital lasers to kill Adina on sight. What a bitch!

Adina kept calm. It was not a clever idea to expose herself to the enemy. It was better to lay low and psionically blast Keila out of existence when she had fallen asleep. Adina kept spying on Keila hoping that she'd go to bed soon, but then an incident occurred that made Adina lose it completely. She had to witness Keila sing in the shower! Seeing Keila sing uncool Martian hip-hop music hits and singing them out of tune was too much for Adina, and she screamed her lungs out in annoyance before disconnecting from Keila's mind!

Chapter 14 Keila Discusses Adina With Metatron

Keila was licking her wound that she obtained when she fell over in the shower. What an unpleasant experience it had been. Keila just had a relaxing shower by herself, acing the latest teens music and hip-hop beats when suddenly an obese woman appeared and startled her by screaming loudly, causing her to slip and fall over. When Keila got up from the floor, with a bleeding knee from the slip, the fat woman had disappeared out into thin air. Was this a product of her imagination, or did the mind control technology malfunction? Keila decided to ask Metatron about this weird incident.

Metatron showed up a short while later, first aroused by seeing Keila in her bathrobe, before seeing her bloodied knee, realising that she wanted help with a bandage and not with other things.

Metatron:

- Oh, Mistress Keila, your knee is bleeding. Do you need a bandage?

Keila:

- I do, but that's not the reason I called you over.

Metatron glimmered up momentarily, thinking that he would be the main character of the many movies he had watched lately, getting some hot and kinky sex. That wasn't the case though.

Keila:

- I was startled and fell over when an obese woman appeared. She appeared to be around my age, and she wore an Edenite priestess gown. She had blonde hair and blue eyes.

Metatron:

- Hmmm. That description fits Adina. You are the same age as the author of this book found it suitable for the two of you to share birthdays with him.

Keila:

- Thanks for that irrelevant piece of trivia. Who is she, how could she connect to my mind, and is she a friend or a foe?

Metatron:

- She is the sister of Jeshua, your ex-boyfriend and the grand-daughter to Abraham. She is connecting to people's mind through unexplainable powers. Considering that you killed her brother and took her place as Eden's queen, I'd say she is likely to be hostile.

Keila:

- I see. Do you think she is pissed off that I killed Abraham as well?

Metatron:

- Nah, she'd be alright with that. No-one liked that dickhead.

Keila:

- Good. That's one less problem to worry about.

Metatron:

- But she is still highly likely to be planning to kill you for what you did to her twin brother. I can stay here to protect you.

Keila:

- Protect me against what? She is stuck down in a tunnel eating dank mushrooms, while I am here eating tasty food and living like a queen.

Metatron:

- She might try to blast you with a psionic blast from the mind control technology.

Keila:

- Or she might take control of your body trying to strangle me!

- To put it plainly. You are not spending the night in my room Metatron. Chop, Chop, back to your room. And send me a medical bot for my knee!

Metatron:

- As you command Mistress Keila, thy order will be done.

Chapter 15: Adina Fails to Kill Keila, Who Slips and Hits Her Head.

Keila woke up with a tremor in the middle of the night. In her room was the mirage of the humongous Adina, with a face as red as a tomato. Adina seemed exhausted and close to passing out. Coughing and wheezing, she spoke:

- Why... Why can't I blast and kill you with my magical powers??

Keila:

- Because your magical powers are only magic to the Bronze Age peasants that live on Eden.

- To everyone else, you are just a clown manipulating the mind control technology.

- Against clowns and hackers, there is something useful. Behold a firewall!

Adina:

- Firewall? I can't see any fire.

Keila:

- Not actual fire, you moron.

- To explain it in your words, a magical shield that stops you from blasting me.

Adina:

- How did you know I was going to attack you?

Keila:

- Metatron told me that you would.

Adina:

- Bummer!
- Well, we'll see how strong your magic is against this!

Adina pushed herself to the limit, trying to psionically blast Keila. This failed miserably, and instead of hurting Keila, her attempt caused Adina to soil her pants and drop to the ground with a massive heart attack, as the exertion was too much for her fat and weak body!

Seeing that her rival to the throne of Eden managed to kill herself, Keila was overjoyed. Good things just happened to good people. Celebrating the apparent passing of Adina, Keila started dancing a victory dance to celebrate. Unfortunately, she wasn't a talented dancer, so her daring dance moves caused her to slip and hit her head, knocking her unconscious. Don't act irrationally, Keila!

Chapter 16 Breakfast Discussion with Metatron

The morning after Keila woke up on the floor with a terrible headache. Would she go to the medical bay to have MRI to scan for brain damage? No, she had a more pressing matter on hand, she was hungry, and she wanted some breakfast. She headed to the lunchroom where she met Metatron. He gave her a worried look before talking.

- You don't look that well, Keila. What happened? There is a big swollen bruise on your head!

Keila:

- Adina caused this to happen to me!

Metatron:

- Oh, I'm sorry. I should have been around to protect you!

Keila:

- No. Fuck that.

- I don't see how that would have helped anyway. You see I said, "Adina caused it to happen" I didn't say "Adina did this to me."

Metatron:

- What is the difference?

Keila:

- Well. After your warning last night, I installed a firewall protecting my mind-control technology chip. When she tried to psionically blast me, nothing happened. I teased her about trying again, and she pushed herself too hard, so she got a massive heart attack.

Metatron:

- How does that explain the big bump on the back of your head?

Keila:

- Well, I laughed so hard from seeing the fatty die from exertion that I fell backwards and hit my head on the bed frame.

- Thus, she caused my injuries, but she didn't make it happen.

Metatron:

- I see. Are you sure you are not going to Medical Bay to check if you've got a concussion?

Keila:

- I will, after breakfast. The pancakes on Tuesdays are just too delicious to miss out. Head injury or no head injury.

Metatron:

- Hmm. Today is Wednesday...

Keila:

- Oh, dearie me! Take me to medical bay at once!

After that, Metatron quickly carried Keila to the medical ward where the AI robots restored her brain to "prime" condition in a couple of days.

Chapter 17 Sexy time: Interrupted

A few days later, Keila had recovered from the self-inflicted concussion, and she realised something. That it had been quite some time since she got laid. This was a problem, as she was forced to close all her social media accounts, including the hook-up app Swoonder, to support the illusion that she was dead.

Fortunately, Keila had a few thousand male subjects on Eden, and some of them were bound to be hot. But before moving on with that plan, she realised something. That she would damage her standing as Eden's god-queen if she started having sex with her subjects. Sex or no sex, her mission to "free" humanity and get revenge on Bjorn Muller was more important.

But what about Metatron? He had an incredibly sexy body despite his more mature age. On the negative side, he was a complete dork and Keila suspected him of being a mid-30's virgin, utterly incapable of hitting the spot. But then the great eureka moment hit Keila. That she could use the mind control technology to control Metatron's movements during sex, thus combining the best of two worlds: Controlled gyration and orgasm. Excited, she dressed up in her sexiest lingerie and called him over to her room.

Metatron came to her room, mesmerised by what he saw. Keila decided to talk first:

- Metatron. Have you found Adina yet?

Metatron was filled with disappointment. Why was his sexy boss dressing up like that to require a status report on the search for Adina? Metatron was considering whether he should tell Keila the truth; that he hadn't been looking for her as he was sick of scouring the tunnels. He decided against it.

- Not yet Mistress Keila. The tunnels are vast, and our efforts have been in vain so far.

Keila:

- That's a bit disappointing. Hmm.

- Anyways, moving on. Metatron, I require you to have sex with me, right now!

Metatron *gasped*:

- But why? You have been rejecting me and teasing me for a month straight with your ridiculously hot body.

Keila:

- Metatron! Never question why good things happen to you, just embrace it.

- But to answer your question: I teased you for fun, and I rejected you because I believe you won't be rocking the bed.

Metatron:

- So, what made you think otherwise?

Keila:

- I realised that I can turn you into the best lover ever, through controlling your body via the mind control technology.

Metatron:

- Wait a second, that's not how I envisioned our love to be! Does that mean I have no control over what I want to do?

Keila:

- Do you want sex or not?

Metatron:

- Well, when you put it that way. Take control of my body, my beautiful Mistress Keila!

Keila:

- Oh yeah!

Keila tried to connect to Metatron's mind that would enable her to have the best sex of her life. Unfortunately, the connection was slow, and a connection error prompt showed up in her mind. Error! Error!
Keila *screams*:

- Why can't I connect to your mind??

Metatron:

- It's probably because of the firewalls we installed to stop Adina from murdering us in our sleep.

Keila:

- Good point. But Adina is dead, so let's turn off the firewalls so we can have the time of our lives.

Metatron:

- Sure, thing boss, that sounds like a flawless plan that can't backfire!

Keila:

- I don't know if you are sarcastic or honest, but hey, let's do this.

Keila connected to Metatron's mind, and it worked better now that the firewalls were disconnected. It was time for some sexy whoop-de-doo! Three minutes into the sex, Adina appeared in the room as a mirage and blasted Metatron unconscious with a psionic blast. Keila gave Adina a furious look!
Keila:

- For fuck sake! I haven't had good sex for months, and now you show up to ruin it all!

Adina:

- I haven't had sex at all, as I am pure and saving myself for marriage.

Keila:

- Well, that's your problem, not mine.
- Why did you kill Metatron?

Adina:

- I fucked up. I was going to control his body to strangle you, but
I sent the wrong command.

Keila:

- Indeed, you did.

Adina:

- It doesn't matter, give me a few minutes, and my psionic powers
have recovered, and I will kill you.

Keila:

- Nah. I'll just kill you now!

After saying this, Keila blasted Adina with a psionic blast. Adina fell to
the floor, screaming in pain before her mirage disappeared from the room.
Was Adina finally dead? This time Keila would go to the tunnels herself to
make sure. But first, she needed to go to the Divine Dimension finding a Zetan technology to save Metatron's life. He needed to survive both for the plot
and for Keila's sex life!

Chapter 18 A One-Sided Fight to Death

Later the same day, Keila took a shuttle down Eden to find and confront Adina. Upon entering the tunnels, she realised that Metatron had done a very sloppy job looking for her as Adina was just a few meters away from the tunnel entrance. Adina spoke to her as she entered the tunnel.

Adina:

- Why have you come here?

Keila:

- Isn't that obvious? I have come to kill you. What else could I have come for?

Adina:

- It was a rhetorical question...

- You have made a great mistake coming here. Even with your "firewall magic" you stand no chance against my immense psionic powers from this close distance!

Keila:

- Is that so? Then blast away Adina.

Adina tried blasting Keila, but nothing happened, and she felt very strange.

Adina:

- What have you done? What happened to my psionic powers?

Keila:

- I turned off the technology. It's just you and me, fighting physically now.

Adina:

- An armed and highly trained rebel of the future against a chubby magical priestess from The Bronze Age? Hardly seems fair.

Keila:

- Life isn't fair. But to make things slightly more interesting, I left my weapons back in the control centre. If you bull-run me and manage to get on top, you can potentially suffocate me with your immense mass!

Adina:

- Okay. Prepare to die Keila.

After saying this, Adina made a bull run towards Keila. In the last second, Keila managed to jump to the side and Adina who had the momentum and a complete inability to change direction continued in a straight line ending up outside the tunnel where she was incinerated by Keila's orbital lasers. Mission complete! Keila avoided her victory dance and entered her shuttle back to the Divine Control Centre.

Chapter 19 Metatron's Revival Disappoints Keila.

A few days later, it was time to revive Metatron by using the Zetan technologies that Keila found in the Divine Dimension. The problem for Keila was that the only way to resurrect Metatron seemed to be to give him a superior God-like power, i.e. a higher tier of mind control technology than she had installed. While this could be a problem as that would technically make Metatron her boss, Keila was convinced that her captivating personality and beautiful looks would be enough to sway Metatron. so that she could still boss him around. Her assistant for the surgical procedure, Samael was less happy.

Samael:

- I don't understand reviving Metatron when I am here to serve you, Mistress Keila?

Keila:

- Because you were dead set on raping and killing me before I became your boss! Metatron, on the other hand, has always been a nice guy!

Samael:

- Those are good reasons. But I am still upset over two people having God chips. Our people have stuck with one god for the last 4000 years.

Keila:

- Well, then it's time to spice things up!

- On the bright side, the death of Abraham nullified your vows of celibacy. You are free to pursue romantic relationships.

Samael:

- Does that mean I can pursue a physical relationship with the beautiful Helena of the Gad tribe?

Keila:

- Yes.

Samael:

- Excellent. I'll do that at once. Best of luck with the surgery, Mistress Keila!

After saying this, Samael rushed out of the room to change his clothes to pursue his crush. Keila realised that she had screwed, as she had to perform the brain surgery on Metatron on hew own, without having any surgical skills!

Fortunately, Metatron's plot armour activated, and Keila performed the complicated procedure successfully. A while later Metatron opened his eyes.

Metatron *blinking slowly*:

- Oh, Mistress Keila, what happened? Did God smite me for breaking my vows of celibacy?

Keila:

- Nah, it wasn't God. Adina killed you with a psionic blast.

Metatron:

- That bitch! Where is she now?

Keila:

- She is dead. The sunburn from the orbital lasers proved too much for her.

Metatron:

- Good!
- Let's get back to where we were when she rudely interrupted us.

Keila:

- But Metatron, are you sure you don't need to rest? You have been dead for three days!

Metatron:

- Well, that's enough time wasted, let's do this.

After that, Keila and Metatron went ahead to have sex. While she was impressed by his dedication to the cause, she was less impressed by his actual performance. And Keila could not control Metatron's body as he had a higher-level mind control chip than she had. Bummer!

Chapter 20 Markus Bauer is Freed from The Mighty Pirate Morgan Henry

Markus Bauer, the Chief Scientist of ISS led by Bjorn Muller, woke up from slumber. He was studying himself through the mirror in the prison cell of Morgan Henry's pirate spaceship. He watched the blue-reddish marks around his eyes where the scuba mask had pressured around his eyes, and he couldn't believe how fortunate he had been. To survive with scuba gear and a tiny emergency pod in deep outer space for long enough to be taken hostage by a pirate ship? It was scientifically impossible and yet here he was.

Markus made a promise to himself that if he came out of this alive, he would change his sexual fetishes from scuba gear to space gear, as space gear was more useful for someone who spent his life working on a spaceship.

The door to Markus Bauer's cell opened, and in came Captain Morgan Henry, wearing luxurious pirate clothes, with a leather eye patch made from buffalo skin, a wooden peg leg and beautiful red and blue-winged parrot on his shoulder. Captain Morgan Henry aimed his flintlock pistol to the head of Markus Bauer, who was rubbing his eyes in disbelief.

Morgan Henry:

- Arrrrrrr! Got something stuck in your eye, aye?

Markus Bauer:

- I must be dead right? I end up in the outer space with scuba gear, and when I wake up, I face a 17th-century pirate.

Morgan Henry:

- Naaaaay! You are alive, and it's the year 2872.

Markus Bauer:

- But what's with the outfit, the eye patch, the pegleg, the gun and the parrot?

Morgan Henry:

- This outfit is my fashion statement. I'm using a wooden peg leg is because I lost a leg during a raid, the parrot is my beloved pet, and this pistol is just for show.

Markus Bauer:

- But why don't you use stem cell technology to grow yourself a leg and an eye?

Morgan Henry.

- You are right. I never thought about that! Thanks a lot.

- Good news for you. Someone paid your ransom. A hefty price to keep you alive. Pervert!

Markus Bauer:

- Why do you call me a pervert?

Morgan Henry:

- We found you wearing scuba gear in deep space. That must be a strange fetish.

- Anyways. Come with me to the loading dock. You are to meet a friend.

Morgan and Markus walked towards the loading dock where Markus was reunited with an old friend, Dr Tzi Chen Cheng, Markus' boss on the Science Commission and occasional secret fuckbuddy. Morgan Henry left, and Tzi Chen walked up to Markus and slapped him. Markus looked at him dumbfounded and spoke:

- Wait a sec. You make your way here to pay my ransom and rescue me, and the first thing you do is to slap me? What am I missing?

Dr Tzi Chen Cheng:

- I told you to not watch gay porn from dodgy Russian websites in the Science Bay! Now we have lost the Science Bay on Bjorn Muller's flagship. How are we going to spy on him now?

Markus:

- I didn't watch Russian gay porn. It just popped up. I think Bjorn Muller caused it to happen, to silence me and get rid of the evidence that Keila is still alive.

Tzi Chen:

- Okay. Then I am not angry at you anymore.

- Yes, Keila's supposed death. What a joke.

- It takes more to fool us at House Cheng, than closing her social media accounts and delivering a bucket of blood and body pieces. Especially since we have hacked the camera on her phone, tracking her every move. The Mighty House Cheng is superior to the House Muller faction!

Markus:

- Oh really. Are you going to publish this information?

Tzi Chen:

- We are. But first, we are going to watch Bjorn hang himself with his lies. Then we announce that Keila is alive to humiliate him.

Markus:

- Good. I want him to suffer for trying to kill me.
- You saved me, is there anything I can do for you, Tzi Chen?

Tzi Chen:

- Yes, I want you to speak to Admiral Max Wellington. I want you to tell him about Bjorn's attempt on your life and then request a transfer to the Proxima Thule Research station. If you are granted access to this station, see if you can convince Keila Eisenstein to attack the station.

Markus:

- Your shifty Chinese bottom. That's an incredibly far-fetched scenario. But I still love you.

Tzi Chen:

- Yes, my big German bear. And yet you know it will happen just like I said. Hee-Hee!

Markus:

- Yes, you are certainly a cunning man. Me likey!

Tzi Chen:

- Indeed.

- Now come with me to my private shuttle. It is a one-week flight back to Earth, and we have plenty of catching up to do.

After saying this, Tzi Chen winked at Markus, and they both boarded the Tzi Chen's shuttle, doing a lot of catching up!

Chapter 21 Bjorn Muller is Having a Terrible Holiday!

Bjorn Muller was trying to enjoy the alcoholic drink and the sunset on the exclusive, luxurious tropical resort where he was spending his holiday. It turned out to be a challenging task. Outside the resort, a large crowd had shouted obscenities towards him for days on end. Inside the resort, the guards gave him hostile looks, the wait staff kept spilling drinks on him, and chefs kept serving him undercooked food.

So why were people giving poor old Bjorn such a tough time? Had the people of Earth finally had enough of his family's tyrannical rule over the planet and the solar system? No, the answer was more straightforward than that: Bjorn was accused of being the cause of the cancellation of *The Bronze Age Fools*. The learning point for Bjorn was that one could oppress poor people on other planets, such as Mars, and Earthlings wouldn't bat an eye, but cause their favourite TV show to be cancelled, and hell will break loose!

Bjorn was considering going back to Hansstadt where he could spend the rest of his holiday comfortably in his suite in Europeum Towers, far away from protesters, poor people, and other rabble. But then he realised something. His father Joachim Muller also lived in Europeum Tower, so if Bjorn went back home, his father might try convincing Bjorn to get married to the horrible freak Alicia White. Bjorn shivered at the thought and realised something. That sometimes being at work was preferable to being on holiday.

With his work ethics suddenly reinvigorated, Bjorn decided to get on a shuttle and hurry back to the Terran Council base on Phobos Moon, where he was stationed. At least no-one dared to argue with him over there!

Chapter 22 Brahma Agrees to Go a Lengthy Walk

In the Divine Dimension, Brahma, one the Zetan Space Gods, decided that it was time to pay his crazy ex, Rangda, a visit. The reason was that he had lost his divine connection to Keila when she for no reason, killed her lover Jeshua. While this unjustified murder could be because Keila was a psychotic madwoman, who had DNA of an alien species, Brahma was convinced that it was because his insane ex-girlfriend Rangda had escaped her eternal prison and connected to Keila telepathically without Brahma noticing.

When Brahma had raised his concern with his boss Zeus, Zeus had been favourable to sending Brahma to check if Rangda was still in her prison cell. But when Brahma had asked to borrow Zeus' spaceship, it had been a negative answer. When Brahma complained about the long walk to get there, Zeus had said *"300,000 kilometres is certainly a long walk, so you better get started! Chop, Chop!"* Thus, Brahma concluded that his boss didn't mind breaking his legs by sending him off on an outrageously long walking journey, and Zeus wouldn't get his vote for the Boss of the Year award.

But how would he find his way to the Rangda's prison? There were no GPS signals in the Divine Dimension, and compasses didn't work either. Fortunately, there was another way. As the Divine Dimension was an endless flat plain, as a flat-Earth-conspiracist pictured how Earth would look, things never fell behind the horizon. Thus, Rangda's eternal prison would be visible from his location, albeit extremely tiny. Since Brahma was an advanced alien species, he had excellent binoculars at his disposal.

Brahma walked up on the top of his house where he would have a free sightline towards the horizon. He turned slowly to study the horizon in a circular pattern. After rotating 359 degrees he finally saw Rangda's prison in the far horizon, and it was a discovery that gave him mixed feelings. On the one hand, it was a relief that he finally saw it after looking for 3 days straight. On the other hand, if he had only turned one degree to the left from his original position instead of 359 degrees to the right, he would have saved himself a lot of work!

Having spotted Rangda's prison, he started his long walk. The hike would take years, and he would constantly be hungry and thirsty. On the flip side, neither hunger nor thirst could kill him because he was a semi-divine alien, stuck in the author's analogy for the 7th heaven, the Divine Dimension!

Chapter 23 No Rest for the Wicked!

Bjorn Muller was back in his spacious and luxurious office at the Terran Council Phobos base. Never had he imagined that he would enjoy his return to work, but the first hour had been quiet and peaceful. The learning point for the average worker, is that if your holiday entails having an angry mob threatening to lynch you; the security guards keeps giving you hostile looks; they waiters keep spilling drinks on you, and the chefs keep giving you expired food, then you are better off working!

Bjorn sat back on his couch and poured himself an expensive glass of Scotch. How relaxing it was to be back at work! The peace ended abruptly when Bjorn's boss, Admiral Max Wellington requested to see him immediately, which reminded Bjorn about the annoying fact, that although he was the son of the Terran Council leader, he wasn't even the boss of his own military base!

Begrudgingly Bjorn made his way to Max's office.

Bjorn Muller:

- You wished to see me, Admiral Max Wellington.

Max Wellington:

- I have received some grave accusations against you, Rear Admiral Muller.

Bjorn Muller:

- The trash bin is over there. You know who my father is, so why even bother accusing me of things?

Max Wellington:

- I also know that I am the highest-ranked officer on this base despite your father's position.

Bjorn Muller:

- Oh, Maxi Jealousy! Who has the most prominent office with the best selection of expensive drinks and women? Burn!

Max Wellington:

- Not meant as a "Burn", I'm just explaining why you are here.
- Besides, I don't drink, and I am loyal to my wife, Magda.

Bjorn Muller:

- Wasn't she and your daughter killed by space pirates last year? Ha-ha!

Max Wellington:

- Grrrr. You're an asshole Bjorn!

- Anyways I am here because I had some grave accusations come in against you.

Bjorn Muller:

- I told you already. The bin is over there. My father doesn't care about Martian whinging!

Max Wellington:

- I think he will care about this: I spoke with Markus Bauer the other day. He accused you of intentionally sabotaging the Science Bay to kill him and get rid of the fake evidence of Keila Eisenstein's death.

Bjorn Muller:

- That's ridiculous. The dislodgement of the Science Bay was due to the Russian porn virus that Markus Bauer downloaded.

Max Wellington:

- How do you know the accident was caused by a Russian porn virus since you never went back to investigate the Science Bay?

Bjorn Muller:

- I know, because I reprimanded Markus Bauer earlier for downloading prohibited X-rated video clips, and for storing a scuba gear in the Science Bay.

Max Wellington:

- Scuba gear on a spaceship? Why?

Bjorn Muller:

- You don't want to know!

Max Wellington:

- A correct statement!

Bjorn Muller:

- Anyways. How does Markus Bauer claim to have survived the accident?

Max Wellington:

- He claims that he equipped the scuba gear and then was picked up, resuscitated, and taken hostage by the infamous space pirate Captain Morgan Henry. Apparently, Tzi Chen Cheng showed up a couple of weeks later and paid his ransom.

Bjorn Muller:

- That's an absurd and far-fetched story. Divine intervention would make more sense!

- Anyways Tzi Chen and Markus have a secret sodomite relationship. Tzi Chen probably told him to tell lies about me to make my life miserable!

Max Wellington:

- How do you know about Tzi Chen and Markus Bauer?

Bjorn Muller:

- They invited me to a threesome once. I was considering it to piss off my father. But then I realised that my brother Benjamin is already doing that, so I dropped that idea.

Max Wellington:

- You do realise that Benjamin is homosexual and not just pretending to irritate your dad?

Bjorn Muller:

- That's ridiculous. The Mullers have perfect DNA. How could we be gay? Besides I have suffered from unrequited love to that bitch Keila Eisenstein for the last four years. How would that happen if I preferred men?

Max Wellington:

- What are you talking about? Did you just confess treason, to disprove that you are gay?

Bjorn Muller:

- Did I? What a shame I hacked the security in this room and turned off the cameras and the audio recordings!

Max Wellington:

- Fuck this shit. I am sending you back to your father. Joachim Muller can deal with you.

- Get the hell out of my office.

Bjorn Muller:

- That's alright. I'll think about you and laugh when I enjoy my life in luxury and abundance on Earth!

After this, Bjorn left the room with an arrogant smile, blissfully unaware that his father was not planning a royal welcoming reception for him when he came back to Earth!

Chapter 24 Keila Finds Advanced Alien Technology

Keila was having a moment of self-doubt. She was doing a "Charlie Sheen", questioning whether she was still "winning" despite everything that had happened. She had gone from a famous revolutionary with a large army to the *"god-queen"* of a bunch of inbred peasants, living such an anachronistic lifestyle that even the Amish seemed progressive and modern.

But Keila concluded: Her visions had told her that she would win, and since she wasn't crazy, this must mean that she would start winning the war soon. But how could this happen? She was "dead" and had a bunch of Bronze Age peasants worshipping her. Bjorn and her enemies in the Terran Council had a vast army and advanced weaponry. What kind of idiot would come out backing her now?

But then Keila realised something. That there must be undiscovered alien technologies in the Divine Dimension, that was all she needed to turn the war against the Terran Council to her advantage. Keila remembered the day when she was connected to the Divine Detector machine and saw the dead Yahweh, Keila knew there were more secrets to look for in that Divine Dimension. She turned towards the naked and hungover Metatron, who was in her bed.

Keila:

- Wake up, Metatron! We have things to do. We need to go to the Divine Dimension and find technologies that we can use against our enemies in the Terran Council.

Metatron:

- That's a terrible idea. Let's bring in some more wine and resume our sex marathon!

Keila:

- Metatron! We have spent three days straight drinking wine and having sex. Don't you want to do something else for once?

Metatron:

- I spent 62 years here without wine and without sex. I have a lot of catching up to do!

Keila:

- Thanks for reminding me of how old you are!

Metatron:

- Just one more day, please. Today is Saturday. Working on Saturdays is illegal in our culture.

Keila:

- Wait for a second! You said the same thing yesterday?!

Metatron:

- I was lying yesterday.

Keila:

- And lying is not a sin in your culture?

Metatron:

- Not when it is for a worthy cause.

Keila:

- That's enough. You are coming with me to the Divine Dimension to find some advanced alien technologies, or I'll close your window of opportunity for sex.

Metatron:

- You drive a tough bargain. Let's go.

Keila and Metatron teleported their minds to the Divine Dimension and entered the Zetan archives in the Divine Palace. As Keila had expected, there seemed to be blueprints for thousands of advanced Zetan technologies there. There was only one slight problem: All the descriptions to the technologies were written in the Zetan language. Unfortunately, neither Metatron nor Keila had any idea how to read the Zetan language. Keila sighed; she was so close to Zetan technologies and yet so far from getting what she needed.

Metatron:

- Seems that we have run into a dead end.

Keila:

- You tell me about it? Why did the Zetans, write in this gibberish language instead of writing in typical 29th century English like the rest of us?

Metatron:

- Good question, but presumably they didn't know about the English language, considering that the English language appeared in the 5th century AD and the Zetan civilisation was destroyed in the multi-millennial war long before that.

Keila:

- Wait. How can you know these things since you can't read the Zetan language?

Metatron:

- Abraham told me.

Keila:

- Your former dementia-ridden boss doesn't seem like the most credible source of information.

Metatron:

- True. Now I remember. I used the AI and a code-breaking program to decipher the Zetan language. It made about as much sense as the "Spacenet Auto-Translate" function, but you'll get a rough idea at least.

Keila:

- Cool. Let's try it on this schematic!
- "Potato's skin will cry and fade away when sharp blades end its life."
- That sounds like a cool weapon!

Metatron:

- Hmm. That sounds like Zetan technology for a potato peeler!

Keila:

- Dammit! Let's keep looking.

Metatron and Keila kept looking. After sifting through useless and plot-irrelevant technologies for days on end, they finally found five schematics that were crucial for the progress of the story. These were:

- **The Zetan Spherical Communication Blocker:** Technology that stopped the enemies' telepathic communications on demand

- **The Zetan Advanced Cloaking Device:** Technology that made spaceships invisible

- **The Zetan Ballistic Energy Absorber:** Technology that stopped bullets mid-air Matrix style!

- **The Zetan Unprotected Bionic Chip Disruptor:** Fool-proof technology that blocked the enemies' bionic microchips, causing them to freeze and look like drooling fools.

- **The Zetan External DNA Modifier:** Convenient trinket that changed the appearance and the outer DNA layer of a person. Affecting everything including their smell to that of another person.

They also found a lot of other technologies that they used to enhance their sex life, but that's outside the scope of this story!

Chapter 25 Markus Bauer Betrays House Muller.

Markus Bauer was sitting by his desk at the Proxima Thule research station located in the asteroid belt. He was sick of his new job already. As bad as it had been working under Bjorn Muller, especially when Bjorn had tried to kill him, working at Proxima Thule was worse!

Proxima Thule was the House Muller's research station for useless research. It was the place where incompetent scientists and guards were sent to work so they wouldn't cause damage elsewhere. Thus, Markus Bauer had to work with a bunch of scientists that had received too many accidental electric shocks during their crazy experiments, and they were protected by a bunch of perpetually drunk and severely obese security guards. Their current project was not any better, and Markus Bauer had been tasked with improving the design for the helium-inflated goat sex doll. What an utterly derogatory task for a prominent scientist like himself!

The breaking point for Markus Bauer was when one of the drunk guards had vomited over him, and destroyed the goat sex doll design. Markus had enough, and he would follow the wishes of his shifty and unreliable on-off lover Tzi Chen Cheng and betray House Muller by contacting the infamous terrorist Keila Eisenstein and urge her to attack Proxima Thule.

But how would he reach Eden with his message undetected? Markus decided for an ingenious plan, to call the Edenites from the Proxima Thule's 24 hrs call centre, pretending to his colleagues that he was making a sales call! After a few signals, Metatron picked up the phone on the other side.

Metatron:

- We are not buying any fucking goat sex dolls. Fuck off!

After that, Metatron hung up. Realising that his cover as a salesman wouldn't work, Markus decided to go for the risky option to call again, this time with his own miniature hologram generator.

Metatron:

- You again? What do you want?

Markus Bauer:

- I am Chief Scientist Markus Bauer. I am calling from the Proxima Thule base. Can I speak to Keila Eisenstein, please?

Metatron:

- Keila is dead, and why would a chief scientist try to sell sex dolls?

Markus Bauer:

- The sex doll sale was just a cover. What I really want to do is to betray House Muller and get you to attack this small and very weakly defended research facility.

Metatron:

- And why would you want to betray House Muller?

Markus Bauer:

- Because Bjorn Muller tried to kill me to cover up that Keila never died. I know she is alive, House Cheng hacked her phone, so they have a live update of what she is up to.

Metatron:

- Those are good selling points. But tell me: what use do we have for Proxima Thule?

Markus Bauer:

- The station is full of prominent Terran Scientists that can help you transform your backward Bronze Age tribes to a futuristic metropolis.

Metatron:

- Considering the useless inventions that have been released from your facility in the past, employing those scientists would bring us even further backwards! From the Bronze Age to the Stone Age!

- I'll talk to you later Markus; I got to see what the boss has to say.

After this Metatron hung up the phone and Markus Bauer had no choice but to bide his time and keep working on his "fulfilling" research project.

Chapter 26 Keila Orders an Attack

After the phone call with Markus Bauer, Metatron went to Eden looking for Keila. He found her sitting on the throne in an empty ancient temple, studying a burning amphora with olive oil.

Metatron:

- Why that long face? And why are you burning olive oil?

Keila:

- The Edenites... They came with offerings today, and they brought me this. I asked them for high-powered weapons. And they bring me olive oil.

- To punish them, I set fire to the olive oil to show my dissatisfaction. The Edenites called me "crazy bitch" and took off. Sob Sob!

Metatron:

- Have you heard about trade? You'd have a better outcome if you sold the olive oil Eden and bought the weapons out of the sales?

Keila:

- Perhaps. I'll try that next time.

Metatron:

- Good.

- I had a call from Markus Bauer. He knows that you are alive since House Cheng's Tzi Chen Cheng hacked your phone. He threatens to tell Bjorn and expose to House Muller that you are alive unless you agree to attack the Proxima Thule research station.

Keila:

- That's awesome! I have been waiting for a sign to attack the Terran Council for a long time. This is it!

Metatron:

- Fair enough. But what purpose would an attack on Proxima Thule have?

Keila:

- Many! I will kidnap their prominent scientists, steal their valuable research data, and sow fear in House Muller with my mysterious random attack.

Metatron:

- Alright. I'll let Markus know we are going and that we will see him in a couple of days.

Keila:

- Are you a bloody idiot? You are going to tell a prominent Terran Council scientist that we are planning to attack his base? Of course not!

- You stay here, while I bring my Edenite militia to attack the outpost.

Metatron:

- Your Edenite militia?! They haven't been trained in modern combat yet! They still think it's the Bronze Age and that a tribal war formation with spears and shields is the way to go!

Keila:

- They'll learn as they go. Prepare my spaceship Metatron. It's time for Keila Eisenstein to fight again!

Chapter 27 The Attack on Proxima Thule.

A few days later Keila and her Edenite militia approached the Proxima Thule research station. With their Zetan stealth technology, there was no problem getting to the base undetected, but Keila faced another issue: Her Edenite militia insisted that a Bronze Age phalanx was the best way to fight! "Ah, fuck it," Keila thought to herself. With her Zetan technologies, she could fight a few incompetent guards herself!

Meanwhile, Captain Berndt Messerschmitt woke up from his nap when the warning indicator blinked in his security office. He looked at the computer screen in disbelief, turned his eyes to the half-empty whiskey bottle, and then looked at the screen again. What he saw was unbelievable. The infamous terrorist Keila Eisenstein had docked with his station, and she was accompanied by a group of men wearing bronze spears and bronze shields. He turned to his colleague Sebastian Marica, to confirm the vision:

Berndt Messerschmitt:

- Hey Marica! Do you also see the terrorist Keila Eisenstein accompanied by a group of Bronze Age warriors on the monitor?

Sebastian Marica:

- Mas Tequila, Por Favor!

Berndt Messerschmitt:

- Why are you asking for tequila instead of answering my question?!

Sebastian Marica:

- I see them. But it must be a delirious hallucination. Thus, I need to drink more to get sane.

Berndt Messerschmitt:

- This is absurd. Call HQ to find out if they are using the station for a movie production today. Aren't these crews from the reality show that was cancelled, *The Bronze Age Fools*?

Sebastian Marica:

- Sorry sir, but it seems like all our communications are down. As if we are blocked by unknown technology. Everything says blocked.

Berndt Messerschmitt:

- Or maybe you just spilled a bottle of booze in the relay again?!
- Get the other guards! Let's confront these clowns.

Sebastian Marica:

- Sorry, Berndt, it's just you and I guarding the entire space station, the rest went on holiday two weeks ago.

Berndt Messerschmitt:

- What? Why didn't anyone say goodbye?

Sebastian Marica:

- They did, but you were too drunk to remember.

Berndt Messerschmitt:

- Bloody Hell! Oh well, time for us to stop this infamous terrorist and her *"Bronze Age Fools"* followers!

Meanwhile, Keila armed to her teeth and equipped with advanced Alien technology, saw two blind-drunk and severely obese security guards walking towards her. Was this all the guards for this Terran Council facility that was filled with expensive machinery and top-end technology? What a lucky day.

She was lifting her rifle and about to shoot them when she got one of her "visions".

Rangda *hissing*:

- Dance and they will die!

Keila *shocked in disbelief*:

- Wait? Who are you, and why would dancing be a better option than shooting the guards?

Rangda *screeches*:

- Hmm, I am Rangda, Your guardian angel! Just obey the vision like you always do.

Keila:

- Cool. Yeah, why not?

Following the conversation with Rangda, Keila decided that the only sensible thing to do was to drop her weapons and start dancing instead. The drunken security guards tried to shoot her, but their aim was off by a mile, and instead, the Edenites had to take cover from stray bullets behind their large bronze shields.

Watching Keila's "seductive" dance was too much for Sebastian, who had been stuck on a "men only" research facility for too long. He got a massive heart attack, clutched his chest with one arm and accidentally shot Berndt Messerschmitt in the head with his pistol while falling towards the floor. Both men died on the spot.

Melchior Dorevitch, Keila's Edenite commander, approached her angrily after the skirmish:

- Mistress Keila! Why did you start dancing, risking our lives when all you needed to do was to shoot them with your pistol?

Keila:

- Why didn't you shoot them with your gun then? Oh yeah, you think a bronze spear and a bronze shield is better than a gun!

Melchior:

- Thank you for the lesson Mistress, Keila. We will start using guns like the rest of humanity.

Keila:

- Good. I hope you brought your gas masks because I will open this canister with sleep-inducing gas to knock everyone on Proxima Thule unconscious!

Without waiting for Melchior's reply, Keila opened the canister. The gas spread across the space station knocking everyone, including her own Bronze Age militia, unconscious. So, Keila being the only one who had a gas mask on, had to spend the next 10 hours dragging the unconscious scientists as well as her own militiamen back to her space shuttle. Being a rebel leader is demanding, especially if you are an idiot!

Chapter 28 Bjorn Muller Reacts to the Proxima Thule Attack

A few days later Bjorn Muller was having a bender together with the courtesans Intisar and Kinette. Bjorn enjoyed the company of Intisar and Kinette as he was an immoral villain who was secretly in love with his nemesis Keila Eisenstein. As he could not have Keila, Bjorn did what any wealthy villain would do; he hired escorts that looked like her. This had angered his very racist father Joachim Muller, who had no real objections to Bjorn's rampant drug and sex abuse but was furious that Bjorn had fired his North European looking escorts and replaced them with Mediterranean looking ones! Bjorn's bender came to a halt when Admiral Max Wellington knocked on his door.

Bjorn opened the door, and Max Wellington gave him a surprised and angry look:

Max:

- Why are you still here?! Didn't I tell you to go back to Earth, before I went on my holiday?!

Bjorn smiled arrogantly at Max:

- You did. But then my latest shipment of courtesans arrived. My father doesn't allow me to have sex with other races at Europeum Tower, so I decided to stay here and get it out of my system.

Max:

- That was one month ago. Why are you still here?

Bjorn:

- You clearly don't have the same appetite that I do!

Max:

- You disgust me!

- Besides if you stayed on the base during my holiday, why haven't you done anything about the attack on the Proxima Thule research station?

Bjorn:

- I considered it, but I didn't know who the attackers were, so I couldn't reward them.

Max:

- Reward them?!

Bjorn:

- Yes, reward them. Proxima Thule was the dumping ground for useless scientists performing pointless research. I wanted to fire them for years, but I didn't want to pay them severance packages. So, I left the station guarded by two incompetent security guards, hoping for it to be attacked, and it finally was. After two long years!

Max:

- Okay. So, you are not concerned about what your corporal Berndt Messerschmidt said? That the base was attacked by Keila Eisenstein and soldiers using Bronze Age weapons?

Bjorn:

- Who cares? Besides his claims are absurd so I assume they are bullshit.

Max:

- Very well. If you don't intend to work while at this base, then please get the fuck out!

Bjorn:

- Sure. But can you lend me a couple of thousand Terran Credits
in cash? I ran out of money, and I haven't tipped my friends for
their excellent service yet.

Max:

- Hell no! Get the fuck out of here before I call the guards!

hearing this, Bjorn finally gave in, and returned to Earth for a long over-
due catch up with his father.

Chapter 29 Not exactly a royal reception.

A few days later Bjorn Muller arrived back into his home city on Earth, Hansstadt. To his great disappointment, he did not receive a royal welcoming reception upon returning home. Instead, Bjorn got detained in immigration as he was carrying an outdated biometric passport. After a few hours, Bjorn was released, and his next disappointment came when he couldn't book a driverless cab to Europeum Towers, as he had neglected to renew his credit card. How could this happen to the son of the mightiest person on Earth, the son of Terran Council Chairman Joachim Muller? After walking for three painstaking hours to get to Europeum Tower, Bjorn found the answer, it had all been orchestrated by his father!

Upon seeing Bjorn, Joachim Muller smirked at him and spoke:

- Welcome back, Bjorn. I hope getting here wasn't too difficult.

Bjorn Muller:

- I would like to report the immigration officers. The idiots didn't recognise me and instead detained me for hours.

Joachim Muller:

- Yeah, so I heard. You were travelling with an expired passport, and they did their job. I will commend them for their duty.

Bjorn Muller:

- But I am a famous person, they should know about me!

Joachim Muller:

- You should carry a valid passport! Any more questions?

Bjorn Muller:

- All the cabs refused to drive me today, so I had to walk all the way from the spaceport to here!

Joachim Muller:

- Yes. We have had too many freeloaders not paying for transport, so I ordered all the cabs to require pre-payment for trips made today.

Bjorn Muller:

- Are you the one behind all the trouble I have had today?

Joachim Muller:

- Yes, I am the one causing you trouble. You must stop thinking so highly of yourself. You're the black sheep of the family. Now I must deal with you as Max Wellington had enough of your idiocies!

Bjorn Muller:

- What idiocies? I am a capable member of this family!

Joachim Muller:

- Capable member of the family? The last six months you have caused the Bronze Age Fools to cancel. You have incorrectly announced the death of the most wanted criminal of the Solar System. You managed to get kicked out of a resort. And you have spent more time whoring and boozing than doing actual work. It would be difficult to be less competent than you.

- You are even incapable of trivial tasks such as renewing your passport and credit card and then you complain about it.

Bjorn Muller:

- Keila is dead. Some idiotic guard who is revived after being shot in the head proves nothing.

Joachim Muller:

- Unfortunately, the "proof" of her death that you presented was even less credible. A closed-down social media account and a bucket of blood with traces of her DNA. What a pile of dung!

Bjorn Muller:

- So, what is your plan for me, father? And who are we having dinner with?

Joachim Muller:

- Wow, you are finally paying some attention. Yes, there are three table settings on my table, and we do have an honoured guest joining us. Your new boss. But first, let's drink some wine and enjoy the sunset in silence.

Bjorn Muller:

- But who...?

Joachim Muller got up and slapped Bjorn and said: "I said, let's enjoy the sunset in silence". After that Bjorn shut up and together, they shared an utterly unenjoyable hour, before the guest of honour Alicia White arrived.

Alicia White was the daughter of John White, who was the faction leader of House White. She was the most ridiculous villain of this story. Being the result of genetic manipulation, Alicia was a human infused with the genome of other predator species to give her superior animal-like senses. She had the ferociousness of a tiger and a pair of sharp retractable claws; she had the cool-headedness of a crocodile and the aggressiveness of a raging bull. On top of that, Alicia had the sense of smell of a bloodhound. While these abilities sound impressive, it had the drawback that she also shared physical features of the animals mentioned, with glowing yellow eyes, menacing fangs, lizard-like scaly skin and a small lump of a tail that resembles that of a croc. Her animalistic behaviour also made her disregard social standards for human-to-human interaction.

Her father John loved her but had chosen to hide her away in the black operations department of House White, where she could do what she did best, killing and torturing other humans.

Bjorn Muller:

- What the fuck is Alicia White doing here?!

Alicia said nothing, and instead, she screeched and gripped Bjorn by the balls and licked him in the face, before speaking with a hiss:

- Your father asked me to come here and put you in place! You have been a naughty boy Bjorn. I want to taste you from head to toe. Hiss!

Joachim studied Bjorn, who was in immense pain and couldn't say a word. Eventually, he spoke:

- Impressive move Alicia, you did what no-one else can do. You got the spoiled brat to shut up!

- You can release him now. I think he's almost suffocated.

Alicia released Bjorn, who was gasping for air, and then she took a seat next to Joachim at the table.

Bjorn, having regained his breath, shouted at his dad:

- I am not marrying that freak! I refused four years ago, and I'll refuse now!

Alicia White:

- Don't worry. I am not on the marriage market anymore. I have found my calling in life.

Bjorn Muller:

- And that is?

Alicia White:

- To eat naughty boys!

Bjorn Muller:

- You mean like figuratively speaking?

Alicia White:

- No, I meant literally. I kill and eat people that are on the House White "kill" list.

Bjorn Muller:

- Stuff that!

Joachim Muller:

- You have been naughty Bjorn; so, make sure you don't end up on Alicia's naughty list. For your own sake!

- Fortunately, I am giving you a chance to redeem yourself. Go with Alicia White and her men to Eden and find out Keila's whereabouts. Then go to Proxima Thule to investigate the attack. If you are successful, I might give you another job when you get back!

Bjorn Muller:

- Hey, wait. I am your son and an excellent leader of men. I don't mind investigating the rumours of Keila's survival, but don't put me under the command of that freak!

Joachim Muller:

- You were chasing Keila for four years, yet you stopped the chase because she closed her social media profile and delivered you a bucket with blood and gore. Alicia, on the other hand, doesn't stop until she personally has ensured that the target is eliminated.

Bjorn Muller:

- But she is a monster. She killed most of the population in the Martian city of Pamshal with a synthetic Ebola virus, just for fun!

Joachim Muller:

- I didn't know that Bjorn, but good on you, Alicia. I commend you for your virtuous deeds.

Alicia White:

- Thank you, Chairman Muller. It's a pleasure butchering those innocents for the glory of the Terran Council. The people of Mars are inferior to our race, and so is an easy target for me.

Bjorn Muller:

- You are both horrible people!

Joachim Muller:

- Thank you for the compliment, Bjorn. I didn't become the Chairman of a brutal plutocratic dictatorship by being a nice guy.

- But time is money! So, you better get ready for your trip to Eden. See you when you get back!

Having said this, Joachim pressed the button to activate the trap doors that were set under the guest seats under the table. Fortunately, he had remembered to set it to non-lethal propulsion, so they propelled and landed safely on a mattress one level below. If Joachim had been forgetful and left the trap doors on lethal killing mode, this story might have had another outcome.

Chapter 30 Metatron Delays Alicia and Angers Keila.

A few weeks later, Keila was in the shower when Metatron contacted her telepathically via the divine technology mind-control god chip.

Metatron:

- Bjorn Muller and a beast-like mutant called Alicia White are here looking for you. Shall we kill them?

Keila:

- No. We cannot expose our revolutionary plans yet. Do whatever it takes to delay them, while I'll travel with an emergency shuttle to Eden and hide.

Metatron:

- Okay, I'll do that.

Having finished his telepathic conversation with Keila, Metatron approached his distinguished guests. He didn't even have time to speak before Alicia grabbed him by the balls and hissed in his ears:

- Where is Keila? I can smell her on you! Hiss!

Metatron evaluated Alicia's statement. He deduced that she was lying. He had just had a shower, and he hadn't even touched Keila afterwards. But then he looked at Alicia again, and another idea struck him. How interesting it would be to have sex with the freak in front of him. Alicia was the first woman he had ever seen with glowing yellow eyes, retractable claws, and lizard skin. And she had a sexy tight body, not an ounce of fat!

But then he felt guilty. Keila was his girlfriend and cheating on her with a mutant freak wasn't nice. Except... It wouldn't be cheating, as Keila had given him permission to have sex with Alicia. *"do whatever it takes to delay them"* couldn't be interpreted otherwise. Having made up his mind, Metatron grabbed Alicia by the crotch and tried to speak with a deep sexy drunken whiskey-drinker voice, but instead came out as squealing in pain like a skinny little girl:

- So.... yikes! You like it rough, hey? They don't call me big Jack for nothing. You and me in the storeroom over there, let's get groovy! A-ha? Ouch! Hmmm...

Alicia White's eyes sparkled brightly, and she looked at Metatron with pure delight. The usual reaction she got for her gripping people by the balls habit, and intense cold-blooded stare was usually fear and terror, but finally, she had found a man that liked her! They then proceeded to the storeroom and had very rough and noisy sex. When they were done, Alicia was so happy, so she ordered Bjorn to come back with her to the spaceship, having forgotten about why they had travelled to Eden in the first place.

For Metatron, things were worse. As it turned out, he wasn't up for the challenge of having sex with the super rough Alicia White. Instead, he had to drag himself to the Medical Bay bleeding and in severe pain from Alicia's sexual madness. And when Keila came back, instead of thanking him for going beyond duty, she was full of jealousy and scolded him for cheating on her with a mutant freak. Aww, Life isn't fair, Metatron!

Chapter 31 Alicia Almost Kills Bjorn Muller During Sex.

A few days later, Alicia White and Bjorn Muller arrived at a House White Black Operations hideout on Mars. Bjorn, who wanted to know what was going on, decided to ask Alicia.

- Alicia, why are we on Mars, and who is this prisoner?

Alicia White:

- We are on Mars because Keila is alive, and this prisoner is Keila's ex-lover, who I am going to torture and eat alive while filming. I will then send Keila the video recording and challenge her for a duel. Which she will accept! Then, I will kill her, and we'll both get rewarded.

Bjorn Muller:

- There are so many far-fetched assumptions in that scenario!

- How do you know Keila is alive? The only thing you did see on Eden was Metatron, and then you went back to the ship for a nap after your shenanigans. How could you know whether Keila is alive or not?

Alicia White:

- Because I found Keila panties in the storeroom when I was having fantastic sex with Metatron.

Bjorn Muller:

- Oh, I see. When were you going to share this piece of evidence, and why don't we bring an army to catch her?

Alicia picked up Keila's panties from her pocket, sniffed them and ate them. Then she smiled and spoke:

- No, I won't get help from the army. Now that I know what she smells like, I know that she will be delicious. Heeee hee!

Bjorn Muller:

- Wait a second. Are you planning to eat her, or "eat" her?

Alicia White:

- I plan a bit of both actually. And after killing Keila, her boyfriend Metatron will be mine!

- But now I will torture and eat the prisoner. You stay in the other room Bjorn; I know how weak your stomach is!

Bjorn left the room and let Alicia do her thing with the prisoner. Between the agonising screams of pain and gore, Bjorn felt that his jealousy was increasing. The first few weeks of the trip, Alicia had been all over him, constantly harassing him sexually with her unwanted advances. But after her crazy session with Metatron, she had lost all interest in Bjorn and kept obsessing over Metatron instead. This was so wrong. Bjorn was the sex god of the solar system, and Alicia should swoon over him so that he could reject her and boost his own ego.

Bjorn made a fateful decision: he would give Alicia the sex of her life, to prove that he was a better lover than Metatron. He pumped himself up with sexual-performance-enhancing drugs and waited eagerly for Alicia to leave the torture chamber. A while later she came out, soaked in blood and Bjorn spoke to her:

- Alicia! Forget about Metatron. I am the true sex god of the solar system, and I can prove it to you, here and now!

Alicia:

- Sure, bring it on "sex god".

As it turned out, Bjorn was not up for the challenge. What made matters worse was that Bjorn kept shouting "Nein" ("no" in German), which Alicia in her frenzied and orgasmic state interpreted it as nine out of ten in intensity and roughness. This was too much for old Bjorn and combined with the effect of the boner pills, it caused him a massive heart attack!

Chapter 32 The Misogynist Bjorn Muller Accuses Alicia White of Rape.

Yesterday the frail and old self-proclaimed "sex god" Bjorn Muller woke up from an induced coma. Apparently, the pathetic old bugger swallowed a vast amount of sexual enhancement drugs so that he could outperform the latest tryst of Alicia White, the mysterious Jack Silver, also known as Metatron. This failed miserably as Bjorn got a massive heart attack during his rendezvous with Alicia, only revivable with advanced technology.

Upon waking up, Bjorn alleged that he repeatedly shouted "Nein (no)" during the intercourse, while Alicia claims that he yelled nine (out of ten of sexual intensity). While neither claim can be proven, bear in mind that Bjorn is a filthy rapist and misogynist with a prostitute addiction, spending equivalent to the GDP of a small Martian country, while Alicia White is the young and beloved daughter of our great Chairman John White.

Martin Orchard-Twig, House White News

Keila turned off the news show. She didn't know whether she was happy or indifferent that Bjorn was raped, but she was annoyed at the idiot that revived Bjorn when he finally had died. Suddenly Keila received an email from Alicia White with the text *"Alicia eating Josh, come face me if you dare"* and a video attachment with Alicia eating a Martian prisoner, Josh.

This made Keila extremely upset. That freaking ugly mutant had already seduced Keila's lover Metatron, Keila's rapist Bjorn and now she was going after Keila's ex Josh? How could that crazy bitch be so obsessed with stealing her seconds? She thought of deleting the email, but then her curiosity got the better of her, and she opened the video attachment. As it turned out, "Alicia eating Josh" wasn't the typical homemade amateur video and instead, it was showing Alicia eating Josh alive.

The video confused Keila. Why was Alicia sending her a video where she gruesomely murdered Keila's ex? Keila had murdered her own ex Jeshua due to divine providence/insanity six months earlier, so why would she care if Alicia killed her other exes? But then Keila realised that Alicia was also the woman who was responsible for killing most people in her hometown as well as seducing Metatron, so it was time to deal with Alicia, once and for all.

Filled with rage, she jumped into a spaceship heading for the abandoned asteroid's station where Alicia had taunted to face her, forgetting to bring important stuff such as weapons, gear, and soldiers.

Facing a homicidal mutant and her squad of Black Operations operatives unarmed and alone, doesn't seem like a good plan, so how will this end? You'll find out soon!

Chapter 33 Keila's Plot Armour Activates Again.

Some hours later Keila arrived at the Moreno outpost, and she realised that she shouldn't have travelled alone and unarmed to face a murderous mutant and her group of trained Black Ops killers. But should she go back to Eden and procure weapons and soldiers? No. Divine Providence guided her, and if she was meant to face Alicia and her men on her own, so be it.

She walked down the corridor and came to the lobby of the abandoned asteroid's old and grimy hotel. Josh's head was on a spike, and underneath it, there was a sign saying *"Keila, your next"*. Deciding to set things straight, Keila dipped her finger in the blood and changed the sign to "Alicia, you're next". When she was done, she heard a noise, and suddenly Alicia and her men surrounded Keila.

Alicia White:

- Keila, we meet at last. From smelling your panties, I know that you'll be delicious.

Keila:

- So, it was you that stole my panties? Fuck you, those were my favourite pair.

Alicia White:

- What are you going to do about it, little girl?
- Looking forward to being eaten?

Keila:

- Is that "eaten" or eaten?

Alicia White:

- I would prefer to do both if you want to, but otherwise just eaten. I am not Bjorn. I might be a genocidal mutant, but I am not a rapist. The Bjorn incident was a misunderstanding!

Keila:

- Okay. Well, I came to kill you, not to have sex with you, so I'll pass on "eaten".

- Anyways I am here now, so let's have this fistfight to the death!

Alicia White:

- Wait, who said anything about a fistfight? Who fights with their fists in the 29th century?

Keila:

- Well, this is a bit awkward, but I came here on a whim to face you, and I forgot to bring any weapons...

Alicia White:

- Okay, fistfight to death will do.
- Now...... Are you ready?!

Keila:

- Yes!

Without saying anything, Alicia swept in and knocked Keila to the ground with a punch to the head. Ouch! What a cheater Alicia was, punching before the bell had rung! But then Keila realised that a fight to the death on an abandoned asteroid hotel wasn't regulated and that she was in trouble. Where was her divine connection when she needed it the most? Keila got up, and Alicia swept in and punched her in the head again!

Then it came to her. The divine connection and premonitions: Suddenly, the mirage of Brahma showed up in front of her. He sighed:

- Aaah, Keila, Keila, Keila. How do you always manage to get into trouble?

Keila:

- I just follow my premonition and your divine guidance, master.

Brahma:

- Did I tell you to fight a dozen armed men led by a mutant with superhuman senses on your own? Hell no, I didn't!

Keila:

- I am sorry grandmaster Brahma. But can you please help me out of this mess?

Brahma:

- No! I have been helping you out of your troubles for five years, but you just keep finding new ways to get into trouble. I am out! You are on your own!

Having said that Brahma disappeared out of Keila's vision and instead she stood face to face with Alicia again.

Alicia White:

- Why are you talking to yourself out in the thin air? Did I punch you that hard?

Keila:

- I am just trying to convince my spiritual connection to save me by intervening with a miracle and kill you to rescue me.

Alicia White:

- And people call me crazy?!
- Where are your gods now?

Keila:

- The first one I called hung up on me. But give me some time, and you'll face divine wrath.

Alicia White:

- I'll call you on that one. Mostly because I am a sadistic killer with added feline DNA, and just like a cat, I like to toy with my victims, killing them slowly for my bemusement. Take this!

Alicia impaled Keila's shoulder with her sharp claws, and then punched her in the face knocking her to the ground. Alicia then licked Keila's blood off her claws and spoke joyfully:

- Aaah! Delicious, just as I predicted. I love to sip a B+ blood type. You should be more like your blood type, sweet and courageous!

Keila:

- Oh, I'll be getting the last laugh, Alicia. Hold on a minute.

Keila realised that she was in trouble. For unclear reasons, the gods that had granted her premonitions had never given her enough speed and strength to beat up a dozen of elite operatives in hand to hand combat! With Brahma refusing her telepathic calls, she only had one option left: To call the evil space demon Rangda.

Rangda *telepathically*:

- Having some trouble, little girl? I am busy but read out the number that's visible on your hand and the code word, and you'll be fine.

Keila:

 - Cool, I'll do that.

Keila looked at the number and code word on her wrist "22131985 self-destruct."
Keila:

 -         Twentytwomilliononehundredthirtyonethousandninehun-
   dredeightyfive self-destruct.

And nothing happened except for Alicia swooping in again, this time biting a piece of flesh off Keila's damaged shoulder.
Alicia White:

 - At least fight me, like your ex Josh did. Your no fun, Keila!

Keila:

 - It is spelled "You're!"

 - Besides, thanks for killing Josh for me, that bastard cheated on me with my best friend!

Alicia White:

 - So why did you come here to kill me then?

Keila:

 - Two reasons; 1: You spread synthetic viruses in my hometown, killing most of the population. 2: I need your DNA, so I can use alien technology to look like you and kill everyone on the Terran Council.

Alicia White:

 - Fair enough. But killing me seems to fail miserably.

Keila:

- True.
- Rangda! Why is the code not working?

Rangda *telepathically*:

- Sorry, Keila, I forgot to tell you. There are meant to be commas between the digits. Thus, read them out as single digits.

Keila:

- Okay! Cool.
- Two, Two, One, Three, One, Nine, Eight, Five self-destruct.

As Keila narrated the sequence, the battle armours of Alicia White and her operatives all self-destructed, killing the entire group. Boom! Keila looked around herself in disbelief and joy. How had Rangda implanted bombs in the battle armours of Keila's enemies her location in another dimension? It was a miracle.

Keila:

- Thanks, Rangda. You are my new inter-dimensional Best Friend Forever.

Rangda:

- Good, hehe. Then you wouldn't mind if I "accidentally" kill your mentor Brahma, would you?

Keila:

- Nah, he left me to die. Fuck him.

Rangda:

- Good. I'll talk to you later.

Understandably the reader now wants to know how Rangda could rig Alicia and her group's battle armours for self-destruction. Obviously, she didn't. Instead, it was Alicia's father John White, the Chairman of House White, who was the culprit/hero behind it. John being evil enough to imbue his daughter with predator DNA to make her more fearsome, was also ruthless enough to predict that she would double-cross him in the future. And like any villain with self-respect, he had a contingency plan. A voice-activated self-destruct sequence in her daughter's and her operatives' battle armours.

But how could Rangda know the activation sequence to the self-destruction mechanism? Simple: she was a supernatural space demon with superpowers!

Chapter 34 Brahma Dies from his Peanut Allergy.

A few weeks later, Brahma finally reached his destination, Rangda's *"inescapable"* eternal prison. He quickly realised that term inescapable was incorrect, as there was a tunnel, an indication that Rangda had dug herself out. But how had she dug herself out from a prison made of the second hardest material in the universe? Brahma realised that he was to blame. After convincing his colleagues to spend years building the inescapable prison to punish Rangda for her crimes instead of just killing her, he had stuffed up in the last minute. Before sealing the door to the prison, he had thrown his engagement ring, which incidentally was made of the hardest material in the universe at her. With such a "useful" tool at her disposal, it was only a matter of time, a few millennia, for the evil space demon to get out, digging herself a hole using the ring. Brahma called out Rangda's name and she appeared and walked towards him.

Brahma:

- Ugh. You have really aged a lot since the last time we met!

Rangda:

- No, this is my true form. The grand beauty of a Xeno-Zetan hybrid, the queen of the Xenos, destined to be the ruler of the galaxy.

Brahma:

- Whatever. You are still ugly, and besides, there are none of your people Xenos left in the divine realms, as we killed them all.

Rangda:

- Really? Is that so? I suggest you have a look behind you.

Brahma turned around, and as he did, his chest was pierced by the sharp claws of a Xeno beast warrior, with the end of the claws sticking out from

Brahma's back. Reacting instinctively, Brahma channelled his Chi-energy and crushed the skull of the Xeno warrior with a well-aimed blow.

Rangda:

- How did you survive that??

Brahma:

- I am just that badass!

Rangda:

- I see... Xenos charge!

Another dozen or so of Xeno beasts emerged, and Brahma had no problem killing them all, despite being mortally wounded and a lot smaller than the Xenos in physical size.

Rangda:

- Very impressive.

Brahma:

- Your Xenos are dead, and you are next. Any last words?

Rangda:

- I don't think so. They might be dead, but they served their purpose.

Brahma:

- And that was?

Rangda:

- To weaken you enough for this!

Rangda pulled out a bag with dehydrated peanut powder and threw it at Brahma's wounds. This was a deadly trick as Brahma, just like many other Zetan had a severe peanut allergy and getting the toxins in peanut powder straight into his wounds was enough to kill him!

Rangda wanted to increase her own power and give Brahma a more spectacular death; however, so she pulled out the magical plot device: The corrupted Zeto crystals "magical" trinkets that radiated evil and destruction. Aiming the trinket towards Brahma shattered and absorbed his soul, causing his head to explode. Witnessing Brahma's headless corpse, Rangda laughed maliciously for an extended period!

Chapter 35 Keila Wakes up with Purple Eyes and No-One Cares

Simultaneously with Brahma's unfortunate passing, Keila held a meeting with her subjects as the "democratic" god-queen of Eden. Being the democratic god-queen had the benefit that none of her subordinates dared to question her decrees or follies, but it also had the drawback that many of them didn't fear her enough to implement her orders.

In the middle of the meeting, Keila suddenly dropped to the floor with severe epileptic convulsions. The seizure was because her strong telepathic bond to Brahma made her feel what he was feeling, so she wasn't feeling very good. Eventually, the shaking ended, and Keila ended up with a much stronger bond to Rangda than she had before. This caused her eyes to turn purple, the same eye colour that Rangda had.

Metatron rushed up to her and spoke:

- Keila, are you okay? You had epileptic seizures, and now you have purple predator eyes!

Keila:

- I am fine, Metatron. In fact, I have never been better!

Keila gave Metatron a foreboding smile that made him wince away from her, before daring to speak again.

- But Keila. You had a severe epileptic seizure. How can you be fine, and what happened?

Keila answered nonchalantly:

- Not much. My spiritual guide Brahma was brutally murdered by the evil space demon Rangda. Rangda has now bound herself to me, making me a lot more powerful. But don't worry, despite being linked to an evil demon, I will use my newfound powers to make the solar system a better place. He-he-he

Metatron:

- That doesn't sound good at all. There must be something we can do to help you.

Keila's shifty and unreliable captain, Melchior Dorevitch joined in on the conversation:

- Stop worrying, Metatron. She said that she was fine.

Metatron:

- Have you ever seen anyone have seizures and then wake up with purple eyes before?

Melchior:

- Nah, but it doesn't bother me. Keila can have whatever eye colour she wants. As for her being possessed by an evil space demon; we both know that such things don't exist. Now let's conclude the meeting so we can have food and drinks.

Metatron:

- So, you are just going to ignore the health and sanity of our leader so that you can eat and drink?

Melchior:

- Yes. Can we have a vote in the assembly, please?

As it turned out, the assembly voted to ignore Keila's condition and proceed to eat and drink as they were all thirsty and alcoholics of biblical proportions!

Chapter 36 Rangda's Long Backstory Compressed.

In, The Divine Sedition, Rangda's long backstory, is written in great detail. But time is money, and Rangda's backstory is not that important for the overall plot, so here comes a shorter version.

Rangda's mother, Kalianka, was a Zetan scientist, who was left behind on the Xeno's home planet Xenora, after a botched research expedition from Zetani to Xenora. Against all the odds, she managed to survive on planet Xenora as she became a goddess/ sex slave/hostage for a tribe of Xenos living on the North Pole of Xenora. Over the years, she taught them everything she knew, fell in love with a Xeno, and eventually an unlikely set of mishaps caused her to fall pregnant, giving birth to a Xeno/Zetan hybrid Rangda. Rangda was born, and together they lived happily for some years until Kalianka died from skin cancer, as her Zetan skin couldn't handle the strong UV index on Xenora.

Losing her mother to skin cancer caused Rangda to snap, and she made it her life goal to annihilate the peaceful and prosperous Zetan galactic empire. As it turned out, Rangda had plenty of time to prepare her Xenos for the unnecessary war as she was immortal and neither aged nor got sick due to her status as the only Xeno/Zetan hybrid in the universe.

Eventually, Rangda had trained the Xenos to fight the Zetans, and she started off with several wins due to the Zetans peace-loving nature and dislike of wars. Eventually, one of the Zetans named Yahweh, came up with a brilliant plan to stop the battle of the two planets: To utilise and mind-control another intelligent species, humans from Earth, to fight the Xenos for the Zetans.

This changed the tide of the war as the humans fighting for their "prophecies and Gods' orders" were as aggressive as the Xenos, but they had a lot better equipment and slaughtered the Xenos on every planet. Rangda realised that if she couldn't beat the Zetans, she'd better join them. Changing her appearance to that of a beautiful Zetan woman, she seduce the Zetan leader Brahma, and infiltrate the Zetan homeworld of planet Zetani. Once she was on planet Zetani, she set off a supernova explosion that destroyed most of the Zetan galactic civilisation, and for this crime, she was sentenced to an eternity in the "inescapable" prison in the Divine Dimension. But now she was free, and she could resume her quest to eliminate all the Zetans and become the evil demon queen ruling the entire galaxy! Mwahaha!

Chapter 37 Rangda Provides Keila's War Strategy.

Rangda studied Keila telepathically from the Divine Dimension. She was starting to get restless with her human puppet, as Keila seemed to be unable to do anything at all on her own. Rangda wanted to involve humanity in a massive war to weaken them enough for a Xeno invasion, but all that Keila seemed to care about, was her fit body and various reality shows. But then Rangda realised that Keila was so useless because Brahma had only spoon-fed her stuff and stopped her from thinking on her own. If this was the case, she could be useful for Rangda's cause.

Unfortunately for Rangda, Keila was too far away from her to connect with, unless they both were suffering from a concussion at the same time. And this was easier said than done. Rangda had banged her head against the wall several times in the last month, but it had all been in vain, as Keila's brain had been in peak performance every time. Oh, what a headache. Literally.

Meanwhile, Keila was studying herself in the mirror after a gym training session. She had a super tight body and excellent features. She should be able to seduce any man in the solar system, and yet she was stuck with Metatron. And it was all because of her purple predator eyes! Every time she tried to give someone a sexy look, they just ran away in terror fearing for their lives. This was so unfair. Keila had failed to cheat on Metatron for months, as a payback for him having sex with Alicia White to "delay her". A bright idea came in Keila's mind. What if she ordered some tinted lenses and to hide her purple predator eyes? Then she'd be sexy again, and men would run after her, instead of running away from her. Filled with joy, she jumped up in the air and then fell over, hitting her head on the bathtub knocking herself out.

Seeing this, Rangda knew that time was short. She ran with full speed to knock herself out against a wall. But she hit it a bit too hard, so although she managed to get a connection with Keila it was a bit patchy. The message Rangda sent was: *"Pose as Alicia White, infiltrate the Terran Council, cause House White to argue with House Rashid, also cause House Muller to argue with House Cheng. Convince the Houses of Earth to open the portal on Earth to the Divine Dimension and fight the Zetans."*

Unfortunately, due to patchy inter-dimensional connection and Rangda's poor English, the message Keila received was: *"Attack the insignificant House Rashid outpost, Aljadid Salam, pretending to be House White, and then rob a House Cheng bank pretending to be House Muller."* It is beyond the scope of this story to tell how they could misunderstand each other this much, although, for Keila, the message she received was a lot more useful for her quest to liberate the Martians from the Terran Council!

Chapter 38 Death to the Infidels!

A month later, Ibrahim Rashid was having his afternoon tea and smoking his shisha in the shade of his tent, erected on the penthouse terrace of Rashid Tower in Rashidium. Aah, this was the life, drinking a cup of delicious tea and smoking a hashish shisha flavoured with lemon myrtle. How could one have a better or more relaxing time scheming ways of making people miserable? Suddenly, the peace was shattered when Ibrahim's personal assistant, Abdul the Eunuch, came in yapping with his high-pitched voice.

Ibrahim Rashid:

- Inshallah Abdul. What is the matter? Has my latest child bride delivery been delayed?

Abdul the Eunuch:

- No, it's much worse than that. Akram Rashid has been killed in a suicide bombing.

Ibrahim Rashid:

- Akram Rashid? Who is that, and why should I care?

Abdul the Eunuch:

- It's your beloved grandson Master Ibrahim.

Ibrahim Rashid:

- Oh yes. That's alright. These things do happen. Besides, I have a large harem of wives and countless children. I must have hundreds of grandchildren, I lost track of most of them!

Abdul the Eunuch:

- You have 182 grandchildren to be specific.

Ibrahim Rashid:

- So, I have plenty of other grandchildren for spares then. No need to worry.

Abdul the Eunuch:

- But Master Ibrahim, Akram was killed by American suicide bombers from House White.

Ibrahim Rashid:

- What?! Whatever the Americans do, we must fight back! How dare those Americans copying our method of warfare and brutally murder my innocent beloved grandson?? Jihad! Death to Infidels!

Abdul the Eunuch:

- But Master Ibrahim. We cannot invade America. It's impossible.

Ibrahim Rashid:

- You are right Abdul. Let's settle for hijacking an American cruise spaceship and brutally murder American tourists. To spice things up, we can send weapons and supplies to factions that hate House White on Mars.

Abdul the Eunuch:

- Excellent plan master. Make the Americans fear us enough to avoid senselessly murdering your family members.

Ibrahim Rashid:

- Good. That's settled. Now when will my child bride arrive?

Abdul the Eunuch:

- I will have to get back to you about that.

Ibrahim Rashid:

- Good. He-he-he!

Chapter 39 Problem with File Attachments

Bjorn Muller was sitting in his luxurious office on the Phobos base where he was back after his rape allegations against Alicia White, which had caused her mysterious disappearance. Fortunately, Bjorn was not a suspect of Alicia's disappearance as her operatives had dropped off Bjorn's lifeless body at the Phobos base and had then quickly taken off, not keen to answer questions!

Bjorn checked the calendar. It was Father's Day back in Europe, but would he call his vile racist father to celebrate the occasion? No, he wouldn't. Suddenly there was a knock on Bjorn's door, and as Bjorn shouted, *"Come in!"*, there he was, speaking of the devil, Joachim Muller, Bjorn's father.

Bjorn Muller:

- What are you doing here? I thought you were celebrating Father's Day back on Earth with your other children.

Joachim Muller:

- So, you remembered that it was Father's Day and yet you didn't call me? You're a terrible son.

Bjorn Muller:

- Still, five minutes to go before midnight. Happy Father's Day Joachim.

Joachim Muller:

- Nice save... If I came for Father's Day...

Bjorn Muller:

- Okay, so why did you come?

Joachim Muller:

- Do you remember the video attachment you sent the other day, the video that would prove that Alicia White raped you?

Bjorn Muller:

- Yes, of course! I have been wondering why you haven't gotten back to me!

Joachim Muller:

- I am here now, but as it turns out, you are an even bigger idiot than I thought. The video you sent didn't prove any of your allegations. Instead, it showed that you raped the terrorist Keila Eisenstein five years ago, an event that was the catalyst for her murdering your grandfather a few weeks later and starting this damn rebellion!

Bjorn Muller:

- Hmm. That wasn't rape. I paid her to act all scared on the video.

Joachim Muller:

- So, you admit to paying the woman that murdered your grandfather just weeks before the murder. The same woman you have been "chasing" for four years? Oh, Bjorn if you weren't my son, you'd be dead by now!

Bjorn Muller:

- Okay. No, I didn't pay her. I raped her. She was my sex slave before she escaped.

Joachim Muller:

- I feel like you are having a severe credibility issue, Bjorn. It's fortunate that Keila is dead so we won't have to dwell on this any further! I hope that she'll stay dead as well.

Suddenly Admiral Wellington rushed in and interrupted the father-son moment:

- I am deeply sorry to interrupt you, but I have an urgent report. The Aljadid Salam outpost in the asteroid belt has been attacked by American suicide bombers. House Rashid has retaliated by boarding an American cruise spaceship and taking 1,000 passengers as hostages.

Joachim Muller:

- American suicide bombers killing Muslims? The world is going crazy. Bjorn, get the fuck out of this office, I need to discuss this matter with Max.

Bjorn Muller:

- But this is my office?!

Joachim Muller:

- I don't care, now get the fuck out! And get yourself some candy!

Having said this, Joachim threw some money on the floor to humiliate Bjorn. Fortunately, Bjorn knew that the only coins his father carried were actual gold coins, so he eagerly picked them up and left his father alone with Max Wellington without throwing a tantrum!

Chapter 40 A Tampered Crime Scene

A few days later, Bjorn Muller arrived at the Aljadid Salam outpost in the asteroid belt as an independent investigator representing House Muller. Bjorn was about as untalented in crime scene forensics as he was in everything else, but his father had sent him anyway as he needed Bjorn's luxurious office on the Phobos base for himself. Bjorn studied the crime scene, and even he could establish that quite a few things were dodgy. The victims had died from multiple bullet wounds, and yet the attackers had blown themselves up. Why would anyone act this way? And how come the attackers were decomposing as if they were dead for a long time while the victims still looked freshly killed. He decided to discuss his findings with the local investigator from House Rashid, Sharif Sim Salabim:

Bjorn Muller:

- Sharif, from what I can tell, these men can't have been the perpetrators, that killed Akram Rashid and his men.

Sharif Sim Salabim:

- Silence you mongrel, how dare you questioning the prophet, peace be with him.

Bjorn Muller:

- I didn't question your prophet Sharif; I questioned your competence! How can men who have been dead for weeks have killed Akram a few days ago? These bodies have been decomposing for weeks!

Sharif Sim Salabim:

- They haven't been dead for weeks. They look more rotten because of their ungodly behaviour, while Akram and his saintly entourage's bodies still look fresh due to the purity and God-loving lives they have led.

Bjorn Muller:

- Okay. But how do you explain that the medical status bionic chip in the attackers' brains indicate that they died three weeks ago when Akram was killed three days ago?!

Sharif Sim Salabim:

- Shut up, Kafir. Don't question me with your fake gods, your artificial technologies, or your fake news. We believe that House White killed Akram, and until you can prove otherwise, be respectful to us!

Bjorn Muller:

- But I just did prove otherwise?

Sharif Sim Salabim:

- You are no longer welcome here; wretched unbeliever. Now leave before we proclaim Jihad on you!

Bjorn Muller:

- Alright, I am leaving now.

After his argument, Bjorn took his shuttle to the closest asteroid bar for some well-deserved drinks. The shit that he had to put up with...

Chapter 41 A Botched Rescue Operation.

A few days later, House White led by the incompetent colonel Mark White, conducted a failed rescue attempt of the prisoners on the hijacked cruise spaceship "America First". This was a tragedy that caused the death of over a thousand prominent Americans, but one man who was very satisfied with the outcome was the Chairman of House White, John White. The terrorist attack had killed off many of his rivals from other powerful families in North America, and best of all was that it was the Muslims fault. Thus, some things hadn't changed in America in the last 800 years since the 21st century. When something goes wrong, always blame the Muslims!

The only smoulder in the beaker for John White was the way his operatives had died. From the images he had seen, it appeared like they have been killed from activating the secret self-destruction mode he had built into their combat gears. What if the same fate had fallen on his sweet homicidal daughter Alicia White, who was still missing? John thought of her maniacal laughter, her cute, sharp bloodstained fangs, and her glowing yellow eyes, and suddenly, he was filled with misery. It wasn't fair that he had lost someone so unique and precious! He wailed and cried for hours, which turned out for the best as he didn't have to fake grief when delivering the press conference about the botched rescue attempt!

Chapter 42 Keila Has a Non-Lethal Abortion

A few weeks later, Keila woke up and felt sick again! Was a stale listeria-ridden rockmelon the culprit this time, or was it something else? Concluding that she hadn't eaten any rockmelons lately she realised that she hadn't had her period in a while. Keila concluded that she might be pregnant. How cool was that, could her divine connection have blessed her with an immaculate conception: The future Messiah of mankind that would unite us all for a better future, in alignment with the True Maker's wishes? If that were the case, it would hopefully be a girl that she would name Sabina. Since most previous Messiahs and prophets had been men, it was time for some girl power!

Keila realised that there was a slight problem with her Immaculate Conception theory. That she wasn't a virgin, as a matter of fact, she had been going at it around the clock with Metatron since she got possessed by Rangda and her eye colour changed to purple. She wouldn't have been the Virgin Mary, even if she wanted it to be so.

There was only one way to find out. To go to the Medical bay and have the medical robot run some tests. The tests gave both positive and negative answers to Keila. On a positive note, she was pregnant with a girl: yeah girl power! On the negative side, it wasn't a case of immaculate conception, but just a plain old traditional copulation, as the father of the child was Metatron.

But what would she do now? Keila had a revolution to start, and besides a normal conception of a girl, was too mainstream and boring. Then she came up with the fool-proof plan, to close her eyes and wait for her visions to tell her what to do. After a while, the vision came, showing her future daughter Sabina at an Edenite adulthood ceremony, 14 years later. The funny thing was, the age of an Edenite girl to be considered as an adult was actually 12, meaning that her daughter Sabina was meant to be born in two years and that she wasn't meant to be pregnant in another year and three months. Woho. So why was she pregnant now? Her visions had shown her the way, and thus she had an entire year and 3 months to lead her glorious revolution against the Terran Council! Using 29th-century technologies, she instructed the Medical bot to perform a non-lethal embryo extraction on her and save the embryo for use the following year, when the time was right. After the procedure, Metatron showed up and was terribly upset with Keila:

- I heard you had an abortion earlier today.

Keila:

- No, a non-lethal embryo extraction. I was hoping for an immaculate conception from a Zetan grandmaster, so I was a bit disappointed when it turned out that you were the father.

Metatron:

- You were hoping for an immaculate conception after having sex every day for two months? How does your brain even work?

Keila:

- I wonder that myself sometimes. But don't worry, my visions told me that I will give birth in two years. So, I had a non-lethal embryo extraction and will give birth to Sabina in two years. Now I just need to liberate Mars from the Terran Council and kill Bjorn Muller. Hey, I got a whole year!

Metatron:

- Wait, your visions told you this? Your suspicious premonitions also showed you that it was a promising idea to confront Alicia White and her goons alone and unarmed.

Keila:

- I did survive, and she died, didn't I?

Metatron:

- Yes, due to a chain of unlikely events!

Keila:

- A chain of unlikely events is my middle name.

Metatron:

- No, it's not, it's Susanna.

Keila:

- Don't be boring, Metatron, you know what I mean.

Metatron:

- Okay, but if you die during this stupid rebellion, I'll insert the embryo into a surrogate mother next year.

Keila:

- Cool. We have a deal.

As it turned out, Keila's vision was inaccurate. This was because, the True Maker, the Supreme God and almighty creator of the universe, the source of her visions, had mixed up the age of the adulthood ceremonies. This was because the True Maker thought that every Jew used the age of 13 for female adulthood ceremonies, but the Edenites who were conservative Jews, used the age of 12. Therefore, if the True Maker had been good at her job, Keila would have stayed on Eden raising her daughter with Metatron in peace. But now due to the True Maker's incompetence, Keila would start a chain of events where Rangda almost destroyed the galaxy. Thus, if you ever have a difficult day at work, remember that even fictional supreme deities can fuck up at times!

Chapter 43 Brahma's Interest in Selective Breeding

Before Brahma met his end due to his severe peanut allergy, assisted by a multitude of grievous wounds caused by Rangda's Xeno warriors, he had a passion for selective breeding. Brahma had one pet project that seemed promising in theory but ended being a complete fuck-up in real life. Brahma wanted Keila Eisenstein and Bjorn Muller to breed as that theoretically, could lead to the birth of the perfect Zetan/human hybrid as Keila had a lot of residual Zetan DNA giving her unique abilities, and Bjorn had Zetan DNA for intelligence, which might seem strange because he was a drunken idiot.

As neither Keila nor Bjorn was Brahma's pets he couldn't just lock them up in a cage and hope for the magic/biology to happen, so instead he used his supernatural Zetan abilities to implant visions to convince them to meet each other and fall in love.

The plan had a major flaw, as Brahma failed to account for the fact the Bjorn Muller was an alcoholic degenerate, and Bjorn's idea of being together with Keila was to lock her up in a small cage and use her as a sex slave. The learning point is that it's difficult to breed lesser species, especially ones that are so unpredictable as humans are.

For four pages of pseudoscience "explaining" Keila's abilities, read the Divine Sedition.

Chapter 44 Keila's Visions Render Markus Bauer Unnecessary to the Plot.

Keila was ferociously punching a boxing bag in the gym. She was angry with her chief scientist Markus Bauer, former Chief Scientist for Bjorn Muller, whom she had put in a lot of effort rescuing.

The reason for Keila's anger was that Markus Bauer had refused to reverse engineer the alien mind control technology that she used to bully people that didn't think or act like she wanted. Being the good character in the story she hadn't used it for homicidal purposes yet. That objection wasn't enough for Markus who thought that Keila shouldn't have unobstructed access to her followers' minds as well as the ability to kill them from afar using the power of thought. What a bummer.

Markus had also objected to Keila's motivation why she needed to produce millions of mind control microchips, as he claimed there were better ways to communicate securely within the group than giving the leader unobstructed power. What a downer. Keila wanted to fire him, but she couldn't because then he'd run back to his Terran Council masters telling them about her, and she couldn't kill because he was right, and she didn't see herself as the villain of the story.

In her anger, Keila got distracted, and the boxing sack flew back at her, knocking her over, and causing her to hit her head on a gym bench. Seeing the stars, she also saw another old mate, Rangda, who was drinking blue Zetan blood from a Zetan skull.

Rangda:

  - Hi Keila. What's up?

Keila:

  - I hit my head again. What are you doing?

Rangda:

- I am just drinking the blood from a stupid Zetan, that we found napping in the wilderness.

Keila:

- Okay, cool. Was it anyone important?

Rangda:

- No, not this time. Not every Zetan is as crucial for the plot as Brahma.
- Can I help you with anything?

Keila:

- Yes, you can. I need the Zetan mind control technology reverse-engineered for mass-production with human technology so I can become the benign god-queen for the Martian population.

Rangda:

- Great. I'd thought you'd never ask. Just open your mind, and I'll transmit the plans to you telepathically.

Keila:

- Cool, how do I open my mind?

Rangda:

- Just bang your head against the wall a few times, that will speed up the connection!

Keila:

- How could that work?

Rangda:

- It just does.

Keila:

- Okay, have it your way.

A few minutes later, Keila had a terrible headache from the repetitive self-inflicted violence to head. On the bright side, Rangda instructions worked, and she now had the blueprint to the reverse-engineered Divine Technology.

Chapter 45 Keila Invokes Rangda to fight the "Infamous" Morgan Henry.

A few days later Keila was on a regular passenger ship that would take her from the mining colonies in the asteroid belt to The Olympus Republic on Mars. To avoid attention, she was travelling with public transport as most vehicles that could go so far was registered and would arouse suspicion. To travel even more incognito, Keila had used the Zetan external DNA modifier to change her appearance and smell to that of another woman. She had also made up another first name, Kristina.

Unfortunately, Keila should probably have worked a bit more on her backstory because when the immigration officer asked for her last name and date of birth, she couldn't come up with anything except her real family name and date of birth. Thus, she was Kristina Eisenstein born on Eden the 22nd of March 2850, and it wasn't her fault that she shared last name and date of birth with an infamous terrorist, that was purely coincidental. Fortunately, the immigration officer didn't bother arguing with her, as he had a new match on Swoonder, and trying to get laid was more important to him, than doing his job.

One who did notice Keila's fake identity was Tzi Chen Cheng. Being a prominent scientist and aware of her survival, he had a bot performing an ongoing search for her on Spacenet. Realising that Kristina Eisenstein from Eden born on the same date as Keila must Keila, he decided to intervene and have her captured! Unfortunately, Tzi Chen didn't have access to his own black operations team, so instead, he had to rely on unreliable and incompetent third parties to reach his shifty objectives: He had to rely on the pirate Morgan Henry.

There was a slight problem with hiring Morgan Henry. Henry Morgan preferred dramatic effect and theatrical appearance over getting the job done. For dramatic effect, Morgan kept wearing pirate clothes, a sabre, and a musket instead of proper equipment. Although he had swapped his pegleg for a real stem cell grown leg after his conversation with Markus Bauer six months earlier.

Keila watched a soap opera in her cabin, when she heard Morgan Henry speaking on the public announcement system:

- Argh, this is the infamous pirate Morgan Henry.

- I demand a parley with Keila Eisenstein, or I'll scuttle this ship. Aye. *Burp*

Keila was petrified by fear. How could Morgan Henry know that she was on this ship, and what would she do about it? Keila had dealt with the army, special-forces, Bjorn Muller, Alicia White, and various gods in the past, but she had never dealt with an infamous real-life pirate. Not knowing what to do, Keila slammed her head into the wall to contact Rangda. Unfortunately, she slammed it too hard, so she almost knocked herself unconscious in the process. Rangda who was playing board games with her Xenos was not happy to be contacted.

- What is it now, Keila?

Keila:

- The infamous pirate Morgan Henry is here to kill me! I am afraid...

Rangda:

- How can you fear a bunch of costume play nerds with peg legs, muskets, and swords when you have modern battle armour, automatic weapons and alien technology that stop bullets mid-air? Just kill them!

Keila:

- You are right, Rangda.

- But there is a slight problem. I slammed my head too hard when trying to summon you. So now I have a severe concussion, and I can hardly stand up...

Rangda:

- The shit that I must put up with...

- Okay, I'll help you. Let me possess your body and give you super-human strength.

When possessed by Rangda, Keila felt how her power grew exponentially. Killing a group of armed pirates no longer seemed like a challenge, so what was the fun in that? Against better judgement, she threw away her weapons and body armour. It was time to kill dozens of bloodthirsty pirates with her bare fists!

From the Divine Dimension, Rangda could see what was happening. What was her idiotic human host doing? Rangda had used some of her psionic powers to make sure that an armed and sane Keila could fight off the pirates. But keeping this lunatic alive would surely drain her energy, and she would be back on scratch. Then again if Rangda didn't keep Keila alive, how would she find someone stupid enough to open the portals to Earth and unleash her Xeno Invasion? Left with no choice, she transferred her abilities, *time slow, telekinesis, and poison lips* to Keila.

Filled with supernatural powers, Keila went out in the corridor to fight the pirates. One of them screamed at her:

- Keila Eisenstein, have you come to surrender?

Keila:

- Nah, I have come to kill you all!

Pirate:

- Argh! Kill the crazy bitch. Fire!

The pirates raised their muskets and fired at her. This didn't take any supernatural powers to dodge, as three of the muskets failed to shoot, one misfired and injured the shooter and the last two that did fire missed by a mile as Morgan Henry and his team hadn't mastered the ancient trade of musket making. Keila ran up to the closest pirate and punched him with such immense force that he went flying for 30 meters, crashing through a wall and interrupted a couple's lovemaking.

Keila now got an idea. Would it be cool to use her superhuman speed to speed-shoot the other pirates with the fallen pirate's musket? Yes, it would! Keila picked up the musket and shot two of the pirates with her superhuman speed; unfortunately, there was a complication on the third shot, the barrel of the musket overheated and exploded injuring her hands. When Rangda saw this, she got so frustrated, so she slammed and tilted the table with the board game in the Divine Dimension. She then used some more of her demonic powers, healing Keila's hands from afar. With her healed hands, Keila picked up the pirate sabre and slashed the other pirates into pieces.

After this Keila used her speed to quickly run onto the pirate spaceship, setting it to self-destruct, before confronting Morgan Henry and his group in the lobby of the passenger ship. Morgan Henry, being such a dickhead, had taken the incredibly handsome captain of the ship hostage and held him at gunpoint. Keila got an idea. If she could save the captain, she could later seduce him to get back at Metatron for having sex with Alicia White. Morgan Henry spoke:

- Keila Eisenstein: I have taken the captain of this ship hostage. Surrender yourself, or we'll kill him.

Keila:

- Accomplices of Morgan Henry. I am Keila Eisenstein possessed by the evil space demon Rangda. I have superhuman powers. Leave me with your captain, or I'll kill you all.

Pirate:

- Fuck this! I am not fighting someone possessed by an evil space demon. I am out. Sorry captain, but you are on your own.

All the pirates mumbled in agreement and rushed towards their own ship, leaving poor old Morgan Henry with the fearsome Keila.
Morgan Henry:

- Stay back, or I'll kill this handsome captain!

Keila:

- Go for it and see if I care.

Morgan Henry, thinking that he might as well bring the handsome captain with him to the afterlife, pulled the trigger, but he shouldn't have. When Keila noticed that Morgan pulled the trigger, she used the time slow and telekinesis abilities in conjunction, managing to turn the Morgan flintlock pistol towards his own head, killing him. A few seconds later, the now disengaged pirate ship blew up killing Morgan Henry's pirate crew.
Keila ran up to the handsome captain who was lying on the floor in shock and spoke to him.

- I saved the day captain; now kiss me so the ending credits can roll.

Handsome Captain:

- I don't know. I am in shock from almost getting killed. Besides, you are bleeding, possessed by an evil demon, and you just killed dozens of men.

Keila:

- Don't worry about those minute details. I am a good girl deep inside, and I deserve my handsome captain, in the end, don't I?

Handsome Captain:

- I guess you are right. You do deserve some kisses!

The Handsome Captain leaned over to kiss Keila, but he shouldn't have. Still being possessed by Rangda, the poison lips ability was still active, so the Captain dropped dead to the ground with foam from his mouth. So much for romance after butchering dozens of pirates, Keila!

Chapter 46 Bjorn Muller Tries to Cover-up that Keila is alive.

A few days later, Bjorn Muller was sitting in his office disgruntled. Despite doing a proper job for once, proving that House White didn't attack House Rashid, no-one believed him. No doubt due to his lifetime of lies and heinous crimes. But, if no-one trusted him, why did his father send him to investigate the attack on the Aljadid Salam base?

Disappointed, Bjorn Muller realised the answer to his question. His father sent him to conduct pointless investigations to make sure that he wasn't involved on important decisions. This was highly unfair. Despite his tattered record of accomplishment, he was Joachim's oldest son, and he was born to be prominent and influential, regardless of his actual work performance.

Suddenly, there was a knock on Bjorn's door. It was his right-hand man Captain Adal Schneider. Bjorn sighed at him and spoke.

- Oh, it's you, Adal. I hoped it would be Fritz bringing me a coffee!

Adal Schneider:

- Have you told Fritz to bring you coffee?

Bjorn Muller:

- No. But he should know that he needs to bring it, as I intend to do some work today.

Adal Schneider:

- How can Fritz know that you intend to work for once? Most of the time, you are busy with drug-fuelled orgies.

Bjorn Muller:

- Good point. I should call him. Otherwise, I might be waiting forever for my coffee. Such terrible service on this base!

- Anyway, I assume you didn't come to bring me a coffee?

Adal Schneider:

- No bringing coffee is Fritz's job. I came to report about another pirate attack.

Bjorn Muller:

- Always just unwelcome news! No coffee and a pirate attack. Tell me some good news for once.

Adal Schneider:

- I was just getting to that. The pirate attack failed, and Morgan Henry and his whole crew are dead.

Bjorn Muller:

- That is good news. I might even forgive Fritz for not bringing my coffee. Who killed them?

Adal Schneider:

- Well, now we are back into unwelcome news territory. It seems your old friend Keila Eisenstein is back from the dead, possessed by the evil space demon Rangda.

Bjorn Muller:

- What are you talking about Adal? Do you have any proof of this absurd theory?

Adal Schneider:

- Yes, I do. Please check this footage of the attack as well as this blood sample that is clearly from Keila Eisenstein.

Bjorn Muller studied the attached documentation and videos for a while. Then he spoke again.

- Being a master detective and a superior human specimen, I have come to a conclusion on this case.

- The woman who butchered all the pirates must be Keila's twin sister, Kristina Eisenstein.

Adal Schneider:

- But Keila doesn't have a sister?

Bjorn Muller:

- Apparently, she does. Look at the passenger manifest "Kristina Eisenstein DOB 22 March 2850."

Adal Schneider:

- But isn't that just a fake alias she used?

Bjorn Muller:

- No, it can't be. Who would use an alias with the same last name and the same date of birth as their real identity? Thus, it must Keila's twin sister.

Adal Schneider:

- But she stated her name as Keila Eisenstein before she killed Morgan Henry?

Bjorn Muller:

- That is just to confuse us. Clearly Kristina doesn't want us to chase her.

Adal Schneider:

- So, what do you want to do?

Bjorn Muller:

- Tell the authorities in the Olympus Republic to arrest her and keep her detained until I have interrogated her.

Adal Schneider:

- What reason should I give them to arrest her? Killing the menace Morgan Henry is a good deed that should be rewarded.

Bjorn Muller:

- Yes, but she also killed Captain Michael Swoon with her venomous lips. That is the crime she is wanted for. Dismissed Adal!

After Adal had left the room, Bjorn Muller was gripped by terrifying fear. His "crazy ex," i.e. rape victim was back from the dead, possessed by an evil space demon that gave her superpowers. With his luck, she would soon come after him! And his father would be furious if it turned out that he had failed to kill Keila last year and fallen for her ploy.

Thus, the only way for Bjorn to save his own skin was if he could kill "Kristina" Eisenstein to silence her permanently! On top of all his problems, his coffee was yet to arrive. Doing the only reasonable thing in the situation, he called his servant Fritz and yelled *"Bring Meinen Kaffee Jetzt, Dummkopf!"*, Before hanging up.

Chapter 47 Keila Meets with Hellas Petrakis.

Keila was sitting in a prison cell in the Olympus Republic, the most prominent nation on Mars. She was angry with the Olympians. Despite that Keila single-handedly had solved their pirate problems, they had refused to grant her an audience with their president, Hellas Petrakis, and instead, they had locked her up in this cell. Keila considered slamming her head against the wall to contact Rangda and be granted super-powers, but she refrained from doing so. Senselessly murdering people was not the best way to make new friends. The door opened, and in came Hellas Petrakis, Keila's old friend and mentor.

Hellas Petrakis:

- Thank you for solving our pirate problem! You wanted to see me?

Keila:

- Yes. It's me, Keila.

Hellas Petrakis:

- Oh really? The Keila I knew was a nutcase, but she didn't have superpowers caused by being possessed by an evil space demon. Besides she was declared dead over a year ago.

Keila:

- But it is me. I closed all my social media accounts to fake my own death.

Hellas Petrakis:

- Is that so? Was that really all it took for Bjorn Muller to proclaim you dead?

Keila:

- Yes.

Hellas Petrakis:

- Damn, that guy is an idiot.

- Unfortunately, I don't believe you. Our DNA scanners say that you are not Keila, but an unidentified Edenite woman.

Keila:

- But I am Keila. Take a blood sample, and you'll find out.

Hellas did take a blood sample, and he was shocked to find out the result: that woman in front of him indeed was Keila Eisenstein. Confused Hellas spoke to Keila:

- How did this happen? How did you survive swapping all your blood with Keila's blood?

Keila:

- No, Hellas. I am Keila. I used mysterious alien technology to change my appearance to that of another woman.

Hellas Petrakis:

- Okay, that makes as much sense as my explanation!

Keila:

- Okay, but look at this. I can revert to my actual appearance.

Keila activated the Zetan external DNA modifier, and her appearance reverted to her true self. Amazed Hellas studied her and spoke.

- That thing would make a large profit in the cosmetic surgery industry! But you are right, you really are Keila. Well, except for your glowing purple predator eyes.

Keila:

- The predator's eyes are the price I must pay for being possessed by the space demon Rangda.

- Anyways, I came here with a bunch of alien technology that will enable us to defeat the Terran Council and liberate the Martians from oppression.

Hellas Petrakis:

- I don't know Keila. Revolution seems like demanding work. I'd rather just have a nap.

Keila:

- Is your laziness the reason for your weak, Greek economy in the Hellas Republic?

Hellas Petrakis:

- No! Our weak economy is the Germans fault. Death to House Muller and the Terran Council!

Keila:

- Good. That's what I want to hear.

- Now please plug this alien mind control chip... I mean this secure communications device into your ear so we can communicate better.

Hellas Petrakis:

- But why would we need that? We are in the same room?

Keila:

- Because I need to go back to Eden and fetch some stuff while you mass-produce weapons with the technologies, I am about to give you.

Hellas Petrakis:

- OK. I'll plug in your secure communications device into my ear and I'll wait for you to call me.

- Ouch, that hurts! What kind of device is this?

Keila:

- Don't worry. It's not an evil alien technology that enables me to see everyone's' thoughts and kill people from afar.

Hellas Petrakis:

- I never asked what the device doesn't do, just what it does.

Keila:

- Oh, right... It's a secure communications device. I am heading back to Eden now. Make sure to mass-produce 20 million copies of this technology and insert in every citizen's brain so we can talk without the Terran Council knowing.

Hellas Petrakis:

- Sure. But there is one problem. You cannot leave the palace as Keila Eisenstein or spies will tell House Muller about it.

Keila:

- What about if I change my looks to my alter ego, Kristina Eisenstein?

Hellas Petrakis:

- Well, Kristina Eisenstein is wanted for murder. Not a useful identity either.

Keila:

- So, what do you suggest?

Hellas Petrakis:

- I suggest you take the identity of Rose Menakis, a law-abiding citizen of the Olympus Republic who died in an unfortunate accident this morning. I can bring you a sample of her DNA.

Keila:

- Cool, let's do that.

A few hours later, Keila Eisenstein/Rose Menakis was on a passenger spacecraft that would take her back to the Asteroid Belt where Eden was located. Keila was annoyed. She had always been a pretty girl, and she thought that was how life was meant to be: enjoying the smiles of the opposite sex and the joy of watching her reflection in the mirror. But with Rose Menakis face life had turned sour. No-one smiled at her anymore, and it was painful to watch her reflection in the mirror. Being ugly wasn't fun, and she could wait to get to Eden and use her real appearance, as the only fault with her actual appearance were her purple predator eyes, and those were easily remedied with tinted lenses!

Chapter 48: A Thrilling Confrontation

A few months later Keila landed on Mars with a small ship and group of Edenite soldiers, which she had convinced to use proper weapons, instead of Bronze Age spears and shields. Keila had received reports from Hellas Petrakis that he had successfully implanted all Olympus Republic citizens with "secure communication" devices, also known as the alien mind-control technology. Keila was curious whether Hellas Petrakis really was dumb enough to fall for her ploy that the microchips just was for secure communication. Keila could keep wondering about that as Hellas is not a point of view character, so his real motivations will remain unknown.

Keila timed her arrival poorly, as she landed just before a large House Muller fleet arrived for an unofficial "state visit".

The term "state visit" was an intentional misrepresentation of what they were doing. Since it didn't sound civilised to call the visit a looting party, so House Muller insisted that it was a state visit. The background to the state visit was that House Muller kept sending inflated invoices for the operation of the magnetic field generators on the Martian North Pole and the South Pole that made Mars liveable through creating a magnetic field that kept the Martian atmosphere in place, stopping it from being dispersed by the solar wind. There was a slight problem with those inflated invoices though that the magnetic field generators were built 500 years ago and should have been paid off centuries earlier. Then again, House Muller was wealthy and had a large army, so they were always right. To make an analogy to the 21st century, House Muller's acted like International Monetary Fund operates today, constantly draining poor countries of money and resources bringing in their corporate hired guns, USA, when someone failed to fall in line.

Realising that both Bjorn Muller and his father Joachim Muller had landed on Mars and wasn't far away, Keila slammed her head at the side of her spaceship to connect with Rangda. She connected with Rangda, who was panting and didn't seem very keen to help.

- What is it now, Keila?!

Keila:

- I am on Mars, and both Bjorn Muller and Joachim Muller are nearby. They are accompanied with a vast House Muller army.

- I was wondering if you could lend me some superpowers, so I could kill them all and end the war?

Rangda:

- Okay, how many are with you and how many of them are there?

Keila:

- I have a dozen followers with me, and they are around 10,000. What do you reckon? Would it be doable?

Rangda:

- Perhaps. If I had all the corrupted Zeto crystals with me, fully charged then maybe.

Keila:

- Okay, can you get those within the next half an hour?

Rangda:

- Considering it took me thousands of years to get the ones I have, and I drained the crystals helping you with killing a few pirates when all that you needed to do was to shoot them. I'd say the answer is no.

- I got to go. I had to kill and drain a few Zetans to charge the Zeto crystals, and now they are hunting me.

Keila:

- Oh really? I am so sorry about that. Are you going to be okay?

Rangda:

- Yeah, I'll be fine. Considering that the Divine Dimension is an endless plain, and we Xenos run faster than Zetans, they'll give up pursuit eventually.

Keila:

- Okay cool. Talk to you later.

When Keila opened her eyes, she and her small group of soldiers were surrounded by a large group of angry German soldiers. The leader of the group Adal Schneider approached Keila.

Adal Schneider:

- Crazy woman, identify yourself!

Keila:

- I am Rose Menakis, an Olympus Republic citizen. The man next to me is Melchior Dorevitch, leader for an Edenite trade delegation sent here to negotiate with Hellas.

Adal Schneider:

- Okay, Rose, your biography doesn't mention your mental illness. Do you have anything to say for yourself?

Keila:

- I am not mentally ill!

Adal Schneider:

- You just slammed your head into the side of your spaceship, and then you spoke with yourself, staring out in the thin air.

Keila stayed silent for second wrestling with an emotional decision to make. She wasn't insane, and Adal had insulted her by claiming her to be crazy. Was the best option:

A: Falsely admitting insanity to Adal to get him to leave her alone?

B: Tell him the truth: that she was the legendary Martian freedom fighter Keila Eisenstein, and she was speaking to the alien space demon Rangda, who had promised to give her superpowers.

Realising that Rangda had refused to give her any powers, Keila chose option A.

Keila:

- I am sorry, but I am insane. My psychiatrist must have forgotten to update my biographical information.

Adal Schneider:

- I see. Unfortunately, the crime "being armed and insane, close to the Terran Council leader" offence carries a 3000 Terran Credits fine!

Keila:

- Damn it. Do you take cards?

Adal Schneider:

- Do you seriously think I am accepting card payments when I soliciting a bribe?

Keila:

- But I don't carry around 3000 Terran Credits in 100-credit gold coins.

Adal Schneider:

- Well, I am sure your Edenite friends can help you out. They are a trade delegation, after all!

Melchior muttered and opened his money bag. How could his idiotic boss come up with these things? Who in their right mind would slam their head against a solid surface and then speak with themselves? He grudgingly handed Adal Schneider the money. Joachim Muller saw what happened and approached the group.

- Tsk. What is this, Adal? Soliciting bribes from the locals? Who did he take the money from and how much?

Melchior:

- It was from me. He stole 3,000 credits. May I have them back?

Joachim Muller:

- Unfortunately, I cannot give you the money back as Adal has to pay me a 3,000 fine for unpermitted bribe solicitation. But Adal can write you an IOU letter collectable from the House Muller bank in Hansstadt on Earth.

Melchior:

- So, you witness your subordinate steal from the innocent locals, and your response is to steal the loot for yourself and then do nothing to rectify the problem.

Joachim Muller:

- That sums things up! Adal confiscate the Martian peasants' weapons, they can have them back when we leave, we have no use for their outdated rubbish.

Melchior:

- Outdated rubbish? What if I told you that we have access to advanced alien technology that will demolish your Terran army on the battlefield and expel the Terran Council from Mars?

Joachim Muller:

- Ha-ha, you are a funny one, I give you that. Here is a tip from me.

Joachim Muller picked up a 100-credit gold coin and threw it at Melchior, a sizeable gift but an insult considering that Adal had just robbed Melchior of 3000 credits. Bjorn rushed in to join the conversation.

- Father, we cannot let these rebels go. What if the crazy woman in the corner there is Kristina Eisenstein possessed by the demon Rangda, twin sister of the terrorist Keila Eisenstein?

Joachim Muller:

- In that case, you should pay her for doing your job when she killed Morgan Henry. But she clearly isn't. Let the peasants be, we must rob, I mean talk to, Hellas Petrakis

After this Keila and her groups, weapons and equipment were temporarily confiscated by the House Muller army, while they were talking to/ robbing Hellas Petrakis. Fortunately, they were given back their stuff when the House Muller army left, as the Mullers had assumed that Melchior was joking when he spoke about advanced alien technology and hadn't studied the confiscated equipment.

Chapter 49 Keila Coordinate War Plans with Hellas Petrakis

After the Terrans had left Keila and her group entered the presidential palace of Olympus Republic, The Muller's had applied German efficiency to the looting, stealing everything of value, even fittings and fixtures. Keila stepped into Hellas Petrakis office where he was sitting on the floor sobbing. Keila worried that she would have to listen about how the Muller's had tortured Hellas and threatened to kill his family, but she spoke to him anyway:

- Are you okay buddy, what happened?

Hellas Petrakis:

- The Terrans came. They stole everything from me. Including my teddy bear collection!

Keila:

- But did they torture you, or threaten to kill your family?

Hellas Petrakis:

- No, of course not. The Olympus Republic is technically a House Muller vassal/ally. It wouldn't make sense to torture and threaten their ally. But they did steal my teddy bear collection. Bu-Hu!

Keila:

- I see. Do you know any nearby toy store, where I can buy new teddy bears to make you feel better?

Hellas Petrakis:

- Don't spread salt in my wounds, Keila. It's bad enough as it is. Besides, my teddy bear collection is priceless.

Keila:

- Okay. Well, I am back with my special forces and my alien equipment. Let's avenge your loss by fighting the Terrans, defeating them on the battlefield, and expelling them from Mars.

- We will win freedom for our people! And steal back your teddy bears

After that, it was decided. Hellas Petrakis pledged the support of his nation, risking the lives of his citizens, to avenge, and if possible, steal back his stolen teddy bear collection!

Chapter 50 Keila Humiliates Mark White.

A few days later, Keila was studying the well-defended perimeter to gadolinium mines in the Tengil Dominion owned and operated by House White. She was angry with her ally, president Hellas Petrakis, who had promised to send soldiers to help her attack the mines but had failed to find anyone stupid enough to participate as he was broke as a beggar. Keila was considering her odds for success. She had a dozen followers, and the base was guarded by a garrison of 1,000 soldiers. While it would be glorious to attack the base with guns blazing, driving the Terrans away, Keila questioned whether she had enough plot armour to survive such a ploy. She concluded that she hadn't. Keila also considered summoning the powers of Rangda to give her superpowers, but she remembered what Rangda had said a couple of weeks earlier, and she didn't want to slam her head against a wall to contact Rangda just to be rejected again. So, she had to come up with another solution, but what would she do?

Meanwhile, Mark White was studying the featureless and cold desert landscape surrounding the gadolinium mine. He was like Bjorn Muller as he was supposed to be a prominent member of his family, but due to his constant fuckups, he wasn't. In Mark's case, his father had condemned him to guard this mine while the mutant freak Alicia White travelled around doing all the "fun" stuff. Mark sighed, he hadn't fucked up anything lately, and hopefully, he would soon be promoted to something more interesting. He logged into his Swoonder account hoping to get some tail, which was easier said than done, as the amounts of females around the mines were non-existent.

The use of gadolinium as a fictional material in a story is as far as the author is aware of a new and unique plot device. Unlike most other fictional materials, such as Vibranium etc. gadolinium does exist and can be bought on eBay for $20, but it's still obscure enough to be used for fictional usage in a sci-fi story. For the sake of the Divine Sedition and Divine Space Gods part 2, gadolinium was a valuable material that was used by the magnetic field generators on the Martian North Pole and the Martian South Pole.

Suddenly Keila got a moment of inspiration and realised how she would be able to infiltrate the gadolinium base. She would organise a Swoonder date with the commander of the fortress, Mark White. Unfortunately, Mark rejected her contact attempt, and Keila felt personally offended until she realised why: She was using the Swoonder account of the unattractive Rose Menakis.

What she needed to do was to use the alter ego of an incredibly sexy femme fatale to make Mark White swoon and give her access to the base and his private quarters. The obvious choice for a sexy femme fatale was herself, but she rejected the idea. Even if Mark White were dumb enough to not recognise the poster girl for the Martian revolution, there would surely be someone who did. But what about her "twin sister" Kristina Eisenstein? Kristina was sexy and a lot less famous than Keila, so she'd be the perfect Swoonder profile. Keila used the Zetan external DNA modifier and changed her appearance to that of Kristina Eisenstein and then she used the Swoonder app and created at perfect 3D hologram replica of her body for her profile.

Mark White was a bit sceptical when he received a second Swoonder request within five minutes. The base was in the wilderness, and there were usually months between interactions on the app. Was this an elaborate plan by the resistance to infiltrate the base and steal the valuable gadolinium? Mark received a nude hologram of "Kristina Eisenstein" and decided that this was his lucky day and not an elaborate ploy to infiltrate the base.

Ten minutes later, Keila and Mark White were alone in his private quarters on the base. Usually checking in new visitors and getting security clearances would take forever but, Mark White, being a prominent member of his faction ignored these steps as he didn't want to ruin the mood, now that he finally was about to get some tail.

Keila:

- So sexy Mark, I hope you are into bondage because I brought all the stuff!

Mark:

- Not really to be honest, can't we just have regular sex instead.

Keila:

- No, because I am a kinky femme fatale, so it's my way or the highway. Besides, I don't see a line of women outside your room.

Mark:

- You are right, Kristina. Have it your way. Tie me up!

After tying Mark to the bed, Keila continued her seduction attempts.
Keila:

- You know what is sexy, Mark? The password to that security console on the wall. Give me the password, and I'll lick you from top to bottom.

Mark:

- Nope. First, we have sex, and then I'll give you access to the mainframe, okay?

This answer gave Keila a conundrum. Was she able to trust Mark and would he give her access to the mainframe after a round or two of sex? She realised that the best way to find out was to ask Rangda, who seemed to be all-knowing. Keila walked up to Mark, gagged him and then she slammed her head into a wall to contact Rangda.
Rangda:

- Nope!

Keila:

- You don't know my question yet?

Rangda:

- I am not giving you superpowers to fight your way out of this heavily guarded base.

Keila:

- That wasn't my question!

- My question is: Will Mark giving me the access codes to the mainframe if I have sex with him first?

Rangda:

- No idea, I don't know him. But why would anyone give up access codes to the mainframes to their casual hook-up after having sex with them?

Keila:

- Yeah, I know. I was a bit sceptical about that too.

Rangda:

- As you should. Men are pigs! I.E. Delicious!

- But fuck him if you want, the access code to the mainframe is Sexystudmark69

Keila:

- Thanks, Rangda.

Rangda:

- Cool. Thanks for having a simple request for once! When are you opening the portals on Earth to facilitate my return to the regular universe?

Keila:

- It's on my to-do list.

Rangda:

- Yeah right!
- Talk to you later Keila

After her conversation with Rangda, Keila logged in on the mainframe and activated the evacuation signal. Keila could see how everyone abandoned their posts and rushed to their transport shuttles, retreating to Phobos. They clearly weren't huge fans of their boss, because no-one came by Mark's private quarters to make sure that he was okay. After the defenders had left, Keila called Melchior, and he arrived with the Edenite troops robbing the place dry of gadolinium and downloading all the files on the mainframe. Before leaving the base, Keila changed to her real appearance and took the ultimate selfie featuring her with a big grin and the bound and gagged Mark White in the background. Keila Eisenstein was back from the dead!

Chapter 51 Joachim Muller is Furious with Bjorn and Max Wellington

Joachim Muller was mad. He was at the Phobos base, and they had run out of his favourite food and favourite drinks. This wouldn't have been an issue under normal circumstances, but now his return to Earth was delayed due to the unfathomable incompetence of Mark White and his soldiers guarding the gadolinium mines. What kind of idiots left their posts and abandoned their commander tied up with an infamous terrorist?

But Mark White and his idiotic soldiers was John White's problem, Joachim had problems closer to home, his idiot son, Bjorn. He assembled Bjorn and Max Wellington to discuss the issue.

Joachim Muller:

- Bjorn! You have been naughty again!

Bjorn Muller:

- Look, how can I be to blame for Mark White and his idiot soldiers losing all our gadolinium supplies to the Martian Humanist Alliance?

Joachim Muller:

- Correct. It's impressive that John White manages to have worse children than I do, considering how retarded my children are. The only son that shows some potential for leadership prefers the company of men. Yuck!

Bjorn Muller:

- But Benjamin can't be gay for real. We Mullers have perfect genetics. He is just pretending to be gay to spite you.

Joachim Muller:

- So, you reckon that your younger brother has pretended to be gay for 40 years straight just to spite me? I have walked in on him in the act more than once; the bastard doesn't understand the concept of locking his apartment door!

Bjorn Muller:

- You should try knocking on the door before walking in?

Joachim Muller:

- Knocking on an unlocked door in my own building? Are you for real?

- Anyways, I have a confession to make. While most Mullers have perfect genetics, you and your brothers are the exceptions.

- You see the scientist who "perfected" your DNA was a mortal enemy of our faction who was very dedicated to his cause and played the long game. Apparently, we murdered his entire town and family 30 years earlier. And instead of planting a bomb or starting a rebellion, he studied hard to become the world's leading expert in genetic optimisation of embryos.

- Obviously, we wanted the best scientist that money can buy, so we hired him. But he intentionally sabotaged every embryo by implanting hidden critical flaws. When we finally caught on and tortured him, he just said "Worth it" gave me the finger and chugged a hidden cyanide capsule.

- The worst part is that while he died quickly, I have suffered in silence for over 60 years over what he did. Jacob Silvergeld, fuck you!

Bjorn Muller:

- But why didn't you tell me? If you had told me about my bad genes, I might had tried harder and with a humbler approach to life.

Joachim Muller:

- I have called you an idiot for over 60 years, and it has taken you until now to get it.

Bjorn Muller:

- Yet, I am not the one falling into the classic German mistake of blaming everything on the Jews.

Joachim Muller:

- Don't worry. I still blame you for your fuckups. I am just telling you why you always fuck up!

- So, with Keila alive and kicking humiliating our friends in House White, what should I do now?

Bjorn Muller:

- Ideally, you'll promote me to a comfortable position on the House Muller board and leave Admiral Max Wellington to deal with all the grunt work on Mars.

Joachim Muller:

- Nope, that's not going to happen! Do you have any suggestions, Max?

Max Wellington:

- I am in support of Bjorn's idea. If you won't fire him from the space navy, then promote him to the House Muller board. Either way, he'll stop making my life miserable.

Joachim Muller:

- Well sorry to make you disappointed gentlemen, but I will give Bjorn one more chance to stop Keila. Fail that, and I might have to end your career permanently Bjorn.

Bjorn Muller:

- I wouldn't mind retirement.

Joachim Muller

- Oh yes, retirement was what I was referring to...

Bjorn Muller:

- Great. Our satellites have spotted Keila travelling on her own, westwards from the Mishra outpost. While we could blow up her vessel with our orbital lasers, Mark White suggested that we attack her with a small army on live television and make a spectacle of her death.

Joachim Muller:

- Just blow her up with the laser! Stop doing stupid things, Bjorn!

Bjorn Muller:

- Sorry dad, but the House White army is already in position. We cannot use the lasers now, or we might hit our allies

Joachim Muller:

- Great! A publicity spectacle orchestrated by you and Mark White. What could possibly go wrong...

As it turned out, a lot could wrong, and Bjorn's idiotic publicity spectacle turned out to be what finally ignited the real Martian revolution.

Chapter 52 Keila Wipes Out an Entire Platoon on Live Television

Bjorn Muller was watching the hovercraft highway between the Mishra Outpost and the Olympic Republic capital Nea Atina. If his satellite were to be believed Keila's hovercraft would be passing by soon and drive straight into the explosive trap rigged for her. The cameras were filming, and it would be a great spectacle. Such a fool-proof plan and yet Bjorn felt the foreboding feeling that this was going to be yet another embarrassing failure. He turned to his colleague Mark White.

- Look, Mark. My father thought that we should blow her up with the orbital lasers. Why are we making things overly complicated?

Mark White:

- Because she humiliated me on social media. She stole my gadolinium, tattooed a dick on my forehead and posted selfies with me tied up and gagged. I am going to do what anyone would do. Have my men kill her in an ambush and then revive her corpse so I can kill her myself.

Bjorn Muller:

- That doesn't sound very brave or heroic. You might as well use the lasers!

Mark White.

- No. If I use the lasers, there will only be an ash pile left of her, and how would I prove her death then?

- So, so, she is passing by our kill zone now, I press this button and boom there she goes! Ha-ha-ha.

Jealous that it was Mark White and not him that would kill Keila, Bjorn had enough, and went back to the Phobos base.

Meanwhile, Keila was flying out of the windscreen in 300 kilometres an hour heading for a deadly head-on collision with a nearby rock when Rangda intervened, paused time, and contacted her.

Rangda:

- Ouch. Seems like you are in real trouble now, less than half a second away from your death...

Keila:

- Wait a second. How did you say all of that in less than half a second?

Rangda:

- I stopped time.
- I am not an overpowered space demon for nothing!

Keila:

- Great stuff, Rangda! Are your evil crystals fully charged yet? I need all the help I can get.

Rangda:

- No, they are not. But I found a way to channel your abilities through draining your life force. You'll age 15 years from the ritual. Don't complain about your aging tomorrow or I'll kill you.

Keila:

- Do you mind if I complain about it to Metatron?

Rangda:

- I don't give a shit if I don't have to hear it.

Keila:

- We have a deal Rangda, I am ready!

Rangda:

- Good. Remember to set the Zetan ballistic energy absorber to reverse. That will slow down your speed enough to not kill you up-on collision. Unfortunately, it will also drain your batteries.

Keila:

- Got it.

Time restarted, and Keila flew headfirst into a rock, bleeding profusely from a big cut on her head. *"You fucking idiot, Rangda"* was her first thought, but then she realised that she had been saved from certain death by her very unlikeable possessor.

Keila wasn't safe yet, though, as all her weapons had been destroyed when her hovercraft blew up. And her magical Zetan technologies wouldn't work either as the batteries were out. And she was facing an army of 40 well-equipped and well-trained soldiers. Ouch. Fortunately, she had a pistol with eight rounds and the ability to temporarily stop time to get an overview. A plan immediately came up in her mind. She would spend the eight shots the following way.

1. Shoot the triggering mechanism on the flying assault drone to keep it stuck in firing mode.
2. Shoot the steering mechanism on the flying assault drone to make it spin uncontrollably while firing to hit unsuspecting White troops.
3. Shoot the latch on the bombing hovercraft to make it drop its payload below.
4. Shoot the safety pin on one of the soldier's grenades to make it explode.
5. Shoot the trigger on the enemy soldier's rocket launchers causing it to fire a rocket at and destroy the enemy tank.

6. Shoot the enemy's heavy machine gun soldier at the exact moment he fired at her, causing him to lose his aim and mow down his friends instead

7. Shoot over her shoulder without aiming to hit the oncoming soldier that was rushing towards her with a machete. Then pick up said machete and throw it in the chest of another soldier.

8. Jump 20 metres up in the air to Mark White's hovercraft, hijack the hovercraft and take him hostage so that the Terran wouldn't fire their orbital laser at her when she made her escape.

Keila resumed time, and everything came to happen exactly as she had anticipated except for her pistol being empty when she reached Mark White, something he felt compelled to comment on:

- Why are you threatening me with an empty gun Keila?

Keila:

- Look, Mark. I just survived an explosion that should have killed me, and then I proceeded to kill or maim the majority of a 40-man platoon in a matter of seconds using only a pistol with eight bullets. I think I am dangerous enough to threaten you with an empty pistol.

Mark White:

- Good point. What do you want me to do?

Keila:

- Shut up and drive as quickly as possible. We must outrun an orbital laser!

After this, they drove as quickly as possible until they were out of sight for the laser. Once Keila and Mark were out of sight, Keila bound and gagged Mark White and left him in the wilderness. But this time she was kind enough to leave him fully clothed. After that Keila hurried to a Martian Humanist Alliance safe house in Nea Atina and slept for weeks.

Now for anyone that feels that this combat scene was farfetched and completely unrealistic, have you seen any triple-A Hollywood action movie released in the last 30 years or so?

Chapter 53 Benjamin Finds an Assassin to Kill Bjorn.

A month later, Joachim Muller and Benjamin Muller were on their way back to Hansstadt after attending a Terran Council meeting in America. The Muller/ White alliance in control of the council had been roasted ferociously for the Keila Eisenstein debacle, and although the other factions had pledged to stop undermining them and stand united against the Martian resistance, both Joachim and Benjamin knew that this would never happen. Their Martian enemies were getting stronger by the day, and instead of standing united against the enemy, all the Terran factions were fighting among themselves trying to benefit from the chaos. Unfortunately, Joachim and Benjamin, were not different from the rest of the Terrans, and they were busy plotting the murder of Bjorn!

Benjamin Muller:

- So, shall I find a skilled assassin that will permanently deal with Bjorn?

Joachim Muller:

- Yes, but it's hard. He is my oldest son.

Benjamin Muller:

- Oh, I understand. It's hard plotting the cold-blooded murder of someone you love.

Joachim Muller:

- No, it's not that. I am a cold-blooded genocidal psychopath. I don't care about emotions.

- What bothers me, is that if Bjorn dies, then you will become my heir, and you won't father any children due to your preference towards men.

Benjamin Muller:

- Wait a second. Is that the reason that you kept Bjorn ahead of me
in the succession order for all these years?

- This is the 29th Century, and no natural conceptions occur on
Earth. All I need to do is to marry a social climber and make some
babies with her in the lab. Then I can spend my days ruling the
planet and the nights I can allocate to sodomy!

Joachim Muller:

- You are right. I never thought about that. Very well, kill Bjorn,
and you'll be my successor.

Benjamin Muller:

- Excellent! I know the right person for the job!

As it turned out, Benjamin had no clue, and the assassin he sent lacked
the skills to do the job properly.

Chapter 54 Bjorn is "Almost" Killed by an Assassin Wearing Lederhosen.

A week later, Bjorn was studying satellite imagery of the Martian surface to examine the chaos. There was a lot of troop movements and fighting on the surface, but there was one big problem. How would he identify his real enemies in the Martian Humanist Alliance from all the other random idiots fighting each other? The Martian political map of 2872 was like a map of Syria in 2017, with a lot of warring factions, each supported by their own powerful foreign backer, fighting for god knows what reason.

Bjorn knew that House Muller was supporting one Martian faction against another faction supported by House Cheng. But he couldn't remember which faction was sponsored by House Muller, and which factions that were endorsed by House Cheng and thus his enemy. Bjorn had an epiphany: His father was correct; Bjorn wasn't good at his job.

With this epiphany, Bjorn had a realisation: that the groups of raiders that were amassing close to the Terran Council's North Pole and South Poles bases were the Martian Humanist Alliance in disguise, preparing to attack and repel the Terran Council from Mars. Excited over his sudden realisation, he was about to pick up the phone and call Max Wellington when there was a knock on the door. It was his coffee delivery.

Bjorn looked at the coffee. It looked terrible, and it wasn't the latte art he liked. How was supposed to drink this shit? And why was the male waiter dressed in tightfitting lederhosen with an opening for the bum? That didn't exactly improve Bjorn's appetite. Bjorn had enough and decided to call out this terrible service.

- Hey! Why are you bringing me this terrible coffee? What's with the lederhosen outfit? Where is Fritz?

German Lederhosen Assassin:

- Scheisse! Fritz ist tot! Ich tötete ihn! Zeit zu sterben, Herr Müller!

The German Lederhosen Assassin pulled up his gun, but he was such a lousy shot, so he shot the coffee cup out of Bjorn's hand instead of shooting him in the head that he was aiming for. The hot coffee, mixed with corrosive poison acid, splashed on Bjorn's arm and burnt him. Bjorn ducked behind his desk looking for a pistol, but all he found was a gold bar. Better than nothing he thought, grabbed the gold bar, and threw it in the head of the attacker knocking him unconscious. *"Great the assassin is still alive, I can torture him and find out who sent him,"* Bjorn thought for a few seconds, and then his trigger-happy and incompetent bodyguard rushed in and killed the assassin permanently with a barrage of bullets.

Bjorn Muller:

  - Why did you kill him? He was knocked unconscious

Jürgen the bodyguard:

  - I heard the shooting and shouting. I thought it was better to shoot first and think later, like I was trained.

Bjorn Muller:

  - But why did you let this conspicuous-looking assassin in, in the first place?

Jürgen the bodyguard:

  - Well, he was dressed like one of your prostitutes.

Bjorn Muller:

  - You idiot. This is a man. Why would I hire a male prostitute?

Jürgen the bodyguard:

  - What do you mean? Am I supposed to keep a tab on your lovers?

Bjorn Muller:

- Knowing who to let in, is your only job!
- Now help me to the Medical Bay you moron. I am injured!

Eager to help, Jürgen grabbed Bjorn's arm to help him stand up. Unfortunately, he grabbed Bjorn, just where the acid splash had injured him. Bjorn shouted at the bodyguard:

- You irredeemable idiot. You can't even help me to the medical bay without worsening my injury. Ttidy up this mess. I'll go myself.

Chapter 55 Bjorn Muller Defrauds the Worker's Compensation Insurance.

A few days later Adal Schneider visited Bjorn Muller in the hospital bay of the Phobos base.

Adal Schneider:

- How are the small superficial wounds from the botched assassination attempt healing? And when are you coming back to work?

Bjorn Muller:

- Sh. Not so loud...

Adal Schneider:

- I beg your pardon.

Bjorn Muller:

- You forgot to mention that my liver, my teeth, my nostrils, my bionic implants, and my mental sanity also got injured in the ferocious attack that almost claimed my life. I don't know if I'll ever be able to work again!

Adal Schneider:

- Now I am completely lost?

Bjorn Muller looked around to see if there was any medical staff member around; after ascertaining that he was alone with Adal, he relaxed and spoke more openly:

- I am claiming worker's compensation insurance, and I want to get my whole body fixed on the insurance company's expense.

With a bit of luck, I can also claim psychological damages and retire with a generous pension.

Adal Schneider:

- I understand, but I am still lost. Isn't your father one of the wealthiest persons in the solar system? Why do you need to defraud work cover?

Bjorn Muller:

- Because my father is a tight arse and claims that I would just spend any money he gives me to buy prostitutes and drugs.

Adal Schneider:

- What about all the money you made as Rear Admiral for the last 20 years?

Bjorn Muller:

- I spent them all: On drugs and hookers.

Adal Schneider:

- Well, at least your father is right about your spending habits.

- Do you really think Max Wellington will sign off on your excessive insurance claim?

Bjorn Muller:

- He'd sign anything if it meant that he gets to mismanage Phobos on his own, without me putting him in place.

Adal Schneider:

- So, that's what you guys have been up to for the last 20 years? I never realised.

Bjorn Muller:

- That's what I do!
- Did you revive and interrogate the assassin sent to kill me?

Adal Schneider:

- Unfortunately, your bodyguard, Jurgen, was too good at permanently killing him.

Bjorn Muller:

- Yeah, that clown won't win employee of the year! First, he failed to protect me against the attack, and then he came in guns blazing when I already had knocked out the assailant.

Adal Schneider:

- Do you think Jürgen was a part of the conspiracy and tried to tie up loose ends when the attack failed?

Bjorn Muller:

- No, Jürgen is too stupid to be in on the conspiracy. Besides, I know who the killer is and who sent him.

Adal Schneider:

- Really? How is that?

Bjorn Muller:

- Simple. My brother Benjamin has this annoying habit of not locking his door. So, a few years ago, I walked in on him, sodomising the assassin.

Adal Schneider:

- So, the assassin was Benjamin's gay lover?

Bjorn Muller:

- Yes.

Adal Schneider:

- Oh no! Benjamin will be so devastated when he finds out that his lover died. It's so sad.

Bjorn Muller:

- Wait a second! My brother sends a guy to kill me, and you pity him. I am the victim here!

Adal Schneider:

- Of course, I pity him. He lost someone he loved. You, on the other hand, is whining about a small burn on your arm.

- Besides everyone like Benjamin. He is so courteous, competent, inspiring, and handsome.

Bjorn Muller:

- Get the fuck out of my office!

Adal Schneider:

- We are not in your office, sir.

Bjorn Muller:

- Sorry, old habit! Get the fuck out of my hospital room!

Chapter 56 "You Have Really Let Yourself Go."

Keila conducted surveillance close to the Martian North Pole, and she studied the gigantic Terran Council Fortress that was guarding the Magnetic Field Generator. Tomorrow would be the day for her daring attack, and it was now or never. Suddenly, there was a beep in the Divine Technology, a notification that Metatron was back in range. Keila felt in relieved. It would be great to speak to Metatron again it had been months since their last conversation.

The Divine Technology had an arbitrary range limit of 75,000,000 kilometres, and as both Mars and Eden were orbiting the sun at different speeds, this meant that they had been out of range for each other the last three months. Technically they could have used Spacenet and social media to communicate, but Keila had learnt her lesson and didn't use social media anymore, realising it was a beacon telling her enemies her location.

Ideally, Keila wanted Metatron to contact her, as he would also have received the notification that she was within range. After ten minutes eager waiting but no contact Keila lost her patience and decided to call the arrogant prick who didn't even love her enough to call her. A confused Metatron answered her psionic call:

- Hey, Metatron, here, who's this?

Keila:

- What do you mean? "Who's this?"
- It's me, Keila, your one true love!

Metatron:

- What are you talking about? Keila is young and beautiful. You must be close to fifty!

Keila:

- But it is me. Remember, when we used the Zetan "lover bind together flowing" sex toy in the Divine Dimension?

Metatron:

- Oh, it is you? You have really let yourself go!

Keila:

- Never remark that a woman looks fat, Metatron!

Metatron:

- I don't think that applies to aging 30 years in a couple of months. What happened?

Keila:

- Ah, you mean the aging.

- I let Rangda possess me and fuel superpowers with my life force. Shit happens

Metatron:

- I told you that you cannot trust that evil space demon. She deceived you and lied to you!

Keila:

- She was straightforward about it. She told me that her superpowers would drain my life force and age me terribly. I reckoned it was a worthwhile trade-off.

Metatron:

- How could you agree to those terms?

Keila:

- Well I know people say they didn't have a choice when they do have options. But I didn't have a choice.

- You see, my hovercraft exploded, and I was flying out of the windscreen in 300 kilometres an hour, heading for a cliff wall. Rangda froze the time just before the collision and offered to give me superpowers that would allow me to survive the impact as well as killing the forty elite soldiers that were after me. I reckoned some aging was a better deal than certain death.

Metatron:

- Okay. Good point.

- Speaking of other things, are you coming back to Eden soon so you can give birth to our daughter Sabina, who is destined to be the chosen one?

Keila:

- Yeah about that... Now that I have aged so much, I don't think I am fertile anymore. Find me a surrogate mother, will you?

Metatron:

- But what about your vision? Sabina being the chosen one and you and I celebrating her adulthood ceremony together?

Keila:

- So, so. I didn't look this old in my vision, so that must have been a phony. I got to go now. I got some German butt to kick and a planet to liberate!

After this, Keila hung up on Metatron and sharpened her plasma sword. She had some German butt to kick. The Bitch was back! Speaking of her back, it was sore due to her rapid aging, so before the ass-kicking started, she needed some well-deserved back massage from a stolen massage robot!

Chapter 57 Keila Attacks the Mighty North Pole Base.

After the extended back massage, Keila was feeling rejuvenated and was ready to kick some German (and American, House White are Americans, but for a movie adaption one can assume that only the Germans will remain the villains) butt. She had developed an attack strategy that was closely reminiscent of every movie ever made, I.E. she led her whole army to a pitched semi-decisive battle, I.E. the storming of the Terran Council North pole base, guarded by troops from House Muller and House White. To win this battle, Keila had adopted another fail-safe Hollywood tactics, marching in the open leading from the front. They encircled the massive base, and on Keila's command, missiles from the Hellas Republic blew up the orbital weapons and satellites that provided the Terran troops with surveillance and air support. When Keila and her army was within close range of the base she contacted its commander Manfred Muller via the hologram generator:

> - This is Keila Eisenstein from the Martian Humanist Alliance. I demand your immediate surrender.

Manfred Muller:

> - That explains a lot. I have been wondering who would be stupid enough to come with their army, out in the open within range for our automated defences.

Keila Eisenstein:

> - I wasn't finished! Before I let you surrender, you must put your head between your legs and kiss your own arse.

Manfred Muller:

> - I can't do that!

Keila Eisenstein:

- Okay, then we'll attack and slaughter you and your men!

Manfred Muller:

- Hold on. I meant I can't bend over and kiss my own arse. I am a high-ranking officer, not a yoga master. Most people are not that flexible.

Keila Eisenstein:

- Okay then. Just surrender, and we'll let you live. Kissing your own arse is optional.

Manfred Muller:

- Thanks, but I think I will to do what my idiotic second cousin, Bjorn Muller, have failed to do for six years straight. I guess I'll just kill you.

- Automated defences, fire at will!

Keila said a silent prayer to a vast assortment of gods (better safe than sorry) that her modified alien technologies would work. Hopefully, the up-scaled Zetan Ballistic Energy Absorber worked or else she and her army would be in a world of trouble soon.

A massive barrage ensued, and the Zetan Ballistic Energy Absorber turned out to work. Now it was just one critical question, which would run out first: The ammunition of the automated defences or the batteries of her energy absorbers? As it turned out, Keila won by a very tiny margin, her batteries were down to half a per cent when the automated defences ran out of ammunition. Some other sections of Keila's army were less lucky though, as not every commander in her army had bothered to read the charging instructions for the batteries. Always read the instructions guys!

After the automated defences had run out of ammunition, Keila implemented the second part of her plan. Her army used Jetpacks to fly over the base's walls and fight their enemies in the courtyard. To make them even cooler, they all charged with plasma swords instead of guns as that were the last thing the enemy would expect. Fighting ferociously Keila made her way to the central citadel. It was time to go in there, kill Manfred Muller, and take control over the base. There was only a slight problem with that plan. The door was locked. Fortunately, there was a ventilation shaft a mere 20 metres climb up, so all she needed to do, was to scale the wall and get in.

Unfortunately, she was the only one in her squad that thought of entering via the ventilation shaft, so when she got in, she found herself outgunned a hundred to one, which without Rangda's superpowers was an impossible equation. Keila ended up getting shot in the shoulder, falling 20 metres before hitting the floor. Ouch, that sounds painful. Was this the end of Keila? Of course not, heard of plot armour, anyone?

Chapter 58 Saved by the Bell!

Some minutes later, Keila woke up from getting a bucket of water over herself. She was bleeding from a bullet wound in her shoulder, and her body was sore from falling 20 metres crashing onto the floor. Now for some readers, this doesn't sound survivable but bear in mind that Mars has a lot less gravity than Earth so it could potentially be survivable, even without Keila's plot armour.

Survivable or not Keila had a more immediate problem; she was chained to a chair and facing the commander of the base General Manfred Muller, and the disgraced Mark White, whom she had humiliated twice. Things looked dire, and how could she be saved this time? It was time to chat with Rangda, but what would she bang her head into to get a connection going?

Manfred Muller:

- So, we meet at last, Keila. You have caused my family a lot of grief.

Keila:

- My pleasure. Out of generosity, I am offering you another chance to surrender.

Manfred Muller:

- You are offering me to surrender when you are sitting chained to a chair in my impenetrable fortress? This is my answer!

Manfred punched Keila in the face, hard enough to establish her telepathic connection to Rangda.

Rangda as a telepathic connection in Keila's head:

- Got yourself in trouble? Again?!
- Don't worry, just stall them and you will be saved by the bell.

Keila:

- Alright. Thanks a lot, Rangda.

Mark White:

- Oh no! You shouldn't have hit her in the head, Manfred. When you punched her, you established Keila's connection to the space demon Rangda. We are in trouble now!

Manfred Muller:

- What are you talking about, you idiot? I thought Bjorn was a moronic pothead, but this takes the cake.

Mark White:

- It's true. When she tied me up during our failed Swoonder date, she slammed her head against the wall, spoke to someone called Rangda, and then she knew my password to the security console in my room

Keila:

- It's not that hard guessing your password when it's the same as your Swoonder account: SexystudMark69

Manfred Muller:

- Ha-ha-ha Mark, you really are the biggest idiot in the army!

Keila:

- He is, isn't he? I am giving you five more seconds to surrender and save your own lives.

Manfred Muller:

- That joke wasn't funny the first time!

Keila:

- Five, Four, Three, Two, One.

After "one" the attachment to a large bell hanging in the ceiling gave way, causing the bell to come crashing down, killing Manfred and Mark on impact. A small piece of debris was then ejected with enough speed to hit and destroy the padlock that kept Keila chained. Thus, Keila was saved by the bell. A while later, the gates to the citadel came crashing down, and the remaining defenders surrendered to Keila's army. Victory to the Martian Humanist Alliance!

Chapter 59 Melchior Sees an Opportunity to get Promoted.

A few hours later Keila gave a televised victory speech to the Martian population. She was a bit stuck on her speech and what lies she should peddle to the people, so she decided to do the right thing and tell the people the truth. Keila looked into the camera, and realised that maybe she should have made a radioed speech instead, as the Keila that people were used to seeing was young, beautiful and athletic while the Keila of present looked like she was 50 years old due to her unnatural aging, had glowing purple eyes, several bullet wounds and a sore back. Ideally, she would need some tinted lenses to hide her demonic eyes and some makeup to look younger, but where would she find these things on a military base at the Martian North Pole?

Instead, the old, weathered and witch-like Keila appeared on Martian televisions, urging the population to take up arms and join in on her assault of the Phobos base. As it turned out, it worked out better than anyone could have imagined. The Martians being used to following fearsome tyrants found the "new" Keila to be utterly bad-ass and a lot more appealing than the young and beautiful version who had been preaching: love, peace and unity.

A few hours later, a massive Martian fleet had assembled, and they were ready to assault the Phobos base. Keila dragged herself towards a small fighter spaceship when Melchior Dorevitch intercepted her in the corridor.

Melchior Dorevitch:

- Mistress Keila!

Keila:

- Hi Melchior.
- Ready to kick some German and American butt?

Melchior Dorevitch:

- Yes. But I am worried about you Keila. Earlier today you got shot, survived a 20-meter fall, and got punched in the head with a metal gauntlet. You should rest and let me lead the charge.

Keila:

- Don't be silly, Melchior; my body is in peak condition.

Melchior Dorevitch:

- Is that so? Then pick up the 1000 Terran Credits gold coin that I just dropped on the floor.

As Keila tried to pick up the coin, she was affected by severe lumbago, and her lower back locked in a very uncomfortable position.
Melchior Dorevitch:

- How's the peak condition? There is an excellent spa and massage robot upstairs.

Keila:

- Mm. I'd kill for a relaxing massage right now.

Melchior Dorevitch:

- No need to kill for a massage. Just leave the killing to me, and just enjoy your victory.

Keila:

- You are right, Melchior. I am wounded, and I deserve a rest. You lead the troops; now that we are united, the Terran expeditionary force doesn't stand a chance.

Melchior Dorevitch:

- One more thing. For me to lead the troops efficiently can you make me a Divine Technology god chip, and make you my right-hand man?

Keila:

- You already are my right-hand-man, and if you want a better mind-control chip, you can have one. Come with me to the base's particle replicator.

After foolishly giving Melchior the technology that would enable him to be Mars' future homicidal god-king, Keila utilised the spa facilities belonging to the late Manfred Muller before falling into a blissful, well-deserved sleep.

Chapter 60 Bjorn Decides to do the Right Thing for Once.

An hour later Adal Schneider and Max Wellington were in a hologram video call with Joachim Muller, broadcasting from the House Muller headquarters on Earth.

Joachim Muller:

- Admiral Max Wellington: Progress Report, please!

Max Wellington:

- All our bases on Mars have been completely overrun. The Martians, who are united at last and equipped with mysterious alien technology are going to attack the Phobos base within the next few hours, with overwhelming force. I suggest that we either sue for peace or quickly abandon this base and regroup.

Joachim Muller:

- I am not allowing either of those options. Where is my weak and incompetent son Bjorn?

Adal Schneider:

- He is still recovering from the assassination attempt that almost claimed his life.

Joachim Muller:

- Adal! We both know that he is just trying to defraud worker's compensation insurance. Bring him in now.

Adal rushed off and a few minutes later, Bjorn was connected to the hologram meeting.
Joachim Muller:

- Good to see your speedy recovery, Bjorn! From dying to top shape in just a couple of days!

- Listen up gents. Now that you are all gathered, I have an announcement to make. You are not allowed to surrender, negotiate, or retreat from the base. If you do either of those, I will order the rest of the army to chase you down and kill you!

Adal Schneider:

- Okay. And what is the good news?

Joachim Muller:

- I didn't mention any good news.

Adal Schneider:

- Ah come on, there are always good and bad in everything.

Joachim Muller:

- Okay then. I'll give you a way out. If you change the gravity generation thrusters on Phobos and aim the moon on a collision course with Mars, then you'll win, and I'll let you live.

Max Wellington:

- But wouldn't a collision between Phobos and Mars cause a massive explosion that would obliterate the moon and melt the entire surface of Mars, killing everyone?

Joachim Muller:

- Yup, but be far enough from the explosion, and you'll win the war and survive the blast!

Max Wellington:

- That's insanely evil and genocidal!

Joachim Muller:

- Yes, I am German!

- Got to go, I got some puppies to drown, just for fun. Talk to you later, gentlemen.

After the call had ended Max and Adal looked at each other in disbelief:
Adal Schneider:

- I am not going to kill billions of people to save my own skin.

Max Wellington

- Neither am I. Where is Bjorn?

Adal Schneider:

- Seems like he is going to do it. We did spend our lives serving an evil family, didn't we?

Max Wellington:

- Indeed, but let's try to repel the attackers. If we can hold the base, there is no need to kill everyone!

Meanwhile, Bjorn was on the way to small fighter spaceship that would take him to the thrusters that created the artificial gravity on Phobos. Bjorn had decided to save Mars. The reason was that his father and brother had sent an assassin after him a week earlier, so death threats didn't bite on him anymore. Even if he were to do die, he would die a heroic death that forever would spite his evil dad!

With the newfound goodness in his heart, Bjorn headed to the other side of Phobos to redirect the moon towards a collision with the sun. He did this to save the Martians from Joachim's genocidal ambitions and to forever bereave his evil family of their base of operations against the Martians.

Chapter 61 Keila Ignores Rangda's Advice and Sets Out to Stop Bjorn.

Meanwhile, Keila woke up from her peaceful slumber with fear and terror. In a nightmare she had seen her nemesis Bjorn Muller adjusting the gravitation creating thrusters on Phobos and Keila knew what this meant that Bjorn planned to kill everyone by making the Phobos moon collide with Mars.

Keila needed to stop Bjorn at once, but what would she do? She decided to slam her head against the closest wall to connect with her spiritual space demon, Rangda.

Rangda:

 - Hi Keila. You look upset, what's up?

Keila:

 - Bjorn Muller is adjusting the thrusters on Phobos. He must be planning to crash Phobos onto Mars and kill everyone.

Rangda:

 - Yes, Bjorn is adjusting the thrusters on Eden, but that is nothing to worry about.

Keila:

 - What do you mean? Nothing to worry about?! I am not going to let that evil rapist kill everyone to save his own skin. I must stop him.

Rangda:

 - I told you already, there is no reason to worry or do anything. Bjorn has turned good and wants to save everyone.

 - I am your spiritual space demon. You can trust me.

Keila *screaming*:

- Fuck you, Rangda! I don't trust you! I will stop Bjorn's evil scheme, no matter what you say. Goodbye, Rangda.

After saying this, Keila closed her telepathic connection to Rangda, and rushed towards a small spaceship that would take her to the dark side of Phobos where she could confront Bjorn Muller!

20 minutes later, Bjorn had adjusted the thrusters on Phobos, and the moon would soon leave Martian orbit and be on a collision course with the sun. It felt good to be the decent person for once, and if he survived all of this, he could resolve all the "misunderstandings" with his crazy ex Keila and start over again. As it turned out, he could address his issues with Keila straight away, as she had come to confront him.

Keila:

- Bjorn Muller! I have come to stop you and your evil schemes once and for all!

Bjorn Muller:

- Keila! Good that you are here. I have changed, and I am one of the good guys now. I have set Phobos on a collision course with the sun to save everyone. Let's talk about our past misunderstandings.

Keila:

- I don't trust you. I will shoot you for what you have done!

Keila looked for her gun, and as it turned out, she didn't carry one. Keila's nurse had found it unsuitable that her patient was having a gun in the hospital bed and had removed it for everyone's safety. When Keila woke up, dedicated on stopping Bjorn Muller she had been too single-minded to notice.

Bjorn Muller:

- Did you forget your gun? Good. Let's sit down and talk like adults.

Keila:

- I won't be your prisoner again. I won't let you crash Phobos onto Mars. I will change the direction of the thrusters. Shoot me if you must!

This gave Bjorn a dilemma. On the one hand, Keila's was his obsession, his unrequited love. On the other hand, if she started changing the direction of the thrusters, she might inadvertently cause a collision with Mars, killing everyone. Bjorn knew what he had to do. He lifted the pistol and shot Keila twice. Bjorn then blew up the console that changed the thrusters and took off, heartbroken that he had killed his "true love" but happy that he had saved everyone. Unfortunately, he had forgotten to refuel his spaceship before taking off, so he ended up on a collision course with Mars.

Meanwhile, Keila woke up, and believed that she was talking to the True Maker. She started spinning a valve that would be impossible to move with manual labour if it was still attached to thrusters. It wasn't connected, however, and easy to turn. After having turned the valve for a while, Keila was convinced that she had saved Mars, and she jumped into her spaceship chasing after Bjorn's ship...

Chapter 62 The Fall of Bjorn Muller.

Bjorn woke up wounded and got out of his crashed spaceship. He could see how his charitable mission had been successful; the Phobos moon was moving away from Mars. He was watching it blissfully for a few minutes until a familiar voice killed the silence, the voice of Keila Eisenstein:

- Bjorn Muller, I have finally won freedom for my people

Bjorn Muller:

- Yes, Keila. I am happy for you.

- How did you survive being shot twice in the freezing vacuum of space, by the way?

Keila:

- It was a Divine Intervention. The True Maker healed my wounds and gave me enough strength to turn the crank connected to thrusters

Bjorn Muller:

- Except that the crank wasn't connected to the thrusters. I was the one who set the thrusters to push Phobos away from Mars' orbit.

Keila had a moment of clarity. Could Bjorn Muller be telling the truth? There was one thing that bothered her, the fact that he shot her twice. Keila decided to bring up the topic:

- But you shot me twice!

Bjorn Muller:

- I had to do it to save everyone. You were dead set on changing the thrusters. Your stubbornness could have caused a collision with

Mars, killing everyone. To protect the people, I had to kill my one true love.

Keila:

- You love me? But I am old-looking, weathered and have fearsome purple predator eyes now.

Bjorn Muller

- Those are the features that make you unique, and I wouldn't want you any other way.

Keila:

- Oh, you are melting my heart; you big bear. Come, give me a hug.

Happy that his unrequited love to Keila finally was requited, Bjorn rushed to hug her, which proved to be a fatal mistake. Just a few steps away from her he slipped, rolled, and accidentally fell off a cliff plunging to his death. So close and yet so far Bjorn!

Chapter 63 A Final Solution.

A few weeks later, the evil plutocrats in the Terran Council had convened for another nefarious meeting, to discuss how to torment the poor people on Mars. There were a few problems for them to discuss. Firstly, their expeditionary army had been defeated and was forced to return to Earth. Secondly, their Phobos base had crashed into the sun and third but not last the Martians had access to alien weapons now, which made them a formidable enemy. But the villainous Joachim Muller had come up with the solution to their Martian troubles, and in the true German tradition, he called the plan: The Final Solution.

The name of the evil plan was a greater source of debate than the project itself, which all the villainous world leaders thought was fool-proof. The Final Solution was to have a giant asteroid "accidentally" crash with Mars, to kill a lot of people and then invade when the dust had settled.

John White:

- I like how you have been thinking about this plan. Having a large asteroid colliding with Mars by "accident" is a stroke of genius. Since we own all the media on Earth, no-one will blame us. But the name? The Final Solution? Things never end well when Germans launch a plan with that name!

Joachim Muller:

- Nonsense. I think it's a great name. What would you name it?

John White:

- So many names to choose from. Either the "America First" or "Make Earth greater than Mars again".

Joachim Muller:

- "America First" for a project primarily funded and executed by Germans? You got to be kidding me.

Ibrahim Rashid:

- The plan should be called the Inshallah plan. Allah indeed wants it to happen!

Joachim Muller:

- Ibrahim. Your faction has been arguing with the Whites and us for centuries, and now you want us to name our evil master plan after your god? It's nonsense.

Tzi Chen Cheng:

- The plan should be called the Nine Divine Beads, and it should be named so because we will use nine small asteroids instead of one medium-sized one.

Joachim Muller:

- You don't think people would find it strange if Mars is hit by nine asteroids within a matter of days? That would surely not be an accident!

- How about this? Since it's a secret scheme, how about we each call the plan whatever we want to call it?

- And remember officially we are trying to save the Martians by the deflecting the asteroid B600 into the sun. We can't help hiring incompetent morons that cause the asteroid to crash with Mars, can we?

Ibrahim Rashid:

- You are right, Joachim. I am impressed and happy that we are now on the same side for once.

- What do we need to do to make this bright future a reality?

Joachim Muller:

- First, we should all sign a blood oath regarding the asteroid strike on Mars. Thus the only way we can cancel the attack is if we all agree.

- Then we need to send a team of specialists to redirect B600 to a collision course with Mars.

- Lastly, we need to send someone gullible enough to protect the asteroid from Martian interference while he believes in the official story that we are redirecting the asteroid away from a collision instead of the other way around.

Santiago Bolivar:

- The last part seems like the hardest. Which commander in our service would be THAT stupid?

Joachim Muller:

- I know the perfect candidate for the job, Supreme Commander Matthias Muller, my brother. He-he-he

Chapter 64 Joachim Muller Fools his Brother, to Escort the B600 Asteroid.

Matthias Muller was Joachim Muller's younger brother and theoretically the second most powerful man on the planet. In reality, he was powerless as he was a good-natured man unsuitable to be the highest military commander of an oppressive dictatorship. Despite being Supreme Commander, he had never visited Mars, and he had taken no steps to prevent the Terran defeat there. Thus, Joachim wanted to get rid of his younger brother, and what better way to do so than having him escort the asteroid B600 that would "accidentally" hit Mars and kill tons of people?

Joachim Muller:

> - Good to see you, Matthias, I have a mission for you. I need you to take a fleet and escort the asteroid B600.

Matthias Muller:

> - But why would I escort the worthless rock B600, when there are so many other more important objectives to achieve in the solar system in the war against Mars?

Joachim Muller:

> - Do I need to give you a reason for giving you an order? Is there any good reason whatsoever to trust the judgement of the military commander said *"Don't worry about Mars, I have full faith in Max and the men we have there"* two days before they were utterly defeated?

Matthias Muller:

> - There was no way I could know that the Martians had access to alien technology...

Joachim Muller:

- There was. You could have sent out spies, checked the satellite images etc.

- Anyways, the reason I am sending you to escort B600 is that the vile Keila Eisenstein is planning to redirect it to a collision course with Earth. You must stop her.

Matthias Muller:

- Oh no! Keila needs to be stopped!
- But I can't go. Who is going to look after my children and my cats?

Joachim Muller:

- Your youngest daughter Hilda is 32 years old, and Just tell your employees to look after the damn cats.

- Let me speak clearly. You escort that rock, or I'll put you on trial for the Mars debacle. Do we have an understanding?

Matthias Muller:

- Yes, brother. I will head off at once.

After Matthias Muller had left, Benjamin Muller entered the room. Benjamin Muller:

- Did he swallow the bait?

Joachim Muller:

- Yes. He will escort the asteroid and then get the blame when it, unfortunately, crashes down on Mars, devastating the planet, killing millions. ha-ha-ha

Benjamin Muller:

- But what if he realises what we are about to do and orders the redirection of the asteroid?

Joachim Muller:

- Worst come to worst; I have an assassin in place. But let's keep Matthias alive if we can, shall we? We need a scapegoat.

Benjamin Muller:

- You are indeed an evil genius, dad.

Joachim Muller:

- Yes, watch and learn and you might be the leader of Earth some-day!

After that, Joachim Muller burst out in an evil diabolical laugh that last-ed for ages.

Chapter 65 Keila Tries Coaxing Matthias Muller to Not Destroy Mars.

A few weeks later, Keila was having a politic strategy meeting with her right-hand man Melchior and a bunch of Martian dignitaries in the late Hellas Petrakis office in the Olympic Republic. As fun as it was leading the Martians to victory against the Terran Council, leading them when it came to day to day issues, wasn't fun. As the unelected president, she had to compromise, listen to boring discussions and the worst part was that no matter what she did, half of the people didn't agree with her and were whining at every step she took. Keila suddenly sympathised with the Terran Council; it was easier to lead a nation as a ruthless dictatorship, crushing everyone that came in her way.

And leading this way was within her reach as she had access to Alien Mind Control technology that could make everyone tremble in awe for her might and power. As the god-queen of Mars, she would lead the Martians to a brighter future! But then Keila realised something. That ruling the Martians through fear, domination and control was eviller than the way the Terran Council had ruled, and that she was the righteous character in the story. Thus, she decided to listen to all the parties hoping for some progress to happen eventually.

The meeting was interrupted when Jasper Svensson, a member of the Martian Science Commission, rushed in. Keila decided to reprimand him:

- Jasper, I know I said I have an open-door policy, but that doesn't mean you can interrupt an important meeting without a good reason.

Jasper Svensson:

- I have a good reason.

- The Terran Council has sent a large fleet lead by Matthias Muller to redirect the large asteroid B600 to a collision course with Mars.

It will collide with us in about five months, killing millions or even billions.

Keila:

- That is a good reason to interrupt us. Thank you, Jasper.
- Melchior: can you send the fleet to defeat the Terrans

Melchior:

- Nope.

Keila:

- That is not the correct answer. The correct answer is, "Yes, mistress Keila, thy will be done!"

Melchior:

- Not really. You see our fleet consists of only unarmed civilian ships and small fighter spaceships.

Keila:

- Well, send the fighter spaceships then?

Melchior:

- Do you really think our pilots can sit in fighter spaceships for weeks on end, with no access to toilets, water, or food?

Keila:

- You are right Melchior. Sending the fighter spaceship fleet doesn't sound like a good plan. I'll better ask someone who knows. I'll contact Rangda.

Keila then smashed her head into the wall to the bewilderment of the flabbergasted Martian dignitaries that were present. Rangda answered:

- Hi Keila. When are you going to Earth to open the ancient portals like you promised me?

Keila:

- Look, Rangda. It's on my to-do list, but I have more important things on my mind. The Terran Council has sent a giant asteroid to collide with Mars and kill everyone.

- How do I stop them?

Rangda:

- Go to Earth, open the ancient portals, and I will help you.

Keila:

- You are useless these days, Rangda. Begone!

After finishing her conversation with Rangda, Keila realised that she shouldn't try to contact Rangda when other people were around. The Martian dignitaries looked at her like she was insane. How ignorant of them! No-one in the room said anything, so Keila felt compelled to talk:

- Jasper Svensson. Can you travel to B600 and try to coax Matthias Muller into not murdering us all? Maybe it's just a silly misunderstanding?

No-one could come up with any better ideas, so Jasper was sent alone on this dangerous and pointless mission.

Chapter 66 Jasper Svenson Inadvertently Kills Matthias Muller.

A few weeks later, Jasper Svensson was eating a peanut butter sandwich on board his ship waiting nervously for approval to dock with Matthias Muller's command ship ISS Blue Earth. The sandwich was delicious made with 100 % Martian extra-strong peanut butter. Martian peanut butter was unique in the sense that it contained 1 million times for peanut allergens than Terran peanut butter did. This was because the plants grown on Mars had been DNA modified to grow on Mars, and thus, had more peanut allergens in them. Jasper wasn't allergic to peanuts, and he loved the robust Martian peanut flavour.

Eventually, Jasper could dock with ISS Blue Earth, where the Terran Security Forces did a comprehensive job making sure that he didn't bring any pathogens or weapons. Jasper was made to shower while different scanners scanned his body to make sure he wasn't hiding anything dangerous. After receiving clearance to proceed, Jasper was given fresh clothes and was instructed to wait in a meeting room where Matthias Muller would arrive shortly.

Meanwhile, Captain Melissa Schiller was pacing back and forth nervously. She was Matthias Muller's secret mistress and the assassin that Joachim Muller had hired to kill Matthias if it turned out to be necessary. Finally, Melissa made her choice. She loved Matthias, and she would never harm him. Instead, she would expose Joachim's evil plan to Matthias and help him stop Joachim as soon as Matthias was done meeting up with the Martian emissary.

In the meeting room Jasper was incredibly nervous. He stuttered, and he couldn't make himself understood by Matthias. Jasper realised that he was very gassy and burped loudly. What happened next shocked him. Matthias Muller dropped to the ground dead from a severe anaphylactic shock. "Oh, shit" was the last thing Jasper thought before Melissa stormed in and shot him in the head.

Having witnessed her lover being inadvertently killed by a very peanutty Martian burp, Melissa Schiller turned evil again, and now that she was in command of the ship, she would make sure that the asteroid crashed on Mars, killing everyone!

Seriously Jasper, all that trouble for a peanut butter sandwich?

Chapter 67 Keila Decides to Listen to Rangda.

Hearing the news of how Jasper Svensson had killed Supreme Commander Mathias Muller with a toxic Martian peanut butter burp frustrated Keila. Although she was impressed by how Jasper had snuck past all the security measures in place, she was frustrated. What had Jasper been thinking? Why had he decided to kill the only important Terran leader that might listen to them and cancel the senseless upcoming mass-murder?

Keila smashed her head against the wall in frustration, and a telepathic inter-dimensional connection with Rangda was established.

Rangda:

- What is it now, Keila? It has been a while?

Keila:

- I didn't contact you.

Rangda:

- Yes, you did. You just slammed your head into the wall.

Kcila:

- That was out of frustration, not to contact you.

Rangda:

- Oh, I see. You should really see someone about that.
- I guess I'll be leaving then.

Keila:

- No, please stay. While you are here, is there anything you can do to stop the Terran Council from killing everyone with the enormous incoming asteroid?

Rangda:

- I told you already. Open the portals on Earth. I'll storm in with my Xeno horde and kill the Terran Council leaders during their monthly meeting. Then I'll activate the blood-pact command console with their blood and use it to redirect B600 into the sun.

Keila:

- That sounds good. But why would you save everyone? I thought you were an evil space demon that loves indiscriminate mass-murder?

Rangda:

- I am, and I do love to murder. But I hate the way you Terrans kill each other. From afar and then wasting the flesh of the fallen. The Xeno way is more honourable. Up close and eating the ones we kill. That's the way you do it!

Keila:

- Okay, I am not going to argue ideology with you, since you are offering to help me. But I have a practical question. How am I supposed to go to Earth and open the portals? I doubt, they'll allow me to pass immigration.

Rangda:

- Fair point. Change your appearance to Alicia White with the External DNA modifier, and then use her ship to travel to Earth.

Keila:

- Thanks, Rangda. That could work.

Rangda:

- I know it will work. He-he-he.

Keila:

- Cool. I'll better head to Eden now so I can change my DNA to Alicia's and use her ship. Talk to you later, Rangda!

Chapter 68 A Long Ride for a Quickie!

A few weeks later, Keila arrived at Eden where Metatron greeted her. She had aged even more in the last few weeks, and she now resembled an 80-year-old hunched woman. Her most prominent feature, the glowing purple predator eyes were still in effect, and they were glowing stronger than ever. Reluctantly Metatron gave Keila a quick hug before backing off from her. This made Keila upset, and she spoke angrily.

- You are an asshole, Metatron. Even Bjorn Muller is a better man than you!

Metatron:

- Bjorn Muller? The man who kept you as a sex slave and then spent the next four years trying to kill you?

Keila:

- He redeemed himself in the end. He said that it was all a misunderstanding and he tried to save the Martians by pushing the Phobos Moon into the sun instead of crashing it unto the surface of Mars killing everyone.

- Bjorn also told me that he would always love me and that I was still beautiful and unique

- He was so excited when I accepted his apology so he ran towards me. Unfortunately, he fell on the way and slumped off a cliff to his death.

- Oh, dear Bjorn, I will miss you.

Metatron:

- So, two minutes of kindness is all it takes to erase a lifetime of villainy, including multiple murders, extortion, misogyny, and rape?

- What's next? Rangda is a good woman?

Keila:

- She is the reason I am here. She agreed to help me stop the Terrans from killing everyone on Mars.

Metatron:

- Why would an evil space demon save the Martians?

Keila:

- She is just appalled by the human way of killing, which is an affront to her culture. In the Xeno culture, the only proper way to murder is up close and personal and then eating the victim.

Metatron:

- She sounds like a nice woman!

Keila:

- She'll be instrumental. She has promised to attack a Terran Council meeting killing everyone and cancelling the order for B600 to collide with Mars.

- All I need to do is to take Alicia White's identity, go to Earth, activate the four ancient portals and wait for Rangda to save the day.

Metatron:

- What's your plan B if the unreliable evil space demon doesn't uphold her promise.

Keila:

- I have thought about that; I am not an idiot!

- In that case, I'll use my Alicia White, identity, request a meeting with the Council, kill everyone and cancel the order B600 order myself.

Metatron:

- Why not go straight for Plan B? That makes a lot more sense and doesn't put the future of humanity in jeopardy!

Keila:

- Nah I stick with plan A. Besides Rangda is not too bad. Her desire to kill and eat people is just part of her culture. I reckon we should be more tolerant of other alien cultures!

- Time for me to use the External DNA modifier and change my appearance to Alicia White, I'll be right back.

Keila walked into the external DNA modifier machine and came out again a half an hour later as Alicia White. It always felt strange to wake up with another person's appearance, but this time it felt extra strange as Alicia had been an extraordinary individual for better or worse, mostly for the worse. One thing felt excellent though, Keila felt and looked the age Alicia had been when she died. Keila came up with an idea to test Metatron. She would try to seduce him as Alicia White. In the best of worlds, she would be able to experience great sex and then be able to scold Metatron afterwards, for choosing Alicia White over her real appearance.

Keila: * Hissing*

- Hey sexy man. Fuck me hard!

Metatron:

- I don't think so, Keila! After my session with Alicia, I could hardly walk for a week.

Keila:

- But it will be fun, the ultimate roleplaying!

Metatron:

- Okay, I guess. Come with me to the "unused storeroom".

Keila and Metatron made their way to their BDSM room for a session of very rough sex. Ten minutes later, Metatron was crawling out from the room bleeding. Keila came after him scolding him for preferring Alicia's body over hers. Déjà vu Metatron, the exact same thing happened a year before.

Chapter 69 "Alicia" Makes a New "BFF" When Passing Earth Immigration.

A month later, Keila and a few Edenites who had changed their DNA to look like Alicia's operatives approached Earth. It was time for one of their toughest challenges that would determine their future: whether they would be able to pass the immigration officers or not. Terran Council immigration rules and border control on Earth had always been notoriously strict, and things hadn't gone looser with the massive war going on in the solar system.

"Alicia's ship" was instructed to dock with Captain Hilda Muller's ship. This was it. How was Keila going to explain Alicia's almost one-year-long absence, without causing any suspicions? Keila was relieved by a big smile of Hilda when they met face to face.

Hilda Muller:

- Oh Alicia, It's been a long time. I am so glad that you finally made your way back to Earth.

Keila:

- Oh, yes, it's nice to be back. It's nice to see you again. How're things?

Hilda Muller:

- Hmm, Alicia, I don't think we have met. I am happy to meet you because of what you did to my disgusting cousin Bjorn. It was comedic gold to see him cry on TV ordering your arrest for sodomising him.

Keila:

- Thanks. Yes, he had it coming.

Hilda Muller:

- Out of curiosity, did you do what he accused you of?

Keila:

- I don't see how I did anything wrong. Bjorn has repeatedly shown the world that he likes it rough. So, I assumed he wanted to be maltreated. As it turned out, he only enjoyed dishing out pain but handled pain like a wimp!

Hilda Muller:

- You are a legend, Alicia. Can I interest you in some House Muller fine wine? I assume you had to drink substandard drinks in your exile.

Keila:

- When it comes to fine wines, I don't mind a few glasses or bottles.

Hilda Muller:

- That's what I like to hear. Together we will run the bar dry!

After that, Hilda and Keila bonded over several bottles of wine. They became best friends forever, or they could have been, if it wasn't for the inconvenient truth: that Keila wasn't Alicia and that she had come to Earth with a mission, to put an end to the reign of the Terran Council.

Chapter 70 Alien Portals Activated.

If one enters the phrase "pyramids + aliens" you get 482,000 results in Google. With this overwhelming amount of "proof" that aliens built the pyramids, it makes sense that the portals between Earth and the Divine Dimension were hidden inside the pyramids. It was Keila's job to activate the portals to pave the way for Rangda and her Xeno hordes.

As it turned out, activating the portals were arduous work. To activate the alien portals, Keila needed to enable them all at noontime at each location within the same day. Thus, she needed to activate the first portal, quickly make her way to the surface to travel to the second portal, and so on. Since there were four switches, located in Central America, the Pacific, Cambodia, and Egypt, it would be a lot of travelling. If Keila had been smart, she'd just dropped off one of her helpers at each location, and they could have activated one portal each with no stress. Unfortunately, she wasn't smart and being convinced that she was *the chosen one* she believed she was the only that could activate the portals. Thus, she had to stress like crazy getting into the activation switch in each pyramid, then rush back to the surface, fly faster than Earth's rotation speed to be on time to the next portal and go again. Simply a very hectic day!

To make matters worse after activating the fourth and last portal in Egypt, no supernatural gateway to heaven opened. Instead, she was arrested by House Rashid police forces for trespassing and vandalism. Bummer!

Chapter 71 Keila Convinces House Rashid Magistrate That She to be Trialled by the Terran Council Leaders.

A few hours later, Keila and her group of Edenites, disguised as House White operatives were on trial at the local magistrate court in the House Rashid capital Rashidium. They faced the local magistrate Mahmoud Inshallah.

Mahmoud Inshallah:

- Alicia White and operatives. For trespassing and vandalism, I sentence you and your agents to each pay 10,000 Terran Credits in fines. Furthermore, you'll be deported back to America where you belong. Do you plead guilty to the charges?

Keila considered her options. Now that the portals hadn't opened, and Rangda hadn't shown up with a horde of monsters, killing the Terran Council leaders and saving Mars, she was in a pickle. Keila would need to get access to the leaders herself, so she could execute plan B, kill them herself, and access blood oath terminal to cancel the asteroid strike on Mars. But how would she get access to the Terran Council leaders? A brilliant idea struck her mind. What if she admitted treason, and requested to be trialled by the Terran Council leaders? Being a high ranking Terran, she couldn't be sentenced to death by a low-level magistrate, so it was an excellent plan.

Keila:

- I plead guilty to the crimes you accuse me of, but I also plead guilty to something far worse. I am liable of treason.

Mahmoud Inshallah:

- Treason? How come?

Keila:

- We have been opening ancient alien portals, trying to enable an alien invasion of Earth.

Mahmoud Inshallah:

- Really? That doesn't make any sense! But sure, if you are keen to die, I'll sentence you all to death for treason!

Keila:

- You cannot sentence me to death for treason, as I am a high-ranking Terran Council operative. Only the Terran Council leaders can sentence me to death.

Mahmoud Inshallah:

- Okay, if you say so. Then I sentence all your operatives to death through stoning. I will pass on your case to the Terran Council leaders that are convening tomorrow morning.

As Keila's Edenite operatives were dragged out of the courtroom, one of them lost his cool and shouted at her.

- Keila Eisenstein. You are a fucking idiot. You condemned us all. I hope you'll burn in hell for this!

Mahmoud Inshallah:

- Alicia, why did you accomplice just call you Keila Eisenstein?

Keila:

- Oh, that's just a derogatory slur in America. He was obviously upset that my actions changed a fine to a death sentence.

Mahmoud Inshallah:

- Oh, I see. Well, good luck with your trial tomorrow.

After Mahmoud had finished speaking, Keila was dragged in chains to the dungeon of Rashid Towers, for her trial the following morning. Although she was a bit sad that her actions would cause the death of her Edenite friends, she was also excited. She had gained access to the Terran Council leadership, and tomorrow she'd kill them all and save her Martian brethren!

Chapter 72 Hilda Exposes Keila's identity and Do Nothing About It.

Later the same evening, in a very fashionable cocktail bar in Rashid Tower, Hilda Muller laid her eyes on the very eligible bachelor Markus White. Being a wealthy high-ranking Terran just like her, and good-looking as well, there was no way that Hilda was going to let this one get away. Hilda walked up to Markus and spoke:

- So, is this where the party is?

Markus smiled at her and replied:

- It seems like the party just got started.

Hilda Muller:

- A shame that your cousin is on trial for treason tomorrow.

Markus White:

- Not really, I don't like Alicia. She is a freak.

Hilda Muller:

- Oh really? I bonded well with her over a couple of bottles of wine the other week.

Markus White:

- You mean you drank the wine, and she drank glasses with animal blood?

Hilda Muller:

- No, of course not. Don't be mean Markus. Look at this selfie of us drinking together.

Markus had a quick look at the picture and then calmly shook his head:

- That's an imposter, Hilda. Alicia has a condition that makes alcohol lethal to her.

Hilda Muller:

- Oh no, we must warn security at once.

Markus White:

- Do we? I don't like my uncle and cousin running House White. I wouldn't mind if the unkillable Keila Eisenstein, masquerading as Alicia White, deals with them.

Hilda Muller:

- You are right. Fuck the leadership. I don't like my uncle Joachim or cousin Benjamin either.

Markus White:

- Good. Let's get out of here before that menace Keila Eisenstein causes her usual trail of death and destruction. I have a lovely secluded island in Seychelles.

Hilda Muller:

- You are such a romantic Markus. Let's go there straight away and enjoy the sunrise while Keila tears our despicable relatives into shreds.

After the conversation, Hilda and Markus went to Markus' private jet for a flight to the Seychelles, where they could enjoy each other's company, watch the sunrise, and bide their time waiting for the menace Keila to do her thing.

Chapter 73 Keila Exposes Herself and Realises a Crucial Flaw in Her Plan.

The next day Keila, still looking like Alicia White, was led to the penthouse level of Rashid Tower, where she was chained to a chair waiting for the Terran Council leaders to sentence her. Although it would be a bit difficult to kill them all, Keila had a secret master plan. She had hidden a container with a highly toxic gas that in a fake tooth. Conveniently, Keila had been immunised against toxin. Once the Terran Council leadership had gathered, John White spoke to Keila:

- Please, Alicia, why are you doing this? Why are you pleading guilty to ridiculous allegations you made up against yourself?

Keila smiled. It was time to reveal her great deceit on prime-time television. She pulled out her fake tooth, meant to be filled with very toxic nerve gas, and spoke:

- I am not Alicia. I am Keila Eisenstein, leader of the Martian Humanist Alliance. I have just tricked you into the same room as me, and within seconds you'll all be dead due to the highly toxic nerve gas I hid in this fake tooth.

The baffled Terran Council leadership looked at her in disbelief and eventually, Ibrahim Rashid spoke:

- Sorry John, but it's clear to me that your daughter Alicia is mentally ill. Bring her back to America and make sure she gets proper treatment.

Keila bit her lip. Why didn't the poison work? She realised the terrible truth. That the Divine Space Gods II: Revolution for Dummies version of her, was a full-blown idiot and not the inspiring heroine from the Divine Sedition! Being a full-blown idiot, she had forgotten to fill up the fake tooth with the deadly nerve gas before she got captured for vandalism. But at least she would show them one thing. That she really was Keila Eisenstein. She deactivated the Zetan External DNA modifier, and she reverted to her real appearance. The delegates stared at her in disbelief and Keila spoke

- Although my master plan to kill you all and save my people has run into a minor issue, I am Keila Eisenstein, and I am completely sane.

After a while, Joachim Muller spoke:

- So, you planned to deliver yourself in chains to be trialled by the Terran Council?

- That's an easy sentence to make. I sentence you to death!

Keila:

- You cannot sentence me to death without reading out the list of allegations against me!

Joachim Muller:

- That list would take hours to read aloud.

Keila:

- I am not in a hurry...

Santiago Bolivar:

- She is right. This is an excellent way to make her death public. I'll fetch the list.

John White:

- Wait for a second, if you are not Alicia, then what happened to her?

Keila:

- I killed her.

Santiago Bolivar:

- Thanks, I'll add that crime to the list!

After compiling his list, Santiago Bolivar started reading out the charges against Keila. There was a lot of them. Keila realised that the only way to get out of this alive was to invoke Rangda, so she slammed her head against the table in front of her. But Rangda didn't answer. Uh-oh was this the end of her? Or could her plot armour activate again? You'll find out in a few lines.

Chapter 74 Rangda Saves the Day!

Two hours later, noontime was approaching, and Santiago Bolivar was still reading up the accusations against Keila. This confused her, she knew that she had been active and caused some mischief, but she had no idea that she had been this busy. Keila's supposed activity level made her proud, she was even more badass than she thought she was.

Keila had only done a small portion of the crimes that Santiago accused her of. But since Santiago wasn't particularly good at his job, and he wanted some well-deserved vacation, he blamed every major unsolved crime on Keila to improve his own statistics.

At noon there was a major bluish bright flash from the pyramids in the distance, when the portals to the Divine Dimension opened, and Rangda and her Xenos swarmed in. Through a stroke of magic, the self-absorbed leaders of the Terran Council did not notice this until the Xenos were nearby when gunfire and people screaming in agony became too distracting.

Suddenly Rangda appeared outside the *"indestructible"* windows of the Rashid Tower penthouse. Rangda emitted a loud shriek, and the windows shattered instantly with a bunch of Xeno beasts storming in. "Ungo, Bungo, Keila" Rangda shouted, and the Xenos ferociously butchered the terrified Terran Council leaders, fetched the blood oath terminal and freed Keila from her chains.

Rangda:

- We meet at last. Now I'll just press this button to redirect B600 to collide with the sun instead of Mars, and that's it. Mission Complete.

Keila:

- Yes, you are my hero. I knew your reputation was incorrect. You are a good guy, just like me.

Rangda:

- What are you talking about, you fool? I killed your enemies because I love to murder. I saved the Martians because I intend to turn them into my slave army to conquer the galaxy. I rescued you because I plan to kidnap you, bring you back to the Divine Dimension, and continuously drain you of psionic energy to fill my corrupted Zeto Crystals.

Keila:

- Oh shit...

Rangda:

- No time to chat. Time to sleep, Keila.

After that Rangda blasted Keila unconscious with a psionic blast and ordered her Xenos to rush back to the Divine Dimension before the Terrans had time to launch a counterattack. It was not yet time for Rangda to conquer Earth, but she'd be back!

Chapter 1: Hilda Muller seduces Markus White.

Hilda Muller studied the super sexy Markus White who was ingesting his fourth cocktail on his private paradise island in the Maldives. This cocktail had something special in it: **Muagra**, House Muller's variant of Viagra, 100 times stronger than the original. Hilda smiled, it had been a while Since she had sex, and her whip and her tight leather outfit was ready.

Hilda approached Markus who had flushes in his face from the potent drug:

- How are you feeling sexy man?

Markus:

- A bit anxious. I am not sure it was the right choice letting the menace Keila Eisenstein, masquerading as my crazy cousin Alicia, to meet up with Earth's leaders.

Hilda:

- Okay, apart from feeling guilty over condemning your uncle and your cousin by letting them get in Keila's way, do you feel anything else?

Markus:

- I do. I feel very horny. Can I borrow your phone?

Hilda:

- You want to borrow my phone?

Markus:

- Yes, I need to call the escort agency at once!

Hilda felt frustrated. She hadn't gotten laid for ages, and alone on a paradise island with a handsome and drugged up man, he asked for her phone to call an escort? Hilda decided to play it cool. She smiled seductively and spoke:

- Sorry Markus, but my phone ran out of battery. Is there anything else I can do for you?

Markus sighed audibly and replied.

- Yeah, I guess.

- Hilda, you're the only available woman. Would you mind having sex with me?

Hilda shone like the sun and replied:

- Oh, Markus, I thought you'd never ask. Stay here while I get changed.

Markus:

- Okay, please hurry.

Hilda left the room and opened her bag that was full of German sex toys and tight leather outfits. Just like a scout, she was always ready, and it was time to get some action!

Chapter 2 An Unpleasant Interstellar Holiday

Ramun, Ungol and Bungol were three middle-aged Xeno gentlemen with singular interest. Watching sports while drinking beer. For most of their lives, they had been able to pursue this hobby without interruptions. The Xeno home planet Xenora was mostly empty after the multi-millennial war; food and drinks were plentiful due to abandoned Zetan AI robots that did most of the work, and best of all their crazy queen Rangda hadn't been seen for millennia.

Unfortunately, Rangda had returned a few years earlier, upset that no-one had tried to break her out from prison. She was hellbent on revenge and was raising an army which forced the three Xenos away from their beloved couch to join the Xeno army, an unwanted change. While Xenos were meant to look fearful, Ramun, Ungol and Bungol looked more like Jabba the Hut with limbs.

Ramun studied the portals in the Divine Dimension leading to Earth. Everyone was rushing through the entrance leading to Rashidium in Egypt to fight and kill the humans, but Ramun had a better idea. What about going through the gateway to the tropical paradise island in the Maldives? He would undoubtedly have a better time there. He called his friends over.

Ramun:

   - Hey guys, come with through this portal.

Ungol:

   - But aren't we meant to go to Rashidium and fight against the human army?

Ramun:

   - Yeah, but I don't feel motivated to fight the humans. But an interstellar holiday would be lovely.

Bungol:

- You are right, I have always wanted to see tropical beaches on Earth. Let's go!

Ungol:

- Hold on. Wouldn't Rangda be furious with us?

Ramun:

- Rangda is always angry. We are better off enjoying ourselves.

Ungol:

- Good point. Let's go.

The three Xeno musketeers walked through the portal to Seychelles and arrived at a beautiful paradise island. Ramun smiled his biggest smile, revealing his blunted fangs.

Ramun:

- This is what I am talking about. This place is going to be great.

Ungol:

- Agreed, but it would be even better with some beer.

Bungol:

- There is a human house over there, they are bound to have some beer.

Ramun:

- No, we better stay away from the humans, or they might call the army.

Ungol:

 - Right, but we can't be without beer. Let's sneak in and steal the beer.

Ramun:

 - Ungol, you're a three-metre-tall 500 kilos heavy man-eating beast. I don't think sneaking is your strength.

Ungol:

 - Stop criticising my weight! I have had a lot of therapy to get over the mean things you said to me over the years.

Ramun:

 - Oh, I am so sorry, I didn't know.

Ungol:

 - Now you do. Let's get those beers.

The three Xenos approached the beach house and what they saw terrified them: Hilda Muller dressed in her tight black leather outfit was having very rough sex with Markus White.
Ungol:

 - Is this how humans copulate? What a freak show! This is worse than watching Rangda when she is angry.

Ramun:

 - I told you we stay clear of the humans...
 - Oh shit, they saw us.

Meanwhile, Markus White spotted the three Xenos, and he emitted a loud girly screech.

Hilda:

- For fuck sake. Man up. You asked me for sex. This is real sex.

Markus:

- Hilda, there are three giant man-eating aliens outside. We are doomed.

Hilda smiled like a madwoman. She had waited for something like this to happen for a long time.

- Finally, some action. Time to kill!

Markus:

- Wait, don't cause interstellar war, and get us killed. Maybe we can negotiate?

Hilda:

- Good point. I'll try that.

Hilda grabbed her plasma sword and ran outside.

- Intruders identify yourselves.

Admittedly I haven't mentioned that the Xenos didn't speak English or German, but believing that they would is ridiculous. They spoke Xenani, but Ramun, who was the most educated in the group, also spoke ancient Egyptian.

Ramun:

- ? ? ? ? ? ? ? ? ? ? (Sorry for interrupting your coitus. May we have some beer. We have travelled far and are thirsty)

Markus turned towards Hilda and spoke:

- It sounds like they are speaking an ancient human language. If we had a phone, we could use the translation app.

Hilda:

- That's the dumbest thing I have ever heard. I can only hear beastly roars. I will deal with them with my plasma sword.

Having said this, Hilda pulled her plasma sword and charged against the Xeno's, chopping Ungol and Bungol to pieces while Ramun was crying on the floor pleading for his life. Hilda was about to turn Ramun into alien sushi when Markus interrupted her.

- Hilda, I got the translation app going, now let our visitor speak.

Using the ancient languages translation app, Ramun and Hilda could finally have a civilised conversation

Ramun:

- ? ? ? ? ? (I surrender, why did you kill my friends)

Hilda:

- I am sorry, I thought you were here to kill us.

Ramun:

- ? ? ? ? ? ? ? ? ? ? ? ? (No, we are deserters from Rangda's army. We don't like killing. We want to drink beer and watch sports.)

Hilda:

- I am so sorry about murdering your friends. If you surrender and become my prisoner, I will lock you up in a cell with unlimited beer and unlimited sports on TV.

Ramun:

- ? ? ? ? ? ? ? ? ? . (That sounds like paradise to me. I am Ramun.)

Hilda:

- I am Hilda, and I feel like we can become good friends. Just stay put.

Ramun did as instructed, and a few hours later, Hilda returned to Hansstadt in triumph having singlehandedly captured one of the fearsome aliens that had destroyed the city of Rashidium and killed the Terran Council Leadership.

Chapter 3 The True Maker Does Nothing to Fix the Mess.

The True Maker (TTM) watched the death and destruction caused by Keila's stupid decision to open the portal for the evil space demon Rangda to invade Earth. How could things had gone this bad? Keila was meant to raise her daughter Sabina, The Chosen One, on Eden together with Metatron. Why had she travelled to Earth and facilitated Rangda's invasion instead? It didn't make any sense.

TTM was certain. When she found out that Keila was pregnant, she had given Keila a joyful vision of her and Metatron raising Sabina together on Eden. She had even given a clear-cut vision showing Sabina's adulthood ceremony with an exact date 13.5 years into the future. How much clearer could she be?

Suddenly, TTM had an epiphany. That the vision she gave Keila, had stuffed up the chain of events. TTM had forgotten that the Jews on Eden celebrated the adulthood ceremony at the age of 12 and not at the age of 13. Thus, if Keila believed in the vision, she would have had an abortion condemning the future of the galaxy. Having an abortion when you were carrying the Chosen One? What's wrong with people?!

Much to her relief, TTM realised that Sabina wasn't aborted, and instead, her foetus was in suspended animation on Eden. What a lucky day. Now she just needed to convince Metatron to find a surrogate mother, so Sabina could be born just in time to stop Rangda on her 12th birthday!

While it might seem like a stupid idea to put faith in a 12-year-old saintly prodigy child to stop an evil space demon from enslaving and destroying the galaxy, it was TTM's primary plan, and never question GOD!

Chapter 4 Metatron is Almost Getting Lucky when he Finds Out About the True Maker's 'Ingenious' plan

Metatron was excited. He had emotionally processed that Keila probably was killed during the Xeno attack against the Terran Council meeting. Metatron was okay with Keila's demise. While Keila was rocking the bed, she was also a psychotic nutcase, and Metatron had realised that she was crazier than she was hot.

The lack of sex was an issue, but Metatron had the solution, he had a date with Melissa of the Gad Tribe and being the god-king of Eden, he was sure to get laid. Things were heating up between Metatron and Melissa when he had an unwelcome interruption. The True Maker showed up in the room as a mirage.

Metatron:

- Who are you?

TTM:

- I am the True Maker.

Metatron:

- Oh, so you are Keila's deity?

TTM:

- As my name implies, I am the only true God of this universe!

Metatron:

- There are a lot of gods that claim that. Anyways I don't have any special powers, so how come I can see you?

TTM:

- Well, I am the deity that created this universe. I can do whatever I want.

Metatron:

- And what do you want? Except for interrupting, that is!

TTM:

- Sabina, The Chosen One, is due to be born in six months.

Metatron:

- I have no idea what you are talking about, old woman.

TTM:

- I need you to find a surrogate mother for the foetus you and Keila put in suspended animation last year.

Melissa:

- I would be honoured to give birth to Metatron's and Keila's daughter, The Chosen One!

Metatron:

- Melissa? You saw the mirage as well?

Melissa:

- Yes.

TTM:

- Great. That settles it. Melissa, I bestow upon you the honour to become the mother of the Chosen One, the Virgin Mary of the 29th century.

Melissa:

- Excuse me, God. I am not a virgin.

TTM:

- Look, Melissa, time is running out, and I am not exactly spoiled for choice. Do you want the job or not?

Melissa:

- Of course. I'd be honoured to give birth to the Chosen One.

Metatron:

- Hold on! What is your plan for my future daughter?

TTM:

- I am going to form her into a peace-loving pacifist, and at the age of 12, she must defeat the Evil Space Demon Rangda Kaliankan and save the galaxy.

Metatron:

- That sounds like a foolish plan.

TTM:

- Lala, I can't hear you. I got to go!

Having said this, the True Maker's mirage disappeared, and Metatron was alone with Melissa.

Metatron:

- You told me you were a virgin earlier today?

Melissa:

- Have you never lied about something on a date?

Metatron:

 - Fair point. Can we have sex now?

Melissa:

- No, we must go to the medical bay straight away and impregnate me with your and Keila's daughter. We can't keep God waiting. Chop, chop.

Metatron:

 - *sigh*. I feared you would say that. Well let's go then.

Having said this, Melissa and Metatron hurried to the medical bay so Metatron could pursue fatherhood with his crazy ex. What an unexpected turn of events, Metatron!

Chapter 5: Keila Wakes up with a Nasty Headache and Chats with Rangda.

Keila woke up after a long sleep, and the whole room was spinning. She had never felt this sick before and she wondered what she drank the night before. Rangda entered the room, and Keila realised that she wasn't recovering from a bender. She was recovering from betraying humanity by opening magical portals, facilitating the invasion of man-eating aliens. Pure angst!

Rangda walked up to Keila and laughed:

- You don't look that well, did you have a lovely rest? Muahaha.

Keila:

- You don't look that pretty yourself. Did the True Maker swap the position of your face and your ass?

Rangda:

- As much as I could flame you, I'll let your reflection do the talking.

Having said this, Rangda pulled out a pocket mirror and handed it to Keila, who had a panic attack when she saw her face. She looked like she was 150 years old, or if that sounds unrealistic, like an 80-year-old smoker who spent most of her life in the sun. Not a pretty sight.

Keila:

- Oh no, my pretty face. How did this happen?

Rangda:

- What? Don't you remember the plot of Space Gods II? I helped you accessing your superpowers, and this aged you.

Keila:

- I do remember. But my looks went from a beautiful 22-year-old to a 50-year-old. Still a lot better than this.

Rangda:

- Now I understand why you are upset. I drained you of your remaining life force. That's why you look like you are 150 years old.

Keila:

- Oh well, at least I will die soon.

Rangda:

- No, you won't. No-one dies of aging, hunger, or thirst in the Divine Dimension. Muahaha.

Keila:

- That doesn't make any sense at all!

Rangda:

- Look, you can address all your complaints to The True Maker and his customer service department. Their email is martin-lundqvistauthor@gmail.com.

Keila:

- I definitely will.

Rangda:

- I thought so. What a shame that you are stuck into place by an invisible forcefield that stops you from moving or acting. Muahaha.

Keila:

- Wait. Why are you doing this to me you evil space demon?

Rangda:

- Silly girl. You answered your question with your question.

- I am doing this because I am an evil space demon. But I also have some other reasons.

- 1: I need to mind control you to mind control your right-hand-man Melchior to become Mars evil God-Emperor, so he can gather a large army and help me defeat the Zetans.

- 2: I need you as leverage against your unborn daughter that your dimwit deity is planning to send after me.

- 3: We are kind of cousins, and I would like to hang out with you from time to time.

Keila:

- Wait how on Earth can we be cousin when you're like 10,000 years old, and I am 25.

Rangda:

- I mean we are not actual cousins. But your great Zetan ancestor is Brahma, who was the brother of my long-dead mother, Kalian-ka.

Keila:

- Weren't you having an affair with Brahma when you infiltrated the Zetans to destroy their civilisation? You slept with your uncle. Yuck!

Rangda:

- Isn't that what all messed up villains do? I mean incest is a recurring theme on Game of Thrones.

Keila:

- Are you also watching Game of Thrones? Few people do in the 29th century.

Rangda:

- I do, indeed. I'll bring my projector next time so we can watch it together. Got to go. I have some evil plans to work on! He-he-he.

Keila:

- Cool, I won't be going anywhere.

As Rangda left, Keila experienced mixed feelings. On the one hand, she had betrayed humanity and were the prisoner of an evil demon queen. On the other hand, she had found her cousin, and she had someone to watch Game of Thrones with, so there was a silver lining to everything.

Chapter 6 Rangda Realises that Melchior Dorevitch is Eviller than She is.

A few weeks, Rangda realised what she had to do. She had to mind control Keila, so she could reach Melchior's mind and turn him evil. While it would be easier to insert a Divine Technology chip in her own brain to contact Melchior, it was too early in the plot to kill Keila, so Rangda decided to do it the hard way. After some connection issues, she saw Melchior as a hologram in front of her.

Rangda:

- Greetings, Melchior. We meet at last.

Melchior:

- Who are you? Did I hit my head?

Rangda:

- I am the Xeno Empress Rangda Kaliankan.

- Hitting one's head to contact me, was Keila's cue. Your cue is even more bizarre. You must drink human blood to contact me.

Melchior:

- Okay. That sounds easy enough. I love to drink the blood of the innocent for breakfast!

Rangda:

- What are you talking about, psychopath? Anyway, I have contacted you to let you know that I have Keila as my prisoner, so you can become the new God-Emperor of Mars.

Melchior:

- I figured that out a month ago when I found out that you kid-napped Keila after invading and destroying Rashidium. I took control over Mars, and I already am the God-Emperor. Muahaha.

Rangda:

- Okay. Uhm. I can provide you with Zetan technologies if you help me conquer the galaxy.

Melchior:

- I already have the Zetan technologies. I stole them from Meta-tron and the Edenites.

- That bastard didn't want to give them to me, so I killed my own mother with a laser to prove my point.

- After that, Metatron realised how badass I am, and surrendered the technologies to me.

Rangda:

- You did what? What is wrong with you?! Hold on a second, I need to discuss something with my colleague.

Rangda turned off her telepathic link and looked angrily at Keila. Keila had given Rangda so much grief for her evil deeds, and then it turned out, Keila's former right-hand-man Melchior was eviller than Rangda was.

Rangda:

- Hey Keila, you have given me so much grief for my evil deeds. How could you hire that psycho to be your right-hand-man?

Keila:

- Well, there wasn't that many applicants to the role, and I was too busy being a super sexy rebel to notice. But yeah, I should have hired literally anyone else!

Rangda:

- Thanks for clearing that up. Go back to sleep, Keila!

Rangda knocked Keila unconscious and considered her options. While Melchior was a scary psycho, she had magical corrupted Zeto Crystals, so he would be easy to control. She re-established her mental connection with Melchior.

Rangda:

- Melchior, I have considered my options. If you join me, I will give you the secret how to turn humans into Xeno-human mutants. They are the vilest and most fearsome beasts in the solar system.

Melchior:

- Excellent. I will do you bidding Empress Rangda!

Rangda:

- Good. I will transfer you the virus that causes the transformation. I need you to build up a gigantic army and then travel to Earth...

Melchior:

- ...And kill and eat everyone? Muahaha

Rangda:

- No. I need you to convince the Terran Leaders to let you move through the Portals to the Divine Dimension so you can help me kill the Zetans. Then we'll eat and kill everyone. Muahaha

Melchior:

- Muahaha

After this, both Rangda and Melchior laughed evilly for an extended period before Melchior, who was less accustomed to lengthy periods of evil laughter started coughing and needed to drink some water!

Chapter 7: Hilda Urges her Xeno Pet Ramun to look Fearsome for a Video.

Hilda Muller was looking at her Xeno prisoner Ramun through the fortified glass door to his cell. He was a sad sight. Having drunk 20 litres of beer Ramun had passed out on the couch and was drooling. He wasn't particularly fearsome either, having a massive beer gut and a slow and dumb face. Worst of all, he had blunted his claws and his fangs to not injure himself when he fell over.

But on the bright side, Ramun was the only Xeno captive that agreed to be paraded like a pet, so Hilda had to deal with what she had. Hilda walked up to Ramun and poured a bucket of icy water over him.

Ramun:

- Mistress Hilda, why did you wake me up like that?

Hilda Muller:

- I need you to look fearful and angry. Roar at the camera and lash out at me and my whip.

Ramun:

- Look. I have seen you with that whip. I am not into interspecies bestiality!

Hilda:

- Yuck, not like that. Roar like you are angry and want to kill me.

Ramun:

- Roaring? Do you think I am a primitive beast? I have learned German and English during my time on Earth. Can't we settle our argument with a civilised debate?

Hilda Muller.

- No, you are doing what you are told, or there will be no more beer deliveries!

Ramun:

- You drive a tough bargain. Let's do this.

Having said this, Hilda and Ramun started their silly charade where she whipped him, and he roared back at her. Due to the silliness of the video, the entire spectacle was in vain, and House Muller decided to use a much more fearsome CGI version of Ramun for their propaganda videos. After Hilda had left, Ramun licked his wounds and wondered what was wrong with humans. He soon got into a better mood when Hilda's zookeeper arrived with a big keg of German beer. Yummy!

Chapter 8: Hilda Convinces the Others to Make Her the Leader of Earth.

Hilda studied the world leaders that had gathered at her headquarters in the Swiss Alps. They were all unfamiliar faces as the menace Keila Eisenstein had caused everyone to die during the last meeting in Rashidium. It was just as good for Hilda, as this meant she was the most experienced world leader left. Hilda thought of sending a *"Thank You"* card to Keila but realised that it would be difficult finding someone stupid enough to deliver said card, as Keila was a prisoner of the Xeno Empress Rangda Kaliankan!

When everyone was seated, Hilda spoke:

- I want to become the leader of the Terran Council. I will show you a video proving that I am the most badass plutocrat on Earth.

Having said this Hilda started a hologram video showing how she, dressed in her German dominatrix outfit whipped the fearsome beast Ramun into submission. The gathered world leaders shook their heads, and the House Cheng delegate Min He Cheng spoke:

- Why did you show us these terrible CGI effects?
- On another notice, are you available this afternoon? *Wink Wink*

Min He's father Ping Chen gave Min an angry look and spoke:

- We are not here to sort out your dating Min. We are here to elect a new Supreme Leader.

- Hilda, can you show us this fearsome beast you have in captivity?

Hilda swallowed hard and felt reluctance. Would she really show the pathetic excuse that was her real Xeno prisoner? She realised that she didn't have a choice and spoke:

- Follow me to the secret House Muller Zoo. We are keeping the beast there.

A while later Hilda had led the delegates to the fortified glass window that surrounded Ramun's cage. Jordan White, the new House White chairperson, exclaimed:

- Hilda! Is this your doing? Did you really tame the fearsome beast turning it into an average obese American?

Hilda cleared her throat and looked away; this was really embarrassing for her after the heroic video she had shown the delegates half an hour earlier.

- Hmm, so the beast became very tame a while after he was separated from his pack.

Jordan White:

- This is amazing, you found a way to pacify the beasts! How did you do it?

Hilda Muller:

- Hmm, German beer and televised sports?

Jordan White:

- You're a genius. I can't believe we never thought about this. I order five full tankers full of German beer. Keep your breweries workings.

Ping Chen:

- I order ten full tankers to protect our borders. And I will vote for you as the Terran Supreme leader.

Enrique Bolivar:

- I order fifteen tankers, and you got my vote as well.

Everyone:

- Three cheers for Hilda Muller, our new planetary leader!

Thus, Hilda Muller was elected to be the planetary leader for Earth. Big tankers of beer were placed near every portal to the Divine Dimension, thus stopping Rangda's evil plan to conquer Earth. While her Xeno warriors were blood-thirsty beasts, they preferred drinking beer over fighting and killing people.

As for Hilda, she was a bit disappointed that history repeated itself again! 900 years after World War 2, the Germans were still better at brewing beer than fighting and winning wars.

Chapter 9: Sabina's Birth is a Disappointment for Metatron.

A few months later, Sabina was born. This was supposed to be a momentous day for humankind, but to Metatron, it was a bit of a disappointment. When the True Maker had told Metatron that Sabina was the Chosen One, Metatron had converted to Christianity, confident that Sabina was the second coming of Christ. But her birth was unremarkable. Despite being born in a stable to emulate Jesus' birth, Sabina couldn't speak as a baby, no angels came from the sky to praise her, and no mysterious men came from the East with gifts.

While Metatron was disappointed at how unremarkable Sabina's birth was, this was an unfortunate coincidence as the True Maker had contracted the flu while visiting another dimension. So instead of performing miracles when "The Chosen One" was born, the True Maker was shivering under the blanket and drinking hot tea in her ethereal palace.

On the bright side, the True Maker recovered eventually, and she spent a lot of time watching Sabina grow up and giving her superpowers instead of dealing with the elephant in the room, stopping the evil Space Demon Rangda!

Chapter 10: Emma Schindler, a Witless Delivery Woman!

Hilda Muller studied the hand-written and scented admiration letter that she had written to Keila Eisenstein. Due to Keila's actions, Hilda was no longer a random military officer in the Muller army, in fear of her evil uncle and perverted cousin. Because Keila opened the portals and let the Xenos in, Hilda was the top dog of Earth, and words couldn't describe how grateful she was.

But who would be stupid enough to travel to the Divine Dimension to deliver the letter? Hilda was not as evil as Joachim or Bjorn, and she couldn't just sacrifice some poor soldier to deliver her vain messages. Hilda was interrupted when her personal assistant Emma Schindler walked into the room. Emma noticed that Hilda was crying and decided to comfort her boss.

Emma Schindler:

- What is the matter, Hilda? I have never seen you cry before! You even used chilly to fake tears on your uncle's funeral!

Hilda:

- I am just so moved by the beautiful poetry I have written. And heartbroken that the intended recipient will never be able to read it.

Emma:

- Oh, poor you. Did you author a poem to your deceased father who was senselessly murdered by a Martian rebel?

Hilda:

- No, but that could be a promising idea. Thanks for suggesting it.

Emma:

- No worries, boss. So, who did you write the poem to?

Hilda:

- To my personal hero. The beautiful and talented Keila Eisenstein!

Emma:

- Keila Eisenstein? The madwoman who opened portals that enabled the invasion by man-eating aliens.

Hilda:

- Yes, if it weren't for her heroic efforts, Mars would have been wiped out by an asteroid strike. More importantly, Joachim would be the boss instead of me.

Emma:

- So, you admire her for selfish reasons?

Hilda:

- Yes. Are there any other reasons in the world?

Emma:

- Never mind. Can I please read the poem?

Hilda:

- Sure, go ahead.

Emma took the heavily scented letter from Hilda's desk and read it. It was filled with excellent prose, and it was almost as skilful writing as you would find in a Martin Lundqvist novel! Emma pondered her options for a while and spoke:

- This is exceptionally good Hilda; you should self-publish it on Scamazon and make a dozen friends give it glimmering reviews. You could earn 20 Terran Credits!

Hilda shook her head and replied:

- No, House White owns Scamazon. I don't want to make them wealthier!

- But, if I could only get it to Keila, a weight would be lifted off my chest!

Emma sighed. She was the definition of a "Yes" woman, and she didn't want to disappoint her boss, even if it meant that she had to bring a letter past a bunch of predatory aliens and deliver a message to the prisoner of their evil queen.

Emma:

- How about if I deliver the letter to Keila?

Hilda:

- Would you do that for me? It sounds incredibly dangerous!

Emma:

- I will be alright. Keila is guarded by a host of man-eating aliens and their wicked demon queen, but Ramun has taught me their language, and you have given them free beer. They'll know that I am their friend.

Hilda:

- That's great, Emma. You are so smart. Deliver the message, and if you make it back alive, I will promote you.

Emma:

- Jawohl Fraulein Muller!

Thus, Emma was sent out on a dangerous and pointless quest to deliver Hilda's love letter to Keila. Learn to say "No" Emma!

Chapter 11: Hilda's Poem Angers Rangda, and Emma Loses her Head!

A few days later, Emma was stopped by a group of Zetans. They didn't seem happy to see her! Zeus approached her and spoke:

- Σταματήστε τον άνθρωπο, είμαστε θυμωμένοι με σας!

Emma was dumbfounded and replied:

- What are you talking about?

Zeus:

- Oh, I am sorry, I used to be a Greek God!
- Are you Hilda Muller's assistant? The Zetans are angry with you!

Emma:

- Why? What have I done?

Zeus:

- Your boss is giving the Xenos an endless amount of beer. But where is our wine? Where is our nectar of the gods?

Emma:

- Look, we had to bribe the Xenos with beer to stop them from invading and killing us all.

Zeus:

- Well, you would better start delivering wine to us, lest we attack and kill you all!

Emma:

- Okay, I'll let the boss know. I need to deliver this message to Keila, Rangda's prisoner.

Zeus:

- I am not going to let you deliver a message to our sworn enemies, the Xenos!

Emma:

- It's just a poem for Keila, Hilda has a crush on her.

Zeus:

- Oh really? Let me look at that letter.

Emma handed Zeus the letter. He read the poem and shook his head in disgust.

Zeus:

- This poetry is awful! What has Keila done to deserve this?

Emma:

- Hilda thinks her poetry is good. Mainly because everyone tells her it is good.

Zeus:

- Okay. Make sure that Rangda doesn't read that poetry, she hates bad poetry more than I do, and wouldn't let that abomination pass unpunished.

Emma:

- Okay, thanks for the heads up!

Emma left the Zetans behind, and eventually, she stood outside Rangda's fortress in the Divine Dimension. Hilda had sent the Xenos a batch of extra strong beer, so all the Xenos had retreated to their fortress where they could recover from their binge drinking session. A grumpy Xeno guard answered the door in the Xeno language which Emma had learnt.

- What are you doing here, human? Give us one reason to not eat you.

Emma:

- I am here to deliver a poem to Keila from my boss Hilda.
- If you eat me, Hilda will stop sending you beer.

Xeno Guard:

- Those are good reasons, please enter!

- Keila is held captive in the small room behind Rangda's room. Don't wake Rangda up. You don't want to see her angry!

Emma:

- Understood. Thanks.

Emma walked down the stairs to Rangda's dungeon. Rangda was snoring loudly in her bed, and next to the bed, was a plasma sword strategically placed. Was this a trap or were the Xeno guards stupid enough to allow entrance to a human while their evil queen was asleep and unprotected? Emma considered her options: She could pick up the plasma sword and chop off Rangda's head, or she could do her job and deliver the message to Keila. Decisions, decisions!

Emma accessed her work description through the bionic microchip in her head. Delivering messages for Hilda was included while murdering sleeping space demons wasn't. *"Well, that settles that,"* Hilda thought and walked into the room where Keila was kept captive.

Keila was excited to finally see a human after being a captive for over a year:

- Finally, I meet a human again. Have you come to save me?

Emma:

- Saving you from an army on man-eating monsters? That's way too dangerous. I have just come to deliver this letter of admiration from Hilda Muller.

Keila:

- Fair enough. Hilda Muller, who is that?

Emma:

- Didn't the two of you meet in Space Gods II, when you pretended to be Alicia White?

Keila:

- Oh yeah, that rings a bell.

Emma

- Anyways Hilda is the cousin of Bjorn Muller and niece of Joachim Muller. She wants to thank you for killing her evil uncle and cousin so she could be the boss of House Muller.

Keil

- Well, this a bit unexpected but thank you for thinking of me.

Emma:

- My pleasure.

- Hilda also sent this poem to you. She would like to pardon you and take you on a date if you ever return to Earth.

Keila:

- Does she know that I look like 150-year-old mummy?

Emma:

- No, but I can let her know.

Keila:

- Cool. Can you read the poem for me? I cannot reach it, as I am covered by a psionic forcefield.

Emma:

- Sure.

While Emma was reading Hilda's poorly written poem, Rangda woke up. She was confused by hearing human voices from Keila's prison cell and decided that she had to investigate. Rangda stormed into the cell and found Enna narrating a woeful poem. Her instincts told her to murder and eat the human intruder, but then she realised that Emma had ignored the chance of killing her in her sleep, so Rangda decided to talk first.

Rangda:

- Who are you, human, and what are you doing here?

Emma:

- I am Emma Schindler, and I am narrating a poem from Hilda Muller to Keila.

Rangda:

- What? Why is your boss sending a poem to Keila?!

Emma:

- To express her gratitude to Keila for opening the portals, causing the alien invasion that killed her unpleasant relatives.

Rangda:

- How rude!

- She should thank me!

- Keila only opened the portals to Earth. It was I who invaded Rashidium and killed everyone!

Emma:

- Well, she also sent her regards to you, but your guard told me how much you hate it when people wake you up.

Rangda:

- If she wanted to thank me, she should have sent me the primordial Zeto Crystal from Earth, so I could conquer the universe!

Emma:

- Hmm, we have never heard of such a plot device before.

Rangda:

- Very well. Please recite the poem for me, and I might let you live!

Hearing this, Emma knew that she was stuck between Scylla and Charybdis. If she refused to recite the poem for Rangda, she would get killed. But remembering Zeus warning, reciting the poem to Rangda was also a terrible option. Emma decided to fake a sore throat and handed the poem to Rangda.

As Rangda was reading Hilda's woeful poem, she was burning with anger and lashed out:

> - This is the worst poem I have read in thousands of years! I will kill you for insulting me.

Having said this, Rangda decapitated Emma with her sharp claws, and then fetched a picnic basket and an old school pen. It was time to send Hilda a reply. Muahaha

Chapter 12: A brutal One-Star Review!

Hilda Muller was preparing for a sexy time with her on and off lover Markus White. The problem with being the most powerful woman on the planet was to find an eligible lover. She needed to find someone who was both handsome, wealthy, and willing to succumb to her violent sex games. This was easier said than done, but fortunately, she had coaxed to Markus to pay her a visit.

Markus approached Hilda tentatively and spoke:

- So, only regular sex and no whips and gadgets today. Agreed?

Hilda:

- Agreed. Only vanilla sex for my sensitive Markus today.

Markus:

- That's a relief!
- Well, let's do this.

Hilda:

- Jawohl! He-he

Hilda and Markus were just getting themselves ready when Hilda's bodyguard Melanie Weber rushed into the room, carrying a blood-stained picnic basket. Hilda gave Melanie a stern look and spoke:

- Melanie! What have I told you about interrupting my sexy times?

Melanie:

- It's an urgent message from the evil Xeno Empress Rangda Kaliankan.

Hilda:

- Very well. Hand me the basket.

Melanie handed Hilda the basket, and as Hilda opened it, she found Emma's severed head and a handwritten note, written with Emma's blood. The letter read

During millennia in prison, I have read millions of poems. This is by far the worst that I have ever read. One Star! Malicious Regards Rangda
PS. Bring me Earth's primordial Zeto Crystal or I'll invade again! DS '
Markus looked at Hilda in disgust and exclaimed:

- I knew that your poems are terrible, but sending them to our enemy and causing your assistant's death? This is the straw that broke the camel's back. We are done, Hilda!

Before Hilda had the time to respond, Markus left the room in anger. Hilda felt deeply disappointed. Being the leader of the planet, she was used to fake reviews to stroke her ego, but Rangda's brutal review had made her doubt her own talents. On top of that, her woeful poem had caused the death of her friend and personal assistant Emma Schindler. Hilda was close to tears when she heard the enticing voice of Melanie:

- I would love to have sex with you, and I love it rough!

Hilda paused for a second. She realised that her life had come to this. In an unexplainable turn of events, she would become lesbian and bang her female bodyguard five minutes after being dumped by her handsome on and off lover. Hilda smiled at Melanie and replied:

- Jawohl, ich werde dich hart ficken, Melanie!

The sex was terrific and made Hilda forget about the severed head in the basket. How convenient that she was converted into a lesbian by the age of 35. No more vanilla sex for Hilda Muller!

Chapter 13: Sabina Convinces Metatron to go to Earth and Visit Hilda for no Reason

A year later, Metatron and his toddler daughter Sabina, were waiting at Europeum Tower for an audience with Hilda Muller. Metatron was a bit sceptical about travelling all the way to Earth to meet up with his former enemy, but when his 2-year-old daughter Sabina had told him with glowing blue eyes that The True Maker and Keila wanted them to meet up with Hilda, he had agreed. He couldn't disobey The True Maker, and a toddler couldn't travel on her own. The door to Hilda's office opened, and she welcomed them with a big smile as they walked in.

Hilda:

  - Welcome, Metatron. This must be your and Keila's daughter Sabina.

Metatron:

  - Yes, that is correct. Thank you for meeting with us.

Hilda:

  - My pleasure. So, tell me, how is Keila in bed?

Metatron:

  - What kind of question is that!

Hilda:

  - Don't worry about that. I am the leader of Earth, and I demand an answer.

Metatron:

- She is amazing. She is both wild and incredibly sexy. Our bed-chamber activities were the reason I tolerated her craziness for so long.

Hilda:

- Damn! What a shame that she is captured by Rangda!
- Anyways, why did you come to visit me?

Sabina's eyes started glowing blue, and she joined the conversation:

- We came because I asked him to bring me to you.

Hilda:

- But you are like two years old? What kind of idiot travels for weeks because a toddler asks him!

Sabina:

- Look. I am the Chosen One, and I speak for The True Maker and Keila Eisenstein.

Hilda:

- Cool. What message does Keila have for me?

Sabina:

- That she loved your poem and sends her condolences for Emma.

Hilda:

- Cool! I knew we were a good match!

Sabina:

- But, my primary reason to come here is to give you a message from The True Maker.

- You must take your army to the Divine Dimension and defeat Rangda to stop the apocalypse.

Hilda:

- What? You want the German army to travel to another dimension and fight? We haven't won an armed conflict since 1870. That is a thousand years ago. Besides we are always portrayed as the bad guys in movies.

Sabina:

- Look, I know it's not ideal, but I can't ask the Americans. They would shoot us on sight, as my mother caused the alien invasion that killed most of their leadership.

Hilda:

- Fair enough. But tell me, why can't the True Maker, just snap her fingers and kill Rangda and Rangda's army? Why does she need a military intervention?

Hilda's valid question was too much for the True Maker to answer, so she disconnected from Sabina's mind, thus reverting Sabina's eye colour and intellect to that of a two-year-old. The clueless Sabina responded and started crying:

- Go Ga, mean lady. Bu-hu!

Hilda:

- That's a terrible reason, come up with something better!

Metatron:

- Calm down, Hilda. The True Maker disconnected from her mind, so Sabina is just like any two-year-old now.

Hilda:

- So, the supreme deity hides when people question her plan? Such a terrible leadership.

Metatron:

- That might be, but it changes nothing. You must send your army to fulfil the divine plan.

Hilda:

- Not going to happen, get the fuck out of my office.

Metatron:

- I won't leave until you agree to help me.

Hilda:

- Yes, you will!

Having said this, Hilda pressed the 'expel annoying visitor' button under her desk, and her AI robots entered the room and forcefully expelled Metatron and Sabina from Hilda's office. Just leave like a civilised person, Metatron!

Chapter 14: Melchior Wants to Eat Sabina Alive, but Rangda has a Much Better Plan!

A few days later Metatron was dozing off at the control panel of his spaceship. Going on a 14-day trip from Eden to Earth without a co-pilot? What a stupid idea! When Metatron woke up, he saw the last person he wanted to see. The cannibalistic God-Emperor of Mars, Melchior Dorevitch.

"Oh shit" Metatron mumbled to himself as Melchior approached him and laughed maliciously:

- Muahaha, we meet again, Metatron!

Metatron:

- Yes, but why? I assume that you haven't come to kill your mother with an orbital laser again.

Melchior:

- No, as fun as last time was, it's one of those things you can only do once!

- Why are you travelling from Earth with your toddler?

Metatron:

- Just doing some sightseeing. My wife is driving me crazy, so I reckoned I would take my daughter on a sightseeing tour until she calms down!

Melchior:

- I don't believe you! Tell me the truth, or I'll eat you alive. Muahaha.

Hearing this, Metatron felt that he was stuck in a difficult situation. If he lied, Melchior would get upset and eat him alive. But telling Melchior the truth, that Sabina was the Chosen One, and had urged Hilda Muller to fight Rangda, wouldn't be popular either. Metatron realised that he was a good guy, so he might as well die as an honest man.

Metatron:

- Okay. The truth is that Sabina is the daughter of Keila and me. She is the Chosen One to stop the evil demon queen Rangda from conquering the Milky Way Galaxy.

Melchior stared at Metatron in disbelief, this was the dumbest thing that he had ever heard:

- I told you to not lie to me Metatron. Now I must eat you alive.

Metatron:

- Please, Melchior. I am telling you the truth. Sabina is the Chosen One!

Hearing this, Melchior attached a bib to his neck and drooled. With a menacing voice, he exclaimed:

- Very well. Thank you for telling me the truth. I will prevent the Divine Plan while having a delicious dinner. Muahaha

Suddenly, Rangda appeared in the room as a mirage:

- Melchior, you cannot kill Sabina.

Melchior:

- What are you talking about, Empress Rangda?

- Sabina is the Chosen One and meant to end your reign of terror. We must stop her!

Rangda:

- No. If we kill her, the True Maker might come to her senses and send someone competent to stop me. But if the fool intends for this child to grow up and confront me, I'll have plenty of time to corrupt all the Zeto Crystals and become unstoppable. Muahaha.

Melchior:

- You are certainly an evil genius, Empress Rangda!

Rangda:

- Yes. Send Metatron and Sabina unharmed back to Eden. The True Maker must believe that her 'ineffable' plan is working.

Having said this, Rangda disconnected from Melchior's mind, and he turned to Metatron.
Melchior:

- Sorry about the misunderstanding, Metatron. You and your daughter are free to go.

Metatron:

- That's a relief. Well, good luck with the coming wars. I will just go back to Eden and reconcile with my wife!

Melchior:

- That won't be easy for you. I'll send her an email, telling her how I caught you asleep and I almost ate her daughter. Good luck. Muahaha

Having said this, Melchior laughed maliciously, and then he and his men returned to their command ship. Metatron felt a deep sense of relief. The True Maker must have intervened and saved his life! But he would need another miracle soon, because how would he explain Melchior's email to Melissa?

Chapter 15 Michael Muller walks in on Hilda Muller having sex.

Hilda Muller was enjoying some fantastic sex with her bodyguard Melanie Weber. During the copulation, she reflected over how strange it was that she suddenly turned lesbian in her mid-thirties, but sometimes good things happened for no reason!

Suddenly, the good times ended when her uncle, Michael Muller, stormed into her bedroom. How awkward! Hilda wouldn't accept this kind of behaviour, so she shouted at Michael:

- Michael! Why are you storming into my bedroom? Why didn't you book an appointment like normal people?

Michael:

- No-one was working. You sent everyone home except Melanie, and she clearly wasn't doing a respectable job guarding your office!

Hilda

- Fair enough. So, what is so urgent that it couldn't wait for another hour?!

Michael:

- The evil God-Emperor Melchior Dorevitch arrived with his whole fleet five minutes ago. He requests to meet you; otherwise, he will destroy this city.

Hilda:

- Oh, so the entire building shaking wasn't from my orgasm? That makes a lot of sense!

- I guess I better meet with this madman before he kills us all. I forgive you for walking in on me having sex, uncle.

Michael:

- Good.

- One more thing. We better promote Melanie to the rank of General before you go.

Hilda:

- Why is that?

Michael:

- It would be embarrassing if your eulogy said that you had sex with a poor person and then got killed by a ravaging madman. It sounds a lot better if you had sex with one of your generals before you died.

Hilda:

- I'd rather survive the ordeal!
- But sure, you can promote Melanie if you want.

Michael:

- Cool!

- Melanie, get a General uniform and go with Hilda to Melchior's command ship.

- I'll hide in the command bunker and retaliate if he decides to murder the two of you.

Hilda:

- That doesn't sound fair at all!

Michael:

- Right, but Melchior specifically asked to see you, so your presence is necessary to avoid our destruction. Good luck, Hilda! Chop, Chop!

Hearing this, Hilda grumbled but acknowledged the wisdom in Michael's word. She put on her clothes and accompanied Melanie to the armoury. As Melanie exited the changeroom in her new uniform, Hilda realised that Melanie looked stunning in a uniform. They would have a lot of fun ahead of them, if they could only survive meeting with the Martian madman!

Chapter 16 Melchior Brings his Huge Army to Threaten Hilda Muller.

Hilda and Melanie flew a small shuttle to dock with Melchior's command ship. Hilda realised that Michael hadn't lied when he told her about Melchior's invasion. The entire Martian fleet had arrived, making Hansstadt uncomfortably cold as the Martian fleet blocked all the sunlight! But what could the psychotic madman want, and why hadn't she sent Michael to meet with Melchior?

Hilda docked with Melchior's command ship, and she realised that the lobby of the spaceship wasn't to her liking. The centrepiece of the lobby was a huge fountain filled with blood and beating hearts. What a terrible and tasteless design! Hilda would never hire Melchior's interior designer!

Hilda was interrupted from disliking the lobby when Melchior Dorevitch approached her:

- Hilda Muller, we meet at last.

Hilda:

- I didn't have much choice, did I?

Melchior:

- Well, you could have sent your uncle. I was expecting to meet with him.

Hearing this, Hilda muttered angrily to herself. Her uncle had lured her into meeting Melchior, instead of doing his job. Hilda reminded herself that Michael would feel the whip if she got out of this alive, and not in a pleasant way!

Hilda:

- I see.
- So why did you insist on meeting me, Melchior?

Melchior:

- I want to bring my massive army to the Divine Dimension, join up with the Zetans and kill Rangda and all the Xenos!

Hilda:

- That doesn't make any sense. You and your army has mutated, and most of you look like the Xenos. Why would you fight against them?

Melchior:

- I had a breakdown with Rangda when discussing Xeno religious doctrine. I branded them heretics, and now they all need to die. Such is the way, when it comes to resolving religious disagreements!

Hilda:

- Fair point. Well, best of luck. The True Maker wants me to send my army to fight the Xenos, but I am much happier if you send yours.

Melchior:

- Great. Would you mind giving us supplies for our holy crusade against Rangda's flawed religious doctrine?

Hilda:

- I knew there was a catch!

- Look we haven't won a war since 1870. That's a thousand years ago. Just bring your army to the portal, and I'll pay you.

Melchior:

- Excellent. Thank you for aiding us in the Holy Crusade for right-eousness.

Hilda:

- Whatever Melchior. I am leaving. Get the fuck out of our territory, and we'll pay you.

Melchior:

- I will. But I will leave enough of my fleet to destroy you if you don't pay. Muahaha.

Hilda:

- Okay, I am out.

On the space shuttle back to Hansstadt, Hilda suffered from a terrible headache. Not only was the army of a madman threatening her capital, but she had also promised this madman freebies, something that would make her accountants a living nightmare!

Chapter 17: Melchior meets up with Rangda and is disappointed.

A few weeks later, Melchior Dorevitch felt like a young man again nervous before a date. He was waiting close to an abandoned temple in the Divine Dimension, and this was the moment he had been waiting for. He was going to meet the wicked Xeno Empress Rangda Kaliankan, his greatest idol.

Suddenly an incredibly beautiful woman appeared. Who was she and what was she doing in this place? Melchior soon found out, as the woman approached him and whispered seductively into his ear:

- Hi sexy. I am Helen of Troy. Would you like to follow me into that temple and get to know me a bit better?

Melchior hesitated for a second. He already had an appointment with Rangda Kaliankan, the wicked Xeno hellbent on conquering the galaxy. Was it wise to make her wait to follow his carnal desires? He looked at Helen again, and decided that Rangda could wait for a while! Melchior smiled, revealed his fangs, and spoke:

- I am Melchior Dorevitch, the God-Emperor of Mars, and I would love to follow you to a private room.

Helen:

- Come with me, oh handsome God-Emperor Dorevitch

Helen took Melchior's hand, and this filled him with anticipation. Having sex with the most beautiful woman in the history of humankind would be even better than eating someone alive. Melchior was aroused, and he drooled like a starving dog. As they entered the private room, Melchior's excitement transformed into shock and awe. Helen had transformed into the hideous and ferocious Rangda, and she was displeased!

Rangda:

- Were you going to make me wait while you were copulating?!

Melchior:

- What would you have done if Helen of Troy tried to seduce you?

Rangda:

- Fair point, I would have considered her proposal.

Melchior:

- So, can you please change back, so we can copulate?

Rangda:

- Nope, I don't have time for that. I am here to give you instructions.

- Meet up with the Zetans and convince them that you are here to help them fight my Xeno army. Once you have gained the Zetans trust, you stab them in the back during the decisive battle. Muaha-ha

Melchior:

- What? Are the Zetans completely retarded? Why would they fall for such a ploy?

Rangda:

- Because I will give you Zetan technology enabling you to hide your grotesque and disfigured Xeno mutations. Furthermore, a small battle between one of your armies and one of my armies, outside the Zetan fortress, will convince them that you are their ally.

Melchior:

- Wait? So, we are going to fight each other?

Rangda:

- Yes, that's the only way to convince the Zetans. I will send Grug-muk the Beer Belly, I am sick of his army drinking beer all the time, forsaking their killer instincts!

Melchior:

- Okay, I will send George Smith and his troops. I am sick of his refusal to eat people alive. Muahaha

Rangda:

- Decided. Muahaha

After laughing maliciously for an extended period, Rangda reversed to her disguise as the beautiful Helen of Troy. Much to Melchior's dismay, she didn't stay to get to know him better!

Chapter 18: George Smith does not convince the Zetans about Melchior's good intentions, but his death does.

A few weeks later, General George Smith was waiting outside the Zetans Valhalla fortress, hoping to secure the Zetans support for Melchior. George was positively surprised when he received the mission. He had feared that a private meeting with Melchior meant that Melchior was about to eat him alive, but instead it turned out that Melchior promoted him to his messenger. How fortunate!

George Smith knocked on the door, and Balder came down to answer it. Balder was severely hungover from drinking too much of the nectar of the gods, which the Zetans had blackmailed Hilda into sending.

Balder:

  - Who are you, and what do you want, human?

George Smith:

  - I am General George Smith, and I have a message from God-Emperor Melchior Dorevitch.

  - He wants to ally with the Zetans to wipe out the Xenos.

Balder:

  - Really? That's the dumbest thing I have ever heard. Melchior wanting to do the right thing? Why?

George Smith:

  - There is a difference between Melchior's and Rangda's religious doctrines and they have vowed to exterminate each other.

Balder:

- Yeah right! What exactly are they arguing about?

George Smith:

- Melchior claims that one should start from the bottom left corner when eating someone alive. Rangda claims that one should start from the top right corner.

Balder:

- That makes no difference whatsoever. The Zetan doctrine forbids us from eating people alive!

- Get away from our fortress!

Balder slammed the door and went back to bed when his father, Odin, approached him.

- Who was it at the door, Balder?

Balder:

- It was a human from Melchior's army. Melchior is seeking an alliance against Rangda.

Odin:

- Why? Aren't they equally evil and best of mates?

Balder:

- Well, according to the messenger, they had a breakdown in religious doctrine, regarding the best way to eat people alive.

Odin:

- Oh, that makes a lot of sense. Humans and other primitive species are known to kill each other for the most frivolous reasons, especially when it comes to religious doctrine! Let this man in so I can talk to him.

Balder walked towards the gate and looked through the opening. Much to his dismay, it appeared that the humans and the Xenos were busy murdering each other outside. Balder shouted to Odin:

- Hey dad. It's too late to save the humans, the Xenos are busy killing them.

Odin:

- What? Rally our Valhalla warriors at once! We cannot let the Xenos murder our future allies.

Having said this, Odin gathered all his troops so that he could join in on the senseless murdering taking place outside their fortress!

Chapter 19: Melchior is rejoicing that his evil scheme is coming into fruition

A few days later, George Smith, accompanied by Odin's army, reached Melchior's army camp. While Melchior was happy that his evil plan seemed to work, he was frustrated that George Smith had survived the battle. In fact, George hadn't survived, but the Zetans had revived George as a favour to Melchior.

Odin approached Melchior and spoke:

- Greetings. I am Odin, and you must be God-Emperor Melchior Dorevitch of Mars?

Melchior:

- Oh, praise the True Maker, you must really have the foresight and immeasurable wisdom oh great Odin.

Odin smiled smugly and replied:

- Yes, I do.
- But your nametag made it easy to identify you!

Melchior checked his uniform, and there was indeed a nametag. Why was he, the god-emperor of Mars wearing a nametag? His tailor would become food for this oversight! Melchior faked a smile to appease Odin.

- Yes, yes. You are right. Thank you for joining our fight against the heretical Xenos.

Odin nodded and smiled at Melchior. He realised that there were a time and place for pointing out that eating people alive was wrong, regardless of how you did it, but that was a future issue. For now, he needed this human madman to deal with Rangda and save the universe.

- It's my pleasure to help you resolve this important theological question and exterminate Rangda's heretical Xenos.

- How do you propose that we deal with Rangda?

Melchior:

- Rangda is bringing her whole army here to kill us, but with the Zetans on our side, we'll easily win.

- My strategy is that you bring all the remaining Zetans here and we fight together in a decisive battle against the Xenos.

Odin:

- That sounds like a perfect plan and not like a devious trap set by an evil mastermind. I'll contact the other Zetans and tell to come here at once.

- Now if you excuse me, I'll house myself and my army into your private quarters. I used to be a god on Earth, and I deserve to live in luxury!

Hearing this, Melchior ground his teeth in anger. But he kept his cool and stuck to Rangda's evil masterplan. Melchior replied with his most sycophantic voice:

- Of course, Master Odin. I am happy to serve!

Odin, who was used to humans acting like this around him, did not notice the falseness in Melchior's voice and felt relieved that this issue had been resolved.

Chapter 20: Helen of Troy, the Clueless Bimbo!

A few days later, Rangda, posing as Helen of Troy, approached Melchior's camp. Frey and Freya stopped her at the gates. Frey looked at her sceptically and spoke:

- Helen of Troy? What are you doing here? Haven't you been dead for over 3000 years?

Freya:

- Don't be silly, brother. She is clearly a Zetan spy who has changed her appearance to infiltrate the humans.

Helen:

- Yes... A Zetan spy is what I am.

Frey:

- Oh really? Who sent you?

Helen:

- I am not at liberty to say, Lord Frey.

Frey:

- Fair enough. But you are not that stupid and ugly bitch Rangda, who must change her appearance to get laid?

Helen/Rangda clenched her jaw in anger, but she had enough self-control to fake a seductive smile. Her 5000 year-long dry spell was about to end, and soon these vain Zetans would fall to her mighty Xenos! Being an inept actress, Rangda replied with a Bimbo's voice:

- Hi-Hi. Rangda? Who is that? I don't know much about politics. Hi-hi

Hearing this, Frey and Freya stared at Helen in disbelief. How was it possible for anyone to not know about the evil Xeno empress Rangda Kaliankan who had destroyed the Zetan civilisation? That made about as much sense as if a human had no idea who Jesus was. Freya shook her head in disbelief and replied:

- You can't be very bright, Helen!
- Anyway, what is your mission here?

Helen:

- Hi-hi I am here to seduce Melchior and spy on him.

Freya:

- Copulating with a human? Yuck on that. But good luck on the spying part. Make sure to repeat all your findings to our Asgardian faction, or you might have an accident.

Helen:

- Oh, I won't have any accident with Melchior, I have protection.

Helen/Rangda walked past Frey and Freya and approached Melchior's private quarters. Melchior stared at her in disbelief as she entered his tent:

- Rangda?! What are you doing here?

Helen:

- Shh, you idiot. I am Helen of Troy, and I have come to seduce you!

Melchior:

- Will you remain Helen of Troy throughout the entire act?

Helen:

- Yes.

Melchior:

- Yippie. Let's do this!

Having said this, Melchior and Rangda proceeded to have very rough and very loud sex that disturbed the entire base. This was because, Melchior being a dickhead, turned on the microphone in his office and decided to broadcast everything on the public announcement system. Copulating with Melchior, Rangda had mixed feelings. On the one hand, it was good to finally have sex again, but on the other hand, it deeply hurt her that Melchior preferred her beautiful human form over her hideous true form!

Chapter 21: Odin sends Frey and Freya on missions.

Later the same day with the nasty noises of Melchior's and "Helen's" love-making disturbing the base, Odin summoned Frey and Freya to his command building. Odin who was tired and grumpy from having his afternoon nap disturbed, hissed in anger:

- Does that sound never end? How can a man last that long?

Frey:

- We discussed that and concluded that he recorded the sound and then plays it on repeat out of malice.

Odin:

- Fucking animal!
- Anyway, it may have disturbed my sleep, but it gave me a great idea.
- Frey, go to Earth and seduce Hilda Muller.

Frey:

- Why me? What I have done?

Odin:

- You're a Norse God of fertility. Seducing and knocking up Terran females are part of your job description.

Frey:

- Yuck. But okay, I'll do it.

Odin:

- Perfect. All done.

Freya:

- Wait for a second! Why did you summon me then?

Odin:

- Oh yes, Freya, my dear daughter. I almost forgot about you.

- I want you to murder Helen of Troy, replicate her looks and take her place.

- We need to know if Melchior is trustworthy.

Freya:

- But that includes a lot of copulation with Melchior!

Odin:

- Evidently.

Freya:

- Stuff that!

- Melchior is disgusting.

- I'd rather go to Earth and seduce Hilda Muller. I have heard she is into women.

Odin:

- What kind of 29th century bullshit is this? No religion allows homosexuality. Do your job, Freya!

Frey and Freya left Odin's office in anger and disgust. They were both extremely disappointed with their assignments. Freya spoke in anger:

- Stuff this. I am not touching Melchior. I am going to Earth to seduce Hilda!

Frey:

- Wait a second. I thought I was the gay fertility god!

Freya:

- I wasn't gay until this assignment, but Melchior Dorevitch, Yuck! I'd rather be with a woman.

Frey:

- I feel you, sister. I would also rather be with a woman than with Melchior!

Freya:

- So, then it's settled? We'll go to Earth together.

Frey:

- But, if you are seducing Hilda, what would my job be?

Freya:

- I have heard Hilda has a very sexy uncle!

Frey:

- Oh la, la. But what about dad?

Freya:

- He will be busy fighting the Xenos. He won't even know we are gone!

Frey:

- Great. Let's go before dad notices we are gone!

Thus, Frey and Freya went through the portal to Earth, hoping for some sexual adventures in Europe. As it turned out, Freya's loathing towards Melchior, ended up causing the Zetans downfall. Because if she had only accepted her mission and murdered Rangda masquerading as Helen of Troy, the story could have ended vastly different!

Chapter 22: A Case of Mistaken Identity.

The next day Odin felt a bit guilty. It was unfair to force his daughter to seduce and copulate with the revolting Melchior. Although Freya's work description said *"fertility goddess"* there was a limit to what he could demand. Odin left his command centre and went out looking for Freya, but she was nowhere to be seen.

Eventually, he came across Rangda posing as Helen of Troy. Odin convinced that Helen of Troy was Freya in disguise, approached Helen and spoke.

Odin *Whispering*:

- Did you carry out the mission I gave you?

Odin's behaviour confused Rangda, but she didn't want to reveal herself, so she replied:

- Yes. Everything is going according to plan.

Odin:

- I am sorry that you must go through with this. Seducing Melchior is too much to ask.

Rangda was still confused, but she decided to go with the flow.

- I am happy to serve my people, the Zetan species.

Odin:

- That is very mature of you. So, where did you hide the body?

Rangda had no clue what Odin was talking about. But she wasn't Rangda Kaliankan the Deceiver for nothing! She smiled, mysteriously at Odin and replied:

- I think it would be better if you don't know.

Odin:

- Okay, but who was it?

Finally, Rangda figured out what was going on. Odin must have sent someone to kill her and take her place as Melchior's concubine. But, why hadn't she faced any assassination attempt? Regardless, Rangda realised that she needed to make up an answer.

- Mbaba Mwana Waresa.

Odin stared at Helen/Rangda with a clueless look and replied:

- Who in the Milky Way is that?

Rangda:

- It's the Zulu goddess of fertility.

Odin:

- Damn. There are just too many Zetan Gods. Impossible to keep track of us all!

Rangda smiled on the inside. Indeed, there were too many Zetans, but that would change soon. Rangda decided to finish the conversation:

- I must go back to Melchior before he misses me.

Odin:

- Yes, of course. Please make sure to report everything you find out.

Rangda:

- I will. Thank you, Master Odin.

Having said this, Rangda hurried back to Melchior's quarters. This had been a narrow escape, and she wanted to stay away from the Zetan leaders to avoid that one of them realised who she really was.

As for Odin, he was overjoyed that Freya had accepted the mission gracefully as he'd expected her to complain a lot. It had been thousands of years, had his daughter finally grown mature and pleasant? Blissfully unaware of Rangda's presence Odin went to bed full of pride over Freya's character development.

Chapter 23: Rangda kills the Zetan Leadership in the Middle of a Great Battle.

A few days later the Xeno army had arrived and was ready to storm Melchior's base. The Zetans were not particularly afraid. The Zetans were godlike aliens, and they had human allies. Against them stood a bunch of brutish and useless aliens who had failed to invade Earth as the temptation to drink free beer had halted their progress. Odin's only concern was that Rangda was nowhere to be seen, but as soon as he had dealt with her incompetent army, he would chase her down!

Meanwhile, Rangda and Melchior finished another round of sex. The time for sex was over, the time to kill had begun!

Rangda:

> - So, so Melchior. Bring some of your bodyguards. We are going to kill the Zetan leadership. Muahaha!

Melchior shook his head and replied:

> - I thought about your plan, Rangda. I concluded that it was stupid, so I came up with a better idea. I had my men rig the Zetan command centre with explosives. As soon as I press this button, I will kill Odin, Ra, Vishnu, Buddha and Tialoc with a massive explosion.

Rangda quickly pulled Melchior's detonator from him and destroyed it. Then she yelled at him:

> - Don't you have any feeling for dramaturgy? You want to kill my eternal enemies off-screen with a massive explosion. Shame on you! I will reveal myself and then chop them to pieces.

Melchior:

- That's stupid and risky. Your eternal enemies might chop us to pieces instead.

Rangda:

- That might be, but it's your only option. Since I destroyed the remote. Gather your elite bodyguards. It's time to kill some Zetans.

Melchior ground his teeth in frustration. Of course, there would be some strings attached to having nonstop sex with Helen of Troy for a week. Rangda was a dimwit and would get them all killed. Yet Melchior wanted to live, so he tried one last attempt at talking Rangda to her senses.

- Look Rangda. The Zetans are eternal godlike aliens. My bodyguards and I are just humans. I think blowing them up is a lot better choice.

Rangda smirked at Melchior and replied:

- You are just going to come as my audience. I have three magical corrupted Zeto Crystals that make me very capable of killing five Zetans at once. Muahaha.

Melchior:

- So why this charade if you could have killed them a long time ago?

Rangda:

- Look, I can kill five Zetans by myself, not five thousand. I am not that unrealistically overpowered! Your men and my Xenos will have to kill the rest!

Melchior:

- Okay, got it!

- Lead the way, boss.

Rangda, Melchior and some of Melchior's bodyguards entered the Zetan command centre. Odin smiled as they approached.

- Welcome Melchior, or should I say future son-in-law?

- We have duped you. Helen of Troy is my daughter Freya in disguise. Show Melchior your real appearance, Helen!

Rangda was a bit perplexed but found the notion interesting, so she revealed her actual appearance. Odin stared at her in disapproval:

- Why did you change your appearance to that hideous monster Rangda? Show your real, beautiful appearance, Freya.

Rangda:

- Who did you call hideous, you old fart?

- I am Rangda Kaliankan, and I have the power of three corrupted Zeto Crystals. Prepare to die Odin.

Odin:

- Oh shit!

After this, the overpowered Rangda swiftly and effortlessly butchered the Zetan leadership. When Rangda had killed the Zetan leaders, Melchior took up a microphone and made an announcement on the PA system:

- Dear Martian Dominion Army. I know this sounds silly, but I am actually evil. So, the Zetans are our enemies, and the Xenos are our friends. Kill all the Zetans. Muahaha!

After finishing his announcement, a bloodbath ensued, which was terrible news for the Zetans as they got exterminated!

Chapter 24: Rangda and Sabina's First Chat!

It was March 2878, and Sabina was having a telepathic chat with her mother, Keila. While this might sound implausible as Keila was Rangda's prisoner in another dimension, Sabina was a 2.5-year-old prodigy child bestowed with supernatural powers by the True Maker herself!

Sabina:

- So, what's new, mother?

Keila:

- With me? Not much. I am still locked up inside this forcefield. I haven't eaten, drunk or had sex in over three years!

Sabina:

- Eww. Don't tell me about your sex life! I am only 2.5 years old!

Keila:

- Fair point. But like I said it's nothing going on there anyway.

- Speaking of other things. Rangda and Melchior joined up and killed all the Zetans. It won't be long until Rangda threatens the future of the galaxy.

Sabina:

- I know. The True Maker told me. It's so annoying that I am the one that's supposed to sort out this mess. I'd much rather live a stress-free life and play with my younger siblings Jasmine and Jordan!

Keila:

- Have you told the True Maker that you don't want the job?

Sabina:

- Yes, but being the Chosen One is not a job that I can resign from! Sigh!

Suddenly Rangda approached Keila from behind and grabbed her head to intercept her psionic call with Sabina. Rangda laughed maliciously and spoke:

- Muahaha. "The Chosen One" we finally get to talk.

Sabina:

- Yeah. I have been waiting for you to contact me and reveal your evil plan. But why did you interrupt my psionic call with Keila? You could have called me when I was free.

Rangda:

- Call you? I don't have your number.

Sabina:

- It's listed in the Psionic Phone Registry. It's 1800 Thechosenone.

Rangda:

- Thanks, I'll remember that!

Sabina:

- Anyways. What is your evil plan, Rangda?

Rangda:

- I thought you'd never ask. I plan to invade Elvonia, home of the Elves, Goldonia, home of the Dwarves, and Grashdunt, home of the Orcs. I will steal and corrupt their magical Zeto Crystals.

- After that, I will return to Earth and steal the seventh Zeto Crystal. Once I have all the Zeto Crystals, I will become unstoppable. Muahaha!

Sabina:

- And once you do, I, the Chosen One, must drag myself to the Divine Dimension and face you? Sigh.

Rangda:

- You don't seem very enthusiastic?

Sabina:

- It usually never ends well for the Chosen One. Look at the Bible, or the Matrix.

Rangda:

- Oh well, may the best woman win?

Suddenly Keila woke up and she was determined that she wouldn't expose her innocent daughter to the evil Xeno Empress Rangda Kaliankan. Doing what any responsible parent would do, she knocked Sabina unconscious with a psionic blast!

It was undoubtedly a good thing that Keila didn't have the custody of Sabina or the Child Protection Services would have to put in overtime!

Chapter 25: Dov Dorevitch Causes a Zombie Apocalypse That is not a Zombie Apocalypse.

The fat, bald and unambitious Dov Dorevitch, brother of Melchior Dorevitch was drinking beer and eating pizza when an explosion shook the building, causing Dov to spill beer all over his greasy T-shirt. As Dov got up from the couch, his crazy Chief Scientist Frank Van Stein entered the room.

Dov:

 - Hey Frank. What's up? Why is the building shaking?

Frank:

 - There is an uprising lead by Colonel Slavonic.

Dov:

 - Who is that, and what is he upset about?

Frank:

 - You fat useless prick! How can you not remember the name of the colonel that's tasked with protecting our capital?

Dov:

 - Hey Frank! Cool down with the attitude. I don't care about these things. All I care about is the results in tonight's Drone Soccer match.

Frank:

 - Well, being Melchior's stand-in, you must care. And people are terribly upset with you.

Dov:

- But why are they upset? I haven't done anything!

Frank:

- Well, you are still Melchior's stand-in. And Melchior polluted the planet, introduced a brutal dictatorship, and ate people alive, so there is that!

Dov:

- Okay, so what do I do? Resign and introduce democracy?

Frank:

- It's a bit late to resign when the rebels have conquered most of the planet and are lined up outside your capital. Besides, the rebels have tried to negotiate many times, and you chose to ignore them every time.

Dov:

- Look, there were better things on TV, or I was getting a massage, or I was having a nap. Life as a dictator is too comfortable to do annoying stuff like politics!

Frank:

- Well, your life is about to end. Unless you approve my evil plan. Muahaha.

Dov:

- Wait a second. Why can't you have a good or neutral plan? Why does it have to be evil?

Frank:

- Because I am the crazy scientist Frank Van Stein employed by the cannibalistic God-Emperor Melchior Dorevitch. Doing good, doesn't exist in my vocabulary.

Dov:

- Yes, it does? You just said it!

Frank:

- Bah, Petty complaints. Regardless I have the solution for you.

Dov:

- Alright! Tell me about your evil plan, Frank. *sighs*

Frank:

- I need your presidential permission to release this airborne Xeno virus, that will convert our population to mindless and cannibalistic Xeno-human hybrids.

Dov:

- So, you want to cause the Zombie apocalypse? That doesn't sound like a good plan at all!

Frank:

- Bah. Don't be silly. The Zombie apocalypse would never work. Dead people walking around mindlessly eating each other. They would starve or thirst to death in days. Melchior wouldn't be happy about that.

- No, the Xenos are just like humans. They can go about their daily lives like any of us. The only difference is that they are loyal to their leader, and they like to murder and eat each other.

Dov:

- But wouldn't they still want to murder me, if that is the case?

Frank:

- No, the Xenos are loyal to their leader Melchior, and you are his substitute during his essential mission in the Divine Dimension!

Dov:

- Cool. Let's do this.

Having said this, Dov went with Frank to Frank's secret laboratory. Dov dropped a few drops of his blood on the blood encryption machine and authorised the release of the Xeno virus in the Martian Atmosphere. As the virus was released, Frank had an epiphany. That he could have murdered Dov and used his blood to release the virus! But now it was too late. Infected by the Xeno virus, he had to remain loyal to his leader Melchior and Melchior's idiot brother Dov, who ruled in his place. Argh!

As Dov walked back to his TV, he was quite content with himself. Frank was right. Infected by the virus, people were busy murdering and eating each other, but no-one bothered him. What a terrific way to stay in power and solve Mars' overpopulation at the same time!

Chapter 26 Rangda's Revelation Change the Genre from Sci-Fi to Fantasy

A few days later, Rangda and Melchior's armies had finished eating the dead Zetans. Like a lazy lion, Melchior was napping comfortably when Rangda stormed in and disturbed his peace. *"Rise and shine my love"*, she hissed unpleasantly.

Melchior got up and responded:

- Oh, Rangda! Please approach me as Helen of Troy. You're not a pretty sight to wake up to!

Rangda:

- Helen of Troy is gone. This is my true form. Besides, you are too ugly for Helen!

Melchior:

- I guess our equal levels of ugliness makes us a good match.

- But why are you waking me up? I need to digest the food before we can take our massive armies and invade Earth!

Rangda:

- The invasion of Earth is postponed! I have a critical mission to complete first.

Melchior:

- What mission? What are you talking about? I thought the plan was to meet up here, kill the Zetans and then join forces against the Terran Council?

Rangda:

- Well, would you have come if I told you that my real plan was to lead our armies around the galaxy looking for magical crystals?

Melchior:

- Of course not, that's a stupid idea.

Rangda:

- No, it's a brilliant idea. You see the Milky Way Galaxy contains seven primordial Zeto Crystals, holding the essence of the True Maker. I own three of these Crystals. The other crystals are found on the elven home planet, Elvonia, the dwarven home planet, Goldonia, the orcish home planet Grashdunt, and the human home planet Earth.

Melchior:

- Wait a second. Did you just change the genre from Sci-Fi to Fantasy?

Rangda:

- No. I didn't. The author did. Anyway, since I am the Xeno Empress Rangda Kaliankan, and you are just a random psychopath who likes to eat people, we'll do as I say.

Melchior:

- But why don't we invade Earth first? You said there was a magical crystal on Earth as well?

Rangda:

- Because Elvonia is easier to invade. The elves are peaceful creatures who still use bows and arrows. Besides, Elvonia is beautiful this time of the year, and elves have delicious flesh.

Melchior:

- Sold! I deserve a holiday on a beautiful paradise planet after all the senseless murdering in the last few years!

Rangda:

- You'll love it. Get your armies ready. We are moving towards Elvonia in the morning.

Melchior:

- Great. I can't wait to kill some elves and have a relaxing holiday.

Rangda nodded and smiled maliciously. She had conveniently left out the fact that their visit to Elvonia wouldn't be much of a holiday as she intended to destroy the planet after stealing the Zeto Crystal. But why would anyone destroy this beautiful planet which could generate a lot of tourism income? Well, Rangda hadn't thought that far ahead, as she liked murdering more than she liked setting up tourism attractions!

Chapter 27 The True Maker Bugs Sabina with Another Mission

Sabina was playing hide & seek with her siblings Jasmine and Jordan like a typical three-year-old when the True Maker rudely interrupted with her latest follies. Sabina shook her head in disbelief and responded:

- You again? What do you want this time?

TTM:

- I had a small set-back. As it turns out, Rangda and Melchior killed all the Zetans, and now they are planning an unholy crusade to find and corrupt the Zeto crystals that contain my soul.

Sabina:

- That's not good. Did you come up with a good plan on how to stop this from happening?

TTM:

- Well, you are the Chosen One, the only one who can stop Rangda. On your 12th birthday, you'll face her and prevail.

Sabina:

- I asked you to come up with a good plan, not to reiterate your lousy plan.

- Why can't you find someone else, and deal with Rangda now instead of waiting for another nine years?

TTM:

- What is the thing with humans these days? Why is everyone questioning my ineffable plan?

Sabina:

- Because you make up your "ineffable" plan as you go, and have no idea what you are doing?

TTM:

- Yet, look at you. A three-year-old who speaks like an adult!

Sabina:

- ...

TTM:

- Ha-ha, got you! Your next mission is to deal with the evil Dov Dorevitch who has turned the Martian population into cannibalistic Zombies. To achieve this, you need to train a bunch of kids to pray to me and be kind and caring to people.

Sabina:

- How is that going to work?

Before the True Maker had the time to answer Sabina's question, Sabina's surrogate mother Melissa entered the room. She gave Sabina a disapproving look and spoke:

- So, here you are, talking to yourself. Dinner is served, and you're coming straight away to eat with your family.

Sabina:

- But Melissa. I am talking to the True Maker, the almighty god of the universe.

Melissa:

- I don't care. I am your mother, and you live in my house. So, you must follow my rules. You can talk to your imaginary friend later.

The True Maker saw an excellent opportunity to avoid answering Sabina's tough questions, so she quickly added in:

- Your mother is right. I am the almighty deity of the universe, but she is the mistress of her house. Go have dinner with your family, Sabina.

Having said this, the True Maker disconnected from Sabina's mind, and Sabina had no choice but to come with Melissa and suffer her terrible cooking!

Chapter 28 Frey and Freya seduces Hilda and Michael Muller.

Hilda Muller was meeting up with Michael Muller in her office. Being corporate giants and the most influential people on the planet, they occasionally had to do some work. Suddenly, they were interrupted when Frey and Freya entered the room. Hilda wasn't used to Norse fertility gods showing up unannounced and exclaimed:

- Who are you?

Frey:

- We are Frey and Freya.

Hilda:

- Oh, you must be Zetans? You are both ridiculously good-looking.

Freya:

- Thank you, Hilda. Being good-looking is part of our job descriptions.

Hilda:

- You are doing great jobs!
- So how can I help you guys?

Freya:

- Well, I am here to seduce you, Hilda.

Frey:

- And I am here to seduce Michael.

Freya:

- So, it would be helpful if you let us do our jobs.

Hilda:

- I would be happy to help!

Hilda winked seductively at Freya. Michael Muller was less comfortable with the conversation and exclaimed:

- Wait? What is going on? Why is the male God here to seduce me?

Frey:

- Well, because I am gay. Obviously.

Michael:

- But I am not gay, I have a family and several children.

Hilda:

- So, so. As happy as I'd be with Freya seducing me, Michael is right. I have a female partner and adding a man to the mix would be better for our relationship.

Freya:

- I understand. Well, I am happy to perform coitus with Michael. He is cute, a lot more attractive than Melchior Dorevitch.

Frey:

- Okay, I'll accept the change. Seducing Hilda was my original mission.

Michael:

- But what if my wife Magda finds out?

Hilda:

- No-one will tell her, and you'll have some good sex for once!

Michael:

- Okay. I accept the sex offer. Please give me a practical lesson in lovemaking!

Hilda:

- Cool, I'll call Melanie and tell her to come over. Then we'll have the best sex ever!

As Melanie arrived, they all got involved in an orgy, and they were having the best sex of their lives. Unfortunately for Michael, having sex with a fertility goddess had a noticeable side effect that wasn't good for his marriage, but more about that later!

Chapter 29: The Invasion of Elvonia

King Mellron of Elvonia, was chanting to celebrate the sunrise. While it was annoying to wake up early every morning to recite prayers, it was worth it. After all, he had been the king over a paradise planet without suffering for thousands of years. If all it took was to chant gibberish to a crystal, then so be it!

King Mellron and his aides were interrupted in their chanting when the portal on the other side of the temple opened. Had those annoying Zetan gods returned with their decrees and follies? While Mellron was grateful that the Zetans had turned Elvonia into a paradise, he was even more thankful that they had stopped showing up!

Mellron saw how creatures showed up on the other side of the temple. They were certainly not Zetans. Some of them looked like horrid humans, while the others were big grizzly-looking monsters that Mellron had never seen before. Mellron grabbed the Zeto crystal and commanded his entourage to grab their bows and meet with the heavily armed invaders.

As they reached the centre of the temple, Rangda yelled out:

- Mellron. I have come to steal your Zeto Crystal. If you surrender, I might let some of you live.

Mellron shouted back:

- I do not fear you. Your accomplices stand no chance against my Zeto Crystal. Leave now!

Rangda:

- I am not leaving without the crystal.

Mellron:

- So be it!

Having said this, Mellron lifted the Zeto Crystal and uttered a command, which incinerated Rangda's bodyguards with a holy white flame. Rangda counterattacked by lifting one of her corrupted Zeto Crystals and uttered a spell that made everyone in Mellron's entourage implode.

Seeing this Mellron exclaimed the obvious question:

- Wait a second. If I set all your bodyguards on fire with holy magic, and you crushed all my bodyguards with unholy magic. What was then the point of bringing others to the fight? And why didn't we target each other first?

Rangda was laughing hard from seeing all the death around her and replied:

- I don't know. You started it.

Mellron:

- Very well. And I will finish it! Simba, Zetani, Humanis!

Uttering his magic command, Mellron noticed that nothing happened. He yelled out in frustration:

- Why won't you die from the magic of my enchanted crystal?

Rangda knew the answer, but she wanted to tease Mellron, so she responded:

- Well, you should ask your boss, The True Maker.

Mellron:

- Good idea! True Maker, why is the Zeto Crystal not working?

The True Maker showed up as a mirage, visible to both Rangda and Mellron and replied:

- You defiled the Zeto Crystal when you decided to use it to indiscriminately murder people.

Mellron:

- But how could I know that would happen? That feature wasn't mentioned in the instruction manual you gave me!

As always when the True Maker was asked a question she couldn't respond to, she disappeared from the room.

Mellron was frustrated and started screaming obscenities to the True Maker:

- Fuck you, True Maker! I have woken up at 5 AM every morning for the last 3000 years to chant gibberish to that stupid crystal, and in the hour of need, you just disappear. What kind of Supreme Deity are you?

As expected, the True Maker didn't respond to Mellron's appropriate criticism, and he turned towards Rangda who was rolling on the floor laughing.

- Oh well, demon. It seems like we both have drained our crystals. Let's make this an epic battle between good and evil!

Rangda got up on her feet, smirked and replied:

- Perhaps. But you forget one thing. I have two more evil crystals that are still charged!

"Oh, shit" was the last thing Mellron said before Rangda blew him up with her unholy magic.

Rangda picked up the fallen Mellron's Zeto Crystal and was laughing maliciously when Melchior approached her. *What? Why did he survive?* she asked herself and as fate would have it, he responded to her question with his first statement:

- Hi Rangda. Sorry I am late. I overslept. What happened here?

Rangda:

- Mellron killed my entourage with his magical crystal. I responded by killing him and his entourage with my magical crystal.

Melchior:

- Whew. How lucky I overslept this morning!

Rangda answered with ground teeth:

- Yes... How lucky!

Rangda's woes worsened when George Smith and Grugmuk the Beer Belly also came into the temple through the portal. How was this even possible, that the three people she hated the most from her inner circle all survived Mellron indiscriminate massacre? Rangda realised that she should have made a roll call before she walked through the portal to Elvonia, to make sure that the people she despised died!

But it was too late now. Burning with anger, Rangda lifted the Zeto Crystal of Elvonia, corrupted it and doomed all life on the planet, as all the life forms on Elvonia were dependent on the benign effect of the Zeto Crystal to survive.

As Melchior watched the plants whither and animals die outside the temple, he felt disappointed, and he screamed out:

- What have you done, Rangda? You destroyed my dream holiday!

Rangda:

- Your holiday just got cancelled. Muahaha.

Melchior:

- Fuck you, Rangda!

Melchior screamed as he walked back through the portal to the Divine Dimension.

Chapter 30: Michael Muller Stares Down a Bottle and Wonders What Went Wrong.

A year later, Michael Muller was sitting drunk and alone in his office, which was now also his home. How could his marriage end this badly? Unlike his relatives, he had stayed faithful to his wife for over 30 years, but when a Zetan sex goddess came to seduce him, he had willingly had a lot of sex with her. Who wouldn't?

Unfortunately, as Freya was also a fertility goddess, she fell pregnant at the same time as Michael's niece Hilda and her partner Melanie fell pregnant to Frey. With this convincing evidence against him, Michael had admitted to his wife, Magda, that his many late-night accounting sessions at Hilda's office, was his encounters with Freya.

Finding out about this, Magda had acted very ungraciously and kicked Michael out of his house. What a bitch. Who wouldn't cheat if an actual goddess came to seduce him? What if Josef had kicked out Mary for her tryst with Yahweh? How different the world would have been!

Stuck with a semi-divine child, Michael had hoped that he could start a second family with Freya, who despite being thousands of years old, still looked younger and fresher than Magda. Yet again, he was disappointed. Frey and Freya had left Earth as soon as Hilda had provided them with a massive droid army to fight the Xenos, and Michael was stuck, being a single dad raising a demi-god child, and no one seemed to care about him.

As for Hilda's, Melanie's, and Michael's children, they never inherited any useful traits for the plot. Presumably, Jenna, Rocco, and Mia became great performers in the adult entertainment industry when they grew up.

Chapter 31: Rangda Plans to Scam the Dwarves of Their Zeto Crystal.

Sometime later, Melchior and Rangda's army reached the portal to Goldonia. Melchior was imagining, how great some fresh dwarven blood would taste when Rangda approached him, carrying silly costumes. She handed Melchior one of the dresses and spoke:

- Put on this costume, Melchior.

Melchior stared at Rangda in disbelief and replied:

- What is this? Are we attending a masquerade? I thought we had a planet to invade.

Rangda

- Well, I thought about it. Dwarves are foolhardy, and their tunnel networks are vast. If we invade, we might have to look for the crystal for years!

- But if we impersonate dwarven deities, they will give us the crystal if we request it.

Melchior:

- Okay.

- So, you plan to use the external DNA modifier to turn us into midgets, so we can trick the dwarves that we are their gods?

Rangda:

- Yeah, I thought about it. But I realised that I didn't have the DNA of the dwarven gods. So, I settled for just dressing like a dwarven deity.

Melchior:

- Wouldn't they question why their goddess is a two-metre-tall monstrosity?

Rangda:

- Nah, why would they? Humanity has a lot of gods that don't look human.

Melchior:

- Fair point.

Rangda:

- I have told you before. I am an evil genius.

- I will pretend to be the goddess Dumathoin, you and George will be playing the gods Moradin and Beronnar.

Melchior:

- Got it. Do you have their lines written down so we can practise?

Rangda:

- No. I'll do the talking. You and George will just stand behind me and nod when I introduce you.

Melchior:

- That's not acting. More like a featured extra.

Rangda:

- Don't bother me with insignificant details. Tell George to get ready. My evil plan is coming into fruition!

- Muahaha

After hearing this, Melchior rushed off to brief George about Rangda's stupid plan while Rangda stayed in the same spot and laughed maliciously.

Chapter 32: Chancellor Randall gives Rangda the Zeto Crystal to avoid hyperinflation

Chancellor Randall was looking out from the door to his underground kingdom. He held a gold nugget in his hand, and he stroke it gently. He loved gold so much, but he would have to part with this piece because dwarves needed to eat. Randall would lead a trade delegation to the town of the surface-dwelling dwarves, those poor buggers who had to work on the farms, in the sun and smell the fresh air. Randall pitied them!

Suddenly, Randall saw something that shocked him. The evil Xeno Empress Rangda Kaliankan dressed in a masquerade costume approached him. Instead of bringing her army, she had brought two humans, dressed in equally ridiculous costumes. *"Ready yourselves,"* Randall said to his bodyguards as he walked out to greet Rangda:

> - Greetings Empress Rangda Kaliankan! I am Chancellor Randall. What brings you to Goldonia?

Melchior smirked at Rangda, and she felt the embarrassment bubbling within her. She was nicknamed Rangda the Deceiver, but her attempt at deceiving the dwarves was dead in its tracks! Rangda replied:

> - I am not Rangda Kaliankan. I am the goddess Dumathoin. I don't understand. Why can't you recognise your own supreme goddess?

Randall's bodyguards broke out into intense laughter, but Randall managed to keep a straight face.

> - Rangda! The goddess Dumathoin is not two metres tall, and she is not wearing cheap outfits from the Dollar Store. Besides you look exactly like this poster.

Randall unpinned a laminated poster from the wall and handed it to Rangda. Rangda studied the pamphlet that was printed thousands of years earlier but was in a miraculously good condition. She realised that her first plan had failed and replied:

- Okay. I admit. I am the Xeno Empress Rangda Kaliankan.

- I have come in peace with a great offer for you.

- Hand me the primordial Zeto Crystal of Goldonia, and I will land the Psyche-16 asteroid, which is full of gold, safely on the surface of Goldonia.

- I'll make you all wealthy!

Randall looked at Rangda and scoffed at her in disapproval:

- Have you ever heard about inflation? Don't you realise that our entire economy would collapse upon the influx of so much gold!

To Rangda's great anger, George Smith got involved in the conversation:

- Chancellor Randall is right, Rangda. You should read up on economic theory. Introducing billions of tonnes of gold won't make anyone rich!

Rangda ground her teeth in anger and eventually responded:

- Okay, how about you give me the Zeto Crystal if I promise to not land the massive gold asteroid on Goldonia?

Randall:

- That's an acceptable deal. We don't care about magical crystals and other superstitions. Just hold tight, and I'll go fetch it for you.

Randall left, and a short while later he returned with the Zeto Crystal. He handed it to Rangda and spoke:

- Here you go, Rangda.

- I hope this token of friendship will you prevent you from invading our planet or destroying our economy.

Rangda:

- Yes, of course. I am a benevolent empress!

Rangda bowed, put the crystal in her pocket and returned to the Divine Dimension.

As they got back, Melchior drooled and spoke:

- So, are we invading now that you got the crystal? Muahaha

Rangda gave him a blank stare and replied:

- Of course not, that would be unnecessary.

Melchior looked at her with sad eyes and replied:

- But Rangda, I am hungry...

Rangda:

- Well, we'll return to Goldonia and buy food like civilised species.

- But I do have an evil master plan for Goldonia.

- I will land that golden asteroid and destroy their economy. You see, I have invaded and destroyed many planets. But I have never destroyed an economy through landing a giant golden asteroid. When you have lived as long as I have, you must come up with novel ways of being evil to keep life interesting. Muahaha

Melchior:

- Well, if it is evil, I am satisfied. Muahaha

After this, they both laughed maliciously over their wicked schemes and shenanigans

Chapter 33: Rangda is Almost Killed During Sparring.

A few months later, Melchior saw Rangda, as she was sparring against her Xenos with ancient-looking swords and shields. Melchior rubbed his eyes. Why in the Milky Way was Rangda sparring with ancient swords and armour? This was the future, if she really had to fight with swords, she should fight with plasma swords, the in-universe version of lightsabres.

Melchior decided to find out and shouted out her name. Rangda got distracted, and she forgot to parry the swing by her nameless Xeno sparring partner and got hit in the head. The strike was hard enough to kill anyone who wasn't powered by evil magical crystals, but fortunately, Rangda WAS powered by evil magical crystals, so she was just a bit dizzy. Rangda approached Melchior on unsteady legs.

Rangda:

- Why did you distract me? You could have killed me. Imagine if the infamous Xeno Empress Rangda Kaliankan was killed when sparring. That would destroy my legacy.

Melchior:

- My apologies, Empress Rangda. I was simply curious why you were sparring with medieval swords. Are we attending a renaissance fair? I thought we had a planet to invade and a magical crystal to steal?

Rangda turned to the side and vomited out a large heap of green bile, and then she spoke weakly:

- Uhm, sorry about that. I am vomiting from the severe concussion that should have killed me!

- I will seek medical aid shortly, but I will reveal my evil plan first!

- I intend to challenge King Gromm for the throne of Grashdunt. The tournament rules are that the fight must take place with medieval weapons in the main battle arena.

Melchior:

- But since when do you care about following rules and respecting local customs? I thought you were Rangda, the Deceiver?

Rangda:

- Well, I'd rather have millions of bloodthirsty orcs fighting for me, than fighting against me.

Melchior:

- But do you really have what it takes to defeat this monstrous orc in single combat? You almost got killed by your nameless henchman during sparring.

Rangda:

- Nameless? Are you for real? I was sparring against Ramban the Strong.

Melchior:

- Is he essential for the plot?

Rangda:

- Not at all!

- Now if you excuse me, I must go to the medical ward to get treatment for my grievous head injury. Talk to you later, Melchior!

Melchior watched Rangda as she was heading to the medical ward, leaving a trail of blueish Xeno-Zetan blood. He shook his head at Rangda's stupid plan. If she almost got killed by her own henchman during training, how was she going to defeat an infamous orc in single combat? On the bright side, if King Gromm killed Rangda, Melchior would be the boss of the army, and he could use futuristic weapons to subjugate the orcs and steal their magical crystal. Muahaha!

Chapter 34: Rangda is saved by a loophole in the competition rules.

A few weeks later, Rangda had recovered from her grievous head injuries and felt as good as new. At least as fresh as someone who was over 10,000 years old could feel. Rangda studied her opponent on the other side of the arena and realised that it would have been a better option to invade the planet with futuristic weapons than fighting the behemoth that was in front of her. Rangda could hear the presenter introduce the fighters.

- In the blue corner, standing at 2 metres and weighing in at 120 kilos, the challenger for the throne: Empress Rangda Kaliankan of the Xenos.

- In the red corner, standing at 6 metres and weighing in at 4 tonnes, the king of Grashdunt, King Gromm.

- Let's get ready to Rumble!

Rangda reflected over the improbability in that she understood and could communicate with the orcs, but anything seemed possible in her life!

The Gong went off, and Rangda charged at the leg of King Gromm and tried to slash him with her sword. Unfortunately, Gromm's thick metal greaves were impenetrable, and the only thing happening was that Rangda hurt her hand and dropped her sword. "Oh, shit," she thought as she noticed Gromm's giant club swinging at her.

Rangda would have been better off dodging than thinking, and she was knocked like a cricket ball, flying straight into the stone wall surrounding the arena. Ouch!

Rangda could hear the presenter and the crowd cheering:

- What a strike by King Gromm. Impressive strength. Empress Rangda is the most pathetic contender for the throne this far!

- Finish her, King Gromm!

Rangda saw the behemoth approaching her and realised that the only way to win would be to cheat. *"Here goes nothing,"* she thought as she pulled out her corrupted Zeto Crystal and used its dark powers to blow up King Gromm.

This upset the crowd, and they started chanting *"Kill the cheater!"* Fortunately for Rangda, Melchior, who could also communicate with the orcs intervened:

- Empress Rangda did not cheat. Using the magical powers of a corrupted Zeto Crystal is not disallowed by the competition rules, chapter 5.4.

The baffled umpires studied the rule book and concluded that Melchior was right. The rules dictated that only weapons invented before 1200 A.D was allowed, but since the Zeto Crystals were eternal objects that had always existed, they were permitted in the duel.

Thus, Melchior saved Rangda's ass from 1.2 million angry orcs and instead of lynching her, they promoted her to be their evil empress! Nice work, Melchior!

Chapter 35: Please take our gold, Zetans!

Meanwhile, Frey and Freya arrived at Goldonia with the robot army they were given as a parting gift by Hilda Muller. Freya wasn't happy:

- I can't believe we left our beloved children with the humans, to travel to the other end of the Milky Way to fight Rangda.

Frey:

- What's the matter, Freya? We are gods to the humans. I am sure they'll look after our kids.

Freya:

- That's the irresponsible attitude that only a man would have.
- Remember what happened to Yahweh's son? He was nailed to a bloody cross!

Frey:

- Come on Freya, most of Yahweh's children ended up fine. It was only the one who was obnoxious and kept pissing off his contemporaries, that was brutally murdered. On the bright side, he became incredibly famous after his death!

Freya:

- If you say so. I just hope that little Rocco will grow up fine.

Frey:

- Oh, I am sure he'll copulate with a lot of humans. As will my daughters. You know what? Once we have killed Rangda and, saved the galaxy, I will go back to Earth to watch them grow up. I will be so proud when they feature in human copulation movies.

439

Freya:

- Human Copulation movies? What is that?

Frey:

- They call it porn. Apparently, it's common for humans to film themselves having sex and then show it to others.

Freya:

- How absurd...

Freya was interrupted from bashing porn, when Chancellor Randall approached her.

- Greetings Zetans. Can you please take most of our gold away?

Freya stared at him in disbelief:

- I do not know which is the most shocking revelation today, that humans' film themselves having coitus or that a dwarf asks me to take his gold away?

Randall:

- Humans' film themselves having coitus. That's absurd.

- While my request might seem strange, it has a perfectly reasonable explanation.

- The dwarven way of life is centred around digging up gold from underground caves.

Frey:

- Yeah, that's an absurd lifestyle when you could fly to the golden asteroid in your star system and collect as much gold as you need.

Randall:

- Anyways. Rangda threatened to land the giant golden asteroid on Goldonia unless we gave her the primordial Zeto Crystal. I realised the implications for our economy and gave her the crystal. Then she landed the golden asteroid anyway, out of spite!

Freya:

- Oh, that's nice of her. That saves you from toiling away for the next 5,000 years in those stupid mines.

Randall:

- The evil witch undermined our economy and destroyed our purpose for living. Gold used to be worth a fortune. Now a loaf of bread is five kilos of gold. You need a wheelbarrow to do your grocery shopping!

Frey:

- Well find something else, that is rare enough to signify value. We really don't care about your gold.

Randall:

- You take away our excess gold straight away. Use your Zetan magic!

Freya:

- There is no such thing as Zetan magic, only advanced technologies. And we never invented technologies to get rid of excess gold. Now piss off.

Randall:

- If you don't steal our gold, I'll kill you. Argh!

Having said that, Randall pulled a knife and tried to stab Freya. Fortunately, Frey had fast reflexes and decapitated Randall with his plasma sword. Frey looked up. They were surrounded by a horde of angry dwarves, and there was only one solution. To run back to the portal as quickly as possible.

Frey and Freya managed to get through the portal and closed it behind them just in time to avoid the angry dwarves, and they collapsed to the ground in the Divine Dimension. The world had turned crazy. Thousands of dwarves had just tried to kill them for refusing to steal their gold. Exhausted from their sprint Frey and Freya passed out from exertion.

Chapter 36 Frey Realises That He Should Have Paid for the Android Antivirus.

An undisclosed time later, Frey and Freya woke up and realised that they were surrounded by Rangda's army. It was just as well that Rangda came to them, so they could finally test House Muller's Xeno killing robots and end Rangda once and for all!

Rangda:

> - Muahaha. The last Zetans. I got you surrounded do you have any final words.

Freya:

> - Your reign of Terror will end today, Rangda. We have brought an army Xeno killing robots that Hilda Muller gave us for rocking the bed and knocking her up!

Rangda:

> - Yes, I can see that you brought a lot of robots. But did you remember to update their antivirus program?

Freya:

> - Of course, we did. Do you think we are completely retarded?

Frey:

> - Uhm, I think my credit card payment for the antivirus bounced.

Freya:

> - What? And you are telling me this now?

Frey:

- Well, the issue somehow slipped my mind.

Freya:

- You are an idiot! That was your only job.

Rangda:

- Muahaha, when I press this button, you're finished.

Rangda picked up a futuristic tablet and pressed a button to hack the drone army. A few seconds later, all the drones turned off.
Rangda:

- Muahaha.
- Any last words?

Frey:

- Oh shit!

After that, the Xeno horde attacked Frey and Freya and tore them into shreds ending the Zetan species. It was unfortunate that they couldn't come up with more profound last words, but such is life!

Chapter 37: The True Maker Sends Sabina on a Mission to Mars

Sabina was playing a video game with her siblings Jordan and Jasmine. It felt nice that the True Maker hadn't bothered her for a while with her prophecies and follies. Without the True Maker in her life, Sabina was just your average spoiled rich kid, with the bonus that she was "The Chosen One" so here surrogate mother couldn't put her in place. Suddenly, The True Maker appeared as a vision, distracting Sabina, and causing her to die in the online video game!

Sabina:

- No, no, no. I have had such an enjoyable time in your absence. What is it now?

TTM:

- Frey and Freya's expedition to lead a robot army to stop Rangda failed miserably, and yet again you're the only hope to save the Milky Way Galaxy.

Sabina:

- How did it fail? I thought you said it was a great plan and I could just sit back and chill, without all this the Chosen One nonsense?

TTM:

- Well, I did, but I overlooked something that Rangda exploited.

Sabina:

- Spit it out!

TTM:

- Uhm. Apparently, there is something called computer viruses. Rangda used that to destroy all the Xeno-killing robots that Frey and Freya had brought to stop her. Alas, the last Zetans are dead, and you are the only one who can stop Rangda.

Sabina:

- Computer viruses? Why didn't they install antivirus and firewalls on the robots?

TTM:

- I am sorry, but neither of those words mean anything to me.

Sabina:

- Wait, aren't you the almighty, omnipotent creator of the universe?

TTM:

- Yes, but I have been around for a trillion years. At my advanced age, it gets harder and harder to learn about new technological innovations!

- Anyways. I need you to go to Mars and stop Dov Dorevitch at once!

Sabina:

- You are an idiot!
- What will happen if I refuse to take part in your foolish plan?

TTM:

- Then I will have to blow up the entire Milky Way Galaxy to stop Rangda.

Sabina:

- You are a terrible boss, but I accept your request. I will tell my dad Metatron that we are heading to Mars to singlehandedly stop the villainous Dov Dorevitch and his dangerous mutant army.

TTM:

- That's the spirit, Sabina. That is why you are the Chosen One!

Sabina:

- Cut it out! I am so excited to die a senseless premature death to do your bidding, don't rub it in. Talk to you later!

Sabina left the room. To her great annoyance, she realised that the mirage of The True Maker kept stalking her until she had convinced Metatron to partake in the foolish divine plan.

Chapter 38: Dov Turns Good and Dies from Drinking Holy Water.

A few months later, Dov Dorevitch was taking part in his daily routine: drinking beer and executing people that angered him, when Frank Van Stein approached him in his throne room:

- A delegation from Eden has arrived Master Dov.

Dov:

- Oh, I hope it's my mum. I haven't heard from her in ages.

Frank:

- Uhm, Melchior incinerated her with an orbital laser to prove a point to Metatron.

Dov:

- Oh. So, she died?

Frank:

- That's usually the outcome when you set people on fire.

Dov:

- Shit! That bastard.
- Anyway, who is coming to visit me then?

Frank:

- Melchior and his daughter Sabina. We are better off blowing up their ship, as rumour has it, she is the Chosen One.

Dov:

- Well if she is the Chosen One, she is just what the Martians need. We will welcome her with open arms.

Frank:

- But what the Martians need is to get rid of our tyranny. The arrival of the Chosen One is not in our interest.

Dov:

- Don't be a sourpuss. I am sure Sabina will be a perfectly safe and cute seven-year-old girl. Do invite them.

Frank:

- I don't like this, Boss. But as you wish!

A while later Sabina and Metatron arrived at the gothic reception area of Dov's Palace. It had a mix of styles. Fountains depicting impaled bodies pumping blood to satisfy Melchior's preferences, and big-screen TVs showing sports with a large assortment of beers to meet Dov's preferences. Dov smirked when he saw Sabina enter the throne room. How could his pathetic advisor be afraid of this little girl?

Without hesitation, Sabina walked up to Dov, grabbed his arm, stared into his eyes, and spoke:

- Dov Dorevitch, stop being evil.

Dov looked back at Sabina with a blank gaze and replied:

- I am no longer evil.

Frank:

- Oh shit!

When Dov suddenly became a good guy, he pondered what his first action as a reasonable person would be. He looked at Frank Van Stein and realised that murdering the villain who released the zombie apocalypse, that wasn't a real zombie apocalypse, would be a great start. He pulled up his plasma sword and cut off Frank's head.

Dov:

- Ah, feels good to be one of the good guys!

Metatron:

- Good guys? You just chopped off the head of your right-hand-man!

Dov:

- It was for a noble cause. Frank was an evil man, so I used my bloodlust to do good!

Sabina:

- That's okay guys. Don't argue.

- By the power of the True Maker, I forgive you if you pledge the rest of your life to do good.

Dov:

- I do. We will turn Mars into the paradise it is meant to be. We will stop Rangda's and Melchior's evil plan to corrupt the Zeto Crystals and conquer the Milky Way Galaxy!

Sabina:

- Great. Welcome on board. Please drink this Holy Water. It will detoxify your body of evil.

Dov:

- With pleasure.

Dov grabbed Sabina's bottle of Holy Water and skolled the bottle. But he shouldn't have as the Holy Water set him ablaze from within and killed him.

Metatron:

- Nice move, Sabina. I didn't think you had it in you to deceive and murder someone like that. But Dov deserved to die!

Sabina:

- I didn't mean to kill him. It was meant to detoxify his body from evil. I don't know why he was set ablaze!

Metatron picked up the bottle and read the warning label aloud:

- Holy Water: Use only as directed. If used by evil, or formerly evil persons, make sure to dilute the product and only consume small quantities to avoid adverse side effects.

Sabina:

- Oh really? I forgot to read the warning label.

Metatron:

- You're an idiot!

Sabina:

- Look! I am seven years old. You are my father. You should have read the warning label for me.

Metatron:

- Point taken. But for the future record, this was the divine plan! I am not going to look the fool who inadvertently killed the newly redeemed arch-villain of our solar system.

Sabina:

- Agreed. Let's say that we meant to kill Dov this way.

Having said this, Sabina and Metatron accessed the PA system and announced that Dov and Frank were dead, and that Metatron was the new leader for Mars. No-one had any objections, and there were celebrations all over the planet, although a few breweries went out of business!

Chapter 39: Hilda Muller meets Sabina and Metatron on Mars

A few months later, Hilda visited Sabina and Metatron in the presidential palace of the Olympic Republic. She was a bit anxious over travelling so far to meet the people that she forcefully expelled from her office on their last meeting, but at least the fat menace Dov Dorevitch was dead, so it was fitting that Hilda showed up to express her support.

Hilda entered the throne room. Instead of blood fountains and beer taps, the room was filled with video games and pink toy ponies. Certainly, an improvement, but not very statesmanlike! Sabina clapped her hands and spoke sarcastically:

- Look what the cat dragged in! I am considering expelling you from my office to get payback for five years ago.

Hilda replied irritably:

- You dragged me all the way to Mars, so you could kick me out of your office. I thought you were the Chosen One, not some spoiled kid!

Sabina:

- Oh yeah. The Chosen One. Now I remember why I asked you to come over.

Hilda:

- And that is?

Sabina:

- I need you to find the primordial Terran Zeto Crystal, also known as the Holy Grail, that is hidden in the Templar Tunnels under the Solomon Temple in Jerusalem.

Hilda:

- I see. So, you dragged me all the way here, to give me, the Leader of the Terran Council, instructions for a job on Earth! Couldn't you just have called?

Sabina:

- Well, I guess. But it's more fun dragging you all the way here.

Sabina noticed how Hilda looked close to explode in anger, but she intervened before Hilda's outburst:

- But honestly. I needed you to come here so I could give you the magical power to unlock the door to the secret chamber where the Zeto Crystal is stored.

Sabina shook Hilda's hand, and Hilda started smiling. It felt good to have some divine powers!

Hilda:

- I feel so invigorated. What powers did you share with me?

Sabina:

- Only the power to sense the location of the Zeto Crystal and unlock the door.

Hilda:

- Come on. I came all the way here. Give me something cool. Like shooting lasers with my eyes or raising the dead.

Sabina:

- No way. I wouldn't be unique if I gave you all my powers!
- Do you accept your crucial mission to save humankind?

Hilda:

  - Yes. Yes, I do.

Sabina:

  - Good. Now I will say something I have been longing to say for the last five years!

Hilda:

  - And what is that?

Sabina:

  - Get the fuck out of my office!

Hilda being smarter than Metatron realised that there was no point in arguing with Sabina. But Hilda felt very annoyed. Sabina Eisenstein, the Chosen One, was such spoiled brat!

Chapter 40: Hilda Finds the Zeto Crystal and Realises That Sabina was Playing Her Around.

A few weeks later, Hilda Muller arrived in Jerusalem. She was exhausted and grumpy. Even though her command ship was luxurious, it wasn't as good her penthouse on Earth. Hilda was also worried about the damage that her uncle Michael Muller would have caused to her faction in her absence. But Hilda couldn't focus on making money yet. First, she had to find stupid Zeto Crystal so the Chosen One could be bothered to save the galaxy from Rangda.

Hilda's mood didn't improve when she met with the manager of the Solomon Temple, Adam Finkelstein.

Hilda:

  - I need access to the Templar Tunnels.

Adam:

  - Why do you bother me about that? They have tours open to the public.

Hilda:

  - Yes, but I need to find a hidden magical relic. I need to find the Terran Primordial Zeto Crystal.

Adam:

  - That name sounds very fictional. Who sent you on that quest?

Hilda:

  - Sabina Eisenstein, also known as, The Chosen One.

Adam:

- Oh, the SpaceTube phenomena? Isn't she cute? I didn't know you were a fan!

Hilda:

- Not really, but someone must save the planet from the evil space demon Rangda!

Adam:

- Okay. If you say so. I will take you and your bodyguards on a guided tour around the tunnels!

Hilda and Adam got up, and they started walking around the tunnels. Eventually, Hilda felt a strange ping in her brain, and she knew what it meant. The Zeto Crystal was nearby!

Hilda:

- I can feel it. The Zeto Crystal is behind that door!
- Now I must use my supernatural divine powers to open the door.

Adam:

- Or you can just open it like ordinary people do. Turn the handle and push the door. The Swingler Sapphire is part of our tour.

Before Hilda had the time to respond, Adam opened the door and showed her the priceless Swingler Sapphire, also known as the Terran Primordial Zeto Crystal. Hilda ground her teeth in frustration. The spoiled brat Sabina could have told her to go to Jerusalem and get the Swingler Sapphire. So much for supernatural powers and premonitions. But then Hilda stopped being angry and realised the breathtaking truth: The Swingler Sapphire was indeed The Primordial Zeto Crystal and she needed to get it for safekeeping!

Hilda:

- Thank you, Adam. This is just what we need. I'll bring this back to our vault for safekeeping.

Adam:

- Not so fast, this priceless religious relic belongs to the Templar Tunnels Museum.

Hilda:

- But I am the Terran Council leader. I need that Crystal to stop Rangda from conquering the galaxy.

Adam:

- That might be. But we still own the sapphire. I am willing to sell it to you. For a price.

Hilda:

- How much?

Adam:

- 1 billion Terran Credits.

Hilda:

- What? That's ridiculously expensive. I can just steal it from you.

Adam:

- Perhaps. But imagine the bad publicity. "German leader stealing priceless Jewish religious relic from The Solomon Temple.

Hilda ground her teeth in frustration. Being German, she was used to being vilified as the bad guy, and if she stole the damn crystal, she would never hear the end of it. She grudgingly paid up and left with the Zeto Crystal. Saving humankind was an expensive endeavour!

Chapter 41: Rangda Finds Out that Hilda has the Zeto Crystal and Devices a Plan

A few months later, Melchior Dorevitch was drinking some elvish blood and reading the news on his tablet via Spacenet. Spacenet, the internet of the future, had such good coverage, so it even reached Melchior in another dimension!

Rangda entered his room and stared at the tablet in disbelief. How could this be possible? The news article had a picture of the Terran Zeto Crystal and the following headline **"Hilda Muller loses the plot; believes she is the Chosen One and pays a billion Terran Credits for the Swingler Sapphire.
"**

Rangda:

- Melchior! Why haven't you told me about this news article?

Melchior yawned and replied:

- I didn't think you cared about celebrity gossip. Who cares if Hilda spends a billion on jewellery? We are going to invade and eat her soon anyway. Muahaha

Rangda:

- That is the Terran Zeto Crystal, you dimwit. And now it belongs to one of our greatest enemies!

Melchior:

- So, if it was available for sale, why didn't you steal it during your last invasion of Earth?

Rangda:

- How could I foresee that such a priceless artefact would be sold as simple jewellery on Earth? Anyway, we need to move at once!

Melchior:

  - Understood. Should I prepare our troops for another invasion?

Rangda:

  - No, I have a much better plan. Muahaha

Melchior:

  - As you wish Empress Rangda, as you wish.

Once Rangda had explained her plan to Melchior and left, he was sitting with a smug smile on his face. The crazy bitch would get herself killed, and then he would be the evil god-emperor of the Milky Way Galaxy!

Chapter 42: Michael Muller is Seduced and Loses His Head.

Michael Muller was checking his calendar appointments. Apparently, Sabina Eisenstein and Metatron were coming by to collect the expensive Zeto Crystal that Hilda had spent a billion credits on. Michael feared for the annual general meeting. Repelling an invasion of man-eating aliens were challenging, but it would be even more difficult to explain to his relatives why Hilda had spent so much money on a sapphire and then gave it away to an eight-year-old girl.

Hilda had claimed that the sapphire purchase was to save humanity from our extinction but that claim seemed far-fetched to say the least!

As Michael prepared himself for the meeting, he got a notification on his work phone. Helen of Troy wanted to meet him. The announcement filled Michael with hesitation. His wife, Magda, had finally forgiven him for his tryst and love child Rocco, whom he had with Freya. Was it wise to have an affair with another Zetan? Then he checked the pictures of Helen of Troy and concluded that he was a dog, and he would cheat on his wife again!

Another notification popped up. It was from Hilda who urged Michael to come down to the reception area to meet with Metatron and Sabina. Michael realised his opportunity: He could have sex with the most beautiful woman in the history of humankind in the chairman office of Europeum Tower!

"Meet me at Hilda's office in five minutes" he texted to Helen, while he hacked Hilda's office and turned off the security cameras.

Five minutes later, Michael was in Hilda's office and very ready to cheat on his wife when Helen entered the room.

Helen/Rangda:

- Good day, sexy.

Michael:

- We don't have much time, but I promise to be quick!

Helen:

  - That's a very off-putting thing to say!

  - How about you show me the Swingler Sapphire? I have heard so much about it, and I would love to see it with my own eyes.

Hearing this gave Michael a moment of hesitation. What if he was getting scammed and Helen was here to steal the Swingler Sapphire? Then he realised that time was short, and he needed to get some booty. Michael opened Hilda's safe and took out the Zeto Crystal.

Michael:

  - This is it, my sexy goddess. It's beautiful, isn't it?

Helen:

  - Yes. Are the security cameras turned off?

Michael:

  - Yes, we'll have a private moment. Without my wife ever finding out.

Hearing this, Rangda started laughing maliciously and revealed her true form.

Michael:

  - Oh, fuck!

Rangda:

  - Michael. I have come to kill you and steal the Zeto Crystal!

Michael:

  - Couldn't you have killed me as the beautiful Helen so I would die happy?

Rangda:

- I could have. But I am evil and want you to die miserably!

"Bitch!" was the last thing Michael exclaimed before Rangda decapitated him with her sharp claws. Rangda then reverted to her beautiful Helen of Troy appearance and put the primordial Zeto Crystal in her purse. Rangda left the office, walking past all the incompetent and unsuspecting guards on the way out

Chapter 43: Sabina Decides That is Time to Deal with Rangda.

A couple of hours later, Hilda, Metatron and Sabina watched the headless Michael in Hilda's office. The first reflection about this is that Metatron wouldn't win the parent of the year award, allowing an eight-year-old to visit a gruesome murder scene. But when your child is the Chosen One, other parenting rules apply!

Hilda studied her empty safe and spoke:

- What a shame. I spent a billion Terran Credits on that sapphire, and now it is gone.

Sabina:

- Wait for a second! The Zeto Crystal was stolen by the evil Space Demon Rangda Kaliankan. The future of humanity is at stake, and you worry about the money?

Hilda:

- Well, the doomsday won't be for a while. But I lost a lot of money today!

Sabina:

- You're incredibly greedy and short-sighted!

Hilda:

- That's capitalism for you!

Metatron:

- So, so, ladies. Let's not argue about politics. Rangda has all the Zeto Crystals and is now unstoppable. So, what do we do?

Sabina:

- Well. I guess I will just have to go to the Divine Dimension and stop her?

Metatron:

- But isn't she unstoppable?

Sabina:

- Well, stopping unstoppable villains is the work of the Chosen One! My time has finally come.

Hilda:

- While you are stopping Rangda, can you also bring back the Swindler Sapphire? The accounting department will make my life miserable over this.

Sabina:

- Nope. Not my problem. My mission is to stop the destruction of the universe, not cooking your books!

Suddenly, the True Maker appeared in the room and felt compelled to join in on the conversation:

- Sabina. You are not meant to go yet. I intend for you to confront Rangda on your 12th birthday just before the galaxy is doomed.

Sabina:

- Or I could just stop her now. You know being proactive and all.

The True Maker:

- That's true. I never thought that far. Well, then, I have no objections.
- Best of luck, humans!

Having said this, the True Maker disappeared, and Hilda tentatively spoke:

- Hey, Sabina. You weirdo. Who were you talking to?

Sabina:

- Oh. I forgot how silly I look when I speak to the True Maker when other people are around. I'll go and deal with Rangda tomorrow. Can you hitch me a flight to the portal in Egypt?

Hilda:

- Sure. Have your beauty sleep, little girl. Tomorrow you'll save humanity, and we'll all be heroes.

- Would you mind resurrection Michael by the way?

Sabina:

- I would mind. The dimwit tried to cheat on his wife and got killed by our greatest enemy that stole our magical crystal. There are more worthy candidates for resurrection!

Hilda:

- Fair point.
- Oh well. See you tomorrow!

Chapter 44: Sabina blasts Metatron too hard to save him from himself.

The following day, Sabina, Metatron, Hilda Muller and a large contingent of House Muller troops stood outside the portal to the Divine Dimension in the ruins of the city of Rashidium. The portal was glowing beautifully, and it would be enticing if there weren't an army of man-eating aliens on the other side of the portal.

Hilda spoke to Sabina:

- Sabina, this is where our ways part. I hope you are not upset that my army and I are not joining you in the battle against the unbeatable demon queen Rangda?

Sabina:

- That's okay. No point for you Germans to face another humiliating military defeat.

Hilda:

- Lucky we are not Americans. Then we'd join you, get our asses handed to us and make it look like we won the war!

Sabina:

- Yes, that would be even sillier.

Hilda:

- Cool. Do you need some weapon and armour? We have the latest and coolest plasma swords and mechanised armour. Way better than those white rags and sandals you are currently wearing.

Sabina:

- I agree. But the divine plan wants me to wear this pathetic outfit.

Hilda:

- Cool. Well, best of luck. I am getting the hell out of here before the shit hits the fan!

After Hilda had rushed off, Metatron looked at his young daughter, and they had the kind of father-daughter moment that only can occur moments before you send your eight-year-old child to face an evil space demon in another dimension.

Metatron:

- I wish I could come with you, so you wouldn't have to face Rangda and Melchior alone.

Sabina:

- You can, the portal is just over there.

Metatron:

- Oh yes, I will stand by you to the end. Together we will face Rangda!

Hearing this, Sabina realised that she had messed up. If Metatron came with her to face Rangda, he would be eaten in two seconds by Rangda's army as he wasn't protected by the True Maker. While it would look good for the future movie for Metatron to make a senseless sacrifice, it would be a nightmare to explain to Melissa and her siblings why she had sacrificed their beloved husband and father for no reason whatsoever.

Sabina:

- No, dad. I cannot allow you to come with me and die for no reason. I'd happily bring some of the German soldiers, but I must keep you safe.

Metatron:

- But what kind of father would I be if allowed my daughter to face
an evil space demon on her own?

Sabina:

- About as bad father as you would be bringing your daughter to
face an evil space demon!

Having said this, Sabina looked anxiously on her watch. It was noontime
and Rangda could destroy the galaxy at any time. Sabina realised that she
needed to finish the family argument the quickest way possible. She blasted
Metatron with a psionic blast, and he dropped to the ground bleeding from
his eyes. Uh-oh did you just kill your dad, while trying to protect him, Sabina? How lucky you can revive him when you get back!

Sabina thought the same thing, and she walked through the portal to
face Rangda!

Chapter 45: Bureaucracy prevails.

Sabina was walking towards Rangda's unholy temple in the Divine Dimension. The Temple was currently a construction site as Sabina had refused to sit by for four years doing nothing while waiting for her 12th birthday. Sabina walked confidently, as she was covered by a magical bright light that stopped all projectiles and burnt everyone that approached her.

Eventually, she reached the gates of the temple, where she faced an impassable enemy. The Construction Site Supervisor.

Supervisor:

- Stop right there. I need to see your licenses to enter this construction site. Furthermore, since you are a minor, I need your legal guardian to sign all the forms for you.

Sabina:

- Hold on. Why are you not burned by my holy white light?

Supervisor:

- Because I am not evil. I am just a bureaucrat who wants to ensure that construction sites are safe. Please provide your full name.

Sabina:

- Oh, I see.

- Keila Eisenstein Silver.

- Well, I accidentally killed my father Jack Silver with a psionic blast just ten minutes ago. But my mother is locked up inside the temple. She can sign the form for me.

Supervisor:

- Okay. What's your mother's name?

Sabina:

- Keila Eisenstein.

Supervisor:

- Okay. I'll call the boss to verify.

The supervisor called Rangda on his hologram phone, and she was responding while she was wearing a bib and baking a cake:

- What is it?

Supervisor:

- Sabina Eisenstein is here to see you.

Rangda:

- You idiot. Why did you put the phone on hologram mode? Do you realise how bad this baking a cake thing is for my image as a super-villain?

Supervisor:

- Apologies Rangda.

- Anyway, she'll need parental consent to enter this construction site, and she claims that her mother Keila Eisenstein, who is your prisoner, can sign the form.

Rangda stood silent for a while and then roared back at the supervisor:

- Are you for real? You expect me to bring my prized prisoner to the gate for a signature. Just let Sabina in so we can have our climactic battle!

Supervisor:

- Sorry, but that is not going to happen. Construction site security is paramount, and our rules must be followed. Otherwise, we'll cancel our contract with you.

Rangda:

- Oh my. Bureaucracy! Not even I can fight it. Very well, I'll bring Keila so we can sign your stupid indemnification forms so we can have our decisive battle!

Supervisor:

- Good. I'll see you in a while.

A while later Rangda came down to the gate with Keila in tow. As Keila signed the papers, Rangda gave the construction site supervisor a hateful glare, but she had to suppress her murderous tendencies, as it was too challenging to commission another construction company to do construction work in the Divine Dimension!

When all the papers were signed, Rangda spoke:

- Sabina, meet me in the main hall in one hour. I need to prepare my outfit and appearance for our ultimate battle. I look ridiculous now, with my bib and flour on my face.

Sabina:

- Fair enough. I am happy to wait for an hour. After all, I came four years earlier than you expected.

Rangda:

- That's thoughtful of you. Keila, you are coming with me. I want you to see your daughter's ultimate failure to stop me from conquering the universe. Muahaha

Chapter 46: A Construction Site Showdown!

An hour later, Sabina was waiting in the main hall of Rangda's temple. It was a pretty sad sight and looked like your average construction site with a concrete floor and full of wooden boxes. Not as menacing as Rangda had wanted it to be! Just as Sabina beat the world record in the mobile phone game "Snake", Rangda and Melchior arrived bringing Keila in chains.

Rangda:

- Muahaha. Our final showdown has come. Today the decisive battle between good and evil will take place.

Sabina:

- Sounds good, I wasn't too keen to wait for another four years!

Rangda:

- Very well. First, you'll face off with Melchior, and if you are victorious, you'll get to fight me. Muahaha.

Melchior:

- I do not want to fight Sabina. I am just the right-hand-man without any magical abilities.

Rangda:

- If you don't fight her, Melchior, I will kill you!

Melchior:

- Damn. I am really stuck between a rock and a hard place am I not?

Rangda:

  - Yes.
  - Attack, Melchior!

Melchior realised that he'd rather take his chances fighting the unarmed eight-year-old Sabina than the evil space demon Rangda. Melchior charged at Sabina with his plasma sword, and when he was about to hit her, she grabbed his arm and uttered:

  - Stop being evil.

This potent and highly effective spell stopped Melchior from being evil. With hypnotised eyes, he turned towards Rangda and uttered:

  - I am no longer evil.

Having said this, he rushed towards Rangda, who replied:

  - For fuck's sake, Melchior!

And then Rangda blew up Melchior with her magical crystals. Rangda turned towards Sabina and hissed:

  - Damn you, Sabina. Damn the True Maker. Now I'll have to find a new evil right-hand-man!

  - To avenge Melchior, I'll have to kill Keila, your mother, Muahaha

Sabina yawned and replied:

  - How predictable.
  - I would suggest you go for it Rangda.

Rangda:

  - You don't mind if I brutally murder your mother in front of you? What kind of "the Chosen One" are you?

Sabina:

- All she contributed to my life was the egg. Melissa was the one who raised me. Besides it's Keila's fault that the True Maker keeps bugging me with this "the Chosen One" nonsense.

Rangda:

- This climactic battle is turning very anticlimactic! Well then. There is no point in killing Keila if you don't even care. Keila, go back to your room!

Keila nodded and did as Rangda ordered. She didn't want to anger her evil captor. Once Keila was gone, Rangda spoke again:

- So, this is it. Are you ready?

Sabina:

- Yes, let's do this.

20 minutes of climactic battle ensued, full of lights, flashes, and explosions. Like your average rave while you're on acid. Eventually, Rangda dropped exhausted to the floor, panting for air.
Rangda whimpered:

- It seems you are winning, Sabina. I drained all my magical crystals.

Sabina:

- Cool. I'll just finish you off with another magic blast!

As Sabina tried to blast Rangda out of existence, she noticed something. Her magical energy was also drained. Rangda also saw this and spoke:

- Muahaha. It seems we are both out of magic power. We'll have to fight this battle with our hands.

Sabina:

- I'd rather not. Hey True Maker!

TTM:

- What is it, Sabina?

Sabina:

- My magical energy got drained. What do I do now?

TTM:

- Don't worry. A good night's sleep will refill your magical energies.

Sabina:

- A good night's sleep? You fuckwit! Rangda is 10 metres away from me, ready to tear me into shreds!

As usual, when the True Maker was confronted with the foolishness of her divine plan, she disappeared without a word.

As for the winner in melee battle between the eight-year-old human girl Sabina, and the ancient bloodthirsty space demon Rangda, the answer is obvious.

After the battle, the True Maker, hating to admit the foolishness of her plan, decided to blow up the Milky Way Galaxy, to stop Rangda from winning and anyone from questioning her!

Chapter 47 Sabina's Spirit Convinces the True Maker About a Good Plan.

The True Maker studied what remained of the Milky Way Galaxy. There was nothing left and everything that lived there, and every character in this story was dead. It was just as well. The True Maker had grown sick of the Milky Way's inhabitants and their constant moaning. The inhabitants of the Andromeda Galaxy were a lot nicer, both to the True Maker and to each other!

Suddenly, the spirit of Sabina tapped the True Maker on the shoulder. She turned around and stared at Sabina in disbelief.

TTM:

  - Sabina? How did you survive that explosion?

Sabina:

  - I guess because I am the Chosen One?

TTM:

  - Oh yeah, the Chosen One. That must be why. Seems like we lost, hey.

Sabina:

  - Yes, and now we'll spend eternity together.

The True Maker suddenly had an anxiety attack. She was a loner and did not want to spend eternity together with Sabina. In fact, she was sick of Sabina already, and they had only interacted for the last eight years. Something had to be done!

TTM:

  - No, that won't be necessary. You see, I devised a plan for how to set things right.

Sabina:

- Cool. Tell me.

TTM:

- I intend to turn back time to 2868. Then your mother can fight Rangda before Rangda gets the Zeto Crystals. Keila is a better fighter than you, so she'll kill Rangda for sure.

Sabina:

- That doesn't sound like a good plan. That would cancel out the plot of Space Gods II & III. Don't you have any better suggestions?

TTM:

- I can turn back time to 2019. You can be reborn during that time and fight Rangda before she gets powerful. You'll get to fight some evil conspiracies on Earth before you reach Rangda, but I will be a lot of fun.

Sabina:

- No. I don't think I'd be a fan of the 21st century. Overpopulation, pollution, war, and Donald Trump. Not a promising idea at all.

TTM got pissed off and shouted back at Sabina:

- Do you have any better plan?

Sabina:

- I do. How about you turn back time half an hour, and make me powerful enough to kill Rangda this time?

The True Maker considered Sabina's plan, and to her great disappointment, Sabina's idea made more sense than her own plan. TTM sighed and replied:

- Okay, Sabina let's do things your way.

Sabina:

- Great. I am stoked to save the universe!

Chapter 48 Ending

Rangda was feeling an explicable sense of Déjà vu when she entered the construction site that was the intended main hall of her future temple. Hadn't she just fought and defeated Sabina in a decisive battle? Obviously not. Regardless felt confident that she would win the battle ahead of her, and she spoke:

- Muahaha. Our final showdown has come. Today the decisive battle between good and evil will take place.

Sabina:

- I know. You told me the same thing 30 minutes ago. You killed me the last time, and the True Maker destroyed the Milky Way Galaxy. But I convinced her to turn back time, so we could fight again.

Rangda:

- So, if I win, the True Maker will destroy the galaxy and turn back time so we can fight again. And if you win, I am dead?

Sabina:

- Yes.

Rangda:

- That's very unfair. How do I really win then?

Sabina:

- You don't. You should never have picked a fight with the True Maker!

Rangda:

- Very well. I'll just keep kicking your ass then!

Sabina:

- No, you won't.

Having said this, Sabina blew up Rangda and Melchior with her over-powered eye lasers, that the True Maker had upgraded her with. Then she used her other powers to make sure that Rangda's and Melchior's armies stopped being evil.

After the galaxy was saved the True Maker appeared in front of Sabina and spoke:

- You did it, Sabina. You stopped Rangda, and you saved the Milky Way Galaxy.

Sabina:

- Cool. Your divine plan really worked, after all.

TTM:

- Honestly, it didn't.

- But the good thing with being the supreme deity is that I can always turn back time and try again until my plan works!

Sabina:

- An incredibly useful ability.

TTM:

- Yes.

- Unfortunately, I'll need to strip you of your superpowers now. We can't have people with superpowers walking around. This isn't Marvel!

Sabina:

- That's all good. I'd prefer being a normal girl anyway. This "the Chosen One" stuff is incredibly stressful!

TTM:

- Good. I'll grant you some wishes now that you saved the Milky Way Galaxy.

Sabina:

- Cool. I want you to resurrect Metatron and make Keila young and beautiful so they can fall in love again.

TTM:

- What? Is Metatron dead?

Sabina:

- Yeah, I accidentally killed him with a psionic blast when I tried to save him from coming here and getting himself killed.

TTM:

- I see. Clearly, I am not the only one stuffing things up.

- Your wishes are granted. Both Keila and Metatron is young and beautiful again. They'll fall in love and be your loving parents.

Sabina:

- Great. That's how the Divine Finalisation should have ended.

TTM:

- I know, right! But that damn writer Martin Lundqvist took the long way to get there!

- Anyway, best of luck Sabina. And enjoy your life.

Thus, Sabina got the ending she wanted. The galaxy was safe from Rangda and Melchior, her parents were reunited, and she had a comfortable upbringing being the princess of Eden raised by her loving parents Keila and Metatron!

The End!

Don't miss out!

Visit the website below and you can sign up to receive emails whenever Martin Lundqvist publishes a new book. There's no charge and no obligation.

https://books2read.com/r/B-A-QIOG-ZKZAB

BOOKS 2 READ

Connecting independent readers to independent writers.

Also by Martin Lundqvist

Divine Space Gods
Divine Space Gods: Abraham's Follies
Divine Space Gods II: Revolution for Dummies

Sabina Saves the Future
Sabina's Quest to Open the Portal in the Sun Pyramid
Sabina's Expedition to Stop the Apocalypse
Sabina Saves the Future: Full Trilogy

The Divine Zetan Trilogy
The Divine Dissimulation
The Divine Dissimulation (Shortened Edition)
The Divine Sedition
The Divine Finalisation

Standalone
Matt's Amazing Week
James Locker The Duality of Fate
The Portal in the Pyramid
Money Laundering in the Laundromat
James Locker: The Duality of Fate (Second Edition)

Sabina's Pursuit of The Holy Grail
Pyramidportalen
Matts Fantastiska Vecka
Divine Space Gods Trilogy

Watch for more at martinlundqvist.com.